"Blackburn's Defend and Protect series is off with a bang in *Unknown Threat*. This heart-racing romantic suspense is one for the keeper shelf! Don your tactical vests and get ready to engage a compelling story that will forbid you from abandoning its pages. Do. Not. Miss. This. One!"

> **Ronie Kendig**, bestselling, award-winning author of The Tox Files

"*Unknown Threat* is a fantastic read! An action-packed opening and sharply drawn characters drew me right in and held me captive. Blackburn has an exceptional gift for weaving twisting plots with characters that walk right off the page. I absolutely adore Faith, the bright and stalwart FBI special agent. I love the attention to detail regarding Secret Service operations. The swoon-worthy romance between Faith and Luke is the perfect slow burn. *Unknown Threat* is an exciting start to a thrilling new romantic-suspense series!"

> **Elizabeth Goddard**, award-winning author of the Uncommon Justice series

"In *Unknown Threat*, Lynn Blackburn has created a page-turning novel with all the elements I've come to love in her books. The hero and heroine are unique and compelling, while surrounded by a rich cast that adds depth to the story. The suspense thread is intense and pulses with energy and pressure. And the romance? It's perfection, with tension to keep me rooting for the characters. It's a perfect read for those who love engaging stories that are threaded with hope."

> **Cara Putman**, award-winning author of *Flight Risk* and *Imperfect Justice*

UNKNOWN
THREAT

Books by Lynn H. Blackburn

DEFEND
AND
PROTECT
1

UNKNOWN THREAT

LYNN H. BLACKBURN

Revell

a division of Baker Publishing Group
Grand Rapids, Michigan

© 2021 by Lynn Huggins Blackburn

Published by Revell
a division of Baker Publishing Group
PO Box 6287, Grand Rapids, MI 49516-6287
www.revellbooks.com

Printed in the United States of America

Library of Congress Cataloging-in-Publication Data
Names: Blackburn, Lynn Huggins, author.
Title: Unknown threat / Lynn H. Blackburn.
Description: Grand Rapids, Michigan : Revell, a division of Baker Publishing
    Group, 2021. | Series: Defend and protect
Identifiers: LCCN 2020038035 | ISBN 9780800737955 (paperback) | ISBN
    9780800739614 (casebound)
Subjects: GSAFD: Romantic suspense fiction. | Christian fiction. | LCGFT: Novels.
Classification: LCC PS3602.L325285 U55 2021 | DDC 813/.6—dc23
LC record available at https://lccn.loc.gov/2020038035

21 22 23 24 25 26 27   7 6 5 4 3 2 1

To my sister, Jennifer—the keeper of decades of memories, the master of mischief, the world's greatest aunt, and the best storyteller in the family. You've made life fun from day one, and I'm thankful every day that God chose you to be my lifelong playmate, advocate, and friend.

—1—

LUKE POWELL'S HEAD THROBBED as he parked his sedan in the empty lot and glared into the nearby trees. The darkness had just begun the slow fade toward dawn, and the US Secret Service special agent could barely make out the trailhead. He used to love Mondays. There was nothing quite like tackling the week and showing it who was boss before the sun had a chance to reach the horizon.

He didn't love Mondays anymore, and he hated running alone. Where was Zane? If he didn't show in the next three minutes—

Headlights pierced the predawn air.

Finally.

Luke climbed from the car and paced in front of it until Zane joined him. US Secret Service Special Agent Zane Thacker didn't speak but fell in beside Luke as they walked toward the trailhead.

Until eleven weeks ago, they'd been a trio. Barring protective details or urgent cases, Luke, Zane, and Thad had met here every Monday morning to tackle the three-mile trail around the lake. Thad was the one who'd introduced them to it when first Zane, and then Luke, joined the Raleigh resident office. It had been Thad's favorite place to run, and since his death in February, Zane and

Luke had continued to meet here every Monday. It was as if they would be spitting on their friend and mentor's memory by failing to go for a run. It was pathetic, but for now it was all they had.

They still couldn't explain to Thad's widow, Rose, why her twins had celebrated their eighth birthday over the weekend with their daddy's buddies instead of their daddy. They could tell Rose all about the explosive that had ripped Thad's car in half. They could tell her there had been a woman of Asian ancestry, somewhere between twenty-nine and thirty-five years of age, in the car with him. But no one could tell Rose who the woman was or why Thad had been at dinner with her—and most devastatingly of all, no one could tell her who had killed them.

Some buddies they'd turned out to be.

"Hold up, man." Zane stopped and propped his foot on a nearby bench. They'd reached the midpoint of the trail, and Luke looked out over the lake beside them as Zane tied his shoe.

"That party nearly killed me." Zane popped to his feet and they resumed their pace, running side by side. "I had no idea eight-year-olds could be so vicious."

"I could have lived my entire life without that experience." Luke loved Betsy and Bobby Baker like they were his own niece and nephew, but their party had been slow torture. He'd spent half the time playing laser tag with Betsy and the other half getting a massive beatdown from Bobby at basketball. The twins had fun. But Luke had been completely unprepared for the chaos, the noise level, and the amount of sugar consumption.

"The twins are great on their own, but I think next year we should see if Rose could choose something calmer," Zane said. "Instead of going to an arcade, maybe we could take them to a movie or something."

"They won't be here next year." Luke had tried to keep the

emotion out of his voice, but based on Zane's quick "What?" he hadn't succeeded.

"She told me last night after the party. She's moving to Texas in June. Her parents have a big ranch, and they're fixing up a small house on the property. The kids will have their own horses, and they'll have cousins and uncles and aunts and grandparents . . ." Luke gave up on trying to make it sound wonderful.

"But what about Thad's parents?"

Thad's parents lived in Virginia, a short two hours away. The move would devastate them. But Luke would bet his next five Americanos that Zane was using them as an excuse to keep from saying what he wanted to say. *What about us?*

"She didn't say much about them other than that they were supporting her decision and she hoped we would as well." Like they had a choice.

"Is this about the woman in the car?" Zane spat the words.

"Thad loved his wife and kids, and he was not having an affair." Luke repeated the phrase that had become his own personal mantra. "There *is* an explanation."

Zane held up his hands in surrender. "Man, you don't have to convince me. I'm asking if we need to convince Rose."

Luke didn't say anything for a quarter of a mile as they continued around the lake loop. The late-April morning was cool and crisp, with a faint hint of something floral in the air. It was shaping up to be a beautiful day in North Carolina. Maybe he would see if Betsy and Bobby could go fishing this afternoon. He'd promised them he would take them sometime, back when he thought he had all the time in the world. Not less than six weeks.

He couldn't blame Rose. Wouldn't. But it still hurt. Was Zane right? Did they need to try to convince Rose? "I don't think this is about the woman in the car. Not directly. I don't think she suspects Thad of infidelity. I think she suspects us of keeping her in the dark."

"She's no more in the dark than the rest of us." Zane swiped at a branch. "Thad was up to something. I don't believe for a second that there was anything inappropriate going on, but whatever he was doing, it got him killed."

They finished the run with no more conversation. What more was there to say that they hadn't already covered a million times?

Luke slowed to a walk as they exited the tree line and approached the parking lot. Zane fell into step beside him.

They were fifteen feet away from Zane's car—the finest late-model sedan the US Secret Service had to offer—when a shot split the air, and Zane hit the ground.

Luke dropped beside him. Another shot, and the ground spat dirt into Luke's face. He strained to hear something—anything— that would give him a clue as to the shooter's location, but his ears throbbed with the sound of his own heartbeat, nothing else.

"Zane?" Luke hissed.

Zane stirred beside him.

Relief flooded through Luke. "You hit?"

"Arm. You?"

"Missed me. Can you move?"

"Do I have a choice?"

Both men crawled toward the relative safety of Zane's car. Two more shots peppered their path, and the distinctive scent of burnt gunpowder infiltrated the morning haze. A third shot left Luke's leg burning like someone had branded him.

But after the next shot, Zane dropped to his chest and didn't move. Luke gave up all attempts at staying low. He grabbed Zane under the arms and dragged him behind his car, leaving a trail of blood to mark their progress. Another crack split the air, and the toe of Zane's running shoe disintegrated before Luke's eyes.

Luke made sure Zane was completely hidden by the vehicle before he stopped and eased Zane's body to the ground. "Stay with me, buddy. Hang in there."

Luke twisted his wrist, tapped his watch until the phone keypad appeared, and dialed 911.

Zane mumbled something Luke didn't catch. While he waited for the call to go through, he patted Zane's pockets, looking for the keys. Zane grabbed Luke's arm and jabbed a finger in the direction of the car before his head dropped back to the ground.

Luke bent lower to get a look at whatever it was Zane had been trying to show him. The 911 dispatcher was saying something, but Luke didn't respond.

The wires hanging from the axle didn't belong. Neither did the slab of C-4 they were attached to.

Two more shots rang out. This time they hit Zane's car.

"We have to move." Luke wasn't sure if Zane was still conscious, but he didn't have time to worry about that. Once more, he grabbed Zane under the arms and dragged, this time away from the car.

His own car was a good hundred feet away, but staying beside a vehicle that was ready to blow wasn't any safer than risking the trip to the other side.

Around the halfway point, the glorious sounds of sirens filtered through the surrounding trees.

Then the ground shook.

And everything went dark.

—2—

MONDAY MORNINGS weren't for cowards.

FBI Special Agent Faith Malone eyed the pile of paperwork on her desk with disgust as she finished off her first Cherry Coke of the morning.

Faith rated her days by the number of Cherry Cokes she had consumed. Normal days? One. Busy days, or days when she was out late the night before? Two.

Days of utter madness called for three.

"Good morning, Faith. Good of you to come to work today."

Faith imagined, not for the first time, what it would be like to whack Special Agent Janice Estes across the face with her empty Coke bottle. Instead, she contented herself with picturing a small rivulet of blood trickling from Janice's nose. "Just like every day and twice on Sundays," Faith said without making eye contact.

"Oh? I thought you were out twice last week." A saccharine Southern drawl disguised her tone but did nothing to hide the venom in Janice's words.

Faith continued to focus on her paperwork. "Nope." Not last week. The week before had been another matter, but no need to bring that up.

Janice wasn't done, and Faith waited for the next dig. She still didn't know what Janice's end game was, but she refused to sink into a verbal sparring match.

"Malone!" The booming voice of Supervisory Senior Resident Agent Dale Jefferson interrupted whatever Janice had been about to say.

"Yes, sir!" Faith paused a second to scan her desk, attempting to memorize the placement of every file and sticky note. Her eyes bounced off the "Faith over Fear" paper holder—a gift from her sister—that had become a painful reminder of how weak her own faith had become. She grabbed her iPad and Apple pencil and walked to her boss's office.

"Close the door." Everything about Dale was . . . off. His tie was askew. His hair was mussed. His eyes were . . . Faith didn't know what this look was. Shattered? A cold dread trickled through her limbs.

"I'm calling a meeting in two minutes. The word is out, and we have to get on top of this."

"Sir? What happened?"

"This morning three separate attacks were carried out on agents from the US Secret Service Raleigh resident office."

The Secret Service? Who? How? Luke? *Please, Lord, not Luke.*

"Two agents were killed. Two wounded, one more seriously than the other. Both of the wounded were taken to the Wake Med trauma unit. That's all I have at the moment. The families of the agents are still being notified."

Faith tried to force sound from her throat, but all that came out was a strangled breath. She cleared her throat and tried again. "Who?"

Dale didn't hear her. "I'll give you the rest of the details in the briefing. We need to go. You have point on the investigation."

Wait. What?

"I want to know who did this. Those Secret Service punks chap my hide on a regular basis, but there's not a one of them who it isn't an honor to serve with. Not to mention that if someone's got it out for the Secret Service, the FBI may be next." Dale grabbed his coffee and a folder from his desk. "Let's go."

Dale strode to the door and pushed it open. Faith tried to make her feet move, but her limbs were heavy with dread.

He paused at the door. "Are you coming?"

"Dale. Who?"

His Adam's apple bobbed twice before he spoke. "Jared Smith and . . ." Dale shook his head hard before continuing. "Michael Weaver."

Not Luke. Faith hadn't realized how disconcerting it was to feel both profound relief and gut-wrenching sorrow at the same time. Dale and Michael Weaver had served together in their early law enforcement days in Illinois. Most FBI agents despised their Secret Service counterparts, and the feeling was mutual. But Michael and Dale's friendship was well-known, and it was because of them that the local Secret Service and FBI agents worked well together. Most of the time.

"I'm so sorry."

Dale's face hardened. "I want to know what happened. You find out who killed him."

"Yes, sir."

Faith followed Dale out the door and down the hall to the buzzing conference room. The chatter ceased when they entered. Faith glanced at the faces now focused on Dale. Word had spread, and the typical Monday morning banter had been replaced with stone-faced tension.

Dale took his place at the front of the room. "Sit."

Should she sit? Did Dale expect her to stand up front with him? For an awkward moment, Faith hesitated in the door before sliding into a chair along the wall.

Two dead. Michael and Jared. Not Luke.

Two injured. Who?

She tried to concentrate on Dale's words, but her gaze was drawn to her coworkers. The grief and shock settling on their expressions. The swiped tears everyone pretended not to notice. The clenched fists. The muttered expletives.

"Details are thin," Dale said. "Michael Weaver was at the gym and dropped during his run. Initial indicators said it was a heart attack, but a paramedic on the scene noticed a puncture mark. Someone shot him with a dart. We still don't know what was in it."

Dale pulled a sheet of paper from the folder. "Jared Smith's condo exploded this morning. There might be no reason to assume foul play, except for the fact that Michael's . . . dead"—Dale paused on the word and then pulled himself together to continue—"and two other agents, Zane Thacker and Luke Powell, were shot this morning and their cars were blown up. Both men are being treated for their injuries but are expected to make a full recovery."

Faith's ears buzzed. Luke Powell? Shot? Treated for injuries? What kind of injuries? "Expected to make a full recovery" didn't necessarily mean that he wasn't in bad shape at the moment.

"Ladies and Gentlemen, we have no idea why, but our brothers and sisters at the Secret Service came under attack this morning. The FBI has jurisdiction to investigate crimes committed against the Secret Service, and I've tasked Special Agent Malone with the lead. You will give her your full and devoted cooperation. I shouldn't need to say this, but in case some of you aren't playing with a full deck, let me remind you. If someone's attacking our brethren at the Secret Service, we could very well be next in their sights. Let's find out who did this. Why they did this. And get justice for our friends. Dismissed."

"Agent Malone." Dale's words were not a request but a command.

"Yes, sir."

"You need it, you've got it."

"Thank you, sir."

"My advice? Start with Jared's place. Then the gym where Michael was killed. Then the spot where Powell and Thacker were shot. Maybe by the time you're done, one of them will be conscious."

Faith bristled at the unnecessary advice. She knew how to run an investigation better than anyone else in this office, and Dale knew it. Did he trust her with this case or not? She considered calling him out on it, but then she saw the sheen in Dale's eyes. This was personal for him.

It was personal for her too. "Yes, sir. I'll keep you in the loop."

Faith half jogged to her cubicle. She filled her bag with her iPad, Apple pencil, extra battery, charging cables, and voice recorder.

"I guess congratulations are in order." Janice was anything but pleased.

What was her deal?

Faith didn't respond while she rummaged through the side desk drawer. Where was her— There. Her fingers wrapped around a container of breath mints. She tucked them into her bag and scanned the other contents. Did she have everything she needed for the day? Who knew when she'd be back in the office.

Janice continued to hover, but Faith had no time for her junk. She lifted her laptop from the middle of her desk, looped her keys onto one finger, and turned to the door. "Gotta run." She tossed the words over her shoulder.

"Break a leg," Janice called after her. It sounded friendly. It wasn't.

Faith's phone rang thirty seconds after she pulled out of the parking lot.

Dale. Probably with more advice she didn't need.

She answered through her car's Bluetooth. "Malone."

"Change of plans." Dale didn't give her a chance to respond or ask questions. "Go to the Secret Service office. They've evacuated the building." *Click.*

Faith performed an illegal U-turn and sped toward the Secret Service office. She listened to the police chatter over her radio. Based on what she was hearing, it sounded like a bomb threat. It was normally a fifteen-minute drive to the Raleigh resident office of the Secret Service, what they referred to as the RAIC. She arrived in ten and had to park a quarter of a mile away. Dale pulled in behind her.

She met him at his car and waited for him to emerge. "What's going on?"

"We'll find out together," he said.

"Do you know how many people are typically in their office?" Faith asked the question more to get Dale talking than out of real curiosity.

"It varies between eight and ten agents and one office manager," Dale said. "Thad Baker hasn't been replaced yet, so they were down to seven agents. Which means as of today, they are down to . . . five. And two of them are in the hospital."

Dale set a blistering pace, and Faith hurried to match it. Three functional agents and an office manager left? She didn't like to draw conclusions, but who had ever heard of a resident office being decimated like this? What had they been investigating that would generate this level of violence against them? Or was it someone who had it out for the Secret Service, or federal agencies in general?

She and Dale reached the police tape. After a quick pause to show their identification, they were allowed inside but then were stopped at a secondary barrier.

"Can't let you in," the officer said. "Everyone's out. The bomb dogs are in there."

"Dale!" A thick Jersey accent punctured the murmuring voices around them.

"Jacob." Dale took the man's extended hand and pulled him into a hug. "I can't believe he's gone."

The two men parted. "You and me both, brother."

Dale pointed in Faith's direction. "You know Faith Malone?"

"Of course." Jacob turned to face her, and his eyes were puffy from tears.

If circumstances were anything other than what they were, she would have given him a hard time for the way his golf foursome had lost to hers and Luke's in the last interagency golf tournament. As it was, she had absolutely no idea what to say.

"I know you and Luke have done a lot of work together. Did they tell you he's going to be okay?"

Jacob's assurance that Luke was going to be fine eased some of her worry. "That's great, sir." Should she shake his hand? She fumbled with her iPad as her mind scrambled. "But I'm sorry for your losses today, sir."

"I appreciate that."

"Faith has the lead on this case," Dale said.

Jacob eyed her with shrewd speculation before he responded. "I'm not sure when we'll get Luke and Zane back in the office, but until then, my remaining agents will give you their full cooperation."

"Thank—"

A commotion from the building interrupted her. Heavily clad figures from the bomb squad stepped out. Dale and Jacob rushed forward. Faith followed.

This was her investigation after all.

"What do you have?" Jacob yelled from twenty yards away.

"Sir, we went through with our dog, and he didn't alert to anything." The woman hidden behind protective gear held up a hand. "But the building hasn't been cleared. ATF wants to do another sweep with a couple of their dogs."

Dale and Jacob launched into a debate about whether to let the ATF handle the bomb aspects of the case. Faith tuned them out. She was usually in favor of keeping the investigation in-house, and the FBI had solid bomb/explosive investigative capabilities. But she knew a couple of the ATF agents from the Joint Terrorism Task Force, and they were top notch. She wouldn't mind them taking care of this part of the investigation.

While Dale and Jacob hammered out the jurisdictional complications, Faith's mind whirled with possibilities. It wasn't easy to get into a federal agency. It's not like the locations were secret, but you needed a badge, you had to sign in, get past security guards. How would anyone have gotten a bomb into their office?

"When can I get back inside?" Jacob's tone made it clear that heads would roll if the answer wasn't "Right now."

"Can't say, sir." The bomb tech backed away. Smart move. "You'll have to talk to my supervisor. She's in the command center vehicle on the other side of the building." She pointed with a heavily gloved hand and then walked in that direction.

"I'll come with you." Dale clapped a hand on Jacob's shoulder. "We'll get to the bottom of this." He turned to Faith. "I suggest you go visit the scenes. There's nothing you can do here at the moment. I'll stay in touch."

Faith fumed as she wound her way back to her car. Nothing she could do? The whole office was on lockdown and could still be in the crosshairs of a killer, and she'd been dismissed from the action.

She slid behind the steering wheel and restarted the GPS directions to Jared Smith's home.

She didn't want to admit it, but Dale had a point. The mess at the Secret Service office would quickly become a jurisdictional nightmare as everyone argued about who was in charge.

The answer was the FBI.

Not because the FBI was always in charge. This wasn't TV, where the FBI always jumped in and took over the case, but in this situation the jurisdictional precedent was set. The FBI not only had the case but also had the resources to do whatever ballistics and forensics might be needed. The ATF would be a welcome addition to the alphabet soup, but they would report all findings to her.

What was so hard about that?

When she pulled to the curb beside Jared Smith's home, she spotted the jackets of six different agencies.

Maybe it wasn't as clear as she'd thought.

— 3 —

FAITH HAD SEEN plenty of death and destruction in her career, but today had been a more concentrated dosage than she ever cared to consume again.

Jared Smith's home hadn't just burned. It looked like a malevolent hand had reached through the walls, crushed every timber into dust, and then dropped a match in the middle of it for good measure.

They'd identified the body from dental records in record time, but he was Secret Service and his files were easily accessible.

In contrast, a section of taped-off indoor track was the only clue that anything unusual had happened at the site of Michael Weaver's death. The forensics team had found the dart, but so far that was their only clue. The gym's video surveillance was already being analyzed in the hope of getting a lead on the shooter. Dale had joined her as she was finishing at the gym, and while he'd been in control of his emotions, she didn't envy the forensics techs she'd left with him at the scene.

Faith had pulled through her favorite fast-food drive-through at two. The chicken sandwich and Cherry Coke—number three so far—had been soothing to her clenched stomach. But now, standing inside the crime scene tape where Luke and Zane had been ambushed, she regretted the decision to eat.

Blood. Their blood. Splattered and spilled.

Luke Powell was in the hospital with one gunshot wound, abrasions, cuts requiring multiple stitches, and according to the agent standing post outside his room an hour ago, a very bad attitude.

Zane Thacker was in the recovery room after having surgery to repair the damage from two bullets. One hit his arm and one pierced through his side, but no major organs were damaged. A bullet had blown off the toe of his shoe, but missed his foot. He was expected to make a complete recovery.

Faith surveyed the scene. The grass around the signs for the trailhead was sparse, but the vegetation on either side of the small dirt parking area was thick and overgrown.

Special Agent Julie Sutton, a young agent Faith didn't know well, approached. "Special Agent Malone? I didn't expect to see you out here. I thought you'd be in the office."

"There'll be time for the office later. For today, I need to see what we're dealing with."

"Of course. I've been here since nine a.m., and I'd be happy to walk you through the scene if you'd like."

"Please."

Sutton pulled out a notebook and pointed in the direction of the trail. "Agents Powell and Thacker met at five forty-five a.m. to run the trail."

"In the dark?" Were they crazy? She walked toward the trailhead, Agent Sutton close on her heels.

"One of the Secret Service agents, Agent Dixon, was out here earlier and he said they run it every Monday. I was skeptical, so I jogged it myself after I arrived. It looks more rugged than it is. Once you get about thirty feet in, there's a smooth dirt path. No rocks, few branches. And once you get to the other side of the lake, the trail is paved almost to the end. You could safely run it with a full moon. Even without moonlight, it would be doable within an hour of dawn by anyone familiar with the trail."

Faith eyed the path. Maybe. She didn't care to run outside. Who was she kidding? She didn't care to run at all. She could run, but why? She pulled her thoughts back to the scene. "Does the trail loop around?"

"Almost. It's a horseshoe, not a complete circle." Julie pointed to another marker at the opposite end of the parking area. "It winds to the far end of the lake, then back around the other side. Assuming they ran the entire path, they came out over there and were walking toward their vehicles when the attack began."

Sutton pointed to the first evidence marker. "I haven't personally interviewed either of the agents yet, but this is what we think happened. The shooter was over there, hidden in the brush. The weapon was a .22 rifle, and the shooter was a horrible shot. My nephew could have hit both of them from that distance. He's seven."

Agent Sutton was right. Caught unaware, even in dim morning light, their bodies would have been easy to see as soon as they exited the trail. How could the shooter have missed? "How many shots?"

"We aren't sure. At least five. But based on the shooter's skill, there could have been more."

Faith walked to the spot where the shooter had been. "We're sure this is the spot?"

"Yes, ma'am. We took photos of everything. Someone was lying here recently, and the angle is right for the shots."

Faith lay down and propped herself up onto her elbows. She pretended to hold a rifle and squinted as if she were looking through a scope.

How had they survived? They were defenseless.

Agent Sutton pointed toward the middle of the parking area. "The first shot was there. Agent Thacker fell. Agent Powell hit the dirt. They both crawled toward the vehicles. The shots followed them as they made their way. One shot got Agent Powell's leg, but it's mostly a burn. Then another shot hit Agent Thacker in the side. At that time, Agent Powell pulled him behind the car."

"How'd you get all this?" There was no way they'd have been able to figure out the time line so quickly, and Sutton already said she hadn't interviewed the agents.

"Agent Powell, ma'am. He blacked out after the explosion, but he came to before the ambulance arrived. He was able to give a pretty thorough report before they took him to the hospital. Agent Dixon passed it on to me."

Luke had been conscious before he left the site? That was the best news she'd heard all day, and it gave her more confidence in the report. If the info was from Luke, injured or not, it was accurate. That man was meticulous. Getting shot wouldn't have altered his personality. If anything, it would have heightened his usual need for details.

Faith continued to peer through her imaginary scope, picturing the scene. Zane falling. Luke pulling him behind the car. If she'd been the shooter, she would have . . .

A horrible realization settled through her. "He wasn't trying to kill them."

"Ma'am?" Agent Sutton's voice pitched an octave higher than it had been earlier.

"The shooter knew the car was set to blow, so he had some fun with them." Faith fought to keep her voice flat and dispassionate. "Then he herded them toward the car. He knew his shots would send them scurrying for safety . . . right into the trap he'd set. He wasn't a bad shot. He was very good."

"That's . . ." Agent Sutton couldn't finish her thought, and Faith couldn't blame her.

Faith pressed her hands into the ground. He'd been here. The person who'd tried to kill Luke. And Zane. He'd been right here. His body had warmed this ground. His breath had fluttered the brush that hid him from view. How long had he lain here, waiting? How long had he worked to know their routine?

"You'll be sorry." She whispered the words to the ground and rose, brushing the dirt of this evil spot from her hands, then her shirt, then her pants. "Let's go see the explosion site." She walked toward the mangled vehicles with Agent Sutton scurrying to keep up.

Faith picked her way around the contorted remains of Zane's Ford Focus. The car had been parked closest to the trail exit, and they'd fled toward it when the shooting started. What was left of Luke's Focus was on the other side of the parking area, near the trail entrance. Both men had been in between the two vehicles when the bombs went off. The open space was littered with bits of metal and melted plastic. She could make out what had once been a wheel to her left, an axle a few feet beyond. And was that the engine?

"My understanding is that Special Agent Powell has some pretty bad contusions from stuff falling after the explosion," Sutton said. "When the first car exploded, he was dragging Special Agent Thacker away. He fell on top of him, and his body took most of the beating from the falling car parts. It's a wonder they didn't both die this morning." Sutton shook her head. "I mean, who survives this?"

"My grandma would say they must be living right," Faith said without any humor. "But I guess the real answer is that it wasn't their time. There must be more for them to do."

Where had that come from? She didn't believe God cared enough to intervene. Not anymore.

Agent Sutton's response was a noncommittal grunt.

Faith turned to the younger agent. "I need your full report ASAP, but you should know that I'm impressed with what you've done here. Good work."

Agent Sutton tried, and failed spectacularly, to stop the grin that made her look like a twelve-year-old who'd borrowed her aunt's FBI windbreaker. "Thank you, ma'am. I'll have the report to you tonight."

Faith nodded at the other agents processing the scene. She'd seen what she needed to see here.

Now it was time to see Luke.

LUKE WAS GOING TO LOSE his ever-loving mind the next time someone knocked on the door. After the visit from the chaplain, he'd told the police officer guarding his door to keep people away. He did not want company.

Everything hurt. His head. His leg. His hands. His arms. His ego.

His heart.

Zane remained zonked in the recovery room, and Luke envied his friend's blissful ignorance. Consciousness would only bring him misery. Michael and Jared. Gone.

How was that even possible? He'd seen them yesterday at the party.

He wanted to throw something. Or yell. Or both. Or worse.

More widows. More fatherless kids. Sure, they all knew the risks associated with their line of work. No one joined the Secret

Service without the certain knowledge that they would, more than once, put their life on the line for someone else.

But no one expected to die in their own house. Or at the gym running laps.

Why, Lord? I can't make sense out of any of this. How many more people do I have to lose?

A tap at the door had him reaching for something, anything, to throw. "Go away!" The words left his mouth even as the gentle eyes of none other than Faith Malone met his.

She didn't flinch. Her mouth twisted into a compassionate grimace. How did she make herself look sorry and sad for him at the same time? What was she doing here?

"Luke." She didn't enter the room. Didn't push the door open another inch. "I am so sorry. I don't know if they told you—"

"I already know about Michael and Jared." The words burned as he said them.

"Yes, and I am sorry for your loss. But did they tell you I'm the agent in charge of the investigation?"

What? Faith? No way. He and Faith had worked together often over the past three years, on everything from a charity golf tournament to a dragon boat race for a cancer fundraiser. And for the past year they had both served on the Joint Terrorism Task Force. She was a good agent, as far as FBI agents went. She was a solid member of the JTTF, but did she have the seniority or experience necessary for an investigation like this? Not that he should have expected any better from the FBI. Leave it to them to put a pretty face on the investigation, knowing full well it would mean the case would go unsolved. Or worse, that they would get the arrest but botch the investigation so badly the perpetrators would walk free.

He'd seen it happen. He'd lived it.

Not to mention that if she didn't solve this case, their friendship, or whatever it was they had, would never survive. Why couldn't it have been anyone but Faith?

"I'm going to take it from the way your expression went from hostile to murderous that you had not yet been made aware of my role in the investigation. I'm going to check on Zane's condition. I'll be back in fifteen minutes."

Faith's face disappeared, then her pale brown hand and perfectly manicured fingertips slipped from the edge of the door. It closed with a faint click.

How could she drop a bombshell like that and leave?

I did tell her to go away.

He stared at the door, but it didn't reopen.

He ought to . . . what? Chase her down the hall? Give her a piece of his mind? Leave the room and refuse to speak to her when she next decided to grace him with her presence? He glanced at his stylish hospital gown, the IV dripping antibiotics into his system, and the bandages on his arms. He didn't need to see the bandages on his leg, or the stitches in his calf. He was trapped.

He slumped against the pillows to wait.

Fifteen minutes later, he heard another soft tap on the door. After a moment, the door eased open. "Is it safe to enter?"

"Get in here."

Faith Malone stepped inside. Barely. The door closed, but she didn't approach him. Instead, she leaned against the wall and studied him. She was as gorgeous as ever, even with dirt staining her knees and the edge of her shirt, a smudge on her cheek, and fire in her eyes. It would be so much easier to keep her at a distance if he hadn't often wondered what it would be like to have her close.

She continued to stand there, iPad in one hand, Cherry Coke in the other.

Faith's Cherry Coke issues were a safe area to pick at her. He hoped. He pointed to the bottle. "How many of those have you had today?" Would she accept the olive branch, lame as it was?

Her chin lifted ever so slightly. "This is my fourth."

"When's the last time you had four in one day?"

"Can't remember."

Luke was pretty sure that was a lie, but he wouldn't press her. Her four Cherry Coke days were her business. Not his. And while he didn't want to admit it, the fact that this morning's events had driven her to a 4CC day? It did something to him. Something he didn't like. It made him start to think things that couldn't be true. Like maybe the FBI wouldn't drop the ball on this investigation. Like maybe Faith would get the job done.

That she'd do it right.

Faith walked to the window and set the drink on the ledge. "I'm sorry about Michael and Jared."

He didn't trust himself to speak, so he tried to nod nicely.

Faith's black hair was straight today, and she tucked it behind her ear. "Do you feel up to talking about what happened this morning?"

Something snapped. "You're being too nice, Faith. Why are you *asking* me? You should be telling me you're sorry for my loss, but you need to hear my version of the story and that's all there is to it. If you're this nice to everyone—"

"I'm not, Special Agent Powell." Faith's brown eyes flashed with unmasked anger. "It's called professional courtesy. Perhaps you've heard of it?"

Ouch.

Faith's face was all angles and hard edges now. She'd told him once that her cheekbones and skin tone were from her Cherokee mother, but her temper was a gift from her red-haired Irish father.

Something told him he did not want to be on the receiving end of the tongue-lashing she was about to unleash. And he knew from past experience that he was in big trouble when she started calling him "Special Agent Powell" instead of "Luke." What was his problem? Why was he being so antagonistic? This wasn't a random agent. This was Faith. He knew her. He liked her. More than he should.

Maybe that was his problem. "My apologies." He waved a hand around the room. "This place is bringing out the worst in me."

She smirked as she sat down. "It isn't this place. It's the potent combination of sorrow, lack of control, and your deep-seated distrust of the FBI in general. I can do nothing to ease your grief or restore your false sense of dominion over your life. I still don't know, nor do I care, why you despise the FBI. All I can do is choose to overlook your disparaging remarks regarding my ability to do my job, and I'm only willing to offer that concession for the next twelve hours."

She tapped the fancy pencil on her iPad and began to write. "Now, Agent Powell, will you please start with your whereabouts this morning and walk me through everything that happened."

He wanted to argue. Wanted to defend himself. Wanted to give her all the reasons for his hatred of the FBI. If she only knew.

But she didn't.

Faith waited, a patient half smile on her full lips. If she was seething in fury underneath that cool exterior, he couldn't tell.

"Fine."

He told her everything.

She listened well, only stopping him twice for clarification. Whenever they were interrupted by hospital staff, which was often, she sat without any sense of frustration or unease, and then as soon as they were alone again, she would prompt him with where he'd left off. There'd been no chitchat. No jokes. She'd been all business.

She glanced over her notes, then asked, "Did you see the shooter?"

"No." He couldn't hide the frustration that leaked around the word. "The sun wasn't up, and we had no cover. I'm sure he was at the edge of the parking area, but I never saw him."

"How many cars were there when you came back from your run?"

"Two. Mine and Zane's."

"Is that unusual? For no one else to be out there yet?"

"We run that trail almost every Monday. I would have expected to see a few cars in the lot by the time we left, but the absence of them didn't strike me as odd. Although, we ran it faster than usual."

"Faster?"

"We were both in a bad mood."

"You run faster when you're in a bad mood?"

He glared at her. "We did today."

"When did you start?"

"Zane was running a few minutes late. We started warming up around five fifty, and we were running by six."

"And you got back when?"

"Six seventeen."

Faith did the math. They'd run a hair faster than a six-minute mile. Impressive. "Why were you in a bad mood?"

"I don't think it's pertinent to the case."

"You're pushing your luck with me, Agent Powell." Faith unscrewed the lid of her drink. "I'll decide if it's pertinent. Why were you grouchy?" She took a swig and set it back on the ledge, then turned to him, waiting on his answer.

"Thad Baker was our running buddy. We were at his twins' birthday party yesterday."

"Ah."

Faith continued to make her notes. She paused after a few moments, and her lips twisted as she stared at what she'd written. When she made eye contact again, her expression was thoughtful. "Thad Baker died eleven weeks ago. To the day."

Luke hadn't made the connection, but she was right.

"Two agents died today. Two almost died. The office was evacuated. Seems to me someone has a vendetta against the Raleigh office. What on earth have y'all been up to?"

Luke did not like where her comments were heading. "Our jobs."

"No doubt. But your jobs have ticked somebody off. And by somebody, I mean the type of somebody depraved enough to lie in the weeds and shoot at you and Zane to herd you over to your cars so he, or she, could blow you to kingdom come. Then escape down the back road in time to blow Jared Smith's condo to bits, and then get to the gym in time to take down Michael Weaver."

Luke couldn't force his brain and mouth to work at the same time. He couldn't do anything but stare at her. Was she serious?

"I haven't ruled out the possibility of three different attackers, but I lay in the spot your shooter did this morning. I saw the tire tracks out of sight of your vehicles. I left there and went straight to Jared's, and then I drove to the gym and went inside. The timing doesn't quite work with afternoon traffic, but I'll drive it again in the morning. I'd be willing to give up Cherry Coke for the day if I'm wrong, but I think with early morning traffic and a well-planned strategy, we could be dealing with one very determined killer." She flipped the cover over her iPad and slipped the pencil into its holder. "I may be reaching, but your attacker could be the same one who blew up Thad Baker's car. I've requested the full case file from the agent in charge of that investigation."

She stood. "I am sorry for your losses, Luke. Truly. And I'm glad your injuries weren't more serious. I'll be in touch."

And with that, she walked out the door.

"Wait!" He called after her, but if she heard him, she didn't respond.

— 4 —

LUKE POWELL WAS an arrogant, egotistical jerk.

How dare he insinuate that she couldn't handle this case.

Faith's annoyance propelled her away from his door and back toward the recovery room. She'd wanted to dump his little ice bucket all over him and watch him squirm in that stupid hospital gown.

Lucky for him, he was rather appealing with his always-smoothed hair all disheveled, not to mention the day-old growth on his usually clean-shaven jaw that highlighted the angular lines of his face in an unexpected way. But that wouldn't have saved him from her wrath if she hadn't seen the raw pain in his eyes—eyes the exact shade of the wood on her grandfather's boat . . .

Get a grip.

Who cared about Luke Powell's eyes? No one. Especially not her. She had a case to solve. And dealing with Luke Powell was going to be . . . complicated. Everything about Luke was complicated. He was infuriating and funny. Churlish and charming. Sometimes she wanted to punch him, and sometimes she wondered what he would do if she kissed him.

Her phone chirped. She stopped and leaned against the wall before she answered. "Agent Malone."

"Are you still at work?" her mother asked.

How many times had she told her mom not to call this number unless it was an emergency? How many times had she asked her to please text, not call, for things that could wait?

She counted to five.

"Are you there? Do we have a bad connection?" Her mother knew there wasn't a bad connection.

Faith counted to five again. "Mom, I can't talk to you right now. You've dialed my work number again."

"Sorry. I don't know how that keeps happening."

Right. "I'm working, Mom. No idea when I'll be home. Everything okay with Hope?"

"Hope's fine. She called this afternoon, but I haven't seen either of you in a while."

"I won't have time to come by this week. Things are—"

"Are you working on the Secret Service case?" Her mom wasn't as obtuse as she tried to appear.

"You know I can't talk about my cases. I'll check in with you later. If you need me, please use my personal phone, okay?"

"Be careful, honey."

"I will. Love you." Faith disconnected the call, checked to be sure she hadn't missed any calls, then retrieved her personal phone from her back pocket and sent a quick message to her sister.

> Hey! Miss your face. I know you're killing it in court this week. When you get a chance, can you research a way to legally stop Mom from calling me on my work number? #notkidding

The blinking dots kept her finger paused over the phone a few moments longer.

LOL! Can't be done. Court's going fine.
Love you!

Love you too.

She slid her personal phone back into her pocket. The next time she was with her mom, she was removing her work number from her mom's contacts.

One deep breath later, she continued to the elevator. Ten minutes later, she was standing outside Zane Thacker's room. When she'd tried to see him earlier, he'd been in between the recovery room and his new room on the fifth floor. Hopefully he'd had time to get settled and would be able to see her now.

"Any news from the outside?" the police officer guarding the hall asked her after studying her badge.

"Nothing new."

"Good," the older gentleman said. "No news is good news. At least on a day like today."

"True." She pointed to the door to Zane's room. "Any changes in Agent Thacker's condition?"

A shrug. "I'm not supposed to know anything, but I heard him talking a few minutes ago. Sounded like he was joking with the nurse. I don't think he's in much pain. Yet. When the meds wear off, he'll be feeling it. You ever been shot?"

"No."

"How about you keep it that way?"

"I plan to try." She liked this officer. He had a calming way about him. He gave her a small salute, then tapped on the door.

A nurse opened it. "Yes?"

"Is Agent Thacker up for a quick visit?" Faith held her badge aloft.

The nurse scowled but opened the door. "Five minutes. I'll be back." She stepped into the hall, and Faith stepped into the room.

Zane Thacker was as opposite Luke Powell as any two people could be. While Luke's complexion leaned toward olive tones, Zane's pale skin accentuated eyes that were the deep blue of the ocean right at the horizon, his hair was a mass of wavy dark-blond curls, and his stubble was . . . red?

He gave her a confused smile. "Faith? What brings you here? I mean, I appreciate the concern for your favorite golf partner, but I didn't realize we'd reached the point in our relationship where you'd come visit me in the hospital. Oh. Wait." He waggled his eyebrows at her. "You came to visit Luke, didn't you? That explains it."

Zane was a bit loopy from the anesthesia, but he didn't have the haunted look so evident in Luke's expression. He was confused by her presence, but not concerned.

Realization hit her hard. Zane didn't know. And she did not want to be the one to tell him.

A soft knock on the door gave her a momentary reprieve. The woman who entered was without question the most gorgeous woman Faith had ever seen in real life. She was at least five foot ten, and as she approached, she made Faith feel every one of her five feet, five short inches. And that hair. Cascades of flowing dark-brown curls shot through with highlights that probably weren't natural but sure looked like it.

"You must be Special Agent Malone," she said. "Special Agent Tessa Reed."

This was the mysterious Agent Reed. She'd been in the Raleigh office for close to a year, but their paths had yet to cross. Faith guessed that she was of Indian or Pakistani descent, but with her accent, she'd probably been raised in the South.

"Yes." They shook hands. "It's a pleasure to meet you, although I wish it were under different circumstances."

Agent Reed's eyes, upon closer inspection, were red-rimmed. She knew. With crushing certainty, Faith understood. Agent Reed had been sent to tell Zane.

Faith tried to convey her sympathies, both for what Tessa had lost and for the task that had befallen her. "I'll come back later."

As she exited the room, she heard Zane. "What's going on, Tess? Why did she leave?"

Fifteen minutes later, Faith twisted the lid off a bottle of water and drank a third of it without pausing. Ugh. Water was so . . . boring.

She settled into a waiting room chair and tapped her iPad, changing the notes she'd written into typed text. Reading over them, she edited as she went along. She needed to get back to the office and analyze every word of the case file on Thad Baker's death.

There was a connection. There had to be. Three dead and two wounded US Secret Service agents in eleven weeks. All from the Raleigh RAIC.

Raleigh, North Carolina, was probably the most dangerous posting in the entire Secret Service now. How crazy was that?

Three dead agents—all of whom had already finished their protective detail and were now on the backside of their careers. The side that shouldn't involve a great deal of risk.

The career path for a Secret Service agent was as varied as the agents themselves, but typically they spent the first phase of their career in a resident office or field office. There they worked mostly on the investigative side of things, primarily related to counterfeit currency and electronic crimes. Anytime a protectee came through the area, everything stopped in order to protect the president, vice president, foreign dignitary, or whoever else it had been determined needed Secret Service protective services. Phase 1 for most agents ran somewhere in the three-to-five-year range. Which meant Luke was a year or two away from Phase 2, and Zane . . . he could go to Phase 2 at any time.

Phase 2 for an agent was the protective detail. This was what the general public thought everyone in the Secret Service did. Agents could be assigned to the presidential detail, the vice-presidential detail, or the details of their spouses, children, or other high-ranking officials. Some agents were the public face of the Secret Service. The suits, the earpieces, the "running alongside the car during the parade" agents. Some worked protective intelligence and did the legwork before, during, and after a visit to ensure all threats were chased down and neutralized before the protectee arrived. Most agents worked a protective detail for no more than five years, and then it was on to Phase 3.

By Phase 3, the agents had a decade of experience and had earned their place as the leaders of the resident and field offices where they were assigned. Some took a management path and climbed the supervisory ladder. Others took the lead on investigations and protective details whenever they arose.

All three agents who were killed had been in Phase 3. Was that significant? Or coincidence? Faith added the question to her notes.

Could the three agents have all touched the same case during their Phase 2 assignments? She'd chase down the idea, but it didn't strike her as the most likely scenario. In big cities, especially cities like New York, the agents did protective work year-round. But in a place like Raleigh, protective details occurred far less often. The Raleigh agents spent the vast majority of their days working on electronic crimes and counterfeiting cases, so while it was possible the connection was political or based on something the agents might have seen or heard during their protective details, that didn't strike her as the most likely angle.

Especially considering that neither Luke nor Zane had gone to Phase 2 yet.

Which pulled her attention right back to Raleigh-specific cases. She needed to see every one they'd worked on lately. Especially cases Thad Baker, Jared Smith, and Michael Weaver had been involved in.

She was going to have to get all up in the business of every single agent in the Raleigh RAIC.

Somewhere a link explained everything.

She drew a circle around the names of Luke, Zane, Thad, Michael, and Jared.

Who was next?

—5—

LUKE POWELL THANKED the Uber driver and fought to keep from wincing as he climbed out of the Prius. He still couldn't believe the doctor told him no driving for a week.

The doctor had also told him to go home and take it easy.

He'd gone home long enough to shower, change clothes, and grab something decent to eat. He hadn't planned on the two-hour nap that followed his meal of leftover pizza, but sliding into work at three in the afternoon gave him a better shot of not being noticed—and improved his odds of not being sent home immediately.

Luke scanned his badge and entered the office.

"Luke!" Leslie Martin, the woman who kept all of them organized, made sure they got paid, and never dropped the ball in the donut department, launched herself from her desk. She put on the brakes seconds before impact, thank heaven, and patted his arms gently, tears pooling, then streaming down her face.

So much for not being noticed. "Hey, Marty." Luke was the only one who called her Marty. It had been their joke since his first day on the job, and at his words, her silent tears became racking sobs.

He couldn't tell her not to cry. He'd have been happy to join her. He pulled her into a gentle embrace.

"Don't pull your stitches." She hiccupped the words as he squeezed her close.

"I'm okay, Marty."

She pulled away, swiping at the black streaks on her cheeks.

He kept one hand on her arm and reached for the box of tissues on her desk. "Here."

She took one. Then another.

Then swatted his arm. "You aren't supposed to be here. The doctor said not until Monday."

How did she know?

"Jacob won't like it." She wiped her nose.

"Luke Powell. My office. Now." The voice of Assistant Resident Agent in Charge Jacob Turner ripped down the hall.

Marty gave Luke a watery smirk. "Told you."

"If he sends me home, I'll buy your lunch tomorrow. But if I get to stay, you have to make me that chocolate cake you brought to Easter dinner." Luke backed toward the hall. "Deal?"

"Deal."

Marty's culinary skills were . . . alarming. Literally. She could set the smoke detectors off while trying to boil water, but she'd mastered one recipe. A succulent chocolate bundt cake that cried for a tall glass of milk or a big scoop of vanilla ice cream. The Weavers had invited everyone to lunch after Easter church services, and Marty's cake had been so popular that Luke had snagged only one small slice before it was gone.

"Hurry up, Powell."

"I think I'll want a salad from—" Luke closed the door of Jacob's office and cut off Marty's voice.

Jacob Turner looked up from his desk. "Sit."

If he sat, he might never get up. "I'd rather stand, if that's okay." Before Jacob could respond, Luke asked, "Did you go home last night?" Jacob's clothes were wrinkled, and he was wearing the same pants he'd had on yesterday when he'd come by the hospital. The bags under his eyes were more pronounced than usual. Like he'd, well, of course he'd been crying. They'd all cried.

Jacob didn't respond to his question. "How's the arm? The leg? The hands? The back?"

If Jacob insisted on cataloging every one of Luke's body parts that had been injured, this would take forever. "I'm good."

Jacob looked over the top of his readers, his expression un-amused.

"I can work."

Jacob continued to eye him. Luke had worked with him long enough to know that he would wait until Luke answered the original questions to his satisfaction.

"They had to put six stitches in the gash on my shoulder. And my arm is achy, but my mobility is good as long as I don't try to lift it above my head. Everything is sore. My leg is on fire. I have stitches in one calf from falling debris. And that blasted bullet skinned me. There's nothing to stitch or fix. I have to wait for the skin to regrow. It burns all the time. The nurse bandaged it with some waterproof stuff and gave me instructions on how to do it myself. I go back to the doctor in a few days for a recheck."

"I heard you're on medical leave until Monday."

"I understood that to be more of a suggestion."

Jacob set his reading glasses on the desk and pinched the bridge of his nose. "You're a pain in my side, Powell."

Luke considered saying something smart like, "Happy to help" or "You're welcome," but before he could decide on the best option, Jacob came around his desk and pulled him into a bear hug.

"I'm so glad you're okay, man." He pulled back and wiped his eyes. "We can't lose any more agents. You hear me? You stay alive."

Luke blinked back the moisture in his own eyes. "I'll do my best."

Jacob returned to his seat. "I've spoken to Dale Jefferson ten times since yesterday. He's assigned Faith Malone to the case. Says she's his best. You know her from the JTTF, right?"

"I do." The JTTF as well as multiple fundraisers and inter-agency events over the past few years. "We spoke yesterday. Briefly."

Jacob took a sip of coffee. "I know you don't like having the FBI run the case, but guess what? I don't care. Put it aside. At least she's someone you already know. If you're determined to be here, then you can be the official liaison between her and this office for the next week. Give her whatever she wants. Help her however you can. I don't care if I see you or not, especially since you aren't supposed to be here in the first place. But if I hear you're giving her grief, I'll send you home. Got it?"

There was no way he would sit out. "She'll have my full coop-eration."

"I thought you'd see it that way."

Luke walked past Marty's desk on his way to his own. Without pausing, he rapped his knuckles on her filing cabinet. "No rush, Marty, but you owe me a cake."

"What? No. I don't—get back here, Luke Powell." Marty's shocked spluttering followed him down the hall. The momentary humor vanished as he stuttered to a stop in front of Jared's cubicle. How was it possible that he wouldn't be back? Who had told his ex-wife? Jared's relationship with his ex had been a train wreck for as long as Luke had known Jared, but he didn't think the ex wanted him dead.

Special Agent Gil Dixon stepped from the cubicle beside Jared's. "What are you doing here, man?" Before Luke could answer, Gil had him in a hug that lasted a few seconds past comfortable. "You're okay?" Gil stepped back, eyes narrowing as he scanned Luke from top to bottom.

"I'll live. And right now, that's cause for celebration." Luke looked down the hall, where Michael's office sat empty.

"True that." Gil ran a hand through his spiky black hair, then over his day-old beard.

Luke pointed to the cubicle beside Gil's. "Where's Tessa?" Even as he asked the question, he couldn't help but wonder how long it would be, if ever, before he would stop wanting to know where everyone was at all times.

"She was at Jared's. Not sure what she was doing. She called Leslie and told her she was swinging by the hospital to check on Zane before she came back. She's bringing coffee for everyone. If you want something, you'd better text her."

Luke pulled his phone from his pocket and shot a quick text.

I'll take an Americano. Quad. Thx.

Her response came seconds later.

What are you doing at work? Zane is ticked.

Before he could respond, his phone rang. Zane. "What's up—?"

"I know they didn't give you permission to go to work." Zane sounded equal parts amused, annoyed, and impressed. "How'd you manage it?"

"Showed up. Better to ask forgiveness than permission. And it's not like Jacob can tell me no. So he assigned me to work with Faith."

Gil grinned. Zane whistled. Faith Malone had been the subject of more than a few conversations, usually involving Thad, Zane, and Gil trying to get Luke to ask her out.

"Not funny." Luke spoke to Zane and glared at Gil.

"It's hilarious and you know it." Gil leaned against the wall. "This is the best thing I've heard in twenty-four hours."

Luke could hear Zane filling Tessa in and the accompanying laughter. "You can all shut it," Luke said. "She's too young for me."

"She's thirty-one." Zane must have put him on speakerphone, because Tessa's voice came through the line at full volume.

"That's older than you, Luke," Gil pointed out. Helpful. Since Gil was already listening in, Luke put his phone on speaker too.

"Not by much." He directed the comment to Gil and then turned back to the phone. "How do you know how old she is, Tessa?"

"I looked her up after I heard she'd been assigned the case." Tessa did not add the implied "duh," but Luke heard it all the same. "She's received a lot of awards. And I talked to a buddy at the FBI, and he says she's the rising star of the office. She's worked some high-profile cases and has the support of upper management. My buddy says she's already turned down a move to a bigger office. The suspicion is that there's some family drama. She's pretty closed about it. He didn't have any other details. But he says whatever it is, it's a problem she leaves at home. He also said if he had to pick one agent to have the lead, it would be her. I don't think anyone in their office was surprised she got the call."

Tessa hadn't told Luke anything he didn't already know, but he had to give her full marks for how succinctly she'd summarized the mystery that was Faith Malone.

"We need a rock-star agent on this case," Zane said. "I don't think I could handle it if we had to deal with that moron who's been working Thad's case."

"What moron?" Luke and Gil both turned to the voice that came from the general direction of Marty's desk.

Faith Malone stood at the end of the hall.

How much had she heard? Based on the smirk she was fighting, he'd guess most of it.

"Janice Estes." Zane's voice rang through the hall.

Was it Luke's imagination, or had Faith shuddered?

"Zane and Tessa, Faith has joined us on this call." Gil, ever the master of diplomacy, smiled at Faith and beckoned her to join them.

"Wonderful," Tessa said. "We're at your disposal, Faith. Whatever you need."

"Same for me," Zane said. "Although in my case, it had best be something computer related."

Faith shook Gil's hand, then took Luke's with a gentleness that surprised him, but he appreciated it. Both of his hands were scraped and burned from yesterday's game of debris dodgeball.

"When can we bust you out of there, Zane?" Gil asked.

"I'm hoping within the hour." Zane's voice had a tinge of desperation. Luke understood.

"I'm going to wait for the doctor to come by," Tessa said. "The nurse said it should be within the next fifteen minutes. Apparently, Zane made a compelling case this morning, and the doctor told him he'd consider letting him go. If the doctor turns him loose, I'll drive him home."

"She means she'll drive me to the office."

"I will not."

"You promised everyone coffee. You have to go to the office."

"We can discuss it later."

The silence from the phone was so tense that Luke couldn't stop from laughing. Gil joined him. Faith smiled. "Okay, you two," Luke said. "I'm going to hang up. Tessa, update us as soon as the doctor makes a decision."

"You got it."

Luke ended the call and slid his phone into his back pocket.

"Are they a couple?" Faith asked.

"No." Gil and Luke answered at the same time.

Faith's eyebrows rose in obvious disbelief.

"Tessa was assigned to Zane when she came on board last year. Zane's headed to Phase Two within the next few months. She was supposed to be his replacement." Gil scanned the hall. "I hope this doesn't mean a delay on his transition to Phase Two. That would be a real kick in the pants."

"Well"—Faith looked around—"is there a conference room I can borrow? I'd say we need to figure out who's trying to kill y'all. If we don't, no one will accept an assignment here, and poor Zane will never get away."

Much to Luke's frustration, his mental approval rating for Faith kept going up. Even though she had to have overheard them talking about her, she hadn't gotten her shorts in a wad over it, so she wasn't too sensitive to be tolerated. She was very sensitive to their losses and hadn't asked for any of the obviously available cubicles all around them but instead requested a neutral space none of them would have an attachment to. He couldn't help but respect that.

And she had a bit of a dark sense of humor. He liked it.

He liked her more all the time. And he didn't like that at all.

—6—

FAITH FOLLOWED LUKE to the conference room and paused inside the door. The table seated twelve. Wall-mounted televisions occupied both of the side walls, while photographs of the president, the secretary of the Department of Homeland Security, and the director of the Secret Service were scattered across the remaining wall space. "Will this work?" Luke was all kindness and civility. He probably suspected she'd overheard most of the conversation about her age and qualifications. She wanted to be ticked off, but the truth was, it was exactly what they would have done at the FBI if the roles had been reversed.

"This will be great. Thanks."

"Can I get you anything? We don't have Cherry Coke in the machine, but Tessa's supposed to be bringing coffee in a little while." He pulled out his phone. "Want me to have her bring you something?"

"No. Thank you. I mainly stopped by today to touch base with Jacob Turner and to make a few arrangements." And to see what happened if she showed up unannounced. "I'll be back first thing in the morning, if that's okay."

"That's fine. I'll take you to see Jacob."

"Thank you."

Before they could leave the room, Jacob entered. "Faith, I wasn't expecting to see you today. Everything going okay?"

"Yes, sir." She took the seat Jacob indicated. Luke settled into the chair beside her. Jacob didn't question his presence.

Jacob took a seat at the head of the table and leaned back in his chair. "Faith, I've assigned Luke to be your liaison with our office. I think it should go without saying, but if at any time you feel that he or any member of our team is stonewalling you, please bring it to my attention."

Faith murmured, "Yes, sir," but there was no time for her to say anything else because Jacob stood and paced.

"Someone killed my people, Faith. We're a small office here, and we don't always see eye to eye or get along perfectly, but we're a family. We still don't have any answers about Thad Baker, and I'll be—"

He cut himself off and took a deep breath, and Faith had a flash of insight. Jacob Turner was coiled tight.

Why?

The obvious answer was grief. Shock. Anger.

But she couldn't rule out the possibility that there was more to it. Three agents had died. Two others could have died. But he was still alive. Was that a coincidence, or was that because he was behind it? Was he trying to cover something up? Protect someone from prosecution or discovery? She didn't really think it was possible that Jacob was responsible for these deaths, but at this point everyone was a suspect.

Jacob ran a hand over his bald head and returned to his seat. "There's no nice way to say this. You have two weeks. If you can't figure out what's going on, I'll be going over your head, and over Dale's head, and I'll be requesting we create a task force. We've waited almost three months for answers regarding Thad Baker's death, and the agent who's responsible for the case has been less than forthcoming. I'm tired of waiting. I want answers, and I want them yesterday."

Faith kept her breathing steady and refused to break eye contact. She wouldn't be bullied by this man. She knew how to do her job, and she knew that short of a miracle, two weeks wasn't enough time to do much of anything. Dale would back her up, and he'd probably be able to talk Jacob out of doing anything drastic.

"I've already talked to Dale." Jacob pointed to the phone. "We've agreed that the Thad Baker case needs to be included in this one. He's going to talk to the agent, and he said she would be available to provide you with all the information you need on this case by tomorrow."

Do not grin. Faith gave Jacob a curt nod. "I'll talk to her in the morning before I come here." Janice had been noticeably absent from the office last night and again today, but she couldn't stay away forever.

All the things Faith suspected Janice of doing flooded her mind, and the urge to smile fled. The way notes had disappeared from her desk, phone numbers jotted down on sticky notes had been changed, even an entire file had gone missing. Janice was already out to get her.

Would this drive Janice to extremes?

Faith shoved all her worries about Janice out of her mind. "If possible, I'd like to interview everyone tomorrow." She hoped her tone conveyed that she wasn't really asking but was trying to be sensitive.

"Everyone but Zane will be available," Jacob said.

Luke fake coughed and Faith heard, "Yeah right."

Jacob shook his head, but she could tell he wasn't as annoyed as he was trying to appear. "If Zane puts in an appearance tomorrow, I'm sure he'll be happy to talk to you. Otherwise, he'll make himself available to you as soon as possible."

"Thank you." She hesitated.

Jacob eyed her from beneath eyebrows that really could use a few minutes with some tweezers. "Is there something else, Faith?"

"I was wondering about the arrangements, sir. For the families?"

Jacob dropped his head. "The bodies were sent to the, er, um, the medical examiner."

Faith didn't miss the way Jacob stumbled over the words.

"Michael's autopsy was this morning. The findings were in keeping with what we expected from the dart that was found. All the toxicology results are being rushed, but it will be a few weeks before we have them. Jared's . . ."

Luke shifted in the seat beside her, and Faith could feel the tension pouring off of him.

"Jared's remains were sent to a medical examiner in DC who specializes in burn victims. We're hoping for results by midweek, but it could be next week." Agent Turner ran a hand over his head again. "Jared didn't have family here. He was from Milwaukee, and his parents are taking care of everything there."

Jacob stood and leaned over the table. The man couldn't be still. "Michael didn't have any family here either. He and Karen, his wife, are both from Illinois. The funeral might be there, might be here. Karen hasn't made any decisions yet. The kids are—"

Jacob turned his back on them and stood facing the window to the outside. The anguish was palpable in the room.

Faith didn't see any reason for Jacob to finish his thought, so she went with a slightly different topic. "I understand Jared Smith was divorced."

"Yes. No kids. His ex-wife is . . ." Jacob turned and looked to Luke for help.

"The woman is a barracuda." Luke made no effort to hide his disgust.

Lovely.

"Jared wasn't a saint. No one will pretend he was. But he didn't deserve the way she cleaned him out. She took everything and continued to bleed him dry. If she's crying right now, it's only because she won't be getting that alimony check."

"Was their divorce over a specific event or—"

"Irreconcilable differences. She hated his job. Hated his travel. Hated the hours."

"How long were they married?" Faith was trying to make sense of what she was hearing.

"Ten years. She thought it was cool to be the wife of the guy guarding the president. Not so much being the wife of the guy who handled the electronic crimes cases in an RAIC in North Carolina. When he didn't get sent to a big city for his Phase Three, she pushed for him to find a new job. But he enjoyed the investigative side even more than the protective side, and he wanted to stay in."

Luke made eye contact with Jacob. Faith couldn't be sure, but given the grief reflected in both of their eyes, she wondered if they were thinking the same thing she was.

Jared's passion for his work may have gotten him killed.

LUKE'S PHONE VIBRATED, and he checked the message.

No coffee for any of you. Taking Zane to pick
up prescriptions, then home. #notsorry See
you tomorrow.

Both Faith and Jacob were watching him. He waved the phone. "Tessa. She's not bringing coffee. She's taking Zane home."

Jacob didn't seem nearly as relieved as he'd expected him to be. "I'm not sure he should be out yet."

"He'll be fine." Jacob was right, but Luke couldn't blame Zane for wanting out of there. "Faith, I'm at your service this week." He glanced at his watch. How was it already 4:30? "Is there anything you want to work on now?"

"Yes." She didn't hesitate. "Since yesterday, we've been focused on the specifics of what happened. Gathering evidence. Studying the crime scenes. Pulling video surveillance from the areas in and around the attacks. I have agents tracking down bomb fragments and looking at tire tracks to give me a vehicle description."

Luke realized she didn't mention how frustrated she was with their lack of progress, which was not because they weren't working around the clock but because whoever had done this had done a good job of covering his tracks.

"I can't shake the feeling that this is connected to Thad Baker, and I want you to fill me in on what the Secret Service knows about his death."

Jacob snorted. "You get full marks for diving into the deep end, Agent Malone." He turned to Luke. "Tell her everything and then tell her the rest of it. I'll be in my office. I have work to do, and my wife and kids have expressed a desire to see me before midnight."

Jacob left the room, and the silence that fell over the conference room was broken by Luke's stomach growling. Twice. Faith chuckled. "When's the last time you had real food, Agent Powell?"

She had a kind smile on her face, and if she hadn't tacked on the somewhat sarcastic *Agent Powell*, he might have thought she was being genuinely nice. As it was . . . "I had some leftover pizza around eleven thirty."

Faith wrinkled her nose.

"What's wrong with leftover pizza?"

"Nothing. But you aren't going to be any help if you can't concentrate on anything because you're hungry," she said. "And I would like to get the Secret Service angle today, if you're up for it."

"I'm up for it." Not really. But he couldn't let her see him weak. Especially after the disaster that had been yesterday.

"Then maybe we should have this conversation over dinner."

Dinner? With Faith Malone? For a split second he could picture them, the way they'd been while working together to plan the interagency golf tournament, sitting on opposite sides of a booth, leaning toward each other, laughing. "Sure. Where do you want to go?"

Faith glanced at her watch. "If we leave now, we should be able to get a seat at Relish without waiting too long. Today seems like the kind of day that calls for comfort food, don't you think?"

"I agree. And you've never met a version of mac and cheese that you didn't find comforting." Relish offered at least seven varieties.

She laughed. A real laugh that reached her eyes and crinkled her face in all the right places. "I won't even try to deny it."

"I'm not complaining. They have great burgers. Let's do it."

Gil Dixon tapped on the door. "Hey, Luke. Sorry to bother you, but I was getting ready to head out. Need a lift?"

Luke's eyes flashed to Faith's. Should he ask Gil to join them? He didn't want Gil to come, but it's not like this was a date or anything.

"Actually, we're headed out in a few minutes to grab dinner and talk about the Thad Baker case," Faith said. "You're welcome to join us."

Gil, the traitor, didn't even try to hide his glee at this news. "Dinner? Where are you going?"

If he'd been close enough to reach him, Luke would have slugged him. As it was, all he could do was watch in mute horror as the drama unfolded.

"Relish. For mac and cheese."

"Relish? That sounds delicious." Gil tilted his head as if he was considering joining them. He cut his eyes once at Luke before smiling warmly at Faith. "I would love to join you."

Luke's fingers twitched.

"Unfortunately, I have a roast in the Crock-Pot that will turn to mush if I don't get home and rescue it. I'll have to take a rain check." He nodded in Luke's direction. "I know he's all yours, but could I borrow Luke for a few minutes before you leave?"

"Of course. I need to check my email and messages anyway." Faith tapped her iPad. "I'll hang out here until you're ready to go."

Luke followed Gil out of the conference room and around the corner to the large open space that held their cubicles. As soon as they were out of sight of the conference room door, Gil turned and walked backward. "How'd you manage it? Did she feel sorry for you for getting shot? Is that why she finally said yes?" Gil laughed at his own joke.

"It's not a date. It's dinner."

"Alone, with Faith. Sounds like a date to me." Gil continued to laugh as he walked to his desk. "Just so you know, I'm calling Zane and Tessa as soon as I get in the car."

"Was there something you needed, or did you drag me out here so you could have a little fun at my expense?"

Gil's expression sobered. "You didn't want me to say yes, did you? I mean, I assumed—"

"Of course I don't want you to come," Luke hissed. "But I also don't need you making it out to be something it isn't."

Gil's grin returned. "Okay. Just making sure we're on the same page. Do you need a ride in the morning?"

"No. Don't worry about it. I'll catch an Uber. But thanks." He left Gil and walked into his own cubicle where his first order of business was to grab a bottle of ibuprofen and pop two tablets in his mouth. After a moment of hesitation, he popped two more. Everything hurt. He could imagine how much worse Zane must be feeling. All he wanted to do was go home, crawl into his bed . . . and wake up in a world where no one was killing off his friends or trying to kill him.

He grabbed his phone and tossed his laptop, notepad, and pen into a messenger bag. As he walked back to the conference room, he scrolled through his text messages—four from his mom in the last two hours—and opened the conference room door without looking up from his phone.

"Mom, I'm not going to argue with you about this."

It wasn't until he registered the tone of Faith's voice that he took his eyes off his screen. She had her back to the door, and he doubted she'd heard him enter.

"I can't." Faith's tone was a study in respectful annoyance.

But if she saw him and thought he was listening in, he had no doubt he would experience the "zero respect and completely annoyed" version of Special Agent Faith Malone. He took a step back. Then another. *Don't turn around, Faith.*

Faith rolled her head in a slow circle. "Don't give me that. Hope understands."

Luke took two more steps. He was back in the hall.

Faith let out a long sigh, then a few "uh-huhs" and "okays."

He reached for the door and pulled it closed.

"I'll check in with you later this week. No, I won't be able to ton—"

Luke knocked on the door, louder than necessary, and pushed the door open for the second time.

Faith turned around and waved him in. "Tomorrow." Her tone left no room for argument. "Okay. Bye." A pause. "Love you too." She ended the call and slid the phone into her back pocket. "Sorry about that."

"No problem." Should he ask if everything was okay or let it go?

Faith was a thundercloud, and all that remained was to see if she would pour down rain or flash lightning. Either option had terrifying implications. Crying women were scary. Angry women were also scary. Women who were crying because they were angry? That was the stuff of nightmares.

"I'm ready whenever you are."

"Great." She gathered all her things.

Gil stuck his head into the conference room. "Powell. Malone. Let's go. We're burning daylight."

"What's *your* hurry? All you have tonight is a hot date with a pot roast." Luke knew the words were a mistake as soon as they left his mouth.

Gil cracked his knuckles. "I didn't think you'd want to share, Powell."

"What I want to know," Faith said, interjecting herself into the conversation with ease, "is what's so special about this pot roast that you would turn down the mac and cheese from Relish."

Her words were playful. And if she'd caught Gil's meaning, she'd done a great job of hiding it.

Gil laughed. "I have a great recipe. I'll share it with you. It's foolproof."

"I think you may be giving me more credit than I deserve." Faith patted her bag. "I love gadgets and gizmos and time-saving devices. But I've never had much success with anything cooking related. I don't even own a Crock-Pot."

Gil stared at Faith in dismay. Luke clapped him on the shoulder. "Not everyone wants to have their own cooking show, man."

They trooped down the hall. "I would kill on a cooking show." Gil stated this as fact, with no hint of arrogance. "I can hear the promos now. They'll play up my Secret Service career. I'll be a hit."

Despite the lightness of the conversation, their situational awareness went through the stratosphere as they exited the building. Luke paused by the door and grabbed a telescoping inspection mirror from the security guard station. They all hesitated before going outside, each of them scanning the parking lot and the cars parked there.

"Give me that." Gil yanked the mirror from Luke's grasp.

"I wonder how long it will take me to hop in a car and take off without checking it for a bomb?" Luke mused as Gil paced around Faith's car, the mirror slid underneath.

"My recommendation is that you don't consider it until we figure out who's behind all this." Gil cleared Faith's car, then moved to his own. "We're good to go."

Luke waited as Gil ran the mirror back inside. By the time he returned, Faith had the doors unlocked and was sliding behind the steering wheel. "Thanks, man. See you tomorrow." The words were part command, part promise.

Gil acknowledged Luke's words with a lifted chin, then climbed into his car. Luke took his spot in the passenger seat beside Faith, and she waited until he had buckled his seatbelt before she followed Gil from the parking lot.

Gil turned left, and Faith turned right.

"I have a suggestion," she said after they were on the highway.

"I'm all ears."

"Let's order the food to go."

"To go?"

"Yes."

"Where would we eat?"

"I have an idea. Trust me. You'll like it."

He did like it.

She'd picked up the food and driven them a few miles out of Raleigh before pulling up to a gated driveway. Luke barely kept his curiosity in check as she entered the code, then wound around the drive and parked beside a small boathouse on a wide river. A luxurious pontoon boat was stored underneath the dock, along with several single sculls.

"Where are we?"

"A friend of my family owns this place. They're almost never here, but they let me use it anytime I want. This is where I row." She pointed to the single sculls on the dock. "Those are mine. And this river flows into a lake about a mile from here. I thought . . ." Her voice trailed off, and she frowned. "I think you could still be a target, and eating in public probably isn't the best idea. And I thought you might appreciate the privacy of this place. I'm guessing our conversation won't be one you would want overheard."

She was right about that.

"Is this okay?" There was something vulnerable in the way she asked the question, and Luke realized that more than giving them a private place to talk, she'd also revealed a piece of herself. This place was important to her, and he doubted she made a habit out of bringing people here, but she'd shared it with him.

"It's perfect."

She smiled at his response. "Let's eat before the food gets cold, and then you can tell me about Thad."

She led him away from the dock and around the side of the boathouse. "Gil is going to be so mad that he didn't come," he said with a laugh. "This is something else." A stone chimney stretched into the sky, surrounded by a low stone wall. Comfortable chairs were arranged around it, and on one side was the largest grilling station he had ever seen.

With practiced movements, Faith lit the gas logs in the chimney and pulled the chairs around a low table. Luke set the food out and bowed his head before digging into his burger. Faith took four bites of her French mac—a mac and cheese loaded with ham, swiss, and mushrooms—before turning her attention to him.

"Are you comfortable enough out here?" She eyed the chair he was sitting in. "It wouldn't surprise me if you left the hospital against medical advice."

He ignored the second observation. "I'm good, and this place is fantastic. Do you row often?"

She swallowed before answering. "I try to get out here at least three mornings a week. Sometimes four. I've always loved being on the water. My grandfather had a boat that would make you cry it was so beautiful. The deepest brown wood, shined to a high gloss. When I was little, we visited my grandparents every summer, and we'd spend days, sometimes nights too, on the lake." She cleared her throat. "We moved to Charlotte when I was in middle school, and I learned how to row through a kids' rowing program. I never looked back."

Her face softened as she talked about the water, about rowing at UVA, about the differences between rowing with a partner, a team, or single. He'd known she could row since their offices had teamed up for a dragon boat race to raise money for breast cancer, but he'd had no idea how deeply she was connected to the sport.

He didn't miss the way she avoided mentioning her family and offered no details about why she'd moved to Charlotte or how she'd come to be in Raleigh. He didn't press. There was time.

He hoped.

He finished off his burger and guzzled down the last of the bottled water he'd brought with him as she polished off her mac and cheese with obvious delight.

"Be right back." She disappeared around the corner, and the sound of the car door opening and closing carried on the air. When she returned, she had her iPad and fancy pencil. She settled back into her seat. "I'm ready whenever you are."

Where to begin? How did anyone describe finding out their best friend and mentor had been incinerated?

Or worse, that his memory and reputation had been incinerated as well?

He cleared his throat. "Let me tell you about Thad first."

Faith didn't speak or look up, but she nodded, and he took that as approval. "Thad is . . . was . . . married to Rose. They have two kids. Twins. Elizabeth and Robert, but they go by Betsy and Bobby."

"Cute."

"They're cute holy terrors. And that was before their dad died. Since then, they're either crying, destroying the house, picking fights with kids in the neighborhood, or cutting their hair." The moment he saw Betsy's dark locks in a swirl on the kitchen floor, he'd known things had reached a whole new level of trauma in the Baker house.

"Understandable." Faith didn't look up, but her pencil flew across the screen.

It was easier to talk without her staring at him. "Rose is trying to cut them a lot of slack, but it's been hard. We all went to their birthday party on Sunday. Pizza and arcade stuff with the kids, then back to the house for cake and ice cream with the family."

He tried to force away the image of Jared teaching Betsy how to swing dance while Michael discussed the latest superhero movie with Bobby.

"We've tried to be there for them, but it isn't enough. We're busy, and we can't be around as much as she needs us to be. And the truth is, our presence is partly comforting and partly agonizing. The very fact that we're alive is a reminder that Thad isn't. And"—here came the hard part—"she's not sure who to trust."

"By she, you mean Rose?" Faith continued writing.

"Yes."

"Why is that?"

Frustration bubbled up. "Like you don't know." He closed his eyes and fought a surge of anger. He could understand that Faith hadn't been briefed on the case in an official capacity, but Thad's death had been all over the news, and the court of public opinion had burned Thad at the stake for infidelity and treachery. The facts had been irrelevant.

It didn't help that actual facts were thin on the ground at the moment.

When he reopened his eyes, she'd stopped writing and was looking at him. She held up a hand in a pacifying gesture. "I know what I've heard, but I'd prefer to hear it from you. Your version might not jibe with what I've been led to understand, and I'm trying to go into this with an open mind."

The anger dissipated, replaced with chagrin. Was it possible he had overreacted to a valid question? "Fair enough."

Faith resumed her writing, and he went back to staring at the river behind her.

"We've tried to piece it together on our end, although we've been blocked more than I think is appropriate from other official entities."

Her gaze flicked to his, then back to her notes. Good. She knew he was talking about the FBI.

"We know Thad went to dinner that evening. It wasn't on his calendar, and there were no emails or text messages mentioning it. The restaurant cameras hadn't worked for over a month, and none of the footage retrieved from patrons' phones shows Thad. We know he got into his car, and we know it exploded a few seconds later.

The memory of that night threatened to overwhelm him. The stench of burning plastic and flesh. The horror of the charred remains. The flicker of hope that it wasn't Thad and the phone call that confirmed it was.

The trip to the Baker home.

The disbelief in Rose's eyes and the way it was replaced with agony.

The funeral.

He dropped his head. There would be two more funerals soon. More crying mothers, more stunned children, more trembling wives.

"Luke?"

He didn't know what kind of look she would have on her face, but he didn't want to see pity or suspicion.

"Luke—"

"Look, we have no idea what he was doing there. We don't know who he met. When we arrived on the scene, we didn't expect to find anyone but Thad in the car."

"How did you discover the second body?"

Luke had to push the reality of it away and be analytical. He could do this. "Some of the body parts didn't match. The forensic anthropologist got involved to sort it out, but there was a serial killer case she had to testify for, and the bodies sat for a week before she got to work. A preliminary report indicated the body might be female, and then someone in the press reported that Thad had been with a prostitute."

"I heard, but my understanding is that there's no proof."

"There isn't any proof, and there won't be because it isn't true."

"We know the other person in the car was female. How can you know for sure she wasn't—"

"You wouldn't have to ask if you'd known Thad."

"And you did." Her observation wasn't dripping with sympathy for his loss, but it wasn't sarcastic either. "Tell me about him."

"Thad loved God, his wife, his kids, and his country, in that order. I don't have to know the details to know that whatever was happening that night, there is a rational explanation that doesn't involve him cheating on his wife."

— 7 —

"HE WOULDN'T HAVE BEEN THE FIRST man to cheat on his wife and not try to hide it." Despite her best efforts, the edge in Faith's voice was sharp enough to slice through granite.

Luke contemplated her for a moment, and her stomach flipped. Yeah. He'd noticed.

"Some men are idiots," Luke said.

True enough.

"Thad wasn't." Luke spoke with conviction, not defensiveness. "He was a gentleman, and I'd bet my last bullet he was giving that woman a ride because it was raining. He loved his wife. His kids were his whole world."

Maybe.

"You don't believe me."

Faith stopped writing at Luke's words, but she kept her eyes on her notes. "It's not my job to believe you. It's my job to find out what happened, which I intend to do without any preconceived notions."

She couldn't tell him that she had no doubt the investigation had been mishandled. Janice wasn't a bad agent, but she had her biases. One of which was that all men were scum. At the first whiff of scandal surrounding Thad Baker, Janice would have gone with the assumption that either he was a traitor to his country or he'd cheated on his wife, and possibly had been guilty of both. And her investigation would have followed the path her assumptions led her. Given that she'd been unable to solve the case, it would seem her path had led her nowhere, which in a roundabout way gave credence to Luke's theory that Thad Baker hadn't done anything wrong.

Faith had more reasons than Janice to hate men—especially men who cheated on their spouse and forgot about their children. But she'd worked hard to keep her personal life and her professional life separate. And unlike Janice, who rejoiced when her harsh assumptions were proven accurate, Faith desperately hoped she would be proven wrong.

Wouldn't it be amazing if there really were a few good men left in the world?

Luke remained silent, and Faith risked a glance. She expected him to be closed off, radiating hostility. Instead, she was caught in a gaze so tender that she couldn't force herself to look away.

"Who hurt you?" Luke's words were soft. The question contemplative.

Faith dropped her pencil. It bounced off her chair and rolled under the table. "I'm sorry. What?" She bent to retrieve the pencil, desperate for a few seconds to pull herself together. It had traveled farther than she'd expected, and a small groan escaped her lips. She slid from the chair and crawled under the table.

But Luke beat her to it. He knelt under the table, pencil in his hand. "I'm sorry."

He meant for the pencil. Right? Or was he apologizing for asking the question? It had been wildly inappropriate after all. Her personal life was none of his concern.

But he was concerned. She could see it. Sense it as she took the pencil from his hand. Feel it as a tremor raced through her fingertips as they brushed his.

It was impossible to scoot from under the table in a dignified fashion. Not that she didn't try. She pressed her hand on the table-top and stood. Then she made a quick adjustment to the weapon at her waist and returned to her seat as Luke resettled into his.

A long silence fell. Faith finally broke it. "You have to have a theory about who killed Thad. My understanding is that the bomb was no hack job but also didn't have a recognizable signature to anyone at ATF. Is that correct?"

"It is." Luke didn't elaborate.

She consulted her iPad. "It wasn't in the news, but Thad had the lead on the Stevsky case . . ."

"He did."

"How'd the Stevskys handle having their patriarch sent to federal prison?"

"He never made it."

"That's right. He died in jail. Heart attack or something. I'm guessing the Stevskys don't believe it was a heart attack?"

"They do not. We kept it out of the papers, but the Stevskys were quite vocal about their desire to take revenge on our office."

"And Thad specifically?" Faith asked.

Luke nodded.

Faith tapped and scanned the iPad, desperately hoping Luke wouldn't realize how furious she was.

She twirled the pen in her fingers. "Did Special Agent Estes investigate the Stevskys?"

"You'll have to tell us." Luke made no effort to disguise his aggravation. "Estes has been a jerk." Luke didn't meet her eye. "She refuses to tell us anything. You'd think we were the ones who blew him up, or that we were in league with Stevsky. Which makes no sense at all."

"I want to hear everything about Stevsky, but I don't want to get too much in the weeds before we clarify a few other things."

She could feel the tension pouring off Luke in waves. "What else do you want to know?"

"I can see why the Stevsky family is the obvious choice for Most Likely to Kill Thad Baker, but who else is on the list? He'd been in this business long enough to put more than Stevsky in jail. Did y'all look at his cases from before he came to Raleigh? And since?"

"We did." There was an edge to Luke's voice. "We investigate too. And we're very, very good at it."

Faith refused to snap back. "I never said you weren't. I'm asking because I don't have any record of it, and I'm wondering if you have an email you might have sent Janice. It doesn't make sense for us to recreate the wheel all because she can't file properly."

She pressed her lips together. She hadn't meant to say that out loud. "Or so I've heard."

"You can't stand her either." There was vindication, and something else—maybe relief—in Luke's voice.

"I did not say—"

"You didn't have to. Even Gil, who gets along with everybody, is convinced that Janice Estes is either grossly incompetent or an evil genius working her own plan to take over the entire world."

It took her a moment to respond. "Be that as it may, do you have the information you provided to her, and is it something I could see?"

Luke was looking at her with an expression she couldn't quite get a read on. He had been angry earlier. Testy. Quick to assume the worst. But now? There was something hopeful in his eyes. Something that might be inching its way toward trust.

— 8 —

FAITH FOCUSED on her iPad. She had no doubt Janice had the missing information and had simply failed to provide it. She hated the thought that someone as inept as Janice Estes had managed to become an FBI agent.

Luke went to the car to retrieve his laptop. When he returned, it only took him a few moments to find the file and send it to her. She opened it and scanned the list. She remembered a few of these cases. Most she hadn't heard a peep about.

And she understood why there had been such a singular focus on the Stevskys.

"Not to belittle the work you've done here, but most of this is relatively small stuff. Minor players. Electronic crimes are important to their victims, but these are not the type of criminals who are likely to escalate to murdering a federal agent. Unless . . . you have classified cases you didn't provide due to national security concerns. Do you?"

Luke grinned at her. "Funny how your coworker never asked about that."

Hilarious.

"We did a thorough investigation on the handful of items not provided to you. Three cases, to be exact. None of which had a particular tie to Thad. None of which had ever been violent in nature. We've officially closed out the investigations into all three. They either have rock-solid alibis or a complete lack of motive combined with zero resources to pull off such an attack."

Part of Faith longed to insist they show her those cases. Let her be the judge of whether they had any merit. But unlike Luke, who had issues with the FBI, Faith didn't have a beef with the Secret Service. She'd always admired them and what they stood for. She'd never met an agent she couldn't respect—at least not on the job. And she had no doubt that this group of agents had been deeply motivated to find their friend's killer. If there had been a minuscule chance that any of the classified cases held the key to a conviction, they would have found it.

"Okay."

Luke gaped at her.

"Let's go back to the Stevsky—"

"That's it?"

"What's it?" Faith knew what Luke was fishing for, but where was the fun in giving in too fast?

"You're okay with me not telling you about the classified cases? Or are you saying okay, and tomorrow you'll have your director on the phone with our director and it will be a whole thing?"

Luke had a vivid imagination. She'd give him that. He needed to relax, but that might be difficult for a man who had lost as many friends as Luke had and had been shot at—was it just yesterday?

"I'm saying okay, which means I'll leave a note in my official file stating I did not personally review the cases—the Secret Service handled that aspect of the investigation—and I was satisfied with their results. I'll let you see the letter. You can sign it if you want to."

Luke frowned. Was he going to insist on seeing the letter? "That won't be necessary."

"Excellent." No point in belaboring things. "Back to the Stevsky case. What can you tell me about that one?"

"Almost everything." Luke tapped a few keystrokes on his computer. "The only pieces of the puzzle missing for us have to do with how the old man died. We didn't have him killed, and we don't know who did it."

Luke spun his computer around so she could see the monitor. "This is the senior Stevsky. Convicted in October of multiple counts of electronic fraud, tax evasion, human trafficking, and just for good measure, counterfeiting."

"He sounds like a real sweetheart."

"You're being sarcastic, but if you'd ever met him, you'd say the same thing. The man oozed a particularly potent essence of kindly grandfather and generous business owner. Everyone in the Raleigh area thought the Stevsky family was the great American story. Immigrants who had come to America and made good within three generations. But the reason they were doing so well was because they were literally printing their own money and ripping people off."

He spun the computer back around. "The Stevsky case was Thad's baby. A few years ago, he got a tip from a confidential informant, and the guy was so scared, he called Thad all the time. Called him when he was at home. On Sundays when he was at church. But the CI was right, and Thad believed his story. Stuck with the case even after the CI decided to relocate for his own safety."

"Where's the CI now?"

Luke brown eyes softened. "He's okay. Lives somewhere out West. He refused witness protection, but Jacob checked in with him yesterday. He's married with a new baby." Anytime Luke talked about kids, his whole demeanor changed. He must enjoy them. For her part, she had limited exposure to baby humans. Or little humans. Or pretty much any human who didn't have a fully formed prefrontal cortex. Although, come to think of it, she strongly suspected a few of the guys she'd dated in college had still been growing their brains. She almost hoped so. It would have given them an excuse for being so stupid.

"Anyone else associated with the Stevsky case who we should contact?" Faith scrolled through the files on her iPad. "Judges? Attorneys? Jurors?"

"Gil and Tessa did that last night and this morning. They made a list of everyone they could think of, including the court stenographer and the handful of reporters who had been allowed inside. They called me this morning while I was still at the hospital to see if I could think of anyone they had missed. All have been put on alert. Local law enforcement is on alert as well. They gave them names and addresses and requested a heads-up if there was any activity near their homes or businesses."

Faith went back through a mental checklist of questions, but these guys had anticipated, and answered, everything.

"I haven't worked any organized crime–related cases in Raleigh. What kind of competition do the Stevskys have?"

"Not much. There are a couple of wannabe families and a few serious gangs, but none of them have the level of finesse the Stevskys had."

"Had?" Faith locked in on the word. "Are they gone? That would create a vacuum someone would want to fill."

"True." Luke's antagonism had lessened. When she questioned something, he wasn't quite as quick to throw up a wall. Good. "We aren't convinced they're gone, primarily for that reason. No one has emerged as the new leader of the family, but no other group has claimed any sort of superiority over the Stevskys. We're leaning toward more of a dormant state. Possibly because they haven't worked out their internal power structure with the death of Stevsky. The other possibility is that they're planning something and are keeping a low profile."

"Well, if they're behind this, they're still keeping a low profile." Faith continued to scan the file. "No one has taken any kind of credit or claimed responsibility. When a federal agency is attacked, the people responsible either shout it from the rooftops or some nobody in their organization lets it slip that they were behind it. Either way, it gets out."

"Yes," Luke said. "But the Stevskys operated with an 'out of sight, out of mind' philosophy. They didn't want credit. They just wanted power and money, at least that's how it was when the senior Stevsky was in control. We don't have a handle on the younger Stevskys. Or how they would react to the loss of the old man under those kinds of circumstances. I've been in touch with my CIs, but no one has heard anything. They've promised to get back to me if anything changes."

Faith stood. She needed to move, and she needed to talk this out. "For the sake of argument, if it was them, what are they angry about? Getting caught? Getting convicted? Or the death of the senior Stevsky? Because attempting to eliminate an entire Secret Service office is no small undertaking. You have to be seriously angry."

Luke scoffed. "Or seriously deranged."

He wasn't wrong there. "Either way, we need to find out how they're doing. Has anyone talked to the sons, daughters, brothers of Stevsky?"

"You'll have to ask Estes." Luke's mouth quirked when he spoke, and Faith got the impression that he was delighted to share this particular bit of information. "We were told to stay away from them. Something about not wanting to clue them in to the fact that we were on to them."

How many antacids had Faith consumed because of Janice drama? And why didn't she have any with her at the moment? "I haven't heard of any FBI movement against Stevsky, but I'll ask Janice tomorrow. What about the competitors? Even if they aren't anything you're worried about, it seems like it would be wise to see if anyone is interested in making a move. Anyone who operates in their world would know that after an attack like this, the Stevskys would be the most likely suspects. It could be an attempt to make them look guilty for something they didn't do."

Luke tapped on his computer. "I'm messaging Jacob now. That's probably something Gil or Tessa could work on tomorrow."

He finished typing and looked at her. "So, are you focusing on the Stevskys?"

Faith couldn't tell what answer Luke was looking for, but it didn't matter. She told him the truth. "They have to be investigated. If you call that focusing, then yes. But if you mean, have I ruled out everyone else and won't be looking elsewhere until the Stevskys are cleared, then no. An investigation like this has to be multifaceted. It has to be both focused and generalized, and it's going to require a true joint effort. I can't speak for anyone else at the FBI, but that's how I do things—and that's how I expect the agents working with me to do things. That includes FBI, Secret Service, ATF, local sheriff, and anyone else. I won't put up with anything less."

FAITH MALONE was a problem.

Luke tried to focus on what she was actually saying and not what he thought she meant. So far, everything she said made sense.

Despite his misgivings, he couldn't ignore the facts. Faith Malone knew her stuff. She was good at her job, and she wasn't afraid to ask tough questions, even if it meant ticking him off.

And right now, with the way her hair was flying around in the breeze coming off the river, she was even more beautiful than he'd realized.

Thad had liked Faith. A lot. When Luke had been assigned to the JTTF, Thad had been thrilled and hadn't hesitated to voice his belief that Luke should ask her out.

It meant nothing that while Faith had been a lot of fun when they'd worked together on a few fundraisers and the annual inter-agency golf tournament, Faith had never given him any indication that she might be interested in knowing Luke outside of work, or the undeniable truth that Luke's family would disown him for bringing home an FBI agent. "She's gorgeous, and she's not going to let you have your own way all the time. She's exactly what you need," Thad had said while they were on their way to help with the protective detail when the last presidential candidate came through town.

"That makes no sense," Luke had countered. "I don't want a woman who's going to do nothing but fight with me. And she's FBI."

"You say that like her being FBI is a deal breaker."

"It is."

Thad had rolled his eyes. "You're going to have to let it go, man."

It wasn't that easy. In fact, it was impossible. But as Faith explained her plans for handling this case, her deep brown eyes sparkling with intensity in the fading light, he had to admit it.

He wished things were different.

Not that it mattered. He couldn't ask her out now even if he didn't have every reason in the world to stay away from her. She was working a case that involved him and his coworkers. She was off-limits.

He could almost hear Thad whispering, "For now."

But it wasn't for now. It was forever.

He'd never realized how depressing that was.

"Luke?" A feminine hand waved in front of his eyes. "You okay?"

"I'm fine." Why was she so worried about him?

"You zoned out for a minute." Faith studied him. "Are you sure you're okay?"

He'd zoned out? He hadn't meant to. He'd been thinking about . . . her. He cleared his throat and sat straighter. "I'm fine. My mind wandered for a second. I can go for a few more hours if necessary. I'm ready for anything."

He could tell he hadn't convinced Faith, but she tapped her fancy pencil on her iPad and nodded. "Okay then, Mr. Ready for Anything, tell me why you don't trust the FBI."

"Who says I don't trust the FBI? The Secret Service and the FBI haven't gotten along in . . . forever." Not liking the FBI hardly made him unique.

"This is way more than posturing or differences in professional culture. Even more than differences in approach to investigations. You have a deep distrust of the FBI." Faith scratched the side of her cheek with one rounded fingernail. "But you strike me as someone who is willing to listen to the facts and see how things play out before drawing an unfounded conclusion. As someone who wouldn't take the long-standing animosity between the Secret Service and the FBI to heart. But you have. Which leads me to believe you have a personal reason. I've never pressed you before. It didn't matter when the only thing at stake was bragging rights. But it matters now, and I need to know what it is."

"No, you don't."

One corner of Faith's mouth twitched. It was the only outward sign that she'd heard him. She didn't respond immediately, and he braced himself for a tirade.

"I'll find out eventually." She didn't raise her voice. There was no hint of agitation. Her confidence was both impressive and irritating. "But until then, you should know that your trust, or lack thereof, in me or my agency is irrelevant to my ability or my desire to do my job."

A phone vibrated somewhere on her person. Not the phone that sat on the table. Her personal phone.

She ignored it.

It buzzed again.

She closed her eyes in clear frustration.

"You should get that," Luke said. "Might be your boyfriend."

Please don't let it be her boyfriend.

She glanced at the phone and fear flashed across her face. "Excuse me a moment." She walked away without waiting for him to reply. She didn't go far. He could hear every word clearly.

"Hello." A pause. "Are you okay?" Her words were terse but held a hint of compassion. "I am." Another pause. "It's okay. Do you need me to—" This time Faith listened for a full minute without so much as a "huh" or "yeah." When she did respond, it wasn't a word. It was a groan, followed by, "You've *got* to be kidding me."

— 9 —

THIS WASN'T THE WAY it was supposed to be. Faith hadn't expected adulthood to be one endless game of whack-a-mole where all she did was beat into submission every new problem that popped up—all the while, standing still. Never going anywhere. Never changing the view.

Faith fought hard to keep all emotion from her voice. "I'm not at home. Send me the link and the log-in. I'll check it out. Can I call you back later?" She ended the call. Why now? Why ever?

She squeezed her hands tight to still them as she returned to Luke. She braced herself for an interrogation, but he didn't speak, even after she took her seat and leaned back in the chair. When she finally looked at him, he held her gaze and didn't look away. His intense focus gave her a glimpse of what it must be like to be questioned by Luke Powell. She didn't like it. "Spit it out, Powell."

He shrugged. "I'm not going to ask you if everything is okay, because I know it isn't."

He had that right.

"You don't have to tell me, but I've been told I'm an excellent listener. You're welcome to vent."

"It's not a life-or-death issue." Faith attempted a light laugh but instead succeeded in something that to her ears sounded more like a seal barking.

Luke squeezed his lips together in a tight line, probably to stop himself from laughing. "Well, thank goodness for that." He spoke with overdone relief. "I'm done with life-or-death issues. I prefer first-world problems all the way. So if you have one of those, please share it with me."

She slid her iPad and pencil into her bag. "My sister is an attorney, here in Raleigh. She also happens to be in a wheelchair, which is the least remarkable or interesting thing about her, but at times has been an issue when it comes to dating. She was in a long-term relationship that ended about six month ago, and she has no interest in changing her status from single to committed. But tonight, one of Hope's friends let her know that there's a dating profile for her on an online dating service. Hope had nothing to do with it, but when she got on there, she did some digging and found there's also a profile for me."

Faith clamped her mouth shut. Why had she told him that? She didn't talk about her homelife at work. Ever. It was a rule that had served her well.

When Luke concentrated, was frustrated, or was worried, he pulled his brows together and a deep line formed between them. The line was deeper than she'd ever seen it, and she'd seen it often enough at JTTF meetings to know she needed to be prepared for anything when he quit thinking and started talking.

She braced herself for the coming barrage, but instead he held up one finger. "I have a few questions."

His deep, steady voice, without a trace of the earlier humor or sarcasm, had a soothing effect. He waited to continue until she gave a brief nod of assent.

"How old is your sister?"

Of all the questions he could have asked, that was not one she'd been expecting, and she answered it without hesitation. "She's twenty-nine."

Luke took that in with a slow nod. "Do you have any other siblings?"

"No." She had no idea where he was going with this, but his questions were hardly intrusive.

Luke gave her a small smile. "Can I see the dating profile?"

"No!"

"Okay. Fine. But do you have any idea who would put up profiles for you and your sister?"

"Hope has a pretty good idea of who did it. And I think she's right."

Luke waited, a mildly curious expression on his face, as though it didn't matter to him one way or the other if she answered his question. But she was almost certain he was dying to know.

She dropped her head in her hands. "Our mother."

"What?"

"You heard me. Our mother. Well, not her directly. Her assistant. Probably."

"Wow."

"Yeah."

She wasn't sure when he'd moved. When he'd leaned toward her across the table, when he'd covered her hand in his. "I'm sorry." The words were soft and low and so sincere that for a brief moment, Faith allowed herself to imagine what would happen if she laced her fingers through his.

"Me too."

"I guess we should call it a night." He squeezed her hand, then released it. "I need to go home and get some sleep. You probably need to figure out how to get that profile down."

She groaned.

"Tomorrow we'll talk about the FBI and the Secret Service and find out who killed my friends."

Faith didn't miss the way he left out the part where someone had tried to kill him, and she appreciated the way he acknowledged that he hadn't answered her question regarding his disgust with the FBI. All in all, it was as good an end to the evening as she could hope for at this point.

She gathered the rest of her things and didn't complain when Luke's hand rested on her elbow as they made their way back to the car.

The drive back to his house was mostly quiet. When he climbed from her car, she expected him to say a quick goodbye and go inside. Instead, he turned back. She lowered the passenger window, and he leaned in.

"Thank you for taking me to dinner tonight and for showing me where you row. When this is over, maybe you could take me out on the water and give me some lessons."

Was he asking her out? No. He was just . . .

"Oh"—he tapped the edge of the car window—"and no matter what I say tomorrow, between you and me, I'm really glad Gil had a roast in the Crock-Pot."

He winked. "Good night, Faith." With that, he turned and walked up his porch steps.

It wasn't until she'd pulled out of his driveway that she realized she'd never said yes to the lessons. But the idea of spending more time with Luke stayed with her the whole way home.

A KNOCK ON THE DOOR, more of a pounding than a knock, woke Luke the next morning. He rolled over and grabbed his weapon from the pillow beside him.

Everything hurt, and he didn't bother to hold back a long groan as his body, stiff from lack of movement overnight, stretched and pulled in painful ways as he got to his feet and flicked on the switch of the small monitor resting on his nightstand.

A few quick taps, and the view from the camera on his front porch filled the screen.

Zane and Gil . . . and Faith?

What were they doing here at . . . a glance at the clock on the nightstand.

9:37 a.m.

What? That couldn't be right. He grabbed his phone.

Dead.

He dropped it back on the nightstand and pulled his iPad off his dresser. It had a charge and confirmed not only the time but also the long string of missed texts that began at 7:30 a.m. and continued to this moment.

He'd slept too hard and too long. An occupational hazard. Especially now.

He texted Gil from the iPad as he gingerly moved through his room.

Sorry. Overslept. Coming.

He could not make himself move any faster. He attempted and gave up on pulling a T-shirt over his head. This was worse than yesterday. Had he ever hurt like this before? He filed through the various sports he'd played, the martial arts he'd studied, and all his training for the Secret Service.

Nope. He was sure. Nothing had ever hurt as much as getting shot, then nearly blown up, then nearly impaled by flying automobile parts.

He eased down the stairs, iPad and T-shirt in his left hand, weapon in the right. He dropped the T-shirt and iPad on the table in his foyer, yanked the door open left-handed, and faced the fury of his two very angry, very worried friends and one FBI agent whose relief, even in his sleep-fogged state, was palpable.

Zane went first. "What's the matter with you? Who puts their phone on silent in the middle of a murder investigation?"

"I didn't—"

"I've lost at least a decade of good years in the past seventy-two hours." Gil's black hair gave every indication that he'd been running his hands through it, often. A known sign of stress for his friend.

"My phone—"

Faith stepped forward. "Gentlemen, as much as I support your right to harass Special Agent Powell, perhaps it would be best all-around if we took this conversation inside." With a quick flick of her fingers, Faith indicated a car parked a few doors down.

Without a word, Luke stepped back and opened the door wide as they all moved inside.

Zane glared at him and everyone. It might have been intimidating had he not also had one arm in a sling and been unable to hide his limp as he went straight into Luke's den and eased himself into a wingback chair.

Gil stayed close to Zane but didn't miss the opportunity to punch Luke's good arm as he passed by.

Faith followed without a hint of frustration. She waited by the door until Luke closed it behind them. "What happened?" Her voice low, calm.

"Phone died."

"I understood you have a house phone." Faith paused by the painting over the little table in his entryway. Her tone conversational. Her body language relaxed.

"Did."

"And?"

"Switched my TV, internet, and phone provider last week. They messed up the transfer. House phone still isn't working."

She gestured toward his den. "Don't be too hard on them, Luke. We all thought—"

"Be hard on *them*? Are you kidding? I'm the one who needs to run for my life." He leaned toward her, speaking low in her ear. "I've been at their mercy before. It's not pretty."

His plea for sympathy earned him a low chuckle and a whispered, "If it gets too bad, I'll protect you."

"Sure you will."

They entered the living area together. Zane glowered. Gil paced and stewed. Best to lead off with a plea for mercy. He focused on Zane. "The house phone still isn't working." Zane knew about his television drama.

"Jared can—" Zane flinched at the sound of his own words. "Crap. How are we ever going to get anything fixed without Jared?"

"Jared was handy?" Faith slipped onto the sofa nearest Zane.

"He'd have been deadly with a power tool. Clumsiest agent I ever worked with in the field." This wasn't speaking ill of the dead. If Jared had been alive and sitting with them, Zane would have said the same. "But give him some wires, a motherboard, a circuit? The man could rig anything."

Luke set his iPad on the table in the foyer but continued to stand near the door, T-shirt in hand. If it were just Gil and Zane, it wouldn't matter, but was it his imagination or was Faith having trouble keeping her eyes off him? Surely not. Still, standing there in shorts, bare feet, bare chest—it wasn't indecent or anything, but it was weird. Then a wave of horror swept over him. He'd been leaning close to Faith, speaking into her ear.

And he hadn't brushed his teeth.

"Excuse me for a moment." He would have loved to have been able to race away, taking the stairs two a time. Instead, he limped from the room and fumed with every step, unable to escape the fact that in a few minutes he would have to reverse the torturous climb.

When he returned to his den ten minutes later with minty breath and smoothed hair and wearing slacks and a fresh button-up, the conversation had shifted gears entirely.

"I know you guys don't want to use FBI resources," Faith was saying, "but if you do need someone, we have a great guy who used to be on our team."

"A great guy for what?" Luke asked.

"Computer forensics. To replace Jar—"

"Why are we worried about replacing Jared? We haven't even had the man's funeral." Luke took a seat across from Faith. Just when he had started to like her more, she did something that ticked him off. Like talking about replacing a man before they'd even paid their respects.

"I'm not talking about replacing Jared specifically, Luke. I'm talking about finding someone with a similar skill set. Your office is now without your main electronic crimes investigator. And you guys deal with a lot of electronic crimes."

"Oh." He'd jumped to the wrong conclusion. Again. Why was he so determined to think the worst of her?

He knew why.

But as he looked at Faith, he had to admit that so far, she'd done nothing but think the best of him—and his agency.

Her face brightened. "I know who you need." She pointedly did not look at Luke but turned to Gil and Zane. "Dr. Sabrina Fleming-Campbell. Do you know her?"

Luke knew who Sabrina was. And he knew her husband, Adam Campbell, but as Faith didn't seem to want to include him in the conversation, Luke kept quiet.

"I know that name," Zane said. "Why do I know that name?"

"Is she the quirky professor from Carrington who works on the human trafficking team?" Gil asked. "Kinda weird, but nice. Genius-level smart."

"That's her." Faith buzzed with energy. "Sabrina is amazing. We've consulted with her on a few cases in our office. If you repeat this, I'll deny it, but she's better than anyone we have at the FBI. She has a reputation for being able to find files and break through firewalls when no one else can. I heard she cracked a defense department–level encryption a few months ago."

"What did you say her name was?" Gil had pulled out a notebook. "Sabrina Fleming?"

"Fleming-Campbell. Hyphenated. She got married recently."

"That's right," Zane said. "I've been diving with her husband."

"She married a Campbell from Carrington," Gil mused. "Interesting."

"What's interesting about it?" Faith asked.

Zane answered the question. "We do a lot of financial crimes investigations. The Carrington Campbells are loaded. One of the wealthiest families in the state."

"I don't think she's the type to care about money," Faith said. "Her standard uniform is skinny jeans and superhero T-shirts, hair in a messy bun, glasses. She's everything you think of when you imagine a computer genius. She's sweet but awkward, so if you call her, be prepared for her to be blunt and maybe even a bit oblivious."

Luke joined Gil and Zane in a snicker at Faith's comment, but her confused expression told him she didn't understand what was so funny. "You just described Jared," he told her. "Although I wouldn't have said he was sweet."

Faith gave him a shrewd look. "Jared wore skinny jeans and superhero T-shirts?"

The men's chuckles morphed into laughter. "Um, no. Jared wasn't skinny. But the man knew his way around a computer far better than he knew his way around people."

The amusement faded, and a somber mood descended. Zane stood. Slowly. His face was smooth, but Luke could imagine how much effort it took for him to keep from grimacing. "Well, as fun as this has been, I need to get back to the office—"

"Oh no you don't." Gil popped to his feet, and Luke couldn't stop the flash of envy at his easy movement. "You go back home. You rest. You—"

"What?" Zane's voice was a growl. "Go home? Kick back in a hammock? Read a book? I don't think so, man."

"Listen, you have legit injuries." Gil pointed to Zane's arm. "You need to take it easy."

"I don't see you telling me to take it easy," Luke said.

Gil rolled his eyes. "You don't even have any holes. I don't want to hear it."

"I have to have holes to be injured?"

"I'm not saying you aren't hurt, but Zane has two holes. He wins."

"Where do stab wounds figure into this theory of yours?" Faith asked the question with overdone seriousness.

Gil matched her tone and took on a professorial air. "Stabbings, while they are more of a slice, count as holes. I'd give full credit for a stab wound. But scrapes are just scrapes. Bruises are just bruises. And getting skinned by a .22"—Gil nodded toward Luke—"is just getting skinned by a .22."

Luke laughed despite himself.

Gil turned to Zane. "I'm afraid I have to agree with the doctor—"

"The doctor can shove it where—"

"Perhaps," Faith interrupted with a tone that earned her all three men's full attention, "Luke and Gil could head to the office, while you and I discuss what happened on Monday. Then I could drop you back off at your house"—she made a hasty adjustment at the look on Zane's face—"or wherever you want, when we're done."

Why did Faith want to talk to Zane alone?

"If that's okay with you, Luke? For us to stay here a bit longer?"

Leaving an FBI agent in his house went against every bit of sense Luke possessed, but Zane would be with her. He wouldn't let her . . . what? What did he think she was going to do in his house? What was wrong with him? This was Faith. He didn't trust the FBI, but he was beginning to trust Faith.

But something about this didn't sit well.

"You're still planning to take me back to my house," Zane said.

"I am." Faith flashed him a bright smile. "You're putting on a brave show, but your skin has a decidedly green tinge to it. Your friends are right to insist that you go home and rest. And if I were a nicer person, I would back them up. But I need to talk to you, and here you are, so I'm offering you the opportunity to stay in the game an hour longer than your friends would agree to. And my guess is, by the time I'm through with you, you'll be ready to lie down. What do you say?"

Gil scoffed. "Wow. Talk about a no-win situation. Go home or stay here and chat with the FBI and then go home. Have fun." He stood. "Luke, you ready?"

This whole needing-a-ride situation had already gotten old. "No. Give me five minutes."

Luke gathered all his stuff for the day and joined Gil by the door. He'd figured out what was bothering him about this. It wasn't leaving an FBI agent in his house. It wasn't leaving Faith or Zane in his house. It was leaving Faith alone in his house, with Zane.

He wasn't joking as he looked from Faith to Zane and said, "Try not to destroy everything, okay?"

—10—

LUKE AND GIL drove away, and Faith turned to Zane. "I wasn't kidding about you lying down. If you need to now, I won't rat you out to your friends."

Zane let out a tiny moan as he returned to the seat. "Thanks, but I'm okay."

"You aren't." She hadn't been joking about the green tinge. Zane Thacker was working way beyond his physical capacity. But she did need to talk to him. And despite what Luke thought, she wasn't nice enough to give the man more time to recover.

"What do you want to know?" Zane closed his eyes. "Did we kill Thad? Did we kill Jared and Michael and have someone pretend to attempt to kill us to cover it all up?"

This was the problem with investigating investigators. They already knew what you wanted to know. So why deny it. "Well, did you?"

Zane flexed the fingers on his left hand. "No."

He opened his eyes then and gave her a wry smile. "But you already know that."

"I have to ask the questions."

"I know. But what you really want to know is who that woman

was with Thad, and if we know about her, and if he was having an affair with her, and if she's the reason they were killed."

"I haven't ruled out the possibility of the affair."

Zane flexed the fingers of his right hand. "You haven't met Rose yet, have you?"

"Thad Baker's wife?" At Zane's confirming nod, she said, "No. I haven't."

Zane rolled his neck in a slow circle. "It takes a special kind of woman to be married to someone in the Secret Service. The hours are long and unpredictable. The duty can be dangerous one day and dull the next. Intense for a week, boring for three. Rose and Thad got married while he was in Phase One, had the kids while he was protecting the vice president, and then moved here when the twins were four. Rose loved Thad, but she is no pushover. She is scary smart, and sometimes she's just flat-out scary. If Thad ever looked twice at another woman, Rose would have taken care of it. And she wouldn't have done it with a car bomb."

The quirk of Zane's brows as he delivered this last line forced a smile to Faith's lips. But she pulled her face back to her usual professional demeanor. She'd seen smart women been made fools of before. "She might not have known. Everyone says they would know, but most don't."

"Most. Maybe. But there's something you should know. No one talks about it, but Rose was CIA before she met Thad. She would have known."

CIA? "That's not in the file."

"Like I said, no one talks about it." Zane fisted the fingers on his free hand, then held it out in front of him and twisted it in small circles.

Was he ever still? "Did the doctor tell you to do these exercises?"

Zane laughed. "I think best when I move. Drives Luke crazy.

I walk around my desk all the time. And I toss a little stress ball. Keeps the juices flowing, annoys everyone except Tessa. She ignores it."

Faith didn't comment. Somehow she didn't think Agent Reed ignored anything.

"We don't know why Thad was at the restaurant, we don't know who he was with or why that woman was in the car. I know everyone wants to think the worst. I guess it's human nature. But I think it could be something entirely other."

"Like what?"

"Luke and I were close to Thad. Closer than is normal for an office like ours. He was intentional about mentoring us. And he was good at it. He was a man of deep faith, and he believed God had put us on the same team for a reason. He had prayed with us and for us over the past few years, and we had become way more than coworkers. Luke and I were lucky to have a guy like Thad as a friend. And that's why the fact that neither one of us know what he was up to makes me think he was planning something, a surprise for Rose."

Not in a million years had Faith expected something like that. "Why would you say that?"

"When you meet Rose, you'll understand. Thad never could pull off a surprise for her. Rose knew when he was going to propose. She knew when he was coming home early. She knew what he got her for Christmas every year. She always knew, and it was a running joke between them. Thad kept trying. She kept figuring it out. And she'd told him that if he involved any of us to help him hide something, it didn't count."

Zane's lips flattened into a thin line. His demeanor shifted, and for a moment, Faith caught a glimpse of the fierce warrior that hid behind the normally gentle eyes. "We need to know what happened. It's personal."

Faith waved a hand in his general direction—the arm in the sling, the bandages she couldn't see but knew were there under his shirt—but he dismissed her.

"It was personal before Monday morning. Thad was a friend. He was one of the good guys. In church every Sunday he wasn't on duty. Prayed with his wife and kids. Took good care of his parents. He set up a rotation of guys in their church to mow a widow's yard last summer. The man was a saint. He didn't deserve to die. His wife didn't deserve to be widowed. His kids . . ." Zane's voice broke. "His kids didn't deserve to go through life without their dad. Someone took him from them. From all of us. The world is a darker place because he isn't in it. He believed in a good God who could be counted on. But I don't get why a loving God would allow it. And I certainly don't see how a God with any sort of real power could let his death drag on with no closure."

Faith studied her shoes. The situation was different, but Zane had just articulated her own despair and confusion.

"I want to believe Thad's death wasn't in vain and there's some deeper meaning behind it all. But I can't see it. What I want is to get ahold of the person who did this. And if they do happen to be the same person who killed Michael and Jared on Monday, well, that would be the icing on the cake.

"If you can figure all that out, you'll get my full cooperation. I don't normally enjoy hanging out with the FBI, but no one wants you to succeed more than I do."

The buzzing of his phone spared her from having to respond immediately.

"It's Gil," Zane said.

"Please, go ahead."

Faith stood and walked toward what she assumed would be Luke's kitchen. The house was open and spacious. More room than a bachelor needed—especially one who worked the kind of hours Luke worked. The kitchen was spotless, with the trace of a lemony cleaner in the air. It looked like the kind of place that would make Gil happy, complete with a gas stove and a large island. Across from the island was a cozy nook with a squishy chair, a lamp, and several stacks of books. Curiosity overrode polite behavior, and she perched on the edge of his chair and picked up a book from the stack to the left of the chair. A biography of one of the founding fathers. Then a travel book focused on scuba diving sites. On the right side of the chair she found a novel and a worn Bible.

Her fingers tapped the edge of the Bible.

She struggled to believe that God was actually good. It was terrifying to admit it. But who could blame her? How could a good God allow awful things to happen?

Her sister—her brilliant, funny, gorgeous sister—hit by a car, the driver of whom had waved her across the street and then gunned it. Faith had been there. She'd seen Hope's body flip over the car, and she'd known before the ambulance arrived that Hope would never walk again.

She ran her hand over the worn leather of the Bible. Luke and Hope would get along great. Hope still believed. Despite multiple surgeries, missing prom and all the normal high school things, having her heart broken by men who didn't think they could have a relationship with someone in a wheelchair—through it all, Hope's faith had grown stronger.

While Faith's had faltered.

"Faith?" Zane's voice called her back from her musing.

"I just wanted to give you some privacy," she said as she retraced her steps.

"No problem. Would you mind taking me to Gil's house instead of mine?" Zane's voice had a faraway quality, and he didn't look at her as she entered the room but instead stared at the television, now on a local news station.

"Is everything okay?"

"I guess it depends on your definition of okay." Zane pointed at the screen. "That's my house."

Faith forced herself not to gape at the scene. The home was fully engulfed in flames as they watched a chunk of the roof fall in. Firefighters were hosing it down, but even to her untrained eye it was clear. The house was a total loss.

"Zane. I'm . . ." She couldn't bring herself to say she was sorry. It was too trite.

He turned off the TV and squared his shoulders before turning back to her. "I guess it's even more personal now."

Fifteen minutes later, Faith pulled to a stop beside Gil's home—a fixer-upper in a part of town that had hopefully bottomed out and was now on the way back. His yard was easily the nicest on the block, but several of the nearby homes had neat lawns and flowers blooming in pots on their steps or in window boxes. Luke, Gil, and Tessa spilled from the door and converged on the car. This must be why Gil had directed them to come to his place and not the office.

Luke yanked the door open. Gil extended a hand and helped pull Zane upright. Tessa took Zane's side with the sling, while Gil took his "good" side, if he even had one at this point. "Come on, buddy."

Faith sat in the car, gripping the steering wheel and feeling like a voyeur as she watched the procession to the house. Luke ran, well, it was more of a shuffling walk, to the door and held it open as Gil and Tessa helped Zane inside. When they were inside, she expected Luke to follow them, but he closed the door and came back to the car. Faith lowered the passenger-side window, and Luke leaned in. "Thanks for bringing him here. It was faster than us coming to my house from the office and then back here. Gil has good food and plenty of it, and we decided to take an early lunch break here. Zane doesn't need to be at his house right now. It's not like there's anything he can do."

"It wasn't a problem." The video from the news of the flaming trusses and beams of Zane's destroyed home replayed in her head and the heaviness of what Zane was facing weighed on her mind and heart. How much more could these guys take? "Can you give me his address? I need to get over there. I'll call you with an update."

"That would be great." Luke gave her the address. "Thanks again."

"You're welcome." He was trying to be stealthy, but she didn't miss the way he steadied himself on the car frame before he walked away. She couldn't bring herself to pull away as he slowly walked toward Gil's house.

He was halfway up the sidewalk when the front door opened and Gil stepped out. "You okay, man?"

Gil walked down the steps but stopped when Luke raised a hand. "I do not need help walking to the door, Gil."

"Fine, tough guy." He took a couple of steps in her direction, which conveniently enough, brought him closer to Luke. "Thanks, Faith." Gil bent down and gave her a small salute.

Then Gil's smile froze on his face, and he crumpled to the ground.

— 11 —

FOR A SPLIT SECOND, Luke didn't believe what he was seeing. Gil, on the ground. Blood. So much blood. Here he was, again. Dragging a friend out of the line of fire. Where? House or car? The house provided more protection, but could he get Gil up the steps? The car was closer and could get them to the hospital, but that would put Faith in danger.

"Luke!"

He didn't turn toward the sound of Faith's voice, but then she was there. Weapon out. Shielding him and Gil with her own body. "The car's closest." Some part of his brain noted the opened back doors of the car. If they could get Gil to the car, he could get in and pull him through.

Luke couldn't stop the groan that escaped as Gil's weight tugged at fresh stitches and bruised muscles, but he pulled him across the yard toward the car. And then Tessa joined them, circling him and Faith as they continued their awkward efforts to get Gil to the car.

"Tessa! Leg!" Faith moved her weapon to her left hand. With her right, she grabbed one of Gil's legs. Tessa grabbed the other one, and with them taking some of Gil's body weight, Luke was able to move faster. He climbed into the back seat and pulled Gil in with him. Faith slammed the door and raced around to the driver's side. She crouched low and kept her weapon drawn.

"Tessa! Run!" Zane stood on the porch, a shotgun on his hip. He and Faith covered Tessa as she ran back into the house. Then Faith was back in the car, tires squealing as she peeled away from the curb.

Faith was yelling something, and it took Luke a second to realize it wasn't at him. She was talking to 911 and prepping a trauma team at the hospital. And she was driving like a professional stunt driver. Or a maniac. Maybe both.

Now that he was fairly certain they wouldn't be shot at, although less certain they wouldn't die in a fiery car crash, Luke searched Gil for the wound. Gil's head and face were covered in blood. Blood ran down his neck, and his shirt and shoulders were soaked with it.

How much more blood could Gil lose? And where was it coming from?

And then he saw it. A hole. In Gil's head.

"Oh, God, please. Please." The prayer had been wrenched from his heart and mind, and he had no other words. "Please. Not Gil. Please, God."

He scanned the back seat of Faith's car. A pale blue sweater lay on the floorboard on the other side of the car from where he sat. He stretched his leg across and tried to pull the sweater toward him with his foot. It took three tries before he got it close enough that he could pick it up. Gil moaned as he jostled him, but at this point, doing something to stop the blood seemed more important than keeping Gil comfortable.

He unfolded the sweater and slid the back of it under Gil's head, then tied the arms together as tight as he could.

Blood seeped through within seconds.

Faith's voice rose above his panic. "Are they ready for us?"

An urgent voice replied. "Yes, but I need you to stay on the line."

"Make sure they're ready." Faith disconnected the call.

Luke appreciated Faith's decision to ignore the 911 operator, because with the way she was whipping through traffic and around curves, she needed to keep her eyes and mind on the road. Seven minutes after leaving Gil's house, they screeched to a halt in the emergency department's circular drive. They were met with scrub-clad, stethoscope-swinging men and women who extricated Gil from the car, settled him onto a gurney, and raced him inside with remarkable efficiency.

And then everything was quiet.

Faith looked at him in the rearview mirror, her eyes wide and manic. "Go inside. Tell them the blood isn't yours or they will have you on a gurney before you can show them your badge."

"No."

Faith blinked a few times. "What?"

"I'm staying with you. Let's park the car. We'll go inside to-gether."

"Luke, I'm fine."

"I know you are, Faith. Okay. I know it." Luke heard the edge of hysteria in his voice and took a deep breath. "But if that mad-man has half the brain I think he has, then he will know this is the closest hospital to Gil's house. I'm sure we beat him, but if he's not waiting to pick off Zane and Tessa, then he could be coming here next."

Faith was breathing heavily, and the sound of it filled the space between them. "Okay."

"Let's park in the regular garage, not the law enforcement spaces. We don't need to make it any easier for him to find your car. He'll know what you're driving now."

"Good idea." Faith put the car in drive and headed through the parking lot like a ninety-year-old with cataracts until she found a space she could back into.

When she turned off the ignition, she leaned over the steering wheel, her breaths coming in quick gasps. Luke climbed out of the back seat and opened her door.

She didn't look at him. "I'm okay. I am. I haven't driven like that in a while. Adrenaline crashing. Give me a second."

Luke leaned against the car, using the door for protection. After thirty seconds, her breathing slowed. After a minute, he thought it was safe to speak. "Faith?"

She didn't look up. "Hmm?

"You could give the guys who drive the president a run for their money."

The faintest of smiles ghosted across her face.

"Ready?"

In answer, she unfastened her seat belt and grabbed a bag from the passenger seat. He held the door open for her, closing it gently after she stood beside him. She drew her weapon and he drew his. "Let's go." Her eyes widened in horror when she saw his blood-stained clothes. A soft "oh" escaped before her expression hardened and she took off toward the emergency department entrance.

Now that his own adrenaline had crashed, Luke struggled to keep up with Faith's quick march, but he couldn't let her see it. This woman had risked her life for him, for Gil, for Tessa, for Zane. She was still risking her life. This case could get her killed.

And she was all in.

He could see it in the thin line of her lips. The ramrod way she held herself. And in the way her hands trembled and she couldn't stop them.

He understood.

His were shaking too.

They tucked their weapons back into their holsters when they reached the door. A security guard took a long look at Faith's FBI badge and let them through.

A nurse who looked like she could play linebacker for the Panthers stopped them as soon as they cleared security. They explained who they were and why they were there, but she didn't take them to see Gil. Instead, she led them to a private room at the end of the hall. "You can't help your friend right now. And you'll scare the patients and their families if they see you looking like you do. It will be all over that social media stuff, and we'll have reporters here in no time flat."

She stepped inside, and they followed her. "You have a private bathroom there, and a shower." She pointed to Luke's shirt. "I recommend you use it. I'll find some scrubs for you to change into."

"Thank you." Luke and Faith spoke in unison.

The nurse let out a deep sigh. "You young'uns have been through a rough patch. If you need anything, my name's Opal. Holler, and I'll get to you as fast as I can." She paused. "Can I get you some coffee?"

"I'd love some coffee," Luke said. "Any chance you have a Coke machine around here with a Cherry Coke?"

"As a matter of fact, young man, we have one in the break room. I'll get the coffee, the Coke, and the scrubs. And I'll get an update on your friend too."

"Thank you."

Opal left the room, and he and Faith stared at each other in the silence.

He didn't want to be alone. He didn't want to leave her alone. But he couldn't stand the way his drenched shirt stuck to him, or the way every time he glanced down he saw Gil's blood. "Give me five minutes?"

Faith's lips curved into a tremulous smile. "It would take you more than five minutes to get all that off"—she indicated the blood—"even if you weren't injured. Don't rush. When Opal comes back with the scrubs, I'll knock."

Luke closed the bathroom door between them.

Within seconds, he realized Faith was right. He was going to need way more than five minutes. His injuries made everything harder than it should have been. Getting out of the bloody clothes left him with blood, Gil's blood, on his face and in his hair. He showered and scrubbed, but the hospital soap wasn't up to the task, and he could only get one of his hands over his head in a feeble attempt to wash his hair.

Faith knocked on the door. "I'm setting the scrubs on the sink," she said. After the door closed, he gave up on trying to get any cleaner. He had pulled on the hospital scrub pants when Faith knocked on the door again.

"I have an update on Gil."

He opened the door and found her standing inches away. "How is he?"

Faith leaned against the doorframe. "The nurse said it's some kind of miracle. Gil's lost a lot of blood, and there's a hole in his head, but the bullet didn't hit his brain. It's too soon to say anything definite, but the preliminary report, it's good."

"Thank you, Lord. Thank you." Luke inhaled, possibly the first deep breath he'd taken in the past hour and, without thinking, reached for Faith. Maybe she wasn't thinking either, but she stepped into his embrace. He held her, her forehead pressed into his chest, and he rested his cheek on the top of her head. Her hair still smelled of something fruity, despite the chaos and drama of the day.

Her hands gripped his waist, and his arms were wrapped all the way around her slim frame. Their breathing was deep, and he had a feeling she was fighting tears the same way he was. Every now and then, a tremor rippled through her, and after the third tremor, he squeezed her closer. Her hands left his waist and wrapped around him, her cheek pressed to his chest.

He didn't know how long they stood there, drawing strength and comfort from each other. He didn't care if it would make things awkward later. He didn't care that she was FBI and that there was no way they could ever be anything more than friends.

Faith Malone wasn't like anyone he'd ever known. And for the first time, he wondered if maybe Thad had been right.

The buzzing of Faith's phone startled them apart. She took a step back, and Luke missed the closeness the instant it was broken.

He released her, and she pulled the phone from her back pocket. "Malone."

Luke tried to get the scrub shirt over his head. Failed.

"Yes, sir. I understand."

Faith tucked the phone between her ear and shoulder and continued to "hmm" and "yes" and "uh-huh" as she took the shirt from his hands, rolled it from bottom to top, and stepped closer. She reached up, dropped the shirt over his head, and then held out one of the arm holes at an angle so he could get his injured arm through. He shoved his good arm in the other hole, and she pulled the hem of the shirt down the rest of the way to his waist.

Was it his imagination, or did her hand linger for a moment longer than necessary before she turned away?

"Yes, sir. He's fine, but would you like to speak to him?" She handed Luke the phone. "Your boss."

He took the phone. "Powell."

"Give me an update. I know what the FBI is saying, but I want to hear it from you. Starting with whether or not you've been shot or pulled anything or need to be back in the hospital yourself. The word I got was you walked into the hospital covered in blood." Jacob finally stopped talking and took a breath.

Luke jumped at his chance to speak. "I'm sore. May have ripped a stitch or two, but I'm fine. The blood was Gil's. All Gil's." He gave him a stripped-down version of the events of the afternoon. "How are Zane and Tessa?"

His question drew Faith's gaze.

"They're fine."

At Jacob's response, Luke gave Faith an "okay" sign, and she sank against the hospital bed in obvious relief. "Where are they?"

"A safe house, and you're headed to one too. Along with Agent Malone."

"Sir, we can't work the case—"

"It's not permanent. Just until we come up with a security protocol. Someone's picking us off, and I'm done losing people."

"Can't I stay here with Gil?"

"Not overnight, but you're going to have to sit tight while we work out the details on where to send you. For now, stay put. Stay sharp." Jacob's growled words left no room for argument.

The call disconnected, and Luke returned the phone to Faith. "My boss is freaking out."

"Mine too." She stood and handed him a cup of coffee, then took a long drink from the Cherry Coke the nurse must have brought while he was in the shower. She tilted the half-empty bottle in his direction. "Thank you for this. I needed it."

"Not much of a coffee drinker, are you?" He took a tentative sip of the brew, then another. It wasn't the worst he'd had.

"Not a coffee drinker at all." She shuddered in feigned horror. "Why would anyone want to drink bean water?"

"As opposed to chemical-laden liquid sugar bombs?" He countered with a pointed look at her Cherry Coke.

And she laughed. A real laugh that lit her up and drew his attention to her lips. It wasn't like he'd never noticed them before. The rose of them against her skin. The perfect proportion of the top to the bottom. They would be soft. He knew it.

And he knew he was in big, big trouble.

—12—

FAITH FINISHED OFF her Cherry Coke and reached for her bag. She retrieved her iPad and pencil and curled up as best she could in the hard pleather chair in the corner of the room.

The fact that the chair was also the farthest she could get from Luke was an added bonus . . . or unfortunate circumstance? She met his gaze and couldn't stop the heat that flooded her cheeks as she caught him staring.

In what universe did she fall apart . . . and fall into a man's arms?

She'd decided a long time ago that men were unreliable and untrustworthy. Eventually, things would get tough, and they would leave.

But Luke didn't leave. When Gil fell, Luke stayed. He'd risked everything to save his friend. And then when she gave him the chance to go inside, he'd refused to leave her alone.

Maybe he was an exception to the rule, but she didn't have the time, energy, or desire to explore that possibility. She had a job to do, and she intended to do it to the best of her ability. She tapped the iPad and brought it to life. Back to business.

"Faith?"

She focused on the screen in front of her. "Yes?"

The bed creaked as he climbed onto it. "Is it safe for me to assume you no longer suspect any of us for these attacks?" The motor engaged as he adjusted the angle of the head of the bed.

The teasing in his voice gave her hope that maybe they could forget the tension and attraction the events of the afternoon had unearthed. She risked a glance and found him smiling, relaxed. Friendly.

Friendly was good.

"I never thought it was any of you," she said. "But I've learned not to trust my instincts."

Luke coughed. "After what I saw today, I'd say your instincts work fine. You were amazing."

She couldn't stop the bloom of delight from his compliment, but she didn't let it distract her. "I trust them in tense situations, but when it comes to investigations, I leave room for the un-expected. I don't assume anyone is innocent. Or guilty. Good or bad."

"Most people are both." He made the statement in an obvious attempt to provoke her.

"Are you always so argumentative?"

"Who, me?"

"Yes, you." She laughed despite herself. "Back to our argument."

Luke visibly objected to her use of *argument*, but she pressed on.

"I agree that people are a mixture of good and bad, but most people aren't murderers. Murder is intense. Murder is a crime of passion. A crime of greed, need, hatred. Some people go off the edge, and their motives are psychological and skewed—the serial killers, the psychopaths. But this doesn't feel like that. This is too intentional. Too planned. Too specific. There's a motive we can't see—yet. But y'all have done something to tick somebody off."

"I'd say we've done a little bit more than tick them off. People tick me off all the time. I don't blow things up." Luke leaned back against the bed, one arm behind his head, the other propped on a pillow. It had to be hurting.

"Have you had any pain medicine today?"

Luke cut his eyes in her direction. "Am I giving you the impression that I'm high on something?"

She couldn't help but laugh at his query. "No. I'm wondering if you need some ibuprofen. That little adventure we had this afternoon? You're going to feel it soon, if you don't already."

"Oh, I'm feeling it. But I don't have any new holes." He turned onto his side to face her, eyes wide.

"Holes." They both said the word at the same time, and they both smiled at the shared joke.

"Gil will be impossible. He has a *hole* in his *head*. He will declare victory for all time." Luke checked his watch, all humor fading from his expression. "Don't you think they should have given us another update by now?"

"It hasn't been that long." Faith glanced at the time on her iPad. "But I feel like I've run a marathon."

"Yeah." Luke closed his eyes. Faith scanned through her notes, looking for something, anything, to give her some direction about where to look next.

"Have you ever?" Luke's question was murmured. Sleepy.

"Ever what?"

"Run a marathon?"

"I hate running. I do just enough to pass my physical fitness."

"Too bad rowing isn't part of the physical. You'd kill it." Luke's speech was slurring in his fatigue.

"Yes, I would."

"Why don't you like running?" He was fading now.

"It's hard to run on water." Luke's eyes were closed, but his mouth twisted up into a small smile at her remark. "And I don't need to run to stay in shape. Rowing is more fun, and it gets the job done."

"It definitely does."

Faith couldn't decide how to take that. But a soft snore from Luke told her that regardless of how he meant it, he was out cold.

She took a moment to study him. His lean body was swallowed in the too-large scrubs, but she'd seen the abs hidden under that shirt. When he woke, she'd have to ask him what he did for exercise besides running. Whatever it was, he did a lot of it.

The hand of his injured arm twitched on the sheet. It sported several deep gouges, one with three stitches, and was covered in purple and green bruises. His dark hair was trimmed short around his ears, but there was enough on top that it fell across his forehead in a way she knew he would brush to the side when he woke. His nose was straight, and his eyelashes were so long they should be a criminal offense.

If her life and heart ever had room for a man, Luke Powell would be the type of man she would want to come home to. A little snarky. A little funny. Confident. Calm. And when he said her name in his deep voice, she felt safe.

A good man in a storm. That was Luke.

Enough drooling over a man she couldn't have. She flexed her fingers. They were stiff and sore from wrestling the steering wheel on the way to the hospital. She swiveled her head in a slow circle, first in one direction, then in the other.

After a few slow revolutions, she tapped her pencil and began to note everything that had happened in the past week. On Tuesday, she'd listed the cases the RAIC office had worked in the past year.

She had left out cases Gil and Tessa worked separately from the others, but now she added them as well.

If she were Tessa Reed, she'd be scared out of her mind right now.

Faith created a new note. She listed each attack. The agent involved. The location. The type of attack. She started with Thad Baker. Car bomb. Restaurant. Two people killed. Six others injured, one seriously.

Michael Weaver. Poison dart. Jogging track. Only fatality. No one else even realized there was a threat.

Jared Smith. Bombing. Only fatality. One condo besides his suffered minor damage. Fire marshal commented in his notes on the precision of the bombing. More explosive material would have destroyed the other units in the vicinity. Less wouldn't have been enough to ensure the destruction of the entire unit.

Zane Thacker and Luke Powell. Shooting/car bombs. Early morning. Remote location. No other injuries.

Zane Thacker. House fire. No fatalities. Midday. No other homes damaged.

Gil Dixon. Shooting. Midday. One shot. Even though the shooter had ample opportunity to take additional shots, he didn't.

With a growing sense of urgency, she studied the list, looking for a pattern that made some sense of the chaos. It had to be here, and she had to find it.

For all she knew, she could be the next one on the list.

LUKE JERKED AWAKE. Why was he in a hospital?

Then reality came flooding back, fast and ferocious. Faith! He threw his legs over the side of the bed.

"If you fall out of the bed, I won't give you a cover story. I'll

tell everyone what happened and laugh right along with them."
Faith sat cross-legged in the same chair she'd been in when he fell
asleep. "Gil will not accept any additional injuries as valid." Her
lips were twisted in an obvious effort to keep herself from laughing at her own joke.

"Thanks a lot." He sat straighter, and then waited for his head
to stop spinning before he stood. "Any news?"

"Opal came by with more Cherry Coke for me." Faith tapped
the half-empty bottle to her left. "Gil was still in surgery, but the
news from the surgeon was positive. Our bosses called. We're being
moved to a safe house tonight. Then a security detail will take us
to your office in the morning."

"Zane and Tessa?"

"Already at a secure location. Zane was ticked off when I spoke
to him earlier. Tessa wasn't any better. They wouldn't let her go
home, and they sent bomb and chemical dogs to her house. They've
checked her car. Nothing has been found yet."

Luke's stomach did a nosedive. "She's next."

"I'm not so sure."

Luke studied Faith. She wore a look of focus and . . . something
else. There was an intenseness to the way she narrowed her eyes
and studied the screen. Luke got the sense that she intended to find
out who was behind these attacks, and she would not be denied.
All investigators wanted to solve their cases, but something about
Faith's drive made him suspect that failure wasn't an option—not
because it would leave a case unsolved but because it would destroy
her. "What makes you think Tessa's not on this guy's list?"

"She's new."

"Not that new. She's been here—"

"Nine months. And she got pulled out after two months here
because there was an unexpected opening for some additional

training. She was gone for two months. Then she was back for three months, then gone again."

"Yeah. Her father died, and she was granted a lengthy leave to go to India for the funeral. She's a second-generation American, but her dad had requested to be buried in India. He'd promised his father. She was gone when Thad died. She didn't get back until a week after the funeral. She felt bad about it, but she wasn't close to Thad."

"Even if I consider the recent attacks unrelated to Thad's death, that still only gives a few months here and no chances to take the lead on anything more than some minor counterfeiting cases."

"True. She's still pretty green. Zane's giving her more responsibility, but she's not running investigations on her own yet."

Faith uncrossed her legs and stretched them straight in front of her for a few seconds before dropping her feet to the floor.

"We can't risk her life on the assumption that she's not in danger, but we—"

A soft tap on the door and a calm "It's Opal. May I come in?" brought Faith's musings to an abrupt end. Faith went to the door, weapon in hand, while Luke sat on the bed, his own weapon drawn.

Opal entered and, after a quick glance around the room, raised her hands in the air. "Don't shoot the messenger."

The door closed behind her, and Faith slid her weapon back into the holster at her back. Luke laid his beside him on the bed.

"Your friend is out of surgery and in the recovery room," Opal said. "His nurse said he'd be up for a visitor in a few minutes."

Faith pointed at Luke. "You should go."

Was she mental? "Not without you." Luke gave Opal the exasperated look he wanted to give Faith. "I'm not sure why she doesn't want to be seen with me. Look at me. I'm rocking these scrubs. I have these cool bruises and stitches. I'm red-carpet worthy."

Opal chose to side with Faith. "Honey, hold out for a man who knows how to put an outfit together and doesn't get shot on a regular basis."

"Tell me about it." Faith shook her head in mock sadness. At least he hoped it was mock sadness. "But in all seriousness, Opal, we need to check with our protection before we leave this room."

"Already got you covered, sweetheart." Opal's delight in being a step ahead was clear. "There are a couple of nice officers outside who are not letting anyone near you. We'll clear the hall and take you up in the staff elevator. It's the same route we take surgical patients, and it's away from the hospital's open corridors. They plan to stay with you until they deliver you to a safe location. You won't be coming back to this room."

Faith let loose an overdone sigh. "Rats. It was starting to feel like home."

Opal smiled at Faith's joke but grew serious as she looked between the two of them. "I like you two, so keep yourselves out of the crosshairs. You hear me?"

Luke climbed off the bed as Faith gave Opal a side hug. "Yes, ma'am. Thank you for taking such good care of us this afternoon."

Opal patted Luke's good arm. "I mean it. No more bullets."

"Yes, ma'am."

"Okay, then let's go."

Luke and Faith followed Opal from the room. The police officers waiting outside their door fell in around them, and their party of five made an awkward trip through the hall and to the elevators. When Opal left them at the recovery room, Luke thought he saw her wipe her eyes.

"I wonder what her story is?" Faith watched the elevator doors close. "She looks like she could be a real battle-ax type, but she's a total marshmallow."

"We should send her a thank-you. Maybe some flowers or something."

Faith turned toward Luke, eyes overflowing in shock.

"What?" Luke's defenses rose like a tsunami. "She was nice to us. And worried about us. What would be wrong with sending her a little token of appreciation?"

"Nothing." Faith whispered the word. "Nothing at all."

He wanted to find out why something as simple as sending someone flowers would surprise her. Was it because she didn't think anyone did that kind of thing? Was it because she was surprised that he'd had the idea in the first place?

Or was it because she wasn't used to anyone showing appreciation for a job well done?

Or for anything at all?

— 13 —

FAITH NEEDED TO GET SOME SPACE before she made an even bigger fool out of herself. *Way to hang your crazy out for the world to see.* Luke couldn't know how the idea of sending someone flowers would make her so . . . ridiculous. And she wasn't about to tell him. She led the way through the doors to the recovery room and promptly found a small section of wall to park herself against. "Go ahead." She pointed toward the room with the police officers standing guard.

Luke searched her face. "Don't leave."

She swallowed hard. What had he seen? Could he possibly know how much she wanted to run screaming from this place? How the need for some privacy was clawing at her insides and driving her nuts? No. He couldn't. But he might be closer to the truth than she was comfortable with. He didn't seem inclined to leave until she responded, so she forced a calmness she didn't feel and said, "I'll be here."

He frowned as if her answer confirmed something he didn't like, but he approached the officer and gained admittance to the small room. Faith closed her eyes and prepared to wait for however long it took. She wouldn't begrudge Luke time with his friend. They'd been through a lot this morning. These Secret Service agents had a tight bond. Tighter than anything she had with her coworkers. Of course, she hadn't given any of her coworkers the chance to get to know her, so maybe it was her own fault.

"Ma'am?" A young voice broke into her musing.

She opened her eyes, and the youngest of the officers assigned to her gave an apologetic smile. "Sorry, ma'am, but they want you over there." He pointed to Gil's room.

Sure enough, Luke stood there, waving at her. "Gil wants to see you."

"Me?"

"You." Luke held the door open, and she didn't have much choice but to enter Gil's room. She took slow steps. Why would Gil want to see her?

"Hey." Gil's voice had a rasp it hadn't had this morning.

The room was tiny, and there wasn't anywhere for her to stand except for right beside the bed. "Hey."

Gil held out a hand. "I want to shake your hand."

She took it, and his grip was firm despite the trauma of the day. "Thank you." Deep emotion laced Gil's words before he winked at her. "I hear you missed your calling as an Indy car driver."

"Maybe I'll try that if this FBI thing doesn't work out." Gil's eyes closed and stayed closed a few seconds longer than was normal for a regular blink, but he forced them open again. Would he even remember this conversation later? "I hope you know I'm keeping score, and you're coming in second in the contest for number of holes. I didn't realize how competitive you guys in the Secret Service are, but I think you've taken it too far this time."

Gil's words were slurred when he spoke. "I'm going to have to think of a loophole I can crawl through to win. Something about the severity of the holes or som . . ." He trailed off, and his eyes did not reopen.

"I'll wait outside. If he wakes up again, tell him we can argue about it later." Faith tried to squeeze behind Luke, but he didn't move.

She was in charge of the biggest investigation of her career. But instead of being in the office, working the evidence and reports as they came in, organizing the investigation and up to her sunglasses in every detail, she was in a hospital with two men, both of whom had nearly been killed by the person she was trying to catch.

And she was trapped.

"Whoa. Where's the fire?" Luke took a small step and pressed himself against the edge of Gil's bed, effectively giving her six more inches. "We aren't being chased. Well, not at the moment."

She eyed the space. She could squeeze through it, but not without rubbing against Luke in a very unprofessional way. For a too-long moment, the walls closed in on her mind. She forced them back, took a few shallow breaths, and chose a light and cheery response to Luke's remark. "Let's hope he doesn't catch us in here. We'd be fish in a barrel." Without giving Luke a chance to continue the conversation, she put both hands on his arm and shoved. "Now, will you please move so I can get out of here?"

Luke did not comply with her request in the way she'd expected. He turned and walked out the door, leaving her trailing after him. She caught up to him at the elevator. "Why are you leaving Gil?"

"Gil's fine. He'll sleep for another hour, and his twin sister, Emily, will be here in about thirty minutes. She's a physical therapist, and she's nice enough, but she's also part Terminator." He gave her an overdone grimace before he continued. "He has police protection, and Emily will make sure he's receiving the absolute best care. Besides, you're the one who has to solve this case, so it's in my best interest and the best interest of my entire team for you to stay sharp . . . and unperforated."

He mixed seriousness and humor so much, it took her a few seconds longer than it should have to catch up to his joke. But she got there. "Unperforated, huh? I have to agree with you there."

"Great. Let's find out what sort of setup they have for us tonight."

The setup turned out to be the top floor of a hotel. Three rooms. One for her, one for Luke and Zane to share, and one for Tessa. The rooms were adjoining and all the interior doors between them were open. Luke walked through the three rooms and approved of the plan immediately. "Yes. Smart. I like it." Zane and Tessa were already there, sitting at a table in the corner of Tessa's room. They were both focused on a shared laptop, and while they acknowledged Faith and Luke, neither of them made any effort to get up.

"Don't you think it's risky?" Faith glanced toward the windows. "We're on the top floor. It's going to be hard to get out if he blows the place up or lights it on fire or something."

Luke paused to allow her to go first through the room he would share with Zane, and then into her own. He paused, still in his room, and leaned against the connecting doorway. "I'm sorry, but have you forgotten what we do? Protecting people is our area of expertise."

She tossed her bag onto the bed, thankful she never went anywhere without an overnight bag in her car. She took a few seconds to familiarize herself with the space. It was clean and comfortable, and she had her own bathroom. She would be fine. "You typically have days or weeks to prepare. And more resources than you have at the moment."

Luke pushed away from the door and settled himself into the

chair in the corner of her room. Did he realize how carefully he moved? She doubted it. He had to be hurting more than he was letting on. "First"—Luke ticked items off on his fingers—"he couldn't have known where we were going to be and couldn't possibly have already set up anything. Second, it's not that easy to blow up a hotel or set one on fire. The world is a dangerous place, but it takes determination to pull off something like that, even without all the local law enforcement agencies in the city on high alert. Third, it makes it harder for him to get to us. Fourth, this is the tallest hotel in the city, and there are very few areas where he can get line of sight to shoot through the windows, and I can assure you that those locations are being watched."

"How do you know all that?"

"This is my city. If a protectee comes to town, we have to know how to protect them here. The protective detail would lean on us to give them information like this. I had a feeling they would put us in this hotel. It's the best choice all the way around."

Faith was impressed. "I guess I think of the local Secret Service offices as being more focused on financial crimes and counterfeiting."

"We are, but that doesn't mean we aren't ready to fulfill our protective mission at the drop of a hat. It's nice to have notice when a protectee is coming to town, but we have to be ready to act on short notice when necessary."

One thing was bothering her though. "Who's left in your office to take care of this?"

"Jacob would have done most of it. Marty, our office manager, would have helped with anything he requested. And the RAIC in Greensboro used to be in Raleigh, and he came over on Monday to help. Our office is down to almost nothing, but there are other RAIC offices in North Carolina. They've sent everyone they can spare."

"The new agents would be unknown to our attacker, so that's good."

"Well, we hope so. We don't know what this guy's deal is. If the motive is connected to one of our current or recent investigations, then we're being targeted specifically and other agents should be safe. If he has a beef with the Secret Service . . ." Luke didn't need to finish the thought. If the attacks were generalized to the Secret Service, any agent was in danger.

But that wasn't how this felt. Ugh. She hated using feelings in an investigation. She preferred facts and evidence. Gut instincts were inadmissible in court. What would she say to their families if one of these new agents were killed? "I didn't think they were in any danger?"

No. There had to be proof. Real evidence that would indicate what the attacker was doing—or what he or she might do next.

She leaned against the wall and closed her eyes. She focused on the case, starting with the shootings on Monday. Then the events of today. There was something there. "The guy coming after you. He's been careful."

"What do you mean?" Luke asked.

"You and Zane were the only people in the area when you were attacked. Those shots couldn't have hurt anyone else. Michael Weaver was jogging on a quarter-mile track with only three other people, and none of them were close by. If this guy had blown up Gil's house the way he did Jared's, he would have run the risk of killing children. Based on the toys I saw in the yard, there are toddlers in the houses on either side of him. The bomb at Jared's was designed to destroy his place but nowhere else. The lady who lived in the unit beside him wasn't there."

No one else was hurt. That bomb. There was something about the bomb. It was there, on the edge of her thoughts. She blew out a breath and forced herself to relax. It would come. She couldn't force it.

"Well, the bomb that killed Thad wasn't a tactical strike. It blew up his car and the two beside it," Luke said. "Six people were injured that night."

"That brings me to my other question. If the purpose was to kill a bunch of Secret Service agents, why wait eleven weeks to kill the rest of you? Maybe the connection we're looking for between Thad's death and this week's attacks isn't there."

"It's there." Luke spoke with confidence, but when she cracked an eye open to look at him, she saw the doubt. "It has to be."

— 14 —

IN THE DARKNESS of his hotel room, Luke woke Thursday morning to the smell of coffee and the murmur of distinctly feminine voices in the next room. He'd jerked awake more than once last night, heart racing, muscles tense, the sound of gunshots echoing in the fading dream. Each time, he'd fallen asleep with a prayer on his lips. He had no idea what was going on, where the threat was coming from, or how they were going to survive this mess. So, he prayed.

It was a lifeline.

He pulled his phone from under the pillow beside him.

8:20 a.m.

The last time he'd checked the time, it had been 4:47. Maybe sheer fatigue had finally pushed him over the edge and into the oblivion of sound sleep. Regardless, he was awake now.

He took a deep breath, clenched his jaw, and forced himself to roll over. Pain pierced his abs, his biceps, his quads. But pain beat being dead.

As his eyes adjusted to the dim light coming from the now-closed door separating their room from Faith's, he could make out Zane lying in a heap of blankets.

"You awake?"

Zane grunted.

Luke used the nightstand as support and pushed himself to a standing position. He shuffled to the door to Faith's room, tapped, and pushed it open.

Faith and Tessa sat at the small table—a coffee cup, a Cherry Coke, and a plate of pastries between them.

"Did we wake you?" Faith gestured to the insulated box of coffee by the sink, and it drew him to it like a three-year-old to chocolate milk. He didn't answer until he poured himself a cup and took his first sip.

"No. I was ready to get up." Or more precisely, glad for the night to be over. He helped himself to a cinnamon roll the size of a Frisbee and bent his head over it. *Lord, bless this food and please keep us alive today.*

Tessa's phone rang, and she stepped to the far corner of the room to answer it.

Faith stood and waved her fingers in Tessa's direction. "I'll see y'all later today."

Luke almost dropped the cinnamon roll. "Where are you headed?"

"The office. They're pleased with the security around my office and yours. So we can get back to work."

"What's on your agenda?" The words were out of his mouth before he could stop them. Why did it matter to him? She was trying to solve the case, which would ultimately keep him alive. He was in favor of her doing her job. Why did he need a play-by-play of events?

If Faith was annoyed by his question, it didn't show. "First I'm going to sort through all the information we've gathered so far and get a time line of what's happening with forensics. Then I'm going to review the security for the funerals. Then I'm going to go over every piece of evidence we have on Thad Baker's case to see if I can find anything that ties them together."

Funerals. Luke's mouth went dry. "I had forgotten about the funerals."

"I can't imagine why," she said.

"When did they decide about everything?" Luke had no idea when the funerals were scheduled or where they would take place, and he had no clue how Faith knew.

"Jared Smith's family requested his body be sent to Milwaukee, and the medical examiner's office is slated to release it later today. They haven't nailed down the funeral arrangements, but it will probably be Saturday or Sunday."

Milwaukee? How long would it take to drive to Milwaukee? Could they go? It felt wrong not to attend the service, but how could they?

"There's been an offer of a private plane to take all of you to the funeral and bring you back. Jacob's considering it."

"What? Who?" And also, when did Faith start reading his mind?

"You'll have to ask Jacob." Faith continued to get ready to leave. She checked her phone, then slid it into her bag. Her hand slipped around her back, and Luke knew she was reaching for the familiar comfort of a weapon.

"It was the Campbells." Tessa returned to the table. "From Carrington. The senior Campbell has a couple of planes here in Raleigh."

Luke understood immediately. "Ah. Adam's grandfather."

"You know Adam Campbell?" Faith paused by the door.

"Yeah. Dive with him. Great guy. Worth more than I'll make in a lifetime, but not snobby."

"I've never met him. I only know his wife, Sabrina." Faith took a few steps toward the door.

"Well, I haven't met either of them." Tessa slid her phone into her pocket. "But I'll hug that man's neck if I ever meet him. We have to pay our respects to Jared."

"Agreed."

Luke's phone buzzed. Rose Baker. "Excuse me." He waved at Faith as she left the room, then Tessa slipped out the door through his room. He assumed she was headed back to her room to get ready for the day.

"Rose. How are you?"

"I know you're in the middle of an investigation, but can you come over?" Rose's voice had an edge of hysteria Luke had never heard. The woman was a rock. Even in the midst of the tragedy of Thad's death, she'd been steady. Solid. Grieving but not without hope. Broken but not destroyed. Her faith made his own seem shallow and inconsequential.

"Sure."

"Now?"

"Rose? What's going on? Do I need to send some agents?" Not that he knew who he would send. Maybe he could get some local officers—

"No. I need to talk to you."

"Okay. I'm downtown—"

"Why are you downtown?" She hadn't heard.

"Um. Let's talk about it when I get there."

"Now." She had a combination mom and agent voice that was kind of terrifying to be on the receiving end of.

Lead with the positive. "No one else has died."

"But someone else was attacked?"

"Gil." Best to be thorough. "And Zane's house."

Rose Baker said a very, very bad word.

Rose Baker never cursed.

"I'm still not driving, and I don't have a car, but I'll get an Uber. I'll text you my ETA and the make and model when I know it."

"Okay."

It turned out a local police officer was available and more than willing to drive him to the other side of Raleigh. "I'll stay close," he told Luke. "Give me a holler when you're ready to go. If I can swing by, I'll pick you up."

"Thanks, man." The men exchanged numbers, and Luke walked up the driveway to Thad's, well, Rose's kitchen door. The officer hadn't moved, and a wave of appreciation for the law enforcement community flooded through Luke. That man did not know him, and he didn't know Rose, but it didn't matter. He knew agents were being targeted, and he was going to do what he could to keep watch.

Rose opened the door before he reached it. She looked him over with a critical eye. "Good grief, Luke. You look like something the cat dragged in. What's going on?"

He entered the familiar room. There was a large island with barstools all around. Muffins arranged on a tray. Coffee in a pot. A little cow filled with heavy cream, even though Rose drank her coffee black. Luke knew his way around this kitchen as well as his own. Maybe better.

But somehow Thad's absence was everywhere. In the missing shoes by the door. The missing jacket on the hook.

"Are the kids at school?" Rose wouldn't tolerate shoptalk around the kids.

"Yes. Talk, Powell."

She poured him a cup of coffee, complete with the perfect amount of cream. He took a seat on one of the stools and talked. He started with Monday morning and kept going until he'd filled her in on the events of last night and even the funeral arrangements for Jared. "I didn't catch the details of Michael's funeral arrangements," he concluded.

"It's looking like next week." Rose topped off her cup of coffee and perched on the stool at the end of the island. "I've been at Karen's most of this week."

Luke dropped his head. "I should have been there too."

"Nonsense." Rose slid the tray of muffins toward him. "We don't need any more dead men. Or women. How's Leslie holding up? How's Tessa?"

Luke took a bite of a muffin and studied Rose. Rose was the consummate professional in everything she did, whether it was hunting down terrorists or making a pound cake. If Rose Baker did it, it was going to be done right. But one thing Rose Baker was not great at was small talk. That had been Thad's area of expertise.

She was making a valiant effort to disguise it, but he knew her too well. He swallowed, took a sip of coffee, and ignored her question. "What's going on, Rose?"

"I'm trying to catch up on what's happening. Jacob must have some kind of lockdown on the media, because there's been very little news coverage."

"Rose."

"They've messed with my family. Again. I'm angry."

He didn't doubt that she was angry, but an angry woman hadn't called him this morning.

Her expression was unreadable as she reached for an envelope resting on top of a basket in the middle of the counter. She handed it to him, then settled back on her stool. "This came this week. I'm not sure when. I forgot to check the mail. Thad always did it on his way home. I never could remember to do it when he was gone. He'd call me and ask me if I'd checked the mail . . ."

Luke didn't want to interrupt her reminiscence. She had a faint smile on her face, and he didn't think this memory hurt too much.

"I thought it was junk mail, but it felt too thick for that, so I opened it."

Luke glanced at the address on the envelope. An ancestry site? He pulled the folded pages out and scanned them. "Thad did an ancestry search? With his DNA?"

That did not sound like Thad Baker. Thad had expressed concerns on more than one occasion about the potential dangers of handing over your DNA to a third party.

"I know. I didn't believe it either. But then . . . well, look at it."

Luke had never looked at one of these reports, so he took his time familiarizing himself with the results. Thad's name was there. Information about his ethnicity was prominent. His great-grandmother had been Korean. His grandmother had been African American. His mom had been Swedish. Thad had joked that he was the entire melting pot in one person.

Luke continued scanning and on one line, hundreds of tiny pieces fell into place.

He traced the words. The name. The lines going back to Thad's grandfather, connecting Thad to a young Korean woman—his distant cousin, Park Mi Cha.

— 15 —

LUKE READ and reread the words.

"This has to be the woman Thad was with. It matches. South Korean, thirty-one years old, female." Rose's voice was tight, steady. Daring him to argue. "She was his cousin."

There was no proof that this was the woman Thad had been meeting with, but what were the odds that it wasn't her?

A wave of relief flooded through Luke. He had known it all along. Thad Baker hadn't been cheating on his wife or his country. Luke had held firm in his belief most of the time, but every now and then, he'd had his moments of doubt. *Forgive me, buddy. I'm so glad I wasn't wrong about you.*

He continued studying the pages. "The date of the application is a week before he died."

"There's no way this is a coincidence." Rose's voice shook. "Thad didn't have this information when he died. My guess is she found him, told him the story, and he agreed to meet with her. I've always been fascinated by genealogy and histories. I've done all of it on my side of the family." She pointed to a family tree, labeled in precise silver lettering, that hung on the wall of their living room. "But I've been limited in what I could find out about Thad's because he refused to do the testing."

A few tears slipped down her cheeks. "Until I saw this today, I had forgotten, but Thad had been teasing me. He said he'd found my Valentine's Day gift, and I would never guess."

Luke continued to study the paper. A small hiccup pulled his attention back to Rose. Tears now dripped from her face.

Luke patted her arm. "This is the first real lead we've had."

"I know," she said. "I'm sorry." She swiped at the tears. "I knew he loved me and the kids. I knew he knew I would kill him if he ever cheated on me." She laughed and sobbed at the same time, and it was one of the most heartrending things Luke had ever heard. "But I wondered if you were lying to me. If you knew who she was to him. If you knew—"

"That's understandable."

"No!" Rose slammed her hand on the table. "It isn't. Not from me. Not about him."

Luke didn't try to talk her out of her rage.

"You tell Jacob." Rose pointed a finger, and Luke wouldn't have been surprised if flames had shot out of it. "That FBI agent who was assigned to Thad's case had better not step one foot on my property."

Rose's extraordinary anger further fueled Luke's suspicion that Janice Estes had made some assumptions—and insinuations—that Rose had not appreciated.

There was no quaver in Rose's voice now. "I want you to find out how Thad met Park Mi Cha, and how they connected. And then I want you to find out why they died."

This case had to be worked by the FBI. There was zero chance of the Secret Service being allowed to do what Rose was asking. At least not completely. Regardless, he had to be careful about how he approached this while Rose radiated fury. "I haven't been impressed with the original agent either."

Rose snorted.

"But I can't leave the FBI out of this, and I think you'll have a different reaction to the agent working the case now. She's solid."

"I don't want to talk to anyone else."

"I know."

Rose paced in a circle around the island.

Luke held the paperwork in front of him. "You opened this today?"

"This morning."

"Would you be willing to look through Thad's things again? Maybe something will jump out at you that didn't mean anything before."

"Sure." She set her coffee mug on the counter. "I'm helping Karen today. There's so much to do for the funeral and the future." She rubbed her temples, and Luke got the impression that while Rose was more than willing to help her friend, she was also struggling with the way funeral planning had ripped the bandage off a still-raw wound. "I'll be racking my brain for anything, and when I get home tonight, I'll look through everything again. I'll text you."

"Can I take this?" Luke flipped through the pages of the report.

"I knew you'd want it. I made copies, but I want the originals back."

Luke folded the document and stuffed it in the envelope. "I know you don't need me to tell you this, but we have no proof she's the woman who was with Thad."

Rose stretched her hands flat on the counter between them. "Are you telling me you don't think—"

"I think it's her too. But this isn't proof."

"Then get it."

Luke called his ride from earlier and was told he could be there in five minutes. Had he been driving around the block the whole time? Could Faith have anything to do with his presence? Regardless, Luke wasn't going to complain about not having to pay for an Uber.

He said goodbye to Rose with the promise of a phone call later in the day and made it back to the office in twenty minutes. It wasn't even 11:00 a.m., but he was already spent. If it got bad enough, he'd grab a nap on the couch in the conference room, but there was no way he was going back to the hotel. There was too much at stake.

He checked in with Jacob and hovered over Marty as she called the hospital for an update on Gil. Thirty minutes later, he was settled behind his desk. His relief that Gil was conscious and doing okay this morning and Zane was coming into the office at lunch was intense. But it was the news that, according to Marty, there was a rumor floating through the world of federal agencies that it had hit the fan over at the FBI office this morning that had him chuckling. He couldn't wait to hear about it straight from Faith.

He had no doubt she'd been involved.

He'd left Faith a message and asked her to call when she had a chance. Who knew when that might be? For right now, it was time to find out who Park Mi Cha was. And if it was possible that Thad's involvement with her was the reason they were both dead.

He knew who he needed, and it only took a minute to find the number and place the call.

"Sabrina Fleming-Campbell." The voice was politely curious.

"Dr. Fleming-Campbell. This is Luke Powell, US Secret Service in Raleigh. We were on a human trafficking task force last year, and I dive with Adam sometimes."

"I remember you, Special Agent Powell. How are you?"

"It's Luke. And, well—"

"You aren't well at all, are you? Your office has been decimated, you've been shot, your friends have been shot, killed, and blown up. All in all, a horrific situation."

Luke had forgotten how blunt Dr. Fleming-Campbell could be. The woman was brilliant, but tact wasn't her forte. "You've summed it up nicely."

"I could have been a little less blunt." Her voice carried uncertainty and maybe some regret. She was hard to read, so he wasn't sure.

"Nah. It's all true, and none of it's a secret. I'm not sure why anyone would think I would be fine."

"Indeed. And my guess is you haven't called me to catch up on social matters."

Did she sound hopeful? She was more of a "get to the point" kind of person. "No, I haven't."

"How can I help you?"

Luke explained about Park Mi Cha and her family connection to Thad, his belief that she might be the unidentified person who was killed in the car bombing, and his questions about whether there might be video footage of her somewhere.

Aside from an occasional grunt, Dr. Fleming-Campbell didn't interrupt him. The only sound coming through the phone was rapid-fire clicking as she typed. After a minute, she spoke. "Can you email me the information you received from Mrs. Baker without violating confidentiality?"

"Not an issue. Rose wants to know more than anyone else."

"I'm sure." The typing continued. "I've sent you an email. Please respond with the information from Mrs. Baker. I'll let you know what I find."

Luke considered his next question. "Dr. Fleming-Campbell—"

"Could you please call me Sabrina? Or Dr. Campbell? I kept Fleming because it's how I'm known professionally, but Fleming-Campbell is a ridiculous number of syllables and highly inefficient, as well as too formal for friends."

"Then Sabrina it is, and it's an honor to consider you a friend."

"Thank you. Is there something else?"

"Yes." He wished he'd called Adam first and let him ask, but there wasn't time for going through third and fourth parties.

"I called you before I checked with the FBI or my boss or pretty much anybody."

"This is on the house, Luke. Don't worry about it. I understand Faith Malone is working the case for the FBI. She's a good agent. One of the best in that office."

"She's been great. I have a phone call in to her, but she hasn't responded yet. When I talk to her, I'll let her know about your involvement."

"Excellent. I have a meeting I cannot avoid this afternoon, but this is my top priority as soon as I return to my desk. I'm good, but even I can't find information that simply isn't there. Be prepared for this to take a few days and for the results to be less than satisfactory."

"I understand." He did, but he also knew he had succeeded in enlisting the help of one of the brightest computer forensics minds in the country. If there was anything to find, she would find it.

"I'll be in touch."

The call disconnected.

Luke set the phone on his desk and rested his head in his hands. *Lord, we need a miracle. Please help Sabrina find Park Mi Cha.*

FAITH STILL HADN'T RETURNED Luke's call. Not because she didn't want to, but what could she say? *Janice is a jerk, and it all went sideways today.*

Dale stopped by her desk. "Come by my office in a few minutes, okay?"

She didn't look up but nodded.

Lord, I'm not sure you're listening. Or if you care. Because, let's face it, you haven't exactly been showing up a lot lately. And I know that may be a sin to think, but it's how I feel, and it makes no sense to me why I would even bother praying to a God who isn't big enough to already know what I'm thinking. I mean, if you don't already know, then you aren't really all that. But the simple fact that I am praying makes me think that somewhere deep inside of me, I do believe you care. Anyway, it's me. Faith. And yes, I can appreciate the irony of a name like that under the circumstances. I bet you got a real kick out of it when Mom and Dad named me. You would have known that thirty-one years later my faith would be in tatters, and I would be sitting in a cubicle praying but also kind of wondering if I'm talking to myself. I don't even know what I'm doing. I need . . . help.

Faith grabbed Cherry Coke number 3, her iPad, and her pencil and wound through the cubicles to Dale's office. She tapped on the door, and he waved her in.

"Close the door." He didn't look up. Was he mad?

She stood behind the chairs in front of his desk, unsure of whether she should sit and settle in or if this would be brief and to the point.

Dale still didn't look up from the computer screen, but he croaked out a hoarse laugh. "Good grief, Faith. Sit down. Sheesh. You're making me anxious hovering like that. Give me a second and we'll talk."

She sat. Tried to still her mind and body. But how was she supposed to give off fewer anxiety-producing vibes?

With a resounding thump, Dale closed the laptop and faced her. "You sure poked the bear this morning."

What was she supposed to say to that? She went with a respectful nod.

Dale laughed. Not a little chortle. No under-the-breath chuckle. A full-blown belly laugh that left him wiping his eyes. When he got some control, he leaned back in his seat. "You aren't worried about this, are you?"

"I lost my temper this morning."

"So? Have you paid any attention to the people you work with? Everyone loses their temper."

"I don't."

"Then it was about time you did."

Dale didn't understand. To lose her temper, to lose control of her emotions? Those were unacceptable situations, particularly in a professional environment.

"It's not the end of the world, Faith. So you yelled at some agents."

"They could—"

"Could what? File a complaint? Get something on your permanent record? Please."

"But—"

"Listen." Dale leaned forward in his seat. "Could you have handled things better this morning? Maybe. But I'm not so sure. Whether you realize it or not, your coworkers simultaneously respect you because you outwork all of them and hate you because you make them look bad on a regular basis. None of them want to be compared to you. None of them want to have to live up to your expectations."

"That's my point."

"No." Dale fisted his hands on the desk, then stretched his fingers wide. "The point is that you're always so in control. Always so efficient and effective. You've set a standard no one in this office can attain. And this morning, when you blasted Janice for the junk she sent you—and yes, it was junk. And when you lit into Troy for not getting the ATF file sent to you. And then asked Walker how long he planned to take to finish the simulation of the shooting because you knew for a fact that he'd gone to dinner and a late movie with some buddies last night, it shocked everybody."

That had been the real low moment. Janice and Troy had failed. Faith didn't feel sorry for them. But Walker? If she'd been in his shoes, she would have told her friends she had more important things to do, but she didn't have a lot of friends blowing up her phone asking her to meet them for pizza. And it's not like he'd left the office early. He hadn't gone to dinner until 8:00 and then went to a 10:00 p.m. movie.

It wasn't realistic to expect to have received significant information between 8:00 p.m. and midnight. But it didn't sit well. Their fellow agents were spending the night in a safe house, and Walker was at a movie? It might not have made any difference in his ability to do his job, but it didn't look good.

"Everyone in this place has been working double time all day." Dale didn't seem angry about that. "My guess is you've been inundated with information. More than you can handle. Am I right?"

"Yes."

"Sometimes people need a good kick in the pants. And you gave them one. So let it go. You're human, and you got frustrated. I'm relieved to know there might be a tiny chink in your armor, because I was starting to suspect you were either part alien or part superhero."

Faith could not stop from bristling at the idea of a chink in her armor any more than she could stop from congratulating herself on being thought of as part superhero. "Regardless, it won't happen again. At least not in public."

Dale rolled his eyes. "Fine. Where are we on the case?"

She sat straighter. "The only reason I can say we've made any progress at all is because we've eliminated a lot of things. We've ruled out all the Secret Service agents in the RAIC office here in Raleigh."

"Shocking," Dale deadpanned.

He wasn't wrong to be underwhelmed by that statement, but she stood by it. "We had to be sure."

"I don't disagree, but I hope you have something better than that."

Uh-oh. "Not anything I can prove."

"How about you give me something you can't prove?"

"I'd rather wait until I have proo—"

"I'd like to hear it now." There was no budge in Dale's demeanor, and Faith was reminded in painful clarity that for Dale, this was the hunt for his best friend's killer.

He had a right to know where things stood, even if she didn't have all the answers. *Here goes nothing.* "I think the same person is behind all the attacks. I think it's one person, working mostly, if not entirely, alone. I think this person has military training. Possibly special forces. I think he is targeting the Secret Service office specifically and that Agents Powell, Thacker, and Dixon are still in danger, but I don't think their families are. If the attacker is a special forces type, he's likely operating with a high level of integrity."

Dale bristled at her word choice.

"Integrity in his mind would be that he would only go after

the people he deems responsible. Not their coworkers, not their families. Based on my observations, he doesn't seem willing to harm innocent bystanders."

Dale frowned but nodded.

"I'm speculating that this is directly related to the Thad Baker case, and I think we need to know more about the woman in the car before we will be able to solve this." Faith stopped talking and took a deep breath while metaphorically holding her breath as she awaited Dale's response.

For longer than was comfortable, Dale didn't speak. He was staring at some point behind Faith, his eyes unfocused, lips in a tight line, head moving up and down in a tiny nod. "That," he said, "was a lot of thinking."

"You asked." Faith didn't quite keep the defiance out of her tone, and she knew Dale hadn't missed it by the way his forehead crinkled.

"I did. But, wow. I'll be better prepared next time."

Next time? Did he mean he expected her to continue not to have any evidence? Or that he expected her to face more difficult cases in the future?

"Why don't you think Jacob and, wait, what's the new agent's name?"

"Tessa Reed."

"Right, Reed. Why don't you think they're being targeted but the other agents are?"

"I think there's a good chance they're not in the crosshairs because their Monday mornings looked like they have for the past three months."

"I'm not following you."

Faith took a sip of her Cherry Coke. "Tessa's morning routine is straightforward. She gets up, does yoga at home, gets ready for the office, and stops at one of three coffee shops on her way in. She's a coffee snob and won't go just anywhere. She rotates them most of the time, but she always goes to the same one on Monday, because Mondays are the only day they serve her favorite lemon poppyseed muffin. She went there on Monday and drove in to the office. I triple-checked. If the shooter had wanted to, he could have added her to his route. She never would have made it to the coffee shop."

She had Dale's full attention now. "What about Jacob?"

"His Monday is set in stone during the school year. His wife goes to the gym, and he takes their youngest to school. He runs the carpool every Monday, Wednesday, and Friday, unless he's out of town. Same order of houses, same time of day."

"And it would have fit on the route?"

Faith could picture it in her mind. "He was typically one of the last to arrive at the office because of the carpool. It would have been tight, but if he'd been targeted, he would have been the last one attacked—after he dropped the kids off but before he arrived at the office."

"Where does Gil fit into this?"

"Gil was completely out of his routine. He told me that most Monday mornings, he swims at the Y. Did you know he'd been on his way to the major leagues before he blew out his shoulder?"

Dale nodded. "Michael told me. Gil has quite the story."

"He really does. Anyway, he typically goes to the Y at five a.m. for an early swim. I asked him when the last time was that he'd missed a swim. He told me the last time he'd missed a Monday was Christmas."

"So where was he on Monday?"

"He'd stayed up to watch the Braves versus the Mets. It went to sixteen innings or something crazy, and he didn't get in bed until after one. He reset his alarm for seven and crashed."

"You're thinking the attacker could have planned to hit Gil first?"

"It's a possibility. We're getting a warrant for the Y's security footage. It's a different location from the one Michael Weaver used. But it would have allowed the attacker to make a loop. Gil, then Luke and Zane, then Michael, then Jared. Jared was well-known for not being a morning person, and he never came to the office early. Luke said he was late a lot. Drove the rest of them crazy. Those Secret Service guys are competitive. All type A, opinionated, kind of aggressive. He said they rode Jared hard about it, but Jared either ignored them or told them to butt out of his business. Nothing changed."

"Okay, so Gil was the first target."

"I think when Gil broke his routine, it messed up everything, but my guess is the attacker had backup plans for everyone he intended to take out. He just had to get in position and wait for his opportunity. He hit Zane's house, maybe thinking Zane would be passed out on painkillers and wouldn't get out in time. And he would have been if he'd been able to sleep. He'd called an Uber around seven a.m. and went to a Waffle House, then instead of going back home, he wound up at Luke's when Luke wouldn't answer his phone. The fire marshal got back to me today. The fire at Zane's was definitely arson, and it went fast. If Zane had been inside, it's likely he wouldn't have gotten out. The attacker may have been shocked when we pulled up at the house and Zane got out of the car. But he hadn't been looking for Zane. He was looking for Gil, and when Gil came out, he got him." Her voice broke on the last few words.

The memory of yesterday—the shot, the blood, the fear—left her blinking back tears. What was wrong with her? She took a deep breath and shook her head as if that would push it all away. "Sorry."

"You were there, Faith." Dale's voice was thick with sympathy. "It's normal to have some strong emotions about Gil's shooting that you don't have about any of the others. It isn't easy to be dispassionate and objective when you watched as a man almost had his brains blown out."

It might be normal, but Faith didn't like it. "I was remembering that Gil had bent down." To talk to her. "He bent down, and it saved his life. The bullet only missed by a fraction. If Gil hadn't moved . . ."

There would be three dead agents.

— 16 —

FAITH LEFT DALE'S OFFICE reassured and relieved. She wasn't going to be fired. Her boss didn't hate her.

She went back to her desk and checked her messages. Just one. From Hope.

> It was Mom. I've gotten the profiles removed.
> And I've talked to Mom. She says it won't
> happen again.

>> Thanks. I know you don't have time to be
>> dealing with that.

> Neither do you. Stay safe.

She hadn't had time to even think about the dating profiles, not in the craziness of Gil's shooting. A flush heated her face at the thought of anyone seeing her on that dating site. Thank goodness Hope had figured it all out.

All in all, this afternoon wasn't ending on a bad note. Had her prayer, if that's what it could be called, been answered? Had God sent help in the form of an understanding boss and a brilliant sister?

It could be a coincidence, but there was a problem with that theory.

Faith didn't believe in coincidences.

She'd texted Luke two hours ago that she thought she'd be done for the day in an hour. He'd texted her back that he was in the office going over all the cases from the past year that could have triggered in someone a pathological need to kill every agent who had worked the case. He suggested she call him when she left work and they would compare notes.

Instead, she ran through a drive-through, inhaled her chicken sandwich, and drove straight to the Secret Service office. The security guard allowed her through, and she found Luke in the conference room. The table was covered with boxes of files. A huge whiteboard propped against the wall was filled with case numbers, random names, and a smattering of photographs.

Faith cleared her throat. Luke turned and smiled.

He had a slow smile. It started in his eyes, touched the edges of his mouth, and then his lips eased into a full grin over the space of a few seconds. It was endearing. Faith couldn't explain why the intentionality of the smile made her feel like it was authentic, unlike the quick, patently false smiles she saw so often.

He put the lid on the dry-erase marker he was holding and pointed to a chair at the head of the table. "Have a seat. We'll compare days."

She pulled the chair away from the table, turned, and sat on the table, swinging her legs. "Mine was interesting."

"So I heard." The way Luke said it, or maybe it was the look he gave her as he said it, sent a thrill of anxious warning down her spine.

"What do you mean, you heard?"

"Good news travels. Also, our office manager? She's friends with yours."

Faith dropped her face into her hands.

"Did you really tell Janice Estes that if she wasn't careful, she could be arrested for mishandling evidence and as an accessory after the fact? And that you'd gladly testify against her because the way she'd handled Thad Baker's case constituted a gross miscarriage of justice?"

Her face still in her hands, she could only nod.

"And"—Luke was clearly enjoying this—"did you also tell an agent that if you had to get the ATF report directly from the ATF after you'd asked him for it three times, you would see to it that he spent the rest of his career in Alaska?"

She moaned.

Luke's howl of laughter bounced around the room.

"It isn't funny." She whispered the words. This was worse than Dale calling her into his office. People were talking about her. Telling their spouses over dinner about the unstable agent who lost it today.

"Faith Malone, I could kiss you."

That got her attention.

FAITH'S HEAD POPPED OUT of her hands like a jack-in-the-box.

And Luke was standing right in front of her. He hadn't meant to say he could kiss her. Not that he didn't want to kiss her. Or that he hadn't thought about it. A few times. Maybe a few hundred times.

Her eyes were huge in her drawn face. Stress and something else, maybe embarrassment, surely it wasn't fear, warred in them.

Perhaps the kiss remark had been inappropriate. She was a coworker, in a sense. A professional. A federal agent.

He leaned closer, but not too close.

"I would never kiss you if you didn't want me to. I would never disrespect you that way. It just came out of my mouth." He couldn't bring himself to lie and say that he hadn't meant it.

"I know."

Did she sound disappointed? Maybe that was his imagination messing with him. He took a few steps back to give her plenty of space, and the sigh that escaped her lips was definitely one of regret.

The faintest pink tinged her cheeks. "My . . . my outburst this morning . . . " It was clear to Luke that Faith was trying to pull the conversation away from kissing and back to the case. "It was unprofessional."

"It was brilliant." Luke held out a fist, and she gave him the most half-hearted bump in the history of fist bumps. "Why are you upset?"

She shifted her position on the table, her legs swinging. "It's hard enough to be a female in this world, Luke. I don't need to add 'maniacal' or 'hysterical' or 'prone to temper tantrums' to my resume."

He couldn't stop himself from laughing. "All you added to your resume today was a subheading under your name that reads 'Do Not Mess with Me,' and that's not a bad thing. I've been yelled at plenty of times for doing something stupid. Sometimes that's the only way to get through to people. Let it go."

She was smiling, but she was definitely not letting anything go. Her grip on the table proved it.

"Fine. What if I change the subject? I have news." He couldn't wait to tell her what he'd learned about Thad's cousin.

"Okay." Before Luke had a chance to speak, Faith's phone rang.

"Hold that thought." She glanced at the phone, her finger hovering over the screen for two more rings.

"Are you going to answer it?"

"I haven't decided." She took a long breath, squeezed her eyes closed, and tapped the screen. "Yes."

Luke turned to the whiteboard and tried to look like he wasn't eavesdropping. If Faith didn't want him to hear the conversation, all she had to do was leave the room.

"Mom, you've called my work number again."

"That's because you won't answer your private number." Luke heard Faith's mom almost as clearly as if Faith had put the phone on speaker.

"That's because I'm working, and there's nothing you can possibly have to say to me right now that is work related. I'm not sure what's so difficult about this for you to understand. You're the one who taught me to keep my professional life professional."

And that was his cue to leave. Luke turned to Faith and mouthed, "I'll wait outside."

She grabbed his good arm and shook her head.

Okay. So he would stay.

"So this is my fault?" Faith's mom's voice was pitched higher than it had been a few moments ago.

"No. It's your fault that I grew up to prioritize my job over every other relationship in my life. It's my prerogative to ignore phone calls from you or anyone else right now because I am working the biggest case of my career, and if I fail, it won't mean the world will miss out on the hottest new paint color. It will mean people, friends, will die."

Faith's mom didn't respond.

"I'll call you in a few days. Please do not call me again unless there's an actual life-or-death emergency."

"Fine."

The phone disconnected.

"Sorry about that." Faith set the phone on the table and picked up her Cherry Coke. "My mother is a piece of work."

"I gathered as much."

"Life hasn't been kind. Some of it she's brought on herself. She doesn't always make the best decisions. But no one deserves some of the stuff she's dealt with. And she . . ." Faith shrugged. "She has a hard time letting go. Of me. And especially of Hope."

"I think most moms have that problem. Mine was blowing up my phone so much on Tuesday, I had to put her number on Do Not Disturb."

"You'd been shot."

She had a point. "I assume this is about Hope and the dating profiles?"

"We can't win. Either she's creating dating profiles and making comments about how much she longs to be a grandmother or she's arguing that if we won't get married, we should just move back in with her. She makes little comments about how she's lonely, how it's a waste of money, etc."

"She says waste of money, you say price of sanity."

"Exactly." Faith tilted her Cherry Coke toward him in an air toast. "I love her. Doesn't mean I can live with her. And Hope needs her independence. She's a bright, intelligent woman who happens to be in a wheelchair."

"Where's your dad?" The second the words left his mouth, Luke knew he'd messed up.

Faith squeezed her bottle so hard the plastic protested with a loud pop.

"Sorry." Luke was in full damage-control mode now. "None of my business."

"My father"—Faith took a drink, as if she needed to wash a bad taste from her mouth—"decided his first family was a bit too much work. He wasn't living his best life with us, what with a teenage daughter in a wheelchair and a wife who was coping by becoming an expert on paraplegia while still working fifty hours a week as an interior designer. She didn't have time to worry about keeping her husband happy, and he decided we weren't what he'd signed up for."

There was no way to respond to that.

"He went in search of another life, and he found one with Gail, a woman who is a whopping two years older than I am."

Yikes.

"Everything we have—my career, Hope's career—we got without any help from him. How could he possibly spare any cash when his new kids, two boys, needed the best preschools, then private schools, then braces? Not that Hope and I ever needed any of that."

The acid in Faith's words could eat through solid marble.

"When you tell me stories about Thad Baker and Michael Weaver—men who loved their wives, were there for their kids, worked hard in their careers but didn't leave their families behind while they did it, I struggle to wrap my mind around it. Partly because I'm not sure I believe men like that are real. But if they are, then how can a good God tolerate their violent departures from this earth while scumbags like the guy who donated some genetic material to make me are still cruising through life like some sort of favored child?"

She looked at Luke and a couple of decades worth of pain shimmered behind her lashes. "Can you explain that? If there are good guys, why don't they get to live out their lives, loving their wives and throwing birthday parties for their kids? Why can't they live to walk their daughters down the aisle? Why does a guy who doesn't even care about his wife or his two daughters get to move on and have Wife and Family 2.0, with no repercussions? He is strong, healthy, and has plenty of cash while Thad Baker is in the ground and Michael Weaver is in the morgue. How is that right?"

She set the bottle on the table and dropped her head.

Luke closed his eyes. *Lord. A little help?*

He opened his eyes, and Faith was staring at him. "I don't expect an answer. I guess this is my day for outbursts and drama. I should go home and swing by here tomorrow morning." She hopped off the desk and walked around the table opposite from where Luke stood. "Is eight thirty okay? I'll bring coffee and a better attitude."

"Faith. Don't go."

She gave him the saddest smile. "It's okay, Luke. Tomorrow." She walked out the door, and he could hear her footsteps as she made her way down the quiet hall.

Follow her? Stop her? Let her go?

He ran around the table and raced down the hall. Well, he tried to race down the hall, but it was more like a wounded lope. He caught up to her as she got to the security guard. "Faith, wait."

She turned. "Luke, I don't want—"

"I know. And we don't have to. I just wanted to say thank you."

Her brow wrinkled. "For what?"

"For staying in the game. For not letting your doubts stop you from believing the best in people." He paused. "For trusting me with huge issues. I can't promise you I have all the answers, but I can promise you I'm a safe place to wrestle with the questions."

She nodded.

"And I like Americanos with heavy cream."

She smiled then. A real one. "I know. Good night."

He let her go then. But he didn't leave the foyer until the security guard had checked under her car and her headlights had disappeared from the parking lot. And he prayed the whole way back to the conference room.

Faith Malone was a hot mess.

And he was about to get burned.

— 17 —

LUKE HAD RETURNED to the hotel for the evening and hung out with Zane and Tessa. Faith had insisted on staying in her own home, either because she was confident she wasn't in danger or because she couldn't bear to be around other people so much that it was a risk she was willing to take.

He and Zane had been ready for bed by ten and Tessa had hassled them about being old, even though she was older than both of them. He didn't care. The sleep had been restorative, both to his body and mind, and he woke up the most clearheaded he had felt since Monday.

Tessa gave him and Zane a ride to the office around seven thirty, and they all gathered in Jacob's office.

Jacob glared at Zane. "What are you doing here?"

"Where else am I supposed to be?" Zane shot back. "My house is a pile of ash. My bed. My pillow. My car. All gone."

Jacob's glare lost some of its ferocity. "I meant you don't have to be here. I'm sure there are things to do about your house."

"You'd think that, but no. My house is still a crime scene. My insurance agent is on it. Luke's offered to let me hang with him until I find a new place. Tessa helped me order a bunch of clothes online, and we had it all shipped here."

"You needed help ordering clothes?" Luke couldn't resist the jab.

"No. I didn't." Zane didn't add "idiot," but his tone suggested it. "But Tess nearly lost her mind when I tried to order some khakis from the wrong store without using any discounts or coupons."

Tessa wasn't having it. "Whatever. If you want to waste your money, fine. I'll leave you to it."

"No, no. That's okay." Zane held up his hands in mock surrender.

"How much did she save you?" Luke knew it was big.

"About three large."

Jacob whistled. "Tessa, can you talk to my wife? Please?"

"Anytime." Tessa all but stuck her tongue out at Luke. "I'm happy to help."

Jacob cleared his throat. "A couple of things before the day gets away from us. First, Karen has decided to have the funeral here, but there's a problem."

"If we attend a public funeral," Zane began.

"We're sitting ducks," Tessa finished.

"Bingo."

"I've never felt sorry for the ducks before," Luke said.

Zane gave him a look of commiseration, and Tessa started to say something, but Jacob kept them on track. "The funeral won't be until next Wednesday. Michael's sister is a missionary in a remote village in one of the former Soviet republics. They didn't get in touch with her until Wednesday evening, and it's going to take her until Monday to get to the States. Karen knows about the problem with us attending and the possibility of the funeral becoming a target, so she's not announcing anything until Monday. If we catch this guy before then, maybe we can attend."

"So, no pressure." Luke couldn't imagine skipping Michael's funeral.

"Jared's parents plan to have a public wake on Saturday, followed by a private graveside service in Milwaukee on Sunday. There's no way we can attend the wake. No one will approve it. But even though there are safety concerns, we've been invited to the graveside service and the local RAIC is working on it. The cemetery is out in the middle of nowhere, and there's going to be a one-mile perimeter to ensure everyone's safety. Charles Campbell has agreed to any security measures we want on his plane. Plan to leave on Sunday morning, but don't advertise it. The goal will be to get out of town and back without anyone knowing we left."

"Lucky we know how to protect high-profile people with public schedules." Zane didn't sound lucky.

"The difference," Jacob said, "is when we have a credible threat, we've been known to ask the protectee to cancel their plans. We'll see where things are on Sunday and make the call then."

Everyone nodded their agreement. What other choice did they have?

"Zane, take it easy. Luke, take it easy. Tessa, don't get shot." Jacob pointed to each of them in turn. "I'm done with seeing my people in the hospital. Now, get to work."

Tessa bounded out of her seat like she'd been sitting on a spring. Luke leaned on the arm of the chair and used it to help push himself upright. Zane groaned, resting both hands on the arms of the chair and heaving himself upward, a hiss escaping through his gritted teeth.

Jacob rubbed his bald head. "Luke. A moment?"

Luke hung back.

"I hate to do this, but I need you to keep an eye on Zane and

Tessa. Tessa's still green. Zane's more beat up than he wants to admit. I know you aren't at one hundred percent, but—"

"It's no problem. I'm on it."

Jacob grunted. "How are things with the FBI? I heard Malone was here for a while last night."

"We're okay." Luke glanced at his phone. "She's supposed to be here around eight thirty so I can bring her up to speed on everything I've learned, and she will do the same."

"Keep me in the loop."

Luke left Jacob's office and headed for the conference room but paused at Marty's desk. "Marty?"

"Yes?" Marty was not her normal sassy self, and that needed to change.

"I hate to be a brat—"

"You live to be a brat," she countered.

"Okay, smarty-pants. Where's my cake?"

"What?"

"Don't what me, Marty. We made an arrangement. You owe me a chocolate cake. I've been dreaming about it. How yummy a nice, thick slice would be with a hot—"

Marty reached under her desk and pulled out a cake carrier.

Luke placed a hand over his heart. "Is that what I think it is?"

Marty lifted the lid and revealed the chocolate cake resting inside. "I keep my promises. I even remembered that you prefer the version without frosting or even powdered sugar." She snapped the lid back on and handed it to Luke.

"You are my favorite," Luke said as he took the cake.

Marty smirked. "Are you talking to me or the cake?"

"Both." Luke winked at her, and she turned back to her computer.

He made it three steps down the hall when she called after him.

"That cake is still warm, and while it is yours, you had better share if you want to keep your job. Brat."

"Who's a brat?" Faith's laughing voice came from the doorway off the lobby. Luke turned and waited as Faith carried two drink holders loaded with hot beverages to Marty's desk.

"Special Agent Luke Powell. Brat extraordinaire." Marty rolled her eyes in his direction. "How are you today, Agent Malone?"

"It's Faith, and I'm fine. Thank you. I didn't know what everyone drank, so I brought an assortment. Can I interest you in a vanilla latte? Or a mocha?"

And just like that, Faith had wrapped Marty around her finger. Luke had never seen it happen so quickly. But Marty was a sucker for a generous act, and Faith had thought of her when she'd made her coffee run.

"I'd take a mocha." Marty stood and approached Faith. "Let me help you with those." Together they set the drink carriers on the ledge around Marty's desk and studied the sides in search of the mocha. "Look at this. An Americano with heavy cream that already has Luke's name on it."

Luke could almost hear the wheels spinning in Marty's head. Time to get Faith out of here. "Awesome. It will go great with this cake you made for me."

Whether she also sensed that Marty was about to pounce or was genuinely curious, Faith helped Luke out. "Marty, did you make Luke a cake? That's so sweet."

Marty eyed Faith and Luke with open suspicion. "Huh. Fine. Yes, I did. It's his favorite. And it will be awesome with that coffee you brought special for Luke." There was challenge in her tone, but Faith, wisely, didn't bite.

"Lovely. I'll take these to the conference room." She turned to Luke. "Do you think Jacob would like a coffee? I have two black—"

"He'll take black. He thinks cream is for wimps. Let's get settled, and I'll run it back to him." There was no way he was going to leave Faith alone with Marty while Marty was having a party with the innuendos.

They set the cake and coffees on the conference room table, and Luke snagged a plastic knife from one of the drawers in the credenza. He'd slid the first slice onto a napkin when Jacob strolled in. "I heard there was coffee and cake."

Luke waved the knife in not-so-mock outrage. "This is my cake!"

"Hand it over."

Luke slid the cake over to Jacob, who took it and the coffee Faith handed him with a quick thanks. Then he left the room, yelling out, "Coffee and cake in the conference room" as he walked down the hall.

"Now the vultures will descend." Luke kept slicing cake.

Sure enough, Zane and Tessa appeared moments later.

"Thanks for the coffee, Faith. You didn't have to do that." Tessa pulled a cup from the holder, read the label, and smiled. "My favorite."

"After your glowing recommendation, I had to try it." Faith took a bite of cake, and her eyes rolled back in her head. "Oh. My. Word." She dashed from the conference room, and Luke experienced the dual desire to know what she was doing and also to be able to move that quickly.

He didn't have to wait long.

"Marty! That cake. It's amazing." Faith's voice carried down the hall. "Will you share the recipe? My sister would love it. Her blood type is chocolate."

It registered that Faith had called her Marty earlier, and neither then nor now did Marty complain. Faith was working her magic on more than just him.

FAITH STARED at the small paper napkin and the smudge of chocolate begging for her to find a way to get it into her mouth that didn't involve licking the napkin.

"Want another slice?" Luke hovered the knife over the cake, a smirk on his face. "I promise it would taste better than the napkin."

How did he know? "No. Maybe later." Definitely later.

He packed up the cake and cleaned the mess around it. He was meticulous, wiping crumbs and even wetting a napkin to tackle a sticky spot on the table. He tossed the napkin into the trash can and declared it to be a three-point shot before settling into a chair and pulling a stapled stack of papers from a folder. "I had a productive day yesterday."

"Let's hear it. I'm ready for something we can sink our teeth into." Faith needed good news. Direction for the case. Anything that didn't contribute to the growing, gnawing certainty that she was a failure.

"We may know who the woman was in the car and why Thad was meeting her."

"What? How? Who? When?"

Luke filled her in on his trip to see Rose Baker, the DNA results, the fact that Park Mi Cha was Thad Baker's distant cousin, and his phone call to Sabrina Campbell.

"Sabrina got back to me last night after you left. Still no hard evidence to prove she was with Thad that night, but Sabrina was able to tell me that Park Mi Cha was supposed to be on a red-eye the night of Thad's death. She didn't get on that plane, and unless she's traveling under an assumed identity, she has not left the States despite the fact that her visa has expired."

"That can't be a coincidence," Faith said.

"Agreed. Sabrina gave me the name of Mi Cha's employer and one known associate. We have a meeting at ten a.m. with Ivy Collins, the CEO of Hedera, Inc., the company Mi Cha was working for as an intern."

"This is fantastic!" Faith caught the tenor of Luke's enthusiasm. "I know you guys are good at investigating foreign nationals, but if there's anything the FBI can do . . ."

"There may be."

Wow. Luke was full of surprises today. "Shoot."

"Sabrina says the known associate is an accountant named David Lee, and she thinks he's in the DC area. She sent photos. He has a distinctive tattoo on his neck. We're working on tracking him down, but he hasn't left the footprint Mi Cha did. The problem is, our DC-area agents are swamped thanks to a state visit from the president of France. And it's not like I can drive up there and knock on doors in my current condition. But your people could."

"I'll get on it. This is great news." She made a few notes on her iPad. "It's strange that no one has come forward looking for this woman, Park Mi Cha. How much thought has been given to the idea that the other person in the car was the target, and not Thad?"

"We considered it over here, but you'd have to ask Agent Estes how much credence she gave to the idea." Luke's dislike for Janice was on full display. "She doesn't like to share information, and she seemed convinced Thad was with a prostitute. As such, she most likely wouldn't have been the target. And there is the sticky point that it was Thad's car, not hers, that was rigged to blow."

Faith processed the information about Park Mi Cha and David Lee. It didn't answer all their questions, but at least it was a solid lead. Finally.

Luke tilted his head to the side. "I have a question."

Something about the way he spoke sent a quiver of apprehension through her, and she braced herself for whatever was coming. "Okay."

"Why didn't you get Thad's case in the first place?"

"What?"

"If they trusted you with this one, why do you know so little about Thad's case? Why weren't you working it?"

"Hope had been sick. She's super independent. Totally capable of handling most aspects of her life, but when she's sick, things can get complicated fast. She got dehydrated and had a nasty case of pneumonia and wound up in the hospital for a couple of days. When the case broke, I wasn't even in the office." Why was she telling him all this? And why couldn't she stop herself? "I don't talk about Hope in the office, so most people assumed I was on vacation."

"Why not talk about Hope?"

"For one, she's a person, not a statistic and not a pity party waiting to happen. She has her life, and she doesn't need my co-workers asking me about her health. You'd be amazed at the things people assume it's appropriate to ask just because someone's in a wheelchair. And also because she's a lawyer, and sometimes FBI agents aren't all that thrilled with lawyers."

"Your boss knows though, right?"

"Dale knows all about Hope, but I don't—"

"You don't want anyone at work to judge you on anything other than your work." Luke didn't ask it. He stated it.

"When I'm at work, that's all that matters."

"You're more than your work, Faith. You're allowed to have a life. A real one."

"I know that."

"Sure you do." Luke made no effort to disguise his sarcasm.

"I don't think—"

"Are you ashamed of your sister?"

"No!"

"Based on your actions, it could be inferred that you're trying to protect your own reputation by not letting people know about Hope, which could imply there's something embarrassing about her. But I don't think that's what's happening. This leaves me thinking you worry that if people found out you have a human side, maybe they wouldn't trust you to get the work done, and maybe they wouldn't assign you the big cases."

"I—" Faith had an argument against this ridiculous assertion. She did. Why couldn't she think of it?

"You were out of the office and missed a big case. Maybe the biggest your office has seen in a while. And it went to Agent Estes. An agent you believe to be incompetent. So not only did you miss out on the big case, but you had to watch someone with an inferior skill set have her time to shine." Luke considered her, speculation all over his face. "I bet she's rubbed your face in it, hasn't she?"

Ouch. "I don't care that someone else got the case. I want to see it handled correctly."

"Okay." Luke fake coughed. "Right. I think you love your sister more than any other person on the planet. You two would have been close anyway, but your dad's betrayal and your mom's"—he considered his words—"unique approach to parenting have given you common enemies and common annoyances, and she's the only person in the world who gets it. I bet she's safe. You don't have to perform for her. But you also feel responsible for her. You'd sacrifice career, relationships, job locations, anything for her, but I bet she doesn't want you to." Luke scratched his chin. "You don't have to tell me I'm right. I already know I am."

Enough of the psychoanalysis. "What does any of this have to do with this case?"

"Nothing specifically. But I have been wondering how someone so clearly on top of things as you are got left out in the cold. And for the record, I'm glad you caught *my* case."

The comment was almost too casual. Like he wanted to say it, and meant it, but also didn't want it to be a big thing. Except that it was.

Luke continued. "For one thing, that Estes woman makes me crazy. But mostly I'm glad because you're good at this. You care. You focus. You want to get the job done and you want to get it done well. It's not enough for you to solve the case. You want a slam dunk. And I appreciate it."

Luke's phone rang. He glanced at the screen and his eyes widened. He held up a finger to her and said, "Hello. Everything okay?"

Faith took the opportunity to take a long drink of her Cherry Coke. Why did talking to Luke almost always leave her with emotional whiplash? She'd wanted to strangle him thirty seconds ago. And now? She studied his profile as he leaned forward over the table, scribbling furiously. Angular features. A tiny bit of stubble that made her wonder if he'd forgotten to shave this morning. Or maybe he'd forgotten on purpose. The muscles in his forearm tightened into firm bands as he held the pen between long fingers. Overall, he had the physique of a runner. Long, lean, strong.

And strongly opinionated.

She didn't like anything he'd said to her about Hope, but mostly she didn't like how much he'd been able to infer about her. Although she hadn't minded that last part.

He said goodbye and placed the phone on the table. "That was Rose Baker. She's looked through Thad's stuff again and hasn't found anything, but if we want to come over tonight and look through it, we're welcome to. Bobby and Betsy have a friend in a play and they're attending, so they won't be home from six to nine."

Luke tapped the pen on the table. "You should know that she told me she doesn't want Agent Estes to step foot on her property."

Faith tried not to snicker. She failed.

Luke didn't laugh. "She also told me she only wants me working on the case, and she didn't want to see you either."

Okay, not so funny.

"The offer to come over tonight while they aren't there is a big step for her. At least she's not insisting I come alone. Could you be free tonight?"

What was the point of pretending she had plans? "Yes."

— 18 —

LUKE CHECKED HIS WATCH. Ivy Collins, Park Mi Cha's boss, should be here in an hour. Faith was on the phone. He could work at his desk, but he didn't want to go back to his cubicle. It was too quiet. Zane and Tessa were there, but without Gil and Jared and Thad, the space felt cavernous and empty. Lonely.

To make it worse, Zane and Tessa were in the middle of a disagreement, and the room crackled with tension. Maybe Faith had been right and there was more than friendship between those two, but Luke couldn't see it. This felt more like a brother/sister argument. Besides, Tessa was driven. Intense. She made Faith look relaxed. There wasn't room on her agenda for a relationship. And Zane wasn't looking either. He was leaving soon. If they survived this case and Zane had a chance to move on to the protective detail, he could be gone as early as the summer.

Luke's chest tightened at the thought. Moving came with the territory, but he'd never expected to develop the kinds of friendships he'd found here in Raleigh. Or that he would wish this group could somehow stay together.

He glanced at Faith. Or that there would ever be an FBI agent he would like. A lot. How had that happened? He risked another glance. Although with the way she was working at the moment, he could stare at her and she wouldn't notice. She didn't even know he was in the room. Her hawk-like focus was impressive and daunting.

And a little frustrating.

What was the point in him liking her if she didn't notice him that way? And when or if she did, what could come of it? Beyond the irritating fact that she was FBI, there was also the fact that their careers would take them in different directions—sooner rather than later.

"Luke?" Faith didn't look away from the laptop.

"Yes?"

"What do you know about Ivy Collins?"

"Nothing more than what I've read on Hedera's website. I hadn't heard of her before, but apparently, she's a big deal. Why? Have you heard of her?"

"I heard her speak at a charity function I attended with Hope. She's quite philanthropic. Young to be in such a position of author-ity. PhD in biochemistry or microbiology. I can't remember exactly. Her company is leading the way in some kind of biomedical re-search. She's only in her early thirties, very well off, entrepreneur-scientist type." Faith leaned back in her chair. "She had a family member with a lot of health issues, and that inspired her to go into research. Somewhere along the way she concluded that while she's a good researcher in her own right, she's an even better business-woman and could do more by running the business."

"Impressive."

"Yeah." Faith's disgruntled agreement confused Luke.

"Why wouldn't it be impressive?"

"Oh, it is. Very."

"Then what's the problem? Do you think she's not as good as she seems?"

"Do you realize she's about the same age as I am and she's changing the world?" Faith gave him a rueful grin. "Makes me feel like a slacker."

Luke tried not to gape at her. "You're too hard on yourself. Who's comparing the two of you? Nobody but you."

Faith huffed. "I have high expectations for myself."

Luke studied her, unapologetically taking advantage of the excuse to look without worrying about getting caught. What was it like inside her head? Did she ever relax? "What do you do for fun?"

Faith's fingers stilled on the keyboard. "Why do you want to know?" Suspicion dripped from every word.

Luke raised his hands. "I'm curious. Besides work and doing stuff with Hope, what do you do for fun?"

"I don't have a lot of time for fun."

She didn't say it like a martyr. More like a crusader. "Come on, Faith. Humor me."

"I'm working." She didn't say, "Leave me alone," but he was sure she was thinking it.

"So am I, but it isn't a complicated question." He got up and walked toward her. "I'll show you how it's done. I'm Luke, and on the rare occasions I have free time, I like to scuba dive. I've done a few triathlons, but mostly I love to run and mountain bike. When I'm home, I read, and I enjoy building things. I bought my house in foreclosure, and I've renovated almost all of it. By the time I leave Raleigh, I should be able to sell it for a profit." He snapped his fingers. "Oh, and I like going to movies with my nephews, but not my niece."

Faith chuckled at that. She'd met Luke's sister and her family when they came to cheer them on in the dragon boat race last year. "What's the matter? You don't like princess movies?"

"I like them fine, thank you very much. She doesn't."

"Then why don't you like to go with her?"

"She doesn't share her popcorn."

Faith laughed out loud. A true laugh that made everything about her softer, warmer, and so very appealing. Luke leaned against the table, two feet away from her. "See. Not hard. Your turn."

Faith wiped the corners of her eyes, still smiling. "I'm pretty boring. I row. That's about it."

"I already know about the rowing. I'm going to ask again. At the end of the day, when you're home and you've finished work . . ." When she didn't respond, Luke prompted her. "This is the part where you fill in the blank."

She turned back to the laptop. "Work is never finished."

"Don't you have any hobbies?"

One shoulder twitched in a half shrug.

"You have to have something. What is it?"

"Nothing. I'm not any good at anything else."

"Who said you have to be good at it? Is there something else you enjoy?"

Again with the half shrug. "I read."

"If you tell me you only read books on productivity and criminal science, I'm going to lose it."

Faith tossed a rolled-up napkin in his direction. "What if I told you I read steamy romances?"

"I'd ask to borrow them."

Faith's eyes widened in surprise. "Luke Powell! You're terrible." She tossed another napkin in his direction. Had she been storing them over there?

He caught it and tossed it back. "Come on, Malone. What do you read?" *Please, let it not be steamy romances.*

"What does it matter?"

Luke fired back. "Why are you making this so challenging?"

She shook her head in slow sweeps from side to side, refusing to make eye contact, her lips twitching in amusement. "It's more fun this way."

"For you, maybe."

Faith laughed a low, throaty laugh. "You're so easy to annoy."

"You enjoy annoying me? So that's it?" Luke pitched his voice in a completely unrealistic falsetto imitation of Faith. "Hi, I'm Faith. For fun, I try to annoy Luke as much as possible."

Faith grinned at him. "It's as good a hobby as any. It's still new, but I feel like I could get good at it if I keep practicing. Perfecting my technique."

Why did the thought of being perpetually annoyed by Faith seem so . . . not annoying? Luke couldn't stop himself. He pushed away from the table and leaned toward her. "You'll have to be careful. A hobby like that could turn into a permanent obsession." He winked, then held eye contact. *Your move, Malone.*

He expected her to back down, but she leaned toward him, her face inches from his, and her voice was husky as she whispered, "I guess I'll have to take my chances."

Would she?

Would he?

Their eyes held, neither of them willing to be the first to make a move or to look away.

"Luke, have you seen—" Zane's voice cut off abruptly. "Oh. Excuse me. I'll come back later."

Faith had her back to the door, but she hadn't moved when Zane walked in, and Luke had matched her response. Now, the slightest uptick of her eyebrows dared him to react. Ignoring Zane, he leaned a few millimeters closer. "This conversation is not over." He caught a flash of surprise—and maybe pleasure? It definitely wasn't fear or anger in her eyes.

"What do you need, man?" Luke shoved away from the table and kept his voice light and calm. He walked over to the credenza with the water pitcher and poured himself a glass, as if being so close to Faith Malone that he could smell her shampoo was a normal part of his routine.

Zane didn't attempt to hide his reaction and openly regarded Luke with a mixture of amusement and shock. "Um, well, I . . ." Zane looked at the back of Faith's head, then back at Luke, then pinched his lips together. Luke wasn't sure if he was trying to stop himself from saying something inappropriate or to stop himself from laughing. Could have been both. "I was wondering if you'd seen my umbrella."

"What do you need an umbrella for?"

"Well, it is mine, so there's that, but also I have to go to the doctor. I'd rather not get soaked on my way to the car."

"I didn't realize it was raining."

"I'm not surprised. You don't seem to be aware of anything outside of this room." Zane grinned his most smart-alecky grin.

Luke didn't bite. "Do you need a ride?"

"Are you offering? Last time I checked, you don't have a car, and you aren't supposed to be driving."

"Good point. Your umbrella is in the corner by Marty's desk."

"Thanks." Zane turned to go.

"You coming back here?"

Zane paused at the door. "Where else would I go?"

Luke didn't have an answer to that, and as Zane left the room, he could feel Faith watching him. When he looked at her, the teasing and flirting were nowhere to be found. She was all business. "Ivy Collins."

"Ivy Collins." Maybe she would have some insights into who Park Mi Cha was.

A NEW VOICE floated down the hall. Light. Feminine. Southern. 9:55 a.m.

"She's prompt." Luke muttered the words around the glass he held to his lips.

Since Zane had left for the doctor, Luke had been all business, and Faith was glad. Sort of.

Luke was a major distraction. No matter how hard she tried to ignore him, if he was in the room, she was aware of his presence. His mannerisms, the way he twirled his pen between his fingers when he was staring at the computer. Or the way he shifted in his seat, something she suspected he wasn't aware of and also something she didn't think was normal for him. It had to be hard to get comfortable with all of his injuries rubbing up against khakis and a golf shirt.

But it wasn't just that. Sometimes she could feel his eyes on her, and she had to force herself not to look up to catch him watching her. It made it so much more difficult to concentrate when she couldn't stop herself from wondering what it would be like to have a man like him around all the time.

Not that she needed a man, but she didn't use to think she wanted one—and now she wasn't so sure.

The phone buzzed and Luke answered. "I'll be right there." He set the phone back on the receiver. "I'll go get her."

He stood, and his entire persona shifted. He wasn't Luke anymore. He was US Secret Service Special Agent Luke Powell, and he was ready to get some answers.

Two minutes later, Luke ushered Ivy Collins into the room. She extended a hand immediately. "You must be Special Agent Malone."

Faith shook her hand. "I am. Thank you for coming in, Dr. Collins." She pointed to the chair to her right. "Please, have a seat."

Ivy Collins was, to Faith's dismay, more lovely in real life than she'd been on the internet or on the stage. Willowy. Fair. Blonde. She oozed femininity. And Luke had noticed. Of course he had.

"Dr. Collins, could I get you some water?" He stood behind the chair to Faith's left, across from Ivy.

"Please, call me Ivy. And yes, thank you." Her smile was soft and her hands brushed Luke's when she took the glass from him a moment later.

Awesome. Ivy had noticed Luke. Of course she had.

Luke took a seat and smiled at Ivy. A warm smile that spoke of friendship and kindness. In that moment, Faith despised Ivy Collins. It was irrational. Faith knew it. But later she was going to have to think about it. Hard.

Before Faith could rein in her emotions and begin her line of questioning, Ivy leaned toward them, earnest and concerned. "I'm still in shock over what's happened. I realize it wouldn't have changed anything, but if I'd had any idea she was the unknown woman from that horrible bombing, I would have come forward immediately."

"We understand," Luke said. "Nothing about this case has been normal."

Faith wanted this interview over as soon as possible. "Dr. Collins, could you tell us what Park Mi Cha did for you?"

"Please, call me Ivy. And yes." Ivy reached into a bag, and Faith experienced a slight twinge of satisfaction when Luke reacted to the motion by surreptitiously reaching for his weapon. He didn't completely trust this new girl. Good.

Ivy extracted nothing more dangerous than a stack of papers. "I brought printouts of everything I could find on her. I have her fingerprints, visa application, the background checks we did—all here." She slid the stack of papers toward Luke.

Faith intercepted them. This was still her case. "Thank you. This should be quite useful."

"It's impressive you were able to compile this so quickly." Luke pointed to the papers.

"I have a wonderful assistant," Ivy demurred. "She does all the heavy lifting for our interns."

"How many interns do you have?" Faith asked.

"I host five to ten interns twice a year. They come in for four months and learn from us. Sometimes they're techy types, sometimes science grad students, but usually they're business majors. We receive ten times as many applications as we have slots available. I only accept four international interns each year because the red tape we have to go through makes it prohibitive."

"She'd been here for four months?" Luke asked as he scribbled notes.

"Yes. She'd completed her time with us. She was supposed to be returning to South Korea the week of the bombing. Her last day at our office had been on the Friday before."

She took a sip of her water before continuing. "It's not unusual for our international interns to take advantage of their time here in the States to do some sightseeing or even interview for jobs at local companies, so we always make sure there is some cushion in their visa to allow for that. Mi Cha began working for us in September and had taken a week in late October to go visit a family friend in Washington State. That was the only time she took off. She didn't have to leave the country until early March, but she was ready to get home."

"Do you know why? Was there something wrong here that she was trying to get away from?" Luke asked.

"No. Nothing like that. At least, nothing that I was aware of," Ivy clarified. "Her mother was ill, and while she was here, the prognosis went from stable to grim. She was close to her mother and was anxious to spend time with her. The last time I saw Mi Cha, I told her to be sure to reach out if she ever decided she wanted to return to the States. I didn't say this to her, but I wondered if she might be willing to consider coming back after her mother passed."

"But when she left that Friday, as far as you knew, she was getting on a plane and you had no expectation you would see her again?" Luke tapped his pen on the side of the yellow legal pad he'd been scribbling on.

"Correct. Has her family been notified?"

"We're still trying to confirm that she's the unidentified person from the bombing. We have a lot of circumstantial evidence but no hard proof. We do know her mother passed away in February, but we haven't spoken to her father yet."

Tears welled in Ivy's eyes. Well, wasn't that special. She was even pretty when she cried.

"Her poor father."

Luke handed her a box of tissues and she took one. "Did she talk about her father much?"

Ivy dabbed under her eyes. "I take the interns to lunch at least three times while they're here, and we did discuss family and friendships. She was an only child, and she was doted on by both parents. I remember her talking about them fondly. Her father was in the Korean military, and they traveled extensively in her teens. And I gathered she enjoyed the travel. Beyond that, I'm afraid I can't say." Ivy held up her palms in frustration.

"That's very helpful," Luke said in a soothing voice.

"I have one more question, if you have the time." Faith wanted to give herself a pat on the back for how civil she sounded.

"I'm at your disposal. Whatever you need." There Ivy went

again with the earnest, eager-beaver attitude. She was making it very difficult to dislike her.

"Is there anything you make or do at your Raleigh office that would be appealing to another country, or have you ever been a target of corporate espionage?"

Ivy nodded, casting a shrewd but, unless Faith was badly mistaken, also appreciative look at her. "We're always on the lookout for that. We have security measures in place to discourage theft of intellectual property. The most stringent is that everyone, from the building maintenance crew to the vice president of operations, has to pass drug tests quarterly and also has to be willing to have their financial records accessed at any time."

"You have permission to look at people's bank statements?" If Luke had been trying to keep the surprise from his voice, he had not succeeded.

"Not me personally," Ivy hastened to assure him. "We have a company that does spot checks on everyone."

"What are they looking for?"

"Anomalies. Too much money or too little, sudden big purchases, etcetera. The type of work we do is highly secretive and would be appealing to certain competitors, as well as a few nation states."

Luke sat back in his chair, tapping the pen on his lips. "Had her records been accessed recently?"

Ivy patted the stack of papers. "It's a little bit different with our interns. They are only here for a short time, and they don't typically establish a large financial footprint. But yes, her records had been checked twice."

She pulled the stack of papers back from in front of Faith, shuffled through them, and extracted a few pages bound with a binder clip. "This contains both of the reports and all the information on the company we use to do them."

Faith didn't have any further questions, and she stood. Ivy and Luke did the same. "Thank you for your time and your willingness to come in."

"Under these horrible circumstances, I wouldn't say it was a pleasure, but I do hope I've been able to help in some way. She was sweet." Ivy turned her attention fully on Luke. "It's awful to think of her and your coworker dying that way."

Luke's acknowledgment was a sharp dip of his head.

"If I think of anything else"—Ivy turned back to Faith—"I'll contact you immediately."

"Thank you."

"I'll see you out." Luke strode around the table and paused by the door to wait for Ivy, who gathered her things with elegance and gentility.

Luke stepped aside for Ivy to go in front of him, but she paused in the doorway. "I was wondering, and forgive me if this is inappropriate to ask."

Great. She was probably going to invite Luke to some sort of gala where he would look fabulous in a tux.

"Your coworker. Special Agent Dixon. Is he going to be all right?"

"He is." Luke answered with a slight lift of his chin and a look Faith recognized. He did not like this question.

Relief spread across Ivy's features. "Good. I knew a boy named Gil Dixon a long time ago. I'm sure it isn't him, but when I heard the name on the news, it brought back a flood of memories. I'm glad he'll be okay."

"So are we." Luke held out his arm, and Ivy took the hint and walked down the hall.

Faith strained to hear their conversation. She couldn't make out any specific words, just the low rumble of Luke's deep voice and the lilting soprano of Ivy's.

What is wrong with me? I do not care. I don't care that she's dainty and lovely and refined, and I'm . . . not. And what was taking Luke so long? How hard was it to send her on her way and get back to work?

Luke was gone five minutes. When his footsteps echoed down the hall, Faith buried her head in her notes.

She didn't turn when he came in the room but was acutely aware of when he stopped behind her chair and leaned over her head. What was he doing? She looked up and found a Cherry Coke dangling from his fingertips.

"I noticed you were almost out."

How did he infuse a sentence that mundane with so much tenderness? Faith wasn't used to people noticing—and meeting—her needs. Much less her wants. Warmth shot through her and she took the Coke, thankful her hands were steady. "Thank you."

"My pleasure." Luke returned to the seat beside her. "I wonder if Gil knows this Ivy girl. She's totally his type."

"His type?" As in, not Luke's type?

"Yeah. Cerebral. Cultured. Looks like she might snap in a strong wind." He did not say that last part as a compliment.

"She is very pretty." Faith twisted the lid from her Cherry Coke and waited for Luke's response.

Luke frowned. "She is. But you say that like being pretty is a bad thing. I would think you would be in favor of a woman turning the world upside down with her brains and abilities and not with her looks." Before she could respond, he continued. "There's something that bugs me about all of this. If she was so close to her parents, how could they not have noticed when she didn't get off the plane? Why hasn't her father been in touch with Ivy wondering where his daughter is? There's something sketchy here."

And just like that, it was back to business.

That was . . . good.

—19—

AFTER A FULL DAY of running down leads and mostly coming up empty, Luke sat in Faith's car and watched from a few houses down as Rose, Betsy, and Bobby Baker drove away from the house, fifteen minutes later than they were supposed to. "Let's go."

Faith pulled closer and parked at the curb in front of the house. "It's so cute."

Luke tried to see it with fresh eyes. "Thad wouldn't have appreciated you saying it was cute."

"But look at it. The porch, the flowers, the wreath on the door. You can tell, even from the outside, that it's a comfortable place."

Luke couldn't argue with that. "Wait until you get inside."

They didn't waste time making the short walk from the car. At any moment, Luke expected to hear the now-too-familiar pop of a rifle, but it never came. Luke opened the garage door using the keypad and was quick to close it behind them. He led Faith into the house, and her voice dropped to a whisper as they entered the empty home. "This feels so . . . wrong."

"Rose knows we're here. It's not like we're sneaking in."

"I know, but—" Faith stopped in the kitchen and turned in a circle, a satisfied smile on her face. "I knew it would be cozy." She held her hands in front of her, as if she were making a point. "This. This is a home. This is a place people live and are welcome to live. You wouldn't have to perform in this house. And you wouldn't have to tiptoe through your days."

"How on earth can you tell that from an empty house?"

"It isn't empty." Faith pointed around the room. "Don't you see it? Pictures on the walls, shoes in the corner. Homework on the counter. There's life here. Good life."

Her voice quavered, and Luke walked through the living room, looking everywhere but at Faith. "There is."

"They didn't deserve to lose their dad."

"No. They didn't."

"Let's find out why they did." Faith's voice was steel.

Two hours later, Luke had a startling appreciation for Faith and her work ethic. After a full day in the office, this woman was working him under the table. All he wanted to do was to close his eyes for a few minutes and maybe forget he'd lost his friends.

Faith was a machine. Methodical. Intentional. Possibly a bit manic. She had dismantled Thad's office one piece of paper at a time and then returned everything to its place in a way that would make it impossible for Betsy or Bobby to know anyone had been there.

"Are you sure Thad didn't have a secret compartment somewhere?" Faith rested her head in her hands. The first hint of fatigue she'd shown.

"If he did, he never told me. And he never told Rose either. She's looked. We've inquired at every bank in town to see if he had a safe deposit box. We've checked the floors and the walls and the ceiling."

Faith sat at Thad's desk. Her eyes scanned the room in a slow progression from floor to ceiling and then back down, as if she had X-ray vision and was using it to look for hidden files in the wall.

There'd been no guarantee they would find anything. It wasn't like Rose hadn't searched everything already. And even though they'd already done it twice in the past few months, Luke had spent part of his afternoon looking through Thad's cubicle at the office, which remained much as he'd left it.

They were looking for the proverbial needle in a haystack, with the added layer of complexity being that the needle might not even exist. But they had to look. TV versions of law enforcement never focused on the dead ends, the hours spent hunting for a lead and finding nothing. In real life, the dead ends were the majority of the work.

"It isn't here." Faith's disappointment layered every word.

He didn't want her to be right, but he was almost certain she was. "Whether it is or isn't, we need to get out of here." He pointed at the clock on the wall. "I do not want to incur Rose's wrath."

"Me neither." Faith widened her eyes in mock terror, then favored him with a gentle smile. "I would never disrespect her that way. Let's make sure everything is put back together."

She pulled her phone from her pocket and scrolled through the photos she'd taken before they started. When she was satisfied that even the small handcuff paperweight was positioned exactly as it had been, they left the house. "Are you going to your house or the hotel?" she asked as they climbed into her sedan.

"The hotel." Luke tried to sound like this was no big deal. He should be grateful for a safe place to rest his head, but he wanted to go home. He wanted to sleep in his own bed. He wanted to get up and have his own coffee from his own French press. He wanted to sit in his chair and start his morning with his Bible and end his day with a good book.

But he also didn't want to die.

Faith's hand on his arm startled him and chased all the negative thoughts away. "It's the smart choice. Your team, your friends—none of them could handle losing you. You know that, right?" Faith's fingers flexed on his forearm. Gentle pressure strategically placed in between bandages.

"I think it's overkill."

"Do it for Zane and Tessa and for your mom and sister. They would worry."

"Yeah." She wasn't wrong, but was he imagining that she might be worried too? "My mom doesn't want me to go home. She also doesn't want me to go to work."

"Moms can't be expected to be anything other than biased in favor of their children surviving the day."

"True."

"Where's your mom?" Faith turned left out of the subdivision, and pointed the car in the general direction of downtown Raleigh.

"Tyler, Texas."

"Is that where you're from?"

"I'm from Plano, just outside of Dallas. My mom and stepdad moved to Tyler a few years ago."

They drove in silence for a few moments. "Is your dad in the picture?"

Luke watched the lights flash across the reflectors in the highway. "No."

He couldn't explain why he insisted on being so disobliging. It's not like he could keep her from finding out. It made more sense to tell her. But how could he explain? He never talked about his family. She kept her own family issues close to the vest, but she had no idea just how much he understood why she did it. He had his own reasons, and he'd bet that many of them were similar to hers.

Except in one very big way.

The phone rang and "Hope Malone" flicked onto the panel set in the dash. "Do you mind?" Faith asked at the same time Luke said, "You'd better get that."

She smiled a thank-you and answered through the Bluetooth. "Hey, Hope."

"Fai—" A sound that had a distinctly breathless quality was all that followed.

"Hope! Hope! Are you there?"

"Go!" Luke hadn't meant to shout, but he had.

"I'm on the way!" Faith's last word was almost a sob.

"Where does she live?" Luke reached for Faith's radio. "I'll call it in."

"Don't. She'll kill me."

"He could have come after her."

Faith's grip tightened on the wheel. "We're five minutes away."

Luke ignored Faith as he flipped her police radio to the correct settings. Faith grudgingly provided the address to the dispatcher.

"The homeowner is a paraplegic. It's possible she's had a fall or is somehow incapacitated, but she's the sister of an FBI agent working a high-profile case, so proceed with caution."

Faith was proceeding with no caution whatsoever. She careened through the streets and skidded into the driveway three and a half minutes after they got the call. She slammed the car into park and grabbed the door handle.

"Wait." Luke reached around her and gripped her wrist.

She pulled away with an elbow into his chest. "Let me go."

"You don't help her if you run in there and it's an ambush or a trap." Faith's arm fell into her lap.

"I have to get to her."

"I know, but let's be smart about it." Sirens blared from multiple directions. "Backup is almost here."

"Luke." The panic in her voice was a vise around his own lungs.
"Hope." And with that, she was gone. Out of the car and running
straight for the front door.

So much for a stealth attack.

Luke limped hard after her and caught up as her key twisted
the lock. She had her weapon out, and he mimicked her as they
entered the home.

"Hope!"

"Faith?" The voice was weak, but it came from somewhere down
the wide hallway to the right.

"We're coming. Hang on."

Lord, I hope you protect idiots. We're gonna need a double portion. Thanks. Luke couldn't keep up with Faith. She ran straight
to the last door at the end of the hall and raced in. "Hope."

Luke entered the room, but the women weren't in there.

"In here, Luke. Help me."

Following the sound of her voice, Luke eased his way through
the bedroom, then the bathroom, and eventually into a large walk-
in closet. The skin on his neck and arms prickled. He didn't like
being in the interior of a house he hadn't cleared, but then he saw
what had happened.

Boxes lay in heaps around an empty wheelchair. The woman
on the floor beside it had a very bloody gash at her hairline. Faith
moved a box and grasped Hope's shoulders. "What happened?"
Luke joined in and pulled the remaining boxes off the woman
trapped under them.

"Thank you," she whispered. "You must be Luke."

"You must be Hope."

"What gave it away?" she asked as Faith helped her into a seated
position.

"The tattoos."

Hope snickered and turned to Faith. "I like him."

Faith wasn't appreciating the humor. "You don't have any tattoos."

"That you know of." Hope offered a fist to Luke, and he bumped it.

Faith shifted a final box away from the wheelchair. "She doesn't have any tattoos."

"It was a joke, Faith. Relax." Hope shifted her arm. "Could you lock the chair please?"

Luke wasn't sure what the protocol was in this situation. Hope was clearly a strong and independent woman. But he didn't know if he could stand aside and watch her struggle to climb back into the chair. All he could do was ask. "Hope, would you allow me to help you?"

Hope frowned, then shrugged. "It would seem most practical, although if you pull a bunch of stitches, don't blame me. Got it?"

Luke slid one arm under Hope's knees, put one arm behind her, and she cooperated by putting her arms around his neck. "Lift with your legs, Special Agent Powell. I'm not sure your insurance will pay for a back injury."

Oh yeah. He liked her a lot. Her skin was lighter than Faith's, but she had the same straight black hair, dark eyes, and strong cheekbones. She wasn't large. Built even smaller than Faith, she was still a respectable weight for him to lift. But he got her up and into the wheelchair without dropping her, so he was prepared to call it a success.

"There's blood on your shirt." Hope pointed toward the bathroom. "I have some stain remover in there."

"It's no big deal. I'm used to having blood on my clothes."

"I prefer to keep my blood on the inside," Hope countered.

"Well, that's boring."

"I WOULD KILL FOR BORING right now," Faith muttered. The remark earned her two groans, in unison. What was happening? Luke and Hope had met thirty seconds ago and already they were tag-teaming her?

"You're an FBI agent." Hope made the statement like she was explaining the law to a four-year-old.

"Really? I had no idea."

"I think she means you don't typically join the FBI when you're in search of a quiet life." Luke had his back toward her now, setting a few boxes on top of each other.

Hope winked at Faith and mouthed, "He's so cute" before speaking in a normal voice. "Exactly. Boring isn't a word anyone would see beside your name in the dictionary."

Luke moved another box, this time with a small grunt accompanying the thud of plastic on plastic. "Are you hiding dead bodies in these things?"

"We got a call." A deep voice spoke from the bathroom.

Faith reached for her weapon, but Luke didn't flinch. "Come on in here, guys—excuse me, and ladies." Luke stepped to the side, and a paramedic and EMT entered.

Hope's flush darkened. "What did you do?" She practically spat the words.

Luke cut his eyes at Faith and twisted his mouth in an "uh-oh, we've been caught" expression. Then he knelt beside Hope's chair, staying out of the paramedic's way. "I know you know what we're working on right now."

She continued to glare at Luke but confirmed his statement with a slight tilt of her head.

"Faith told me you were probably okay, but I couldn't risk it. Don't be mad at Faith. This is on me. I've lost friends this week, and my paranoia levels are at an all-time high."

Hope looked to Faith, and Faith mumbled, "Um . . . yeah." Not because she was trying to put the blame on Luke, but because she was in shock that he'd somehow managed to both crawl under the bus and drive over himself at the same time.

Luke pushed back on his heels, then stood, hands on his hips, surveying the closet. "Hope, would it make sense for you to move either into the bathroom or even all the way into your bedroom?"

The young female paramedic piped up. "Works for me."

"Sure." Hope frowned and looked down at her chair and the four people squeezed in around her. "It is a bit tight in here."

It took shifting three more boxes to clear a path wide enough for Hope to navigate the wheelchair out of the closet.

"Go with Hope." Luke waved a hand toward the closet. "I'll try to get everything stacked on the other side so we can fix this."

Faith hesitated in the doorway. "I'll be right back."

"Hey." Luke stood among the boxes. "I can repair this shelf tonight. If I make a run to a home improvement store, we can get her back in the closet business right away. But if you don't want me to be here, I totally get it."

Faith looked around the closet. This master suite had been a huge selling point for Hope when she bought the house. The closet was the size of a small bedroom, with wire shelving around all the walls. The room was large enough for her to maneuver easily in her chair, and the double rows of shelving on two sides allowed most of her clothes to be hung in easy reach on the bottom shelf.

The top row held off-season clothes, and the upper shelf held boxes of memorabilia that Hope never looked at but wasn't willing to part with either. But now? The upper shelf had pulled free of the wall. The clothes had mostly stayed on the hangers, but all the boxes stacked on top had slid down, crashing into Hope and tumbling onto the floor.

Asking Luke to do any form of manual labor was wrong. She wouldn't ask him for herself. But for Hope? "I'm reasonably handy." It was a weak attempt at getting him to rescind his offer.

"Great! With two of us working, it will take even less time." He shooed her away. "Go see if Hope needs to go to the hospital. Then we'll go from there."

This was ridiculous. Why did he have to wind up being a decent guy? She did not want to like him. She definitely did not want to be indebted to him. And she could never tolerate needing him. That was unconscionable.

She slid her fingers through her hair, untangling snags and snarls. A quick glance in the mirror as she walked through the bathroom did nothing to improve her confidence. She looked exactly like someone who had worked a fourteen-hour day. She paused before the door to Hope's bedroom and leaned against the wall, rolling her neck in two slow, tight circles. She did not have the energy to stay up another several hours working on the closet. They could pull out the clothes needed for tomorrow. But what about the day after and the day after? The way this case was going, who knew when she would be free to come back to help Hope. They should probably get the room at least semi-functional.

Could Luke really fix it? He was so exhausted, he probably wasn't thinking clearly, but he radiated confidence. Strength. Safety.

There were risks being here, but overall, they were minimal. Right? If her theory was correct, she wasn't in danger. Neither was Hope. And the attacker would try to avoid harming her or Hope. Luke might still be at risk, but as long as he was with her or Hope, was he in less danger?

Luke was an answer to a prayer she didn't even know she'd prayed. Hope had probably been praying for a handy, smart, good-looking guy to drop into her life. But not Faith.

"Okay, ma'am." The female paramedic's deep Southern drawl floated through the door, and Faith pushed herself off the wall and into Hope's room. Hope sat in her chair, pressing a large white cloth to her head. "I'm afraid that gash on your head needs stitches. It's too deep for us to bandage. And it's too close to your face to leave it to heal on its own. A good doctor will stitch that up, and you'll never even be able to see the scar in your hairline."

Hope favored Faith with a spectacularly sour expression. "This is all your fault."

"Your closet crashed on you, you got hit on the head with multiple heavy objects, and there's a bloody gash on your forehead. You can blame a lot of stuff on me, but not this." Faith turned to the paramedic. "If I promise to take her to the hospital, can she skip the ride in the ambulance?" Faith tapped the FBI badge at her waist.

"I think we could make an exception." The older EMT grinned at Faith and Hope. "You two remind me of my girls. They would squabble and squawk, but at the end of the day, they had each other's backs."

Hope gave a dismissive flick of her hand. "That one would like to see me wrapped in bubble wrap."

The EMT chuckled. "Yeah. Well. There are worse things than having someone love you, missy." He winked at Hope, patted Faith's arm, and walked out with his bag.

The paramedic gathered a few remaining items and focused a laser gaze at Hope. "Get stitches. You'll be sorry if you don't."

"I will."

"She will," Faith said at the same time.

"Tonight. Now." The paramedic spoke with authority for someone who didn't look like she was old enough to be out of high school.

"Yes, ma'am." Hope offered a small salute, then an extended hand. "Thank you." The paramedic shook her hand and left.

When she was gone, Hope shifted in her chair. "I hate you right now."

"I know."

"I guess we'd better get it over with."

"Yep."

"My car?" Hope asked without needing to. Her car was easy for her to get in and out of, and it was really a no-brainer.

"Keys?" Faith prepared for Hope to argue, but there was no way she was letting her drive.

"In the kitchen." Hope rolled herself toward her dresser where her phone rested. "Are we taking Luke with us?"

"I don't know." What was she supposed to do with Luke? Leave him here? Let him take her car even though he wasn't supposed to be driving? He wasn't supposed to be shifting heavy boxes and repairing closets either, so did it really matter at this point?

"He likes you." Even in a whisper, there was confidence in Hope's remark.

"He's a friend."

"For now. It won't be long."

Faith couldn't stop herself from remembering Luke's "I could kiss you" remark. Not so much because of what he'd said. It had been an off-the-cuff comment, not a statement of serious intent. But when he'd realized what he'd said, he'd gotten serious. Fast. And he hadn't said he didn't want to kiss her. Just that he never would without her consent.

Right now, with everything going down the toilet, she couldn't help but wonder what it would be like to have someone who was her person. The one she could count on to stay with her through the tough stuff and not run for cover when things went sideways.

"Ladies, may I join you for a moment?" Luke called from the closet.

"Of course." Hope lowered her voice and said, "Such a gentleman."

Luke came through the bathroom and entered the bedroom with a hesitant step. "What's the verdict?"

—20—

"STITCHES." The sisters spoke at the same time. Faith's tone carried a hint of "obviously."

Luke clapped his hands. "Excellent." He turned to Hope. "Did Faith have a chance to mention the possibility of me fixing the closet tonight?"

Hope and Faith exchanged a look that made Luke miss his sister in a way he hadn't experienced in a long time. There was an entire conversation happening that he couldn't hear. After a few moments, Hope smiled at him. "This is the first I've heard of it. Do you moonlight as a contractor?"

He tried to assume an air of nonchalance. "I take jobs when I can get them. It's a tough market."

Hope laughed. Faith didn't laugh, but she didn't throw anything at him either. And for the moment, he was going to consider that yet another win.

"I have an idea, if y'all would consider it."

Hope nodded for him to proceed. Faith stood behind her, arms crossed.

"I'm not supposed to be driving, but I can get an Uber to the home improvement store. They're open until midnight on Fridays.

If I leave now, I can get what I need, Uber to my place and get my tools, and then get back here. I can put up a shelf and a rod in a few minutes. I might be done before you get back."

Hope didn't respond for a few moments. Luke could imagine how hard she'd fought for her independence, and a moment like this could feel like it was being taken away. But he was offering friendship and kindness. Would she accept it?

She sat taller in her chair and looked at him. He could see the battle warring behind her eyes, and he waited to see what would win.

"Okay."

"Okay?" Faith gasped the word like a woman who'd swallowed a hot pepper and was calling for something to drink—part shock, part misery.

"Okay." Hope turned to face Faith. "He's here. He's willing. He's not going to rob me blind while we're gone. He's not going to go away until I'm back and you're settled for the night, so he might as well have something to do while he waits. He might be a danger to himself or others if he shows up at the hospital, but if he keeps it unpredictable, he might survive the night."

"Hope!" Faith looked from him to Hope. "Why would you say that?"

"We all know it's true. No point in beating around the bush. Besides, I need to be able to get in there tomorrow. It's what makes the most sense. Now, let's go before I bleed to death."

And with that, she spun the wheelchair and zipped out her bedroom door.

Faith was left standing in the room, mouth slightly ajar. "I'm sorry."

"Why?"

"You shouldn't be—"

"Shouldn't what? Use a drill for five minutes? I can handle it.

It will take me longer to get to the store and back than it will for me to fix it."

"Faith! Let's go!" Hope's voice had a teasing lilt to it.

"She's waiting."

Faith closed her eyes in obvious frustration. "Please don't get killed."

There was zero humor in her words or expression, and he responded in kind. "I promise I will do my best."

Ninety minutes later, Luke returned to Hope Malone's house. Faith had texted that the stitches were done and they were headed back, which Luke found highly suspicious. No one got out of the emergency room on a Friday night that fast. Faith had flashed her badge. That was the only explanation. Not that he blamed her. He would have done the same.

Faith had told him to go ahead and go inside, so he let himself in through the garage and immediately went to work. He was moving slow. His arms and back hurt, and his head throbbed. But his heart needed this. He couldn't bring back his dead friends. He couldn't rebuild Zane's house or heal Gil's head, but he could fix this closet and make it better than it was before.

He removed the old shelf and made small pencil marks on the wall for the locations of the new brackets. When he was finished, the new shelf would be secured into the studs and in a way that they would never, ever come off the wall again.

Fifteen minutes later, the alarm chimed and Faith's voice carried through the house, echoing across Hope's wood floors. "It's us. Don't shoot."

"Back here." He spoke around the screws he had pinched in his lips.

Luke was in a bit of an awkward position, one bracket on the wall, screw on the tip of the drill when Hope came to the door with Faith right behind her. He took a quick glance and gave them what was more of grunt than a greeting before drilling the bracket into place.

"Um. Faith?" Hope spoke in a theatrical whisper that carried over the sound of the drill.

"What?"

"Can we keep him?"

Luke dropped two screws.

Faith's horrified "Hope!" didn't stop Hope's unrepentant laughter. "Relax, Faith."

Faith came into the room and surveyed Luke's handiwork.

He stepped down from the stool he'd found in the garage and waited for her verdict.

"You've been busy. Thank you."

"You're welcome. Although"—he risked a glance at Faith—"I would already be done if my help hadn't run off."

Hope shook her head in mock dismay. "It's so hard to get good help these days."

"You two are hysterical." Faith stepped around Hope and pushed the sleeves of her sweater up on her forearms. "I'm here now, and you're standing around shooting the breeze."

Hope spun around. "I'm going to get out of the way. I'll be in the kitchen, and I'll have coffee ready in about ten minutes. Decaf?"

"That sounds great." Luke spoke to Hope's retreating form, then turned to Faith. "Is she okay?"

"She is. She's going to hurt tomorrow."

"No doubt." He could relate.

"How can I help?"

Faith hadn't been kidding when she said she could help. She anticipated what he needed, helping with screws and the level.

They had the new brackets in the wall and the new shelf set on it before Hope reappeared.

"This is amazing!"

"Give us five minutes, and we'll have the boxes back on top."

The five turned into ten as they swept the floor and removed the old shelf to the garage for a later trip to the curb with the trash. When it was done, Luke sat at Hope's small kitchen table and sipped his coffee. Faith had a small cup too.

"I didn't think you liked coffee," Luke said.

"That"—Hope pointed at Faith's cup—"is not coffee. It's hot chocolate. Because some people never grew up."

Luke tried to hide his smile behind his cup. The two sisters picked at each other, but there was no question that they loved each other very much. "Not to be overly nosy, Hope, but I'm curious how that"—he pointed down the hall—"happened? Were you trying to do some pull-ups on the shelf or something?"

She laughed. "No. I have some notebooks on the bottom shelf, and I was looking for a specific one when the top shelf collapsed."

"It collapsed because y'all had overloaded that pitiful wire shelf with more than it could have ever hoped to hold. We need to reinforce the shelf on the other side too. But I don't think you're in any immediate danger."

"My deepest appreciation, again. To both of you." Hope looked between him and Faith. "I can't be late tomorrow, and I wasn't sure how I was going to get out of that closet!"

Faith narrowed her eyes at Hope, and Luke thought she might say something about Hope living alone or how she could have called 911, but she went in a different direction. "Tomorrow's Saturday. Why can't you be late? Another big case?"

Hope dabbed her lip. "Not big. But important. I've been in court all week, but I have a pro-bono client I've been working with for a while. She runs a bed-and-breakfast/boardinghouse here in Raleigh. Her clientele is almost exclusively Asian. She's a second-generation Korean American, married to a man who is Japanese and Taiwanese. She gets the cultures and her food is to die for. With all the tech and research going on here in the Triangle, word got around. She'll have boarders who will stay for a few days when they are here for a meeting or up to a couple of months when they are here for a project or even when they are moving here but haven't found an apartment yet."

Luke had never heard of this place. Not that it mattered in the grand scheme, but if they had a head of state from that part of the world coming in, it would be a good idea to take a look at who was staying there.

"So, what's wrong?" Faith prodded.

"It's an estate issue. Her home is in a historic district. It's beautiful and worth quite a bit of money. There's a big business in town trying to buy up the whole block. The residents and businesses are banding together to try to hold it off. About a month ago, she shut down and went to visit family in California. She got home two days ago and called me in a panic. The house reeked, and when she investigated, she found someone dead. She didn't recognize him until they found his ID. He'd eaten at her house, and she thought he was a friend of one of her boarders."

"Did he squat in her house while she was gone and have a heart attack or something?" Faith leaned back in her chair and closed her eyes. Fatigue flowed from her, and Luke stopped himself from pulling a strand of hair away from her face.

"No." Hope's voice was rough. "It looked like a suicide."

Faith dropped her head. "How awful."

Luke could feel the tips of his ears burning. He should keep his mouth shut. This was none of his business.

He sipped his coffee and tried not to concentrate on Faith and

Hope's conversation, but it was no use. They talked about the body and the way the police were handling it so far. With every moment, his agitation grew until he had to speak up. "Hope, do me a favor. When you get the report on this guy, will you double-check to be sure it's a suicide and not a murder? And find out if there were other problems, beyond depression or mental health issues. Maybe something that could have contributed."

"Okay."

He'd tried to keep his voice dispassionate and clinical, but Hope's expression told Luke he had not succeeded. Leave it to him to bring the evening to a depressing end. He needed to get out of there before he made an even bigger mess of things. He was about two more sentences away from blabbing about fathers and suicide and how much he hated the FBI.

"Thanks." He finished his coffee in one long drink and set the cup down with more force than he'd meant to use. "I'm going to get an Uber back to the hotel." Faith protested, but not as hard as he might have expected her to. "Will you text me when you get home and let me know everything's secure?"

She nodded in affirmation, but he could see the questions. Questions he did not want to answer.

But she would find out sooner or later.

When she did, how would she react?

And why did he have to care?

WHEN LUKE'S UBER pulled away, Faith closed the door and turned to help Hope clean up.

"What was that about?" Hope set her coffee cup on the kitchen counter. "Luke's fun, but he knows how to shut down a party."

Faith had noticed too. "My guess is that he's lost someone to suicide and he's more sensitive to it than maybe even he realizes."

Hope flashed a mischievous grin. "Maybe he needs someone to comfort him. If Mom had known about Luke, I bet she wouldn't have bothered with that dating profile."

"Hush."

"Why? You like him. He likes you. It's obvious."

"You're delusional."

"I am not. I think God knew you'd never go looking for a man, so he dropped a very nice one right in front of you." Hope waggled her eyebrows. "You can't tell me you don't find him attractive."

"Of course I find him attractive. So do you. Why don't you ask him out?"

Hope smirked. "Not my type."

"He's totally your type. You two hit it off—"

"He's the brother type for me. Not the lover type."

"There's a man for you, Hope. Why not Luke?"

Hope patted her arm. "Because he's already yours."

"Quit saying that. I'm not—"

"I know you're not going to lie to me. You promised."

Faith had. When their world fell apart and it felt like they were the only two people who could be trusted, she had promised. They both had. No lies. No holding back the truth. Faith was the one who told Hope about their dad's affair. Hope was the one who told Faith their dad was getting remarried. They were a team. Bound by blood and tragedy and, perhaps even more importantly, choice.

Faith flopped into a chair. "He's a good guy, and I am attracted to him. But it feels like every time we start making progress toward a real friendship, relationship, whatever, he throws up a wall."

"Then it's lucky you aren't scared of heights." Hope laughed at her own joke.

"You're impossible."

"You're awfully defensive." Hope's grin turned into something more speculative. "You aren't afraid of anything. Never have been. Why not go after him?"

"I can't. Not right now."

"Please."

"I'm working a case—"

"What's the problem?"

Arguing with Hope had never been an easy thing to do. It was particularly difficult when she was right. "I'll think about it."

"I bet you're thinking about it—all the time." Hope stretched out her arms, and Faith leaned down to give her a hug. "Go home. Sleep. And tomorrow, find out what's going on in his heart. I think you'll be able to handle it, whatever it is."

Faith went home and texted Luke as she'd promised. He replied immediately, almost as if he'd been waiting on her, and they texted for a few minutes before she went to sleep.

What would her life be like when the case was over and she wasn't texting Luke Powell every night?

To her surprise, Faith slept hard. A deep, dreamless sleep. She woke with a sense of renewed purpose.

Hope's insistence that Luke was "the" man for her was freaking her out. Hope had a discerning spirit and an unrivaled intuition. Faith hadn't always trusted Hope's gut. If she had, it would have saved her a lot of heartache with guys back in college. But she'd learned her lesson. In recent years, on the rare occasions she'd had an opportunity to go out with someone, she'd always run it past Hope, who had always given her sound advice.

But this was the first time, ever, that Hope had openly championed a man. It would be a lot easier for Faith to dismiss it if she could stop thinking about Luke, which was impossible given that he was an integral part of this case.

Faith pulled a Cherry Coke from her fridge. Down to two. She needed to go to the store on the way home tonight.

Her drive into the office was uneventful, and the building was mostly deserted. A stack of reports sat on her desk that weren't there yesterday. Quite a few agents had been hard at work last night, and this was the result of their labors.

She picked up the first one. ATF believed the bomb that blew up Thad Baker's car had some indications of a professional design and some signs that made them think an amateur had done it. The bottom line was that they didn't know what they were dealing with.

But this was interesting. The explosive at the heart of the bomb that destroyed Jared Smith's home was the same as the bomb in the Thad Baker case. It would be another week or so before they had the chemical composition to know if it was the exact same, but the ATF report indicated the explosive wasn't a common variety . . . so what if it was the same?

She tucked that thought aside and picked up the next file. The Stevskys had gone quiet since their patriarch had died in prison—unless you count killing Thad, although there was no evidence to prove they had done that. Multiple agents had interviewed them this week. All the Stevskys denied any dealings in the death of Thad Baker or the more recent events. Were they truly not behind this? The conclusion drawn by the agents who had written this report was that there was a real possibility the Stevskys were innocent. Well, not innocent, but not guilty of this particular string of crimes.

It would be so nice if there was a way to prove they weren't involved. But how? Faith added that to the swirl of questions her subconscious was mulling over.

The next file contained the fire marshal's report on Zane's house. Arson. Not a shocker. The fire marshal had already given her his thoughts over the phone, and the report didn't offer any new insights.

Then the ballistics on Gil. This was interesting, although not surprising. The same gun that had been used to shoot Zane and Luke had been used to shoot Gil. Which meant their bad guy was a marksman. The agents had located the spot where the shot that hit Gil had come from. It confirmed Faith's theory that the shooter was intentional. Not scattered and random. Not willing to kill anyone who happened to get in his way.

A killer with morals?

What did that even mean?

— 21 —

LUKE HAD GONE TO WORK early after a long night during which he woke up more than once in a panic. He'd had to stop himself from texting Faith at 3:00 a.m. to see if she was okay. Spring thunderstorms had rocked the night, and the dreary day matched his mood.

He was back to his search for information on Park Mi Cha when his phone rang with a distinctive ringtone.

Bill. Not his favorite CI, but not someone he wanted to ignore either.

Luke snatched the phone. "Hello."

"Got a minute?" Bill's voice was rough, too rough for someone who'd just turned twenty-two.

"That depends. Got something for me?"

"I might."

"I'm listening."

"You're barking up the wrong tree." Bill spoke with unusual urgency.

"Which tree would that be?"

"The Stevsky tree."

"The Stevskys claimed they were the wrong tree for several

years. Turned out they were the right one. Why would this time be any different?"

"They didn't do it." A tinge of desperation filtered through Bill's voice. "And it isn't any of their competitors either."

"To be clear, what didn't they do, exactly?" Luke had learned a long time ago that it was crucial to pin Bill down to the specifics.

"You, your buddies, Baker. They didn't do any of it. They don't kill Feds. Killing Feds is dumb, and they're a lot of things, but they aren't dumb."

"Stevsky wasn't dumb, that's true. But I wouldn't necessarily say that's true of the current leadership or of any of his competitors. How do you know they're not involved?"

"Doesn't matter. I know."

That wasn't going to be enough. "Let's say I'm willing to believe you about Stevsky. How can you be sure it isn't Stevsky's competitors setting them up?"

"'Cause they had a meeting. They're all in danger from this guy they're calling the Tiger."

"The Tiger?"

"There's an Asian guy around. He's prowling around like he's stalking prey. And he's got a tiger tattoo. Someone started calling him the Tiger, and it stuck."

"Did this Tiger kill Thad?"

"No idea. Maybe? This guy is bad news. He's made some interesting purchases. A few people have seen him. Not me," he said quickly.

"Why are you telling me this?"

"Everyone's feeling the squeeze. Every Fed in the state is on alert. The local cops are edgy. Killing cops, killing Feds, that's not how things are done around here."

Bill had a point. Killing law enforcement officers was more

rampant in some parts of the country, but not here. Well, it hadn't been before this week.

"Like I said. Killing Feds is dumb. Everyone knows killing Feds brings heat. No one wants that."

Was he telling the truth, or was this an elaborate ploy to take the suspicion away from the Stevsky family? "Where's this Tiger hanging out? And if y'all are so worried about him, why don't you take him out?"

"Now, that would be illegal." Bill feigned shock.

"Right." Like that had ever stopped them before. "So, where is he?"

"No one knows for sure. He showed up and started killing agents. We figure y'all done gone and ticked off some bad dudes. And I'm not gonna lie. We don't care much. But the heat is ridiculous, and we're over it."

"How long have you known this guy was in town?"

"A few weeks."

Luke took a deep breath in through his nose and blew it out slow. *Count to five, Powell. Count to five.*

"You could have called on Monday. Why wait until now?" Luke knew why. They wanted to let this stranger do their dirty work for them, then they could get the benefit. That was until he brought down the wrath of the entire law enforcement community and it got too hot for them to work.

Bill must have understood where Luke's thoughts were heading because he reacted fast and, possibly, honestly for the first time. "Look, we didn't know who he was or what he was up to. Okay? None of us knew. There might be some sick, twisted souls who found some enjoyment in the events of Monday, but there was no way to expect this."

"I don't know, Bill. Stevsky's crew has been furious with us since the old man went to jail. And they lost their ever-loving minds when the man died. They made lots of threats. How do you know Stevsky's sons didn't hire this Tiger to do their dirty work?"

Bill's voice lowered. "I was there, man. When the Stevskys and the others met. This Tiger is a loose cannon. He's not good for any of us. And we don't kill Feds. I already told you that."

Wait a minute. A random puzzle piece fell into place. "Do you know who killed old man Stevsky?"

Bill stayed quiet a few moments too long.

"You do, don't you?"

"How would I know who killed him?"

That was the first thing Bill had said that Luke knew for certain was false. This could change everything. If the Stevskys already knew who killed the elder Stevsky, then they would know it wasn't anyone in the Secret Service or any other law enforcement agency. They would get their revenge, but this wouldn't be it.

Luke could push Bill further, but he had what he needed. Well, some of it. "This Tiger? What does he look like?"

"Man, I wouldn't know. All I know is people say he's Asian."

"Height? Weight?"

"I heard not tall. And I heard lean and fast, and he stalks people like a tiger."

"He stalks people? How would you know you're being stalked?"

"You know when the guy jumps out at you out of nowhere and starts asking questions."

Luke wasn't convinced, but if someone had been in physical contact, then maybe he was a real person. "What did he ask?"

"He needed a rifle."

Luke could believe that. "Accent?"

"Not much. English was good."

"Was it you?"

206

"Nah. Buddy of mine. Scared him pretty bad, and he's not the type to scare, if you know what I mean."

Luke did. Some of Stevsky's men were the meanest people Luke had ever had the misfortune to know anything about. Scaring them would require a special kind of awful.

"To recap. You're telling me that the Stevsky family isn't targeting the Secret Service because you already know we didn't kill the old man and because no matter what, you don't come after Feds. You're saying you didn't kill Thad and you aren't responsible for the events of this week. And you're also telling me that none of the usual suspects here in Raleigh are responsible, and you'd appreciate it if law enforcement would ease up off your backs. And to help with that, you're willing to give up this Tiger guy and send us chasing after him."

Bill snorted. "Sums it up pretty well."

"How do I know you didn't make up the Tiger? You took a calculated risk, killed off some agents, and now it's too hot. You want us to back off, maybe drop our guard, so you've made this guy up."

"Man, I wouldn't drop your guard at all. Not until you find this guy." Bill's rapid response had a ring of authenticity to it. "None of us are dropping ours."

"Are you looking for him too?"

"Only to stay out of his way, but there's some chatter about trying to get rid of him. He's messing things up for us."

That was an epic understatement. "You gonna call me if you get a lead on where he is?"

Bill hesitated but then said, "Yeah. I am."

"Why?"

"If we take him out, it ends, but y'all don't quit looking. You never quit. Not after something like this. But if the Feds get him, he goes to jail, everybody relaxes. Things go back to the way they were."

Luke considered the logic. It didn't seem like something most of the gangs in town would come up with, but Stevsky had always been a smart criminal. Maybe his sons weren't idiots. Could they have dragged the other criminal elements along with them?

FAITH'S PHONE BUZZED.

Luke.

Why did her shoulders relax at the sight of his name on the screen but then tense as she answered the call, nerve endings trilling through her arms and fingers?

"Hey." That sounded casual enough. Right?

"Are you busy?" Luke did not sound casual at all.

"What's up?"

"Are you free for lunch?"

Faith glanced at her watch. It was 10:30 a.m. "Now?"

"No." She could hear the amusement in Luke's voice. "Unless you didn't eat breakfast and want to make it brunch."

She hadn't eaten much, but she wouldn't mention it.

"We need to talk."

Was this about last night? About the case? Both? Neither? "Okay. My office or yours?"

"I can come to you. But we need to be able to talk in private."

She considered her options. If Luke came to the FBI offices, he would attract attention. If she went to his office, the only place with any privacy was the conference room, and that was minimal. "Why don't I come pick you up and we'll eat in the car?"

Luke didn't respond right away.

"Is that a problem?"

"No." Luke drew out the word. "I'm just trying to decide how much risk you would be in, driving around with me."

Well, that was . . . chivalric. And depressing.

"I think we'll be fine as long as we stay unpredictable."

"Maybe."

"I'll pick you up in an hour."

"Okay. Call me when you get here, and I'll come out. I don't want you to get out of the car."

"Why not?"

"We don't know if he's watching our office. You can't be hurt or caught or . . ."

"I'm not a helpless little girl, Luke."

"Gil isn't helpless either. Neither is Zane. Neither am I. And I can assure you, Michael and Jared were two of the toughest men on the planet."

Coming from a man who worked in an organization known for attracting alpha males, his point couldn't be missed.

"This has nothing to do with your femininity, and I never said it did. This isn't a commentary on your skill or any perceived weakness. I'm tired of losing people I love, and I'm not willing to risk you in any way."

Faith almost dropped the phone. What? No. He hadn't meant that he loved her. Just that he was tired of losing people he loved. Right? "Luke—"

"Besides, Hope's kind of scary, and I don't need her on my case forever."

"Okay." Faith recognized Luke's attempt to pull the conversation away from a dangerous ledge. That was a jump they simply couldn't make. "I'll see you in an hour."

When she pulled into the parking lot, Luke was nowhere to be seen. But when she rolled to a stop by the curb, he darted out from behind a low wall. He dodged a few puddles, climbed in, and tapped the dash. "Go!"

She floored it, tires spinning on the wet pavement, and didn't ask any questions until they had cleared the parking lot and were back on the road. "Um, what was that about?"

"Sorry. Paranoia. I have this image of our shooter waiting to pick us off as we leave the office."

"And by we, you mean you."

"Well, Zane came in about ten minutes ago and no one shot him, but yes, mostly I mean me."

Water sheeted across the surface of the highway, and Faith changed lanes and altered her speed. "How is Zane?"

"He says the pain is managed with ibuprofen. But his entire life is a big headache."

"Right. How about Gil?" Faith did care about Zane and Gil, but mostly her goal was to keep Luke talking about topics that did not involve whether he did or did not love her.

"I called him this morning. He's hoping he gets out today. Tessa's trying to convince him to come hang out at the hotel with Zane, but Gil says there's no way they need to be in the same place at night. He says it makes us too much of a prime target."

"He isn't planning on going home, is he?"

"It doesn't matter what he's planning. We don't have the manpower to protect him at home, so home isn't an option."

They drove in silence for another mile. "I honestly thought he was dead." The words flew out of her mouth before she could stop them. They hadn't talked about that horrific afternoon. The gunfire. The fallen friend. The fear.

"Me too." Luke reached his hand across the console and squeezed hers for a second. Then he released it. "I don't think

I've thanked you. Not properly. But you . . . you were amazing. Absolutely amazing."

Something warm spread through her. It started with her fingers, the same fingers Luke had touched, and flashed over her in a sensation of belonging and something she did not want to deal with.

She was standing on the edge of . . . something. A lake? An ocean? Whatever it was, currents and forces were pulling at her the way ocean waves tunneled the sand out from under bare toes. She could walk in, and it might be wonderful. She could walk away and wonder, forever, what might have been. But the one thing she could not do was stay as she was, standing in the same spot. The longer she tried, the more tenuous her hold on . . . what? What was she holding on to? Why was she resisting? It would be much easier to walk in and let the waves carry her.

She risked a glance at Luke, expecting his gaze to be fixed out the window. Instead, he was focused on her.

And somewhere in her heart, she took one step in.

She shifted her gaze back to the road, but the heat of his eyes on her sent prickles all over her skin. Had he noticed?

She pulled into the drive-through of a local deli. "Is this okay?" She hadn't thought to ask before.

"If you're happy, I'm happy." There it was again. Did he mean about the food? Or about more?

They ordered, and he helped her unwrap her sandwich so she could hold it one-handed as she drove. "Okay. Let's hear it. What did you want to talk to me about?"

Around bites of his burger, Luke filled her in on the conversation with his CI, stopping once to take her sandwich from her and readjust the paper around it so she could continue eating without dumping chicken salad into her lap.

"What do you think?" Luke asked.

"I think we need to put out some feelers and see if we can back up his story. If every crime element in Raleigh is scared of this Tiger, he won't be the only one who can tell us about him."

"Agreed." He glanced at his phone. "Would you mind dropping me at the hospital instead of the office? I want to check on Gil and see what he has to say about all of this."

"Sure." She waited a few seconds, trying to get a feel for the water where she now stood. "Mind if I join you?"

"I'd love it." He let the words hang there, long enough that she suspected he meant all three of them. Then he added, "Gil would too. He has a male nurse today. He's less than thrilled."

Relief and resignation collided. Relief that they'd moved to safer, lighter topics. Resignation, because while it had taken a bit longer than normal, there was the wall. Again.

How long did she have to keep reaching out to him? How long would it be before he made a move in her direction?

Would he ever?

And if he didn't, did she want to move toward him anymore?

"Gil doesn't know it, but Jacob doesn't want him out of the hospital. He's well protected where he is. But he's chomping at the bit to get out."

Fifteen minutes later they'd parked and cleared hospital security. Faith held back in the hall. "I'll wait. He—"

"Oh no you don't. He's been wanting to see you. Get in here." Luke grabbed her hand and pulled. She could have easily broken the hold. It wasn't hostile or even demanding. It was playful, and it shocked her so much that she allowed Luke to tug her into Gil's room.

Gil's bruised face brightened when his gaze locked with hers. "Faith! My favorite FBI agent! Get in here and give me a hug." She couldn't resist his enthusiasm and did as requested. He grabbed her hands, looked her full in the face, and with no hint of humor or drama simply and fervently said, "Thank you."

"I didn't do anything." She tried to deflect and pull away, but his grip tightened.

He shook his head. "Don't deny what you did, Faith. Don't deny it to me and don't deny it to yourself. You were brave. You were fierce. When the chips were down, you went all in and pulled me out. You saved my life. Saved Luke's too. He never would have left me, and we would have been sitting ducks."

Faith shuddered at the mental image Gil's words painted as his hands squeezed hers, gentle pressure emphasizing his words.

"You didn't have to." He glanced at Luke. "He had to. We're friends. Dying would be better than having to go back to work and pretending he hadn't let the guy use me for target practice. But you were out of it, and you ran into it."

"I didn—"

Gil wouldn't let her finish. "You're amazing. Don't ever stop believing that. God has you doing his work with that powerful and ferocious approach you have to everything you do. It's a gift, and I'm honored to know you."

Every fiber of Faith's being begged for release. To escape this intense man who wasn't afraid to say what he felt and by sheer force of his will was making her feel things that terrified her. Not for him. Not about him.

But about herself.

—22—

LUKE LEANED against the door. He could hear every word. He could see Faith's profile. Until this moment, he wouldn't have believed her to be afraid of anything, but her fear of Gil's words was palpable.

"I'm not sure I see it the same way, Gil, but thank you." Her husky voice tugged at Luke's heart.

"You'll come around." Gil grinned at Faith and released his hold on her. She stepped back. Almost jumped back. Like she needed some distance, and maybe she did. Faith didn't strike him as someone who enjoyed talking about feelings.

"Did y'all bring me food?"

"Nope. But I think you'll like what I have." Luke filled Gil in on the events of the day. "Think you could check in with your CIs and see if we can corroborate any of this?"

Gil didn't hesitate. "Sure."

"Whoa. Whoa. Whoa. You aren't working this case, remember?" Faith held up her hands between the two of them. Anyone watching would think he and Gil were fighting and she was trying to break it up.

"We aren't working the case." Not technically. "We aren't arresting anyone. We're following up on leads that could potentially have an impact on any number of Secret Service cases." Luke appealed to Gil to back him up.

"What he said. Absolutely." Gil grinned at Faith, totally ruining everything Luke had been trying to set up.

But Faith didn't get mad. "I can't stop you from contacting CIs. Just be careful."

Gil extended his arms, palms up, and shook his head, confusion all over his face. "I don't understand why you think we need to be careful. I'll acknowledge that I personally have been injured. I have a hole. In. My. Head." He paused for effect, then pointed at Luke. "Pretty boy over there, he doesn't have holes. Just scrapes. But they were caused by real bullets, so . . ."

Luke turned to Faith. "What did I tell you? Holes. I knew he would bring up the holes."

Faith laughed, and her laughter was infectious. They were all laughing until Faith's phone rang. She glanced at it. "It's Dale. I'll be right back." Faith slipped out into the hall.

The door closed behind her, and Gil leaned against the pillows, arms folded behind his head. His missing hair was . . . disconcerting. "Talk fast."

"About what?"

"Faith."

"What about her?" As soon as the words were out, he knew they'd been a mistake.

Gil sat forward on the bed, eyes flashing in amusement and satisfaction. "I knew it."

"There's nothing to know." Another mistake. What was he, a sophomore in high school denying he had a crush on Lizzie Sullivan?

"When did you two become a team? And when did you quit despising the FBI?"

"We aren't a team. We're working together on this case."

"Right. Like, what's the word for it? Oh, right. A team."

"Funny."

"I'm waiting."

"On?"

"The answer to the question you conveniently ignored. Did you forget?"

He hadn't forgotten. He and Faith did have a connection that was intensifying. He didn't know what she was to him anymore, but words like *colleague, coworker, friend*—none of those covered it. Not even close. "I still hate the FBI."

"Looks to me like you're in love with the FBI." Gil smirked.

Those were fighting words, and Gil knew it. "Be glad you have a hole in your head."

"I can take you. We both know it. But I led with a question I want an answer to. What's the deal? Have you kissed her yet?"

"Kissed her?"

The door slammed open. No warning tap. Faith stood in the doorway. "Luke. We need to go."

"Why?" Luke was already moving, knowing the answer to the question wouldn't change anything. She said they needed to go. He was going.

"Hope's suicide victim? It wasn't suicide. He was murdered."

"Okay." Murder was awful, but what did that have to do with him?

"The dead guy is a known associate of David Lee."

The boyfriend?

"Hope's client knew Park Mi Cha and David Lee. She's at Hope's office now, and she's willing to wait for us."

Luke moved as fast as he could to Gil's bed. He clasped his shoulder, and Gil mimicked the gesture.

"Stay safe," Gil said.

"You too."

FAITH DROVE. Luke didn't argue, but he did buckle up the second he slid into the passenger seat, muttering all the way about how things would change on Monday when he was cleared to drive.

He must be forgetting he still didn't have a car. Not that Faith intended to remind him of that painful fact.

She concentrated on her driving, chafing at traffic and street-lights and the thunderstorms that wouldn't move out. They were obstacles on her path to Hope's office and a possible breakthrough in this case.

She'd half expected Luke to pepper her with questions, but aside from a few murmurs and one full-blown gasp, which he tried to cover with a cough, he stayed silent. Was he thinking about the case, or was he so terrified of her driving he didn't want to risk distracting her?

When they parked at Hope's office, the storm had intensified. Luke made no move to exit the car. Instead, he turned to her and asked, "What do we know?"

"Hope took your words to heart last night. She came in early and pulled all the records she could find before she met with her client. She spoke with the detective working the case and discovered that the autopsy was scheduled for today. She thought that was odd—they don't always do autopsies on Saturdays—and she intended to put a bug in his ear. Just a quick 'Hey, any chance it wasn't a suicide?' But he beat her to it. Commented that something was sketchy about this case. At first, she thought he was referring to her client, but he assured her he had no doubt of her client's innocence."

"Being on the other side of the country does make it difficult to pin the murder on her." Luke's comment was dry but not sarcastic.

"Precisely. But when Hope pressed him, all he would say was he didn't think everything matched with a suicide and he was going to be present at the autopsy. She asked him to let her know if anything didn't point to suicide."

"What didn't?"

"That's what had Hope all in a tizzy. When the detective called her, he told her the ME's report would be available in the system tonight, and she was planning to rule it a suspicious death. Due to the decomposition of the body, a few things were impossible for her to conclude with certainty, but she thinks the guy didn't hang himself but was hung. The detective agrees, although he admitted some of that is gut feeling and he has no proof."

"And how is this victim associated with David Lee?"

"Hope's client says they ate dinner together several times while Park Mi Cha was there."

"Anything else I need to know before we go in there?"

"Yes. Hope says this woman is an angel, and if we play good cop/bad cop, she will never speak to either of us again."

Luke's shoulders fell, and his entire body relaxed as he awarded her one of his truest smiles. "Your sister is both hilarious and terrifying. I'll behave."

"Thank you."

They sat there, smiling at each other, and the atmosphere in the car sparked with something she couldn't explain.

A bolt of lightning split the air, and the car shook with the force of the thunder that accompanied it. Before she knew what was happening, Luke had shoved her head down and draped his body over hers. She could feel his breathing coming in gasps. "Luke?"

He jerked upright and helped her lean back. "Sorry. My body reacted to the sound before my brain caught up to what it was." He reached for her face and turned it toward him with the lightest pressure. "Are you okay? I didn't slam your head into the gear shift, did I?"

"No damage done." Except maybe to her traitorous heart. Could he tell how much his touch on her face was messing with her?

"Except to my pride." Luke dropped his hand and his head. "Stupid overreaction."

Now it was her turn. She reached for his hand and squeezed. "It wasn't stupid. You're being targeted by an unknown assailant. And it did sound like gunfire."

He wasn't buying it. She could see red streaks tracing up his neck and into his cheeks.

"Luke?"

"Hmm?"

"Thank you."

"For what? Saving you from a thunderstorm?"

"For being willing to save me from whatever it was." Now she'd done it. He was staring her full in the face, and she couldn't back down from what she'd said or the way she'd said it. Might as well go all in. "I'm not used to men who want to protect me or are willing to sacrifice themselves for me."

Luke shook his head in obvious frustration. "You weren't in danger."

"But you didn't know that."

He gave her a weak smile. "Well, you know how it is. Hope would kill me if you got killed in the parking lot of her office."

She squeezed his hand. "Nice try." She leaned toward him and planted one soft, lingering kiss on his cheek.

She pulled away, and the light stubble on his chin left her lips

219

tingling. She could feel his breath on her face and see a vein throbbing in his neck.

"Faith." Her name was a soft moan, and the longing in it sent a wave of desire through her. One she was unprepared to resist. She did the only reasonable thing she could do.

She pressed her lips to his.

—23—

LUKE'S BRAIN COMPLETELY SHUT DOWN. He wasn't thinking about the FBI or being a target of a disturbingly determined killer.

There was only Faith.

He cradled her face in his hands and kissed her, not so much like it was their first kiss, but like it might be their last.

The storm raged around them, but in the privacy afforded by the rain, they were alone.

He had no idea how long he kissed her, but at some point, his mind reengaged and reined him in. He pulled back and pressed his forehead to hers. He wasn't ready to look at her. Wasn't ready for what he would see in her eyes. Would it be surprise? Confusion? Fear? Or something else? Maybe the same something else warring inside him that he couldn't define.

Regardless of what had happened between them, he was still Secret Service. She was still FBI. They still had careers that would soon diverge and take them away from each other.

Nothing had changed.

But nothing would ever be the same.

Faith sat back in her seat, and he mimicked her. "Luke?"

He finally looked at her. "Yes?"

Her bemused smile eased some of the tension. "That was . . . I mean . . . wow."

They were on the same page there. Wow was an understatement.

She breathed out a sigh. "I'm not sure what we do now."

"Me neither." It wasn't romantic, but it was the truth.

They sat in silence, both of them staring through the rain, which had lessened enough that Luke could make out the door to Hope's office.

"We should get inside." Faith sounded like going inside was the last thing she wanted to do. But if they didn't go inside, there would be more kissing. Luke knew it, and he was pretty sure Faith knew it too.

"Yeah."

"Can you grab the umbrella behind my seat?"

"Sure." While he reached behind her seat, she flipped the visor mirror open and ran a finger under her lips. She snapped it closed as he handed her the umbrella. He couldn't resist teasing her a little. "Your lipstick is fine. How's mine?"

To his relief, she laughed and inspected his face. "Um . . . may I?" She stretched a tentative hand toward him.

Oh boy. This was how things started a few minutes ago. She rubbed her thumb across his cheek where she'd kissed him. "You're good."

Luke winked. "Hope will never know?"

Faith dropped her head, but he could see her grin. "I don't know how she does it, but she'll know." She didn't give Luke a chance to comment but fluffed out her umbrella and grabbed the door handle. "On three?"

"On three." He settled his hood over his head.

"One, two, three." They both climbed out. Faith opened the

umbrella and held it high for Luke as he joined her. They huddled close as they skirted puddles and were laughing when they reached the door. Luke held it for Faith as she shook the umbrella and scurried inside. She dropped the umbrella into a corner, and he pulled off his raincoat and hung it on a coatrack.

"There you are." Hope came around the corner, face drawn in concern. "I was getting worried."

Guilt pierced him. What could he say? "Sorry, Hope, but I was making out with your sister in the parking lot" didn't seem like an appropriate response.

"I didn't think the rain would ever let up. I'm glad you got in when you did. Follow me." Hope turned back to the hall she'd come from.

Luke caught Faith's eye, and she was biting down on her lip in what had to be an effort not to laugh. She shook herself slightly, and he could see the professional persona reemerge as she followed Hope. He was confident that he could get himself together as quickly as she had.

They entered a cozy area, more a sitting room than a conference room, filled with sofas and chairs and a low coffee table, designed to put people at ease. The spacing in the room had to have been intentional, as it was also roomy enough for Hope to maneuver without bumping into anything.

A small woman sat in a wingback, sipping from a teacup. She set it on a saucer and stood when they entered.

"Mrs. Lin," Hope said, handling the introductions. "This is my sister, Special Agent Faith Malone of the FBI." Faith stepped forward and shook the woman's hand. "And Special Agent Luke Powell of the United States Secret Service." Luke gave a small bow as he took Mrs. Lin's hand. It was warm from the tea, the skin wrinkled and rough in a few places. She had the hands of a woman who had worked hard her entire life, and as she gave him a tremulous smile, her fear was palpable.

They sat, and Hope picked up a legal pad from the coffee table. "Mrs. Lin, you are under no obligation to speak to these federal agents."

Mrs. Lin picked up her tea and took a sip. "Hope, I'm not afraid of *them*."

Luke wasn't sure she was being completely honest, but he appreciated her courage. "Mrs. Lin, so far all we have is circumstantial evidence, but we believe Park Mi Cha was in a car with my friend, Thad Baker, and was killed in a car bomb in February. We've been piecing things together, and we believe she had found him through a DNA registry site and knew they were related through their grandfather. But beyond that, we know almost nothing about her, and we can't locate her father or anyone who knew her well." He didn't mention Ivy Collins. "Anything you can tell us would be a huge help."

She nodded and straightened in her chair. "Park Mi Cha." Her eyes filled with tears and she blinked rapidly.

Faith snagged a tissue from a box on the table and handed it to Mrs. Lin.

"Thank you." She dabbed under her eyes. "Mi Cha was a sweet girl. So excited to be in the States. She booked a room with me for her entire time here. Her parents wanted her to have good food and some cultural familiarity. I don't know how she heard of me, but she booked her room before she left Korea."

Faith was writing on her iPad at a furious pace, and Luke trusted she'd get the details. He wanted to focus on listening to every word. Was it significant that Mi Cha's family had known to book a room with Mrs. Lin? Maybe. Maybe not.

"When she arrived, she was nervous about her new job. She

wanted to make a good impression and make her parents proud. Her mom had been sick, but she was stable. Mi Cha would never have come if she'd known her mother's health would fail so dramatically while she was gone."

"Did you talk to her a lot?" Faith asked.

"I did. Her mom had cancer. They were hoping to find a donor for a transplant, but it was proving to be difficult because her mother's biological father was American. He was half-Korean himself, and he'd been in the American military. Her grandmother got pregnant but didn't know it until he was already back in the States. The way Mi Cha told the story, her grandmother had been sent to stay with family in a remote village. They told everyone in the village that her husband had died. You have to understand—having a child out of wedlock was frowned upon, but having a child with an American father was even worse, even if he was half-Korean."

She gave them a rueful look. "Her family wanted her to abandon the baby, but she refused. She had loved the American, and she loved the baby. In the village, the baby, Mi Cha's mother, was accepted. She looked Korean and had almost no Caucasian features, so no one knew. Mi Cha's mother didn't know the truth about her father until she was in her twenties."

"Did her grandmother marry?"

"She did. She married a boy in the village who raised Mi Cha's mother as his own. I'm not sure if Mi Cha would have ever been told about the American if her mother hadn't gotten sick. But when they began searching for donors, her mother told her the whole story. Mi Cha signed up on all the DNA registry sites and prayed for a miracle. And she got it. She found a relative who lived out West somewhere, and that relative had a sibling in Raleigh. She was so excited to find him. Scared too. She confided all this to me but made me promise not to tell anyone."

"She found Thad." Luke wished Thad had told him.

"I don't think he believed her at first. Here was this Korean girl telling him they had the same grandfather. His grandfather had never mentioned he'd fallen in love with a Korean girl to anyone, including his American wife, but to be fair, he'd never known he had a Korean daughter."

Faith turned to Luke. "Is Thad's grandfather alive?"

"No. He died before the twins were born. I remember Thad saying how much he wished he'd gotten to see them."

"What about his grandmother?"

"She's passed as well."

Hope cleared her throat, and Faith and Luke, like naughty schoolchildren caught talking in class, sat straighter and gave her their attention. "We need to discuss the person who might be trying to kill you and the connection to the dead body in Mrs. Lin's establishment," she said as she turned to Mrs. Lin. "Can you tell them about David Lee's connection to Mi Cha?"

Mrs. Lin wrung a tissue in her lap. "She was a sweet girl." The words were defensive, apologetic. "I don't know what she saw in him. I'm not even sure if she liked him."

"Did you?" Faith asked.

"No." Mrs. Lin's face clouded. "He was no good. Too possessive. They'd only known each other a few weeks and already he was showing up unannounced, texting her all the time, getting angry if she couldn't go out with him when he wanted her to."

"What did Mi Cha say about it?"

"She told me not to worry about it. Said he was nice, and he took her to fancy places, and she was having fun. That it didn't matter because she would be back in Korea and would never see him again."

"This David Lee. Was he Korean?"

"Yes, but he grew up in the States. His parents moved here when he was two. At least, that's what he told me. I don't know if it's true. I didn't trust him."

"Did she talk to him about Thad?"

"No." Mrs. Lin shook her head furiously. "She had me cover for her a couple of times. To say she was at a work dinner when she was meeting her cousin."

"Do you know why she didn't want to tell him?"

"She told me she was honoring her mother's wishes. Her mother knew what Mi Cha was doing, but no one else did. Not even her father. I'm not sure her father knew that her mother wasn't one hundred percent Korean."

"Was Mi Cha afraid of what would happen if he found out?"

Mrs. Lin shrugged. "Who can know? Love. It's a funny thing. Sometimes the things you think matter don't matter anymore when you're in love. Love changes people."

Luke forced himself not to look at Faith.

"People say it's best to fall in love with someone who is very much like you. I guess that's true sometimes. But sometimes love happens, and the joy of it is discovering how to love someone who isn't like you at all." Her expression gentled. "That's how it was for me. I met my husband, and I didn't care that he was Taiwanese and Japanese. And he didn't care that I was Korean. We loved each other, and that's what mattered. It was hard. My family didn't like him. His family refused to meet me for a decade. But it was worth it."

She smoothed out the tissue. "I told Mi Cha to give her father some credit. From what she told me, her father adored her mother and was terrified of losing her. I felt like he would be able to handle the news. But she didn't want him to know until she was sure Thad, or someone on the American side of the family, was a match."

"That would have taken some time," Luke said.

"It would, but she thought they had time. Then her mother's condition worsened. Mi Cha was going to stay in the States for another week, but her mother called and told her to come right away. She packed everything, shipped stuff home, and was flying out the night she met your friend. That's why I wasn't worried when she didn't return. I wasn't expecting her."

Faith tapped the iPad. "Do you know where she met this David Lee?"

"In my house." Mrs. Lin dropped her head. "I'm known for my Korean suppers. Friday nights we do a big business at dinner. Not just my patrons, but people from all over the city. He saw her sitting at the table, and they started talking. Flirting. That was the first week after she arrived."

"And the man found in your hotel last week?"

Mrs. Lin's eyes filled with tears again. "When the police told me who he was, I didn't recognize his name. But when they showed me a picture, I knew he was David Lee's friend. He never stayed with me. Neither did David. I have no idea how he came to be there. Dead."

"His name was Jesse Thomas." Hope scanned her legal pad. "Thirty-two. He was reported missing last week by his boss. Raleigh police searched for him when the report came in but couldn't find him anywhere. The detective on the case said it was like he'd just disappeared."

"What did he do?" Faith asked.

"He was an accountant. Single. No kids. No family in town."

Luke's phone buzzed. One quick glance told him the call was from Zane. He stood and nodded to the others. "Excuse me a moment, please."

He answered the call but didn't speak until he was in the hall. "Hello?"

"Luke, are you all right?"

"I'm fine. I'm in Hope Malone's office talking to a lady who knew Park Mi Cha. She knew about Thad and—"

"That's awesome, but has Faith gotten a call recently? Maybe one she's ignored?"

Alarm bells clanged through Luke's system. "What's happened?"

"Janice Estes was attacked."

"Define attacked."

"Run off the road. Then shot at. She abandoned her car and took off through a wooded area. She was near Carrington and managed to call 911. Their county officers responded."

"Who caught the case? Anyone we know?"

"Gabe Chavez." Gabe was a homicide investigator and dive team member in Carrington County. Luke and Zane had gone diving with him several times. "Janice mentioned the attacks on us, so he called the office to get some input."

"I guess I should have asked this earlier, but is Janice okay? Was she injured?"

"According to Gabe, she's physically fine, but he said it's like dealing with a wet cat. Said she'd all but hissed at him when he asked her if she thought this attack was related to her investigation into Thad's death."

"Did you tell him she's like that all the time?"

"I did. He said being shot at has clearly not improved her personality."

"Well, I'm not sure it's improved mine either, so I guess we can't fault her for that."

"I guess." Zane didn't sound convinced. He despised her even more than Luke did.

"What was she doing in Carrington?"

"She has a little house on a couple of acres near the county line. Commutes into Raleigh every day."

"Maybe that's part of her problem. Carrington's great, but that commute would make anyone crazy."

"I don't think she needs an excuse. She's just a horrible person." Zane let out a long sigh.

"Being a horrible person isn't usually enough to get you shot at, although she might be the exception." Luke had considered it a few times. "Did she get a look at her attacker? Did they catch him?"

"They did not catch him, but she insists that he's young, Asian, and she's seen him before."

"Where?"

"That's where it gets interesting."

— 24 —

WHERE WAS LUKE?

That phone call must have been important, and he'd been gone five, no, six minutes.

She was still chatting with Mrs. Lin, but there wasn't much more to learn. Mrs. Lin didn't have security cameras, although she was going to have her son install them right away. Forensics hadn't found anything unusual at her inn. The room Jesse Thomas had been found in had already been scrubbed by a crime scene recovery service, and the inn had reopened yesterday. Any evidence that might have been there was either cleaned away or muddled by dozens of fingerprints, shoe prints, and random hair and skin samples.

Luke paused in the doorway. Finally. When their eyes locked, he tapped his watch and gave her a look that told her everything was okay but something significant had happened and they needed to wrap up this interview. She didn't know how she knew that's what he was telling her. She just knew.

By the time Luke returned to his seat, he was the picture of ease. He didn't interrupt Mrs. Lin as she explained that she typically had four long-term boarders, meaning they intended to be there a week or longer. The remaining four rooms were reserved for any stay less than a week.

"In any given month, you could have anywhere from fifteen to fifty people in and out of your doors. Not to mention the dinner patrons," Luke observed. "Do you remember them all?"

Mrs. Lin shook her head. "I'm sure I don't. Although part of what has made me so good at what I do is that I have a knack for faces and names."

"If we come up with a few suspects, would you be willing to look at some photographs and see if the pictures trigger any memories?"

"I'd be happy to. Anything. Mi Cha, she was special. A bright light with a bright future. She didn't deserve to die." Mrs. Lin shuddered.

"I understand, Mrs. Lin. I truly do." He looked from Faith to Hope and then back to Mrs. Lin. "We appreciate your cooperation, and we don't want to take any more of your time. I would imagine you have a full house as we speak."

She gave him an appreciative look. "You should come. I would fix you something special."

"Mrs. Lin, when this is all over, I will take you up on that." Luke stood and extended a hand to Mrs. Lin. She took it and stood. Faith followed suit, and Hope led them back to the office's entryway. The rain had finally eased to a heavy mist, but the thick clouds made the late afternoon darker than it should have been.

Luke volunteered to walk Mrs. Lin to her car. The door had barely closed behind them when Hope turned on Faith. "What was that all about? The phone call."

"You'll find out when I do."

"What do you think about Jesse Thomas?" Hope rolled her

neck in a slow circle, a wince crossing her features at one point. She had to be sore from her run-in with the closet shelves.

"My gut tells me this David Lee knows more about Mi Cha's death than he's told anyone. And Jesse Thomas may have known more too. I don't know if David Lee is a victim or a suspect, but either way, we need to talk to him."

She spotted Luke half sprinting, half hobbling across the parking lot, and her chest tightened. Was he safe? Would he make it inside? And would she ever stop worrying about that?

"One more thing." Hope came closer and lowered her voice. "Is he as good a kisser as I thought he would be?"

"What?" Faith had messed up. She knew it as soon as the word left her mouth. She might as well have said, "Yes, in fact, he's better than I imagined."

"I knew it!" Hope crowed in delight.

"Knew what?" Luke asked as he blew into the room.

"Nothing." Faith glared at Hope as Luke turned his back toward them to hang his raincoat back on the coatrack. "What was your phone call about?"

He turned back to them, eyes bright. "You'll never believe it."

He was right. Two hours later, Faith was still trying to get her mind around it. Janice Estes had been attacked by David Lee. She was sure it was him. But . . .

"Do you think Janice would lie about her attacker?" Luke asked the question from the passenger seat of her car as they drove toward Carrington to talk to Janice.

Faith didn't respond right away. She didn't want to speak ill of a fellow agent, but . . .

"It's not like it would be the first time an FBI agent had lied to put suspicion on the person he thought was responsible for a crime." The bitterness in Luke's words sent a shock wave through Faith's exhausted system.

"What are you talking about?"

"Do you believe her?" The words were more accusation than question. She must have greatly underestimated Luke's disgust for Janice Estes.

"I don't know." It was the truth.

"Figures." Luke muttered the word to the window.

"What is your problem?" What she really wanted to know was what had happened to the guy who had kissed her senseless in this very car a few hours ago. This Luke was angry. Testy. Argumentative. Suspicious.

He didn't look at her, but she got the sense that he was fighting a battle for control. A battle he was not winning. She could come up with only one explanation. She'd known Luke hated the FBI. Known it for a long time. Something about this case was dredging up feelings and emotions she suspected had been festering for years.

Two heavy sighs later, she tried again. "We have thirty minutes before we get to the sheriff's office. I think this would be a great time for you to tell me why you hate the FBI so much."

"It doesn't matter."

"I think it does."

He didn't answer.

"Would you like me to tell you the story I've pieced together?" Still no answer. "I did a little digging."

If Luke got any more tense, he was going to spontaneously combust, but this conversation was long overdue. Well, maybe not long overdue. She'd only cared for a few days, but they had been an intense few days. Was there any hope for them to have a relationship? She had no clue. But one thing she knew for sure was that if they didn't resolve this issue, all the other issues with their different career paths wouldn't mean squat.

"I know about your dad."

Luke stared out the window.

"I read the reports. Your dad was completely innocent, but he lost everything."

Luke didn't react.

"The agents were trying to get the big guy behind it all, and they couldn't reveal what they knew about your dad and his business partner without blowing the case and risking the identity of an agent who was deep undercover."

Luke twitched. Finally, a response. She had wondered if he had ever known about the undercover agent. She had her answer.

"That agent had a wife, three kids. They were protecting him. But in the process, they left your dad floundering. There was a lot of discussion about how to fix the situation. But . . ."

"Yeah. But. But Dad had already died from suicide. He couldn't see he hadn't lost everything. Not really. He still had me. Still had my sister. My mom."

"Luke—"

"I know. Okay." Luke's voice reverberated through the car. "I know about mental illness. I know about depression. I know he loved us. I know he didn't want to leave us. I know that now." The anger fled as fast as it had come, and the next words wrenched out of him in a harsh whisper. "But when you're eight and your dad kills himself, you don't understand the pain and desperation he experienced. All you wonder is why you weren't enough to live for."

Should she touch him? Should she pull over and put her arms around him? Would he let her? Would he believe her if she told him that while the circumstances were different and not nearly as tragic, she, too, had dealt with the abandonment of her father? That she often wondered why she hadn't been enough for him to stay?

"The FBI," he said, spitting the letters, "used him and left him to fend for himself. They let people believe he was guilty. My grandfather thought his son had stolen from all those people. Did that report you read say anything about the way my grandfather wept when he was told the truth? How he went to my father's grave and begged him for forgiveness? How he lived with regret for the rest of his life?"

It hadn't.

"When I told my family I wanted to go into law enforcement, do you know what my mom said? She said that was fine, as long as I stayed away from the FBI."

Oh no.

"She wasn't kidding. Most families hope their kids grow into law-abiding citizens. In my family, a few nonviolent criminal enterprises would be preferable to joining the FBI."

"I'm sure that's not—"

Luke looked at her now. His eyes held a despair that left her shaken.

"It's not an exaggeration. I've learned to tolerate the FBI. But my family hates the FBI. And they always will."

The words fell like a death sentence on her heart.

Tears pricked the corners of her eyes, but she blinked them back. It was dark now, and they rode the rest of the way in a heavy silence interrupted only by the GPS giving her directions.

She put the car in park and dropped her head to the steering wheel. *Lord? I thought you were helping? This doesn't feel like help. What am I supposed to do now?*

Luke cleared his throat. "Thad always told me my anger was going to mess my life up one day. That it hindered my relationship with the Lord. That it hindered my relationships with . . . with others. I thought I'd given it over to God. I thought I'd forgiven the people I blamed for decades. I thought I'd put it behind me. But here we are."

There was pain in his words. And they rang with defeat.

"I am sorry, Faith. You have no idea how sorry." He opened the door and stepped into the darkness.

— 25 —

LUKE WAITED OUTSIDE the car, breathing in the rain-cleansed air. He'd have to get an Uber home. Fine. He deserved whatever it cost him and then some.

But for now, they had to talk to Janice Estes and find out what was going on. Janice Estes had nothing to do with the Stevsky case. She'd known Thad in a professional capacity, but Luke didn't remember Thad ever mentioning her. And if she'd known Mi Cha, then wouldn't she have said something?

Unless she *was* somehow involved. But how could she be? He had to admit it was unlikely.

Faith's door opened, and the Faith that climbed from the car was a professional. Determined. Focused. And not in any way, shape, or form friendly.

He deserved that. Had expected it.

He hadn't expected the pain that sliced through him when she gave him a cold nod and walked into the sheriff's office, leaving him to hobble after her.

When they entered the building, they were greeted by a familiar face. "Luke, man, it's good to see you." Investigator Ryan Parker grabbed him in a quick bro hug, then turned to Faith. "You must be Special Agent Malone." He extended a hand and Faith shook it. Quick and efficient. "It's a pleasure to meet you. I'm Ryan Parker. I came in when Gabe called. I'll get you signed in and take you to our conference room. Gabe has been talking to Agent Estes, so I'll let him fill you in."

They walked to the front desk and showed their badges and weapons before being cleared to enter.

"Any news on the shooter?" Faith asked as they waited on the elevator.

Ryan shook his head in frustration. "Nah. Your agent lives on the edge of nothing out there. And with the way it was raining earlier? We won't find anything. All we can do is hope he doesn't know this area and gets himself lost. We've put out a BOLO."

"Why? That tips our hand." Faith was not happy.

"We have to protect our residents." Ryan was understanding but defended the move without apology. "We have an armed shooter roaming around on foot in a part of the county where folks are known to leave their doors unlocked and don't expect a stranger to be a danger. They have to be warned. Our officers have gone door to door to most of the residents on that side of the county to make sure they know to call if they see anything suspicious."

"How many people are we talking about?"

"About a hundred. That part of the county is sparsely popu-lated. Mostly chicken farmers and older couples who've lived here forever. It's not unusual for some of them to own fifty to a hundred acres. Most of it pasture or woods. Carrington's a big county, and once you get past the city and the lake, it's a lot of open land."

Faith blew out a breath. "He could be anywhere."

"I know this isn't what you want to hear, but yes."

Ryan paused at the door to the conference room, knocked twice, and entered without waiting for a response. Luke held back, and Faith took the lead. This was her case. Her fellow agent. –

Despite everything that had happened, the look Janice gave Faith had Luke twitching to step between them. She exuded hatred and cold fury. "What are *you* doing here?" Janice apparently didn't feel the need to disguise her dislike for Faith.

"It's my case." The words were pleasant enough, with only a hint of an inflection on the word *my*, but Faith's meaning was clear. She had every right to be here. She knew it. Janice knew it. Everyone knew it. And Janice could cooperate, or their boss would know it.

"I'm tired of being treated like some sort of regular citizen." The way Janice snapped her words reminded Luke of an alligator. There was a vicious streak in her, and if she ever got you in her jaws, she would destroy you.

Was she planning to destroy Faith? Could she have set all of this up? Was there even a shooter?

Gabe stood and extended a hand. "Special Agent Malone, I presume?" At Faith's nod, he grinned. "It's a pleasure. Welcome to Carrington. Anything you need, just holler. We have snacks." He pointed to a tray of goodies on the table. "Can I get you a coffee? Tea? Hot chocolate?"

"Do you guys have Cherry Coke?" The question earned Luke a glare, but he didn't care.

"Maybe? I can check the machine." Gabe walked over to Luke and threw a light punch at his good shoulder. "You hanging in there, man?" The question was spoken in a low voice and rang with sincere concern. Coming from Gabe, that meant a lot. Gabe was the class clown 90 percent of the time, but he was as solid as they came.

"I'm good. I'll be clear to dive in a few weeks, once everything heals. You guys need to let me join you on a training exercise."

"We'll do it." Gabe pointed to the door. "You want coffee?"

"Is it fit to drink?"

"Man," Gabe put on a lofty air, "we have an espresso machine. I'll fix you up. Be back in a few." Gabe and Ryan left the room, and left Luke wondering if he should join them.

"Janice, I need you to tell me what happened. From the beginning." Faith sat, her iPad and pencil at the ready. She hadn't ordered Luke out, so he maintained his position by the door.

Janice took a cookie from the platter and broke it in half. Her attitude had shrunk with the size of her audience. Her hostility remained. "I was driving home. No big deal. It's Saturday night, for crying out loud. We've all worked nonstop"—she glanced at Luke—"since Monday."

Did she just glare at him? Like it was his fault a madman was running around Raleigh shooting at agents?

"I was tired. It takes me forty-five minutes to get home. A little less on a Saturday. It'd been such a nasty day, and I wasn't in a hurry. I listen to audiobooks on the commute. I read four or five books every month that way."

Did she want them to give her a gold star?

"I wasn't paying attention. Decompressing. Listening." She frowned at the cookie. "If he hadn't revved the engine right before he hit me, I wouldn't have seen it coming."

"He sped up?"

"I guess he did. He must have. I hadn't noticed anything. Then I heard a truck barreling down on me. Because of the rain, I couldn't tell make or model. Just big, loud, dark. I thought it was some jerk trying to prove how big he was, and I slowed down. Figured he could ride my bumper for a few minutes. My turn was only a mile away."

Leave it to this idiot to antagonize someone already demonstrating signs of road rage.

"But he didn't stop. He didn't back up. When he first tapped my bumper, I assumed it was aggressive driving gone bad. I sped up a touch, expecting him to fall back when he realized what he'd done. But then he hit me again. Harder. That's when I knew he was doing it on purpose."

She took a bite of the cookie. Chewed. Swallowed. Continued. "I still thought it was some road rager. Maybe a drunk. I considered slowing down more, but I wasn't in the mood to deal with the drama. I sped up. By that time, I was almost at my turn, but I decided to drive past. No sense in leading a maniac to my front door."

She had that part right.

"But as I sped up, so did he. Eventually he hit me so hard, it pushed me over to the side. I'm a good driver, and I was able to recover. Anybody else would have spun out of control."

Arrogance aside, she was probably right about that part too.

"I started looking for a place to get off the road. I thought I would pull over, he'd drive by, I'd get a license plate, call it in, and go home. The locals could pick him up. He'd fail a sobriety test, and that would be the end of it. I barely slowed, pulling over in a little parking lot and whipping around so I could tear back onto the road and head back in the other direction before he realized what had happened. But he whipped into the next entrance of the same lot and drove straight at me." She took another bite of the cookie. "These are good."

Faith didn't respond. She'd barely responded to anything Janice had said, other than to write faster.

"He slammed into the back corner of my car. I tried to pull forward, but the car wouldn't respond."

"You were in the vehicle when he hit you. Then you exited your vehicle?" Faith spoke with so much formality, you'd think she didn't even know Janice.

"Yes. And that's when he started shooting."

Faith looked at Janice then. "Did he hit you?"

"No."

"Come close?"

Janice shrugged. "Hard to say. I'm not an idiot. When the shots started flying, I ran into the woods. I expected him to drive off."

"But he didn't."

"Nope. Parked that truck and came after me."

"What was he shooting?"

"Handgun. Don't know what kind. Definitely not a rifle or a shotgun. I hunkered down in a spot thick with some evergreen bushes and called 911. I told them I was an FBI agent, gave them my location, told them I was being fired on, and waited for the Carrington locals to show up."

"Lucky for you they were nearby."

"Yeah. I have to give them credit. They got there a lot faster than I thought possible."

"When did you get a look at the guy? You gave Gabe a description."

"After I got myself tucked away, I saw him by the streetlight before he ran into the woods after me. He's David Lee."

"How sure are you?"

"I'm sure."

"How sure?" Faith pressed.

Janice's lip curled, but she answered. "David Lee has a tattoo. It's clear in all the photos you've found of him. It's some kind of animal tail. Maybe a tiger. Not sure how far down it starts, but it comes up from his collar, over his neck, and a little bit up one cheek."

Luke had seen it. It was quite distinctive. He hadn't thought it looked like a tiger tail. He'd assumed it was a snake of some kind.

But if Janice was right and it was a tiger tail, could this David Lee be the person Bill had called him about?

"Any thoughts as to why he would come after you?" Faith asked the question casually, as if she were asking about the weather and not attempted murder.

"How on earth should I know? It's *your* case. You figure it out." Janice stood. "Will that be all, Special Agent Malone?"

"Not quite, Special Agent Estes. I'd like to know how you've seen photographs of David Lee. How do you know his name and that he has a tattoo?"

Janice tossed her hair. "You leave things on your desk. You shouldn't."

Faith didn't look as surprised as Luke had expected her to. Had she suspected Janice of snooping around her desk? "One more thing. Why didn't you go public with the stats from the ME and the forensic anthropologist when you got them? If you'd gone public with the details that we were looking for a missing woman, twenty-nine to thirty-five, of Asian ancestry, we might have gotten a hit a month ago."

Janice looked at Luke, a malevolent gleam in her eye. "I thought she was a prostitute. No one would have noticed she was missing, or even if they did, they wouldn't have come forward."

"Why would you think Thad Baker was with a prostitute?" Faith got the question out before Luke had time to react.

"Men his type are like that, aren't they?" Janice was enjoying this way too much. "Too-good-to-be-true Christians. Won't go in for a normal affair, but they're all in for the kinky stuff."

"There's nothing about Thad Baker that could have led you to that conclusion." It was a good thing Faith was defending Thad, because if Luke opened his mouth, the things that would come out would not be very Christian at all.

"You'd think so." Janice turned her attention to Luke. "Maybe you didn't know Thad as well as you thought."

Something was tugging at the fibers of Luke's memory. Maybe six months ago. Less than a year. Thad had come in from a task force meeting, baffled that he'd been hit on. "Could she not see the ring?" Thad had said, sticking out his left hand.

"Maybe you hit on him and he turned you down and you're not sorry he's dead." It had been a calculated guess. When Thad had made the statement to him, Luke wasn't sure it was Janice who'd hit on him, but he was sure now.

She went stark white, except for the bright red streaking up her neck. "You . . . he . . ."

Faith hadn't flinched when Luke had spoken. Now she leaned toward Janice. "Is Special Agent Powell correct?"

The specifics were falling into place in Luke's mind. "It *was* you. You came on to Thad. More than once. He finally had to tell you that if you didn't stop, he'd file a complaint." Thad never told him who the agent was. But looking at Janice Estes, Luke could see it all. Janice was tall, blonde, coolly confident in her abilities. Single, unattached, and with no desire to change that status. Not looking for anything more than a good time. She'd set her sights on Thad.

"Janice." That one word spoke volumes. Disbelief and disgust mingled with an edge of fury. Faith was about to blow.

Janice winked at Luke. "He was stuck with a chunky monkey and a couple of rug rats. I was offering him a good time. He declined. His loss. I promise you, I've never had any complaints, and none of my lovers have gotten blown to bits."

"We know who Park Mi Cha was. She wasn't a prostitute. She was a scientist, working on a PhD and here in Raleigh for four months as an intern." Faith's voice held an edge Luke had never heard. "You made an erroneous assumption based on your own biases and hatred for the man. My report will make it clear that you've hindered this investigation, and that it is my belief your incompetence has led to the deaths of two United States Secret Service agents and the attempted murder of three others."

— 26 —

FAITH STOOD. She had to get out of this room. Away from Janice. Away from Luke. Away from everybody. "Go home, Janice." She tried to keep the disdain from her voice.

She knew she had failed.

When she turned to the door, Luke had already opened it. "Happy?" The word sliced from her lips. "Another FBI agent who didn't do her job, and people died because of it."

He looked stricken. His hand reached toward her, then fell away as if he'd thought better of it. Wise decision.

The Carrington investigators stood at a discreet distance. She waved them over. "Are we even sure she was shot at?"

Gabe and Ryan exchanged looks of surprise before Gabe answered. "She was definitely under fire. No one saw it, but a local resident heard it. Called it in. There were spent casings in the parking lot. And the truck is still there. Damage to the front end visually matches the damage to her car. We have roadblocks up, masquerading as sobriety checkpoints, but so far nothing but a few random tickets for not having licenses."

Someone did shoot at her. But who? "What about the truck? Does it belong to David Lee?"

Ryan took this one. "No. Stolen."

"Where was it stolen?"

"Richmond, Virginia. I take it you don't believe her story?" Gabe asked the question gently, but it still stung.

Luke stared at the floor, and for the life of her, she couldn't decide if she was glad he was staying out of it or sorry he wasn't commiserating. Maybe it was a little of both. "If I were you, I would reevaluate everything Agent Estes said. She has not earned the right to be trusted."

"I'll keep that in mind." Ryan crossed his arms. "Does this mean we shouldn't assume we're looking for David Lee? None of us saw him. She could be throwing the search in the wrong direction."

How had it come to this? Her entire investigation was a disaster.

"Honestly? I don't know. I've had trouble with her before, but this is a low I didn't think she was capable of reaching. I was wrong." The words were acid on her tongue.

"I'll keep you in the loop." Gabe extended a hand, and when she took it, he gave it an unexpected squeeze. "It's going to be okay, Agent Malone. We aren't FBI, but we're good at what we do, and you can trust *us*. And while I know this is hard to believe, we like this one"—he tossed a nod in Luke's direction—"and we're in favor of keeping him around for a while."

"Thank you."

They exchanged numbers and made sure everyone had correct contact information, and then Gabe and Ryan walked them out. When they got to the front desk, the guys exchanged handshakes and fist bumps. They said their goodbyes, and Faith forced herself to stay calm. She still faced an hour-long drive in a car with Luke. And because of his injuries, she had to do the driving.

All she wanted was to go home. To wash this day—this never-ending day—out of her hair and maybe, by some miracle, out of her mind.

Luke held the door and she exited. The night was dark, cool, misty. No starlight penetrated the clouds. When the door had closed behind them, Luke paused on the top step.

She didn't turn around. She didn't stop. "I'm not going to leave you here."

"I can get an Uber."

Tempting. So tempting. "That's ridiculous." She'd almost reached her car. "Get in the car."

"Wait!" Luke rushed back up the stairs. Well, as much as he was rushing anywhere these days.

"What?"

He was inside only a moment before he returned with a long telescoping object in his hand. He didn't speak as he used it to check under her car for a bomb.

She blew out a relieved sigh when he stepped back. "It's clear. Let me return this. If you're sure you don't mind, I'll accept the ride back to Raleigh."

"I'm too tired to care about anything right now. I want food and I want sleep. Let's go."

Fifteen minutes and a drive-through stop later, they pulled onto the highway and headed to Raleigh. At least the traffic shouldn't be a problem.

They didn't speak until they were on the outskirts of the city. "Do you think it was David Lee?" Luke asked the question that had been bouncing around in Faith's brain since they left the sheriff's office.

"I don't know." It burned to admit it, but she didn't.

"For what it's worth, I didn't think she was lying. Not when she originally said it. It wasn't until she showed her hand about

Thad that I began to question everything. But . . . for the sake of argument, if it was David Lee, does that mean David Lee is our assailant? That he's revenge killing because he somehow believes the Secret Service is responsible for Mi Cha's death? The way Mrs. Lin talked, he could be the type."

"He's supposed to be an accountant though," Faith said, pushing back. Not because she thought he was wrong, but to further test the theory. "How would an accountant have the skills to blow up Jared's house and shoot the dart at Michael, or the skill to shoot at you and Zane the way he did? I'm not knocking accountants, but you don't expect that."

"What if he isn't an accountant? Or he's an accountant now, but he has some kind of special forces training?"

Faith could see that. "Let's say it was David Lee coming after her, and he's not an accountant. He's a criminal or former military or grew up in a militia and knows about guns and bombs. Even if that were true, which, let me remind you, we have zero evidence of, why come after Janice? She isn't helping us solve the case. And if my theory is correct about Mi Cha's involvement with the Secret Service being the motive behind the attacks, that's another reason for this shooter to leave Janice alone. Janice never met Mi Cha and didn't even know it was her in the car with Thad until this week."

"You're right." Luke's agreement was grudgingly given.

"Could you talk to Sabrina tomorrow? Share what we know and see if that changes anything in her search? She's been looking for David Lee in the DC and Raleigh areas. Maybe she can expand her search to Carrington as well."

"I can do that."

Luke was being very polite, and she could feel his desire to keep things from being awkward. But how could they not be? From kissing her senseless to stabbing her with a metaphorical knife to the heart, he'd put her through a lot today. But she couldn't let herself think about the kissing, or the anger. She didn't have the emotional capacity to deal with any of that.

She pulled up to the door of the hotel, and Luke climbed out. "Thank you for driving."

She nodded and drove away almost before he had the door closed.

She went home. Cleared her house, weapon in hand, before setting the security system and kicking off her shoes.

She showered.

She went to bed.

She did not text Luke.

— 27 —

LUKE THANKED THE AGENTS and officers providing security and then tiptoed into his room. Zane was snoring. Tessa was asleep in the adjoining room, the door cracked. He swallowed his meds, took a shower, and crawled into bed. He hated what he'd done. Hated how stupid he'd been. Hated how his body ached and screamed for rest. Hated how his phone remained silent.

When he woke the next morning, he lay in the bed and for a blissful moment remembered the kiss. Then he remembered the way he'd ruined it all.

And he remembered today was Sunday and Jared's funeral was this afternoon.

Zane rolled over in the other bed. "You awake?"

"Yeah."

"Want to fill me in?"

"No."

"Went that well, huh?"

"You have no idea."

Zane crawled out of bed and spent a few minutes in the bathroom. Luke used the opportunity to check his phone.

A call from his mom. One from his sister, which was almost

sure to be from his niece. She liked to steal her mom's phone and call him at random times when her mom didn't know she had it.

No calls, texts, or emails from Faith.

Zane reentered the room. Athletic pants, T-shirt, bare feet, and a to-go cup of coffee. "Spill it."

Luke ignored him. "Where'd you get that?"

"The detail brought some this morning. It's in the hall."

"Huh." He'd slept through it.

"Spill."

"I need coffee."

"We don't have all day."

"I'm feeling the love, man." Luke opened the door and found a small room service tray in the hall with several coffees, his favorite Americano among them. He nodded at the officer standing guard, grabbed the Americano and a chocolate croissant, and returned to the room. He took several sips and then flopped down next to Zane at the small table in the corner of the room. "I blew it."

"What did you do?" Zane didn't argue with you when you owned up to being an idiot, and he wasn't the type to try to make you feel better when you screwed up. More the type to help you not screw up again.

"Went off on the FBI."

Zane's response was to take a sip of coffee and stare at him.

"I told her I didn't trust the FBI and implied that I didn't trust her either. And for good measure, I mentioned that my family would rather I went into a life of crime than become an FBI agent."

That earned him a raised eyebrow.

"I did apologize."

Zane rolled his eyes.

"But we didn't leave on good terms."

Zane tipped his coffee in Luke's direction. "I would think this conversation about the FBI was a bit overdue. Your feelings on that agency are well-known. She needs to know how you feel before things get too far, unless . . ."

Here it comes.

"How far *have* things gotten between you two?" Zane didn't ask in a voyeuristic way. Not even in a nosy friend way.

It made it easier to answer honestly. "We've kissed."

"Often?"

"No."

"Are we talking more than a quick peck?"

"Yeah."

"Who started it?"

"She kissed me on the cheek. As a thank-you. But then . . ." Luke set the coffee on the table and picked at the edges of his croissant. "I'm an idiot."

"We already knew that, but what happened after the kiss?"

"We went inside to talk to Hope's client. The one who owns the boardinghouse."

"And then?"

"Then you called to tell me about Janice Estes. It was on the way to Carrington that I lost it."

"Did she text you last night?"

"No." Luke could hear the petulance in his voice. He sounded like a whiny teenager.

"Did you text her?"

"No. It's her move."

"In what universe?"

"I blew it. I said I was sorry. She's icing me."

"She has every reason to." Zane had a knack for stating the obvious.

"Then why would I—"

"Leave her thinking you're as big of a jerk as you were yesterday? You may be right. She's not worth fighting for. Not worth a little humiliation." Zane struck a thoughtful pose—one hand on his chin, a lofty air to his tone. "When she figures out who's trying to kill us, she'll go back to her FBI world and you'll go back to your Secret Service world and you won't ever think about her again. Or get twitchy when you have to work together on the JTTF. Or punch a hole in a wall when she shows up one day with a diamond on her finger. Or, even better, when she doesn't show up at all because she's been promoted and she's in New York."

The picture Zane painted was the most depressing scene Luke had never wanted to imagine. "What am I supposed to do?"

"Begging would be a good place to start. It would require you to acknowledge your feelings. Own them. Risk having her stomp on your heart and crush you. Might not be worth it."

"I can't change my family."

"Why are you worried about whether she'll get along with your mom?"

"How do I offer my heart for crushing when it's not like she'd be getting a happily ever after. I'd be inviting her into a life where my extended family is opposed to her presence from day one."

"First, you don't know that. You're projecting your own FBI issues onto everyone else. Second, Faith won you over. Why would you think she can't win your family over? Your mom will love anyone who saves your life, so when Faith finally solves this case, you'll be able to introduce her as the woman who kept your heart beating. Your mom and sister will love her."

Why hadn't Luke thought of that?

"Lastly, when it comes to the happily ever after, no one in the real world gets that. That's not what marriage is. God designed marriage for a lot of reasons, but if you keep looking for someone who will never argue with you or you'll never disagree with, then you are on a true mission impossible."

"Wow. You're a real champion for marriage, aren't you?"

Zane ignored him. "Don't you remember Thad telling us how much trouble he had getting Rose to date him? The CIA and FBI get along about as well as the Secret Service and the FBI, and that's without a family tragedy in the mix. They made it work. Why can't you?"

"Why are you so gung ho about Faith? You barely know her."

"But I know you. You like her. You like being around her. I think she might be the one. Thad thought so too." He held up a hand as Luke tried to speak. "I'm not telling you that you can repair the damage, but how will you know if you don't try?" Zane stood. "Counseling session over. I'm getting a banana. Then I want you to fill me in on the case."

Tessa tapped on the adjoining door. Her eyes were bloodshot, and she looked like she'd had a rough night. She already had a coffee in her hand, but by the looks of her, she would need several to get through this day.

"You okay?"

"Headache." She took the seat Zane had vacated.

When Zane returned, he frowned at Tessa but took a spot on the edge of the bed. "Let's hear it."

"Wait!" Tessa ran into her room and returned with her phone.

Ten seconds later, Gil's voice came through the speaker. "I'm not sure who got me stuck here another night, but it was not cool."

"Hush and let Luke fill us in on what happened last night, or I won't go with your sister to get your suit." Tessa's threat meant nothing to Luke, but it must have meant something to Gil because he hushed.

Luke started with the phone call from his CI. Then the dead

body. David Lee. The attack on Janice Estes. And the connection between Janice and Thad.

"We're going to owe those Carrington guys a steak dinner when this is all over." Zane rubbed a hand over his face.

"What do we do now?" Gil's question wasn't rhetorical, but no one had an answer.

Zane gave Luke a very pointed look.

"I'll call Faith and ask her if there's anything specific she wants us to do. And I'll check in with Sabrina. I left her a message last night, but it was late. I'm not sure if she's working on it today. It is Sunday."

Tessa and Zane looked as confused by that as Luke felt. Could it have been only a week ago that they were at the Baker twins' party? That Jared and Michael were alive, and no one had been shot? How could so much have gone so wrong so fast?

Zane leaned toward the phone. "Gil, you sure you're up for the flight? Do the doctors know you're getting on a plane?"

"They do, thanks to my big-mouth sister. There's a good doc here. Marine. He gets it. He gave his permission."

"With caveats," Tessa interjected.

"Has my sister been talking to you?" Gil's outrage was tempered with amusement.

"Someone has to make sure the guys in this office don't die, and the way I see it, the women are the only ones left standing. I've talked to your sister"—Tessa turned to Luke—"and I've talked to Faith."

"Today?" his voice cracked on the word and Zane chortled.

"What did I miss?" Gil asked.

"Luke's an idiot." Zane answered before Luke had a chance to defend himself.

"What's new?"

257

"This time he was an idiot to Faith." Tessa didn't glare at him, but it was close. She was definitely on Faith's side here.

"When did you—" Luke started.

"What did you do?" Gil spoke over him. "You kissed her, didn't you? Did it go badly?"

"Can we not do this? I need to get some work done, Gil needs to get out of the hospital, and we all need to go to the airport."

"That's fine." Even through the phone, Luke could tell that Gil was up to something. "Tessa, you can fill me in on the plane. See y'all in a few."

Before Luke could respond, Gil had disconnected the call. Zane stood and clapped his hands. "Sounds like a plan." Then, "Oh no."

"What's wrong, man?"

Zane looked like a lost puppy. "I don't have a suit."

Tessa stood, patted his arm, and walked toward her room. "Already taken care of."

"What?"

"How?"

She looked at the two of them. "I talked to Jacob earlier this week. Then I talked to that tailor you take everything to. The suit was ready yesterday. Jacob has it. He'll bring it to the airport." Tessa sounded both smug and defensive, and she didn't hang around for questions. She slipped into her room, closed the adjoining door, and locked it.

Luke turned on Zane. "What did *you* do?"

Zane didn't make eye contact. "I didn't do anything."

"How did you not know she'd ordered you a suit? And gotten it altered? And why didn't she tell you? What is going on with you two?"

Zane still didn't look in his direction. "Nothing. Absolutely nothing."

Luke stared at Zane's back. He'd never heard his friend speak with so much bitterness. Or was it anguish? Had there been a real thing, beyond friendship, between him and Tessa? "Do you want to talk about it?"

"No."

Luke waited.

Zane turned then. "When this is over. Not now."

Fair enough. "I'm here for you, man."

"I know." Zane strapped on a holster. "Let's stay focused on surviving today."

"Sounds like a plan."

— 28 —

FAITH HADN'T SLEPT GREAT but had dragged her exhausted body to the river for a row and then dropped by Hope's house to check on her. When Faith's phone rang at ten-thirty, she didn't answer it. Luke Powell could take his texts and his jokes and his strong arms and his handyman skills and his soft lips, and he could just—

"If you don't answer it, I will." Hope rolled past her. "Stop acting like a teenager. Give him a chance."

"I shouldn't have given him the first chance, and I don't do second chances."

"Maybe you should start."

The phone rang again. Hope lunged and snatched it before Faith could get to it. Her finger tapped the screen, but instead of putting it to her face, she held it out to Faith. "Talk to him." She mouthed the words, but there was still a threat in them. If Faith didn't, Hope would.

Faith took the phone. "Special Agent Malone speaking."

Hope gave her a "why do I even try" look before having the courtesy to leave the room.

"Good morning, Faith." Luke's deep voice sent shivers down her spine. Three words and she was a mess. "I won't keep you, but I need to let you know two things. I talked to Sabrina this morning. She's widening her search parameters for David Lee and trying to locate Mi Cha's dad, and she'll be in touch."

"Thanks for letting me know." That was good. Professional. No hint of the tears threatening as Luke's now-familiar voice came at her in such a formal way.

"Which leads me to the next thing. I asked her to be sure to include you on any findings." There was the knife to her gut. "And not to go through me." And the twist.

He cleared his throat. "I won't have reception most of the day, and I don't want anything missed."

Wait. This wasn't him trying to get out of talking to her? Then why—?

"Once we leave for the airport, we'll be at the mercy of the security detail in charge of this. They aren't getting paid to cover our backsides—totally volunteer—and we don't want to do anything that will make their jobs any harder."

The airport? Security? The lights came on then. Not a light bulb. More like the lights of a football stadium. "You're going to Jared's funeral?"

The screech. The panic. No way he could have missed it. Well, she didn't care. "You . . . you can't! All of you together? You'll be sitting ducks. He could have, I don't know, something to take down an airplane. You know how this works better than I do. You cannot take this risk. I'm sorry Jared is dead. But it doesn't make any sense for you to die just because you need to go to his funeral. I'm sure that's not what he would want."

Hope had returned to the room and sat staring at her, eyes wide in shock.

"Faith." When he said her name that way it sounded like a caress. She crumpled into the recliner. "You're right. We do it all the time with very real threats."

"You don't have an entire presidential detail there. No Air Force One. No armored vehicles. We don't even know who we're looking for. How can you stop him?"

"I can't go into detail over the phone, but we have a good plan. Jacob's been working on it most of the week, and Jacob's the best at this. I'll text you when we're back." There was a long pause. "If you'd like me to."

She didn't want him to need to text her. She didn't want him to go. Didn't want to feel this panic clawing through her body at the thought of Luke dying in a burning plane. She held the phone away from her mouth as she pulled in a deep breath. "Yes," she managed to say. "Please."

"Listen, Faith."

Here it comes. The "let's forget about yesterday and be friends" speech. She braced herself.

"When this is over, can we talk?"

That was somewhat better than being friends, but what was with this "when this is over" nonsense? Would this ever be over? How long did he expect her to wait for this talk? And what if he died today? *Pull it together.* "Sure. I'd like that."

"I have to go. But one more thing."

"Yes?"

"I miss y—."

The call disconnected. Should she call him back? Had someone turned on some sort of jamming signal? Had he said "I miss you?" What else could it have been? "I miss yesterday?" Highly unlikely. Although "I miss the way we were yesterday before five in the afternoon" would have been acceptable.

"What did he say?" Hope reached for the phone, and Faith handed it to her.

"They're going to the funeral."

"I got that."

"And he wants to talk." She put air quotes around the word talk. "Whatever that means."

She'd already told Hope everything this morning. The kiss. The argument. The hurt.

"Sounds to me like he wants to talk." Hope patted her arm. "The real question is whether or not you want to hear what he has to say."

"What is that supposed to mean?"

"He has some childhood trauma—"

"I have my own childhood trauma. He hardly has a corner on the market."

"But you're angry with him for his childhood trauma, and the biases and attitudes that come with it, while you continue to cling to your own. Do you see the inconsistency there?"

"Our father had no reason to leave."

Hope waved a hand over her wheelchair.

"Your accident was his excuse. He couldn't handle it. And I don't think he loved Mom anyway. It was the excuse he needed to convince himself that it was okay to sleep around and eventually to start over. And Mom didn't stop him. It's not the same. Luke's father was put through hell. Tormented by accusations and loss, none of which were his fault and all of which he was helpless to fix. His death was a tragedy. Our dad's disappearance was because of his own selfishness. I don't know how you can even tolerate him."

Hope tilted her head to one side. "When's the last time you talked to Dad?"

Faith had no idea. "Sometime last year maybe?"

"Try three years ago."

"I'm not counting."

"He is."

Faith turned on Hope. "Don't you dare try to make me feel guilty. He's the one who messed up. He's in the wrong. Not me."

Hope didn't flinch. She had her lawyer face on. Impassive. Thoughtful. If Faith's words had hurt her, she didn't show it. "Fine. Don't talk to Dad. But don't block Luke over something our dad did fifteen years ago. Luke's a good guy. He messed up. He wants to talk. I think you should hear him out, especially since you're in love with him."

Faith spluttered but couldn't get a real word out of her mouth before Hope continued. "Don't try to argue. You melted when he called. And you lost your mind when he told you he was getting on an airplane."

"It's stupid. A ridiculous risk. He'll get himself killed."

"Why do you care?" Hope delivered the question in a low voice.

"How could I not care? He's a friend. Gil, Zane, Tessa. All of them. They're friends now. It would be a tragedy if they—"

"It would be a professional tragedy, to be sure. But would it be a personal tragedy? Until a week ago, you barely knew any of them. Seems to me that the one person you can't bear to lose is Luke. And as such, you owe it to yourself, and to him, to at least listen when he talks. If he doesn't have the sense to realize he messed up, then you need to get over him and move on. No sense in getting stuck with a guy who doesn't know how to apologize."

He'd already apologized. She'd left that part out when she'd talked to Hope earlier.

"You'll regret it if you don't." With that dire pronouncement, Hope left the room. "I'm headed to church," she called out as she went to the door. "I'll see you later. Love you."

"Love you too." Faith whispered the words into the air.

Then she sank to her knees. "God? It's me, Faith. Again. Luke. He's . . . I don't know?" From somewhere in the deep recesses of her brain, she remembered a Sunday school teacher telling her the Holy Spirit, who Faith had been terrified of, was able to translate tears and sighs and emotions into words. That she never had to be afraid God couldn't understand her prayers—because he could. Faith hoped that was true, because her powers of speech had failed her. All she could do was kneel on the floor and hope God knew what to do with her.

She knelt long enough that her knees screamed for her to move, but she didn't get up. She twisted around and sat cross-legged. Was Hope right? And what about Luke?

She couldn't blame him for hating the FBI in general, and he definitely didn't hate her specifically. She could almost feel his hands on her face, his lips on hers. That kiss. It had been unexpected, but not a mistake.

Luke meant something to her, and she was pretty sure she meant something to him.

"God? I still don't know about forgiving my dad. He doesn't deserve it. But maybe I could start with forgiving Luke for being so ridiculous? And maybe I could, you know, not be so angry with you about everything? I'm not sure how to do that. I've been angry for a long time, but I don't want to be."

She continued to sit until her frantic thoughts slowed and were replaced with memories. Good ones.

He'd always been there. He was still there. Here. Now.

Peace settled over her, and for a little while she sat, enjoying it. But in time, an urgency that wasn't panic but was intentional prompted her to move.

It was time to stop a killer.

When she got to work, she went straight to Dale's office. She wasn't surprised to see him sitting behind his desk, fuming. If he had been in a cartoon, steam would have been billowing from his ears. As it was, he growled, "Get in here," when he saw her standing at the door.

"Good morning." Faith sat in the seat across from him.

"You're awfully cheery. Are you on something? How many Cokes have you had this morning?"

"One." Number two was in her bag.

She filled him in on the case. As she talked, Dale chewed on a toothpick. He didn't interrupt, but he had shredded the toothpick before she finished.

Faith ended by giving him her thoughts on Janice Estes. She didn't hold back.

Dale shook his head. "I'm still stunned that she handled this all so badly."

"Have you talked to her?"

"Only to tell her to be in my office Monday morning. I have a meeting with one of our lawyers this afternoon. Can you believe it? But that's how it goes these days. I can't just fire her."

Janice had failed Thad, Mi Cha, and all of their families. Her biases and prejudices could have resulted in two more deaths, and all the devastation that had rained down on the Secret Service agents this week. Injuries and explosions and bullet wounds and the loss of Zane's home. It was too much.

Faith couldn't undo any of it. But she could make it stop. She had to.

Five minutes later, she was back at her desk. She dialed Sabrina's number.

Sabrina answered on the second ring. "Good morning, Faith. I don't have any new information yet, but I'm chasing a lead that has potential."

"That's the best news I've heard lately. I was hoping we could brainstorm a little, because I'm wondering if David Lee isn't who we think he is."

"What do you mean?"

"We know from Mrs. Lin that he was controlling. Obsessive. I don't have anything against accountants, but that's not how we typically describe them, unless maybe we're talking about taxes."

"I'm not following you, Faith." Sabrina wasn't unkind, but she wasn't one to sugarcoat her questions. "Anyone can be anything at any time. Some of the worst psychopaths in our history have had normal jobs, and no one suspected them of any criminal involvement."

"I know, but what if in this case, the mild-mannered accountant is a cover?"

"Why would you think that?"

"I don't know. Something Mrs. Lin said about how on top of things Mi Cha's parents were. How protective and prepared. Those aren't people who don't notice that their daughter hasn't come home. And those aren't the kind of people who don't raise all kinds of drama over it. They should have been talking to the embassy and anyone they could find." Faith waited for Sabrina to poke holes in her theory.

"I see your point."

Faith slumped in her seat in relief. If Sabrina could see it, then Faith wasn't completely reaching.

"I know you're already looking for David Lee and Park Mi

Cha's father, but while you're trying to locate them, could you also do some digging into who they really are? Something isn't adding up."

Sabrina's only response was a flurry of keystrokes Faith could hear over the line. She waited. Waited some more. Was she writing a book?

"Done. I have a contact in Seoul. Outside of state department parameters. He owes me big-time, and he'll get back to me quickly. I'll be in touch." Sabrina disconnected the call, and Faith was left staring at her phone.

"Thanks," she said to thin air.

—29—

IT WAS 4:12 P.M., and despite his earlier bravado, Luke was relieved when their airplane landed safely on an airstrip north of Raleigh.

And more relieved when they got word the second plane had touched down on a different airstrip to the east.

Now, to get everyone back to the hotel.

The funeral had been . . . depressing. No funeral was a comedy festival, but not all funerals were so full of despair. Jared's funeral had held so little hope. His ex-wife had shown up long enough to cause a scene. His parents had been broken. Too much like Thad's parents had been at his funeral. And what could he say to comfort them? He couldn't tell them they'd found the killer. Couldn't tell them they knew why Jared had died. Couldn't promise them justice.

"We have to do this again on Wednesday?" Zane grumbled at the window as they drove back into Raleigh.

"It will be worse." Jacob ran a hand over his bald head. "Kids."

Kids. Michael's kids. Guilt cascaded through Luke when he realized he hadn't seen the kids or Karen. Then he remembered he'd been busy trying to stay alive—and not bring his big, targeted backside anywhere near them.

He turned his phone back on, and it worked. Finally. The team who had volunteered to help with security had been good but aggressive. They'd insisted on no electronic communication in case a phone had been hijacked. It wasn't a bad idea, but it was weird to be on this side of a protective detail. If Luke survived to make it to a long-term detail assignment, he'd have to remember this feeling.

He shot a text to Faith first thing. He'd promised.

On the ground.

He'd been hoping for a warm welcome or relief or maybe tears. What he got was a terse order.

Get to your office. ASAP.

Followed by another.

Check your phone.

Well, wasn't that cozy. Maybe she hadn't been worried after all.

Text alerts echoed around the car as his, Zane's, and Jacob's phones all reconnected to the outside world. Luke had expected a few texts, but this was more than a few. He scanned the list. Then stopped and read more slowly. Then checked his email. "We need to go to our office. Not the hotel."

"Okay." Jacob didn't question it. While he directed their driver to change course, Luke showed his phone to Zane. When Jacob was finished, Luke told him. "Sabrina found video footage of David Lee."

"Where?"

"Lots of places around Raleigh. He'd changed his appearance

and was staying at some hourly hotel. BOLOs are out, and all the local cops are looking. Faith has called some CIs, and they're looking too."

"What else?" Jacob asked.

"No details, but Faith says Sabrina found something big. She's organizing her thoughts and will want to share it with us when we get there. Maybe a video chat or something. Who knows?"

Jacob didn't look up from his phone as he spoke. "We'll have the car drop us at the office and then take Zane back to the hote—"

"No way." Zane leaned forward in his seat. "I'm going with you. I can get an Uber later. If there's any chance this is the guy who used me for target practice, I want to look into his eyes."

Luke didn't blame Zane, and he wouldn't mind having his buddy with him. Gil would have a duck when he learned he'd been left out of the loop, but it was for the best.

They arrived at their office ten minutes later.

"'Bout time," Gil spoke from Marty's desk as Tessa perched on the edge of it. "You didn't really think I was going to the hotel, did you?"

Luke didn't have time to argue with him. "Where's Faith?"

"Already in the conference room. She's on the phone with some-body at the FBI. She knows we're here." Gil smirked at him. "But thanks for being worried about me. You know, being in the office when I'm supposed to be taking it easy and all. Tessa here said you'd be upset, but I see how things stand."

Luke didn't respond as he hurried down the hall, drawing up short a few paces from the conference room. He needed to prepare himself. He was a professional. Faith was a professional.

Faith stepped into the hallway, head down, phone in hand, and ran straight into Luke. His arms reflexively wrapped around her as he steadied her, and for a moment she was pressed against his chest. When she looked up, her face inches from his, the desire to kiss her overwhelmed him.

So much for being a professional.

But he couldn't. He wouldn't. She would have to make that move.

But she didn't. She took a half step back and he dropped his arms. Her expression was tight as she crossed her arms and whispered, "I don't like this, Luke."

He almost apologized but stopped himself. This wasn't about them or about him touching her. This was about the case. "What is it?"

"I don't know." There was a hint of despair in her words. "The pieces of the puzzle, they're here in front of me and I can't figure it out."

They were standing close, heads bowed and almost touching. He placed his hands on her elbows and squeezed. "You don't have to figure it out alone, Faith. Let's hear what Sabrina has to say, and then let's work it together. We'll figure it out."

Luke released her, but her arm traced his as he pulled away and her hand found his. "Luke?"

"Yeah?"

"I'm glad you're not dead."

There was barely a hint of forgiveness, but her words carried the hope of it. "Me too." He squeezed her hand, and the small smile she gave him as she reentered the room filled him with warmth.

Maybe she would forgive him. Maybe they could talk it out like adults, and their fathers' choices wouldn't dictate their future.

Luke turned around and looked straight into the eyes of a very appreciative audience. Zane leaned against one wall, Gil the other. Tessa stood in the middle. Was she wiping her eyes? Jacob stood back from all of them, phone in hand, not paying attention to the drama that had riveted the others.

As Luke approached, Zane, Gil, and Tessa gave him a round of silent applause. He ignored them. "Conference room. Everyone. Now."

They followed him, Jacob bringing up the rear. Faith was on the phone, standing in the far corner of the room as they all found seats.

"Did you make up?" Tessa whispered.

"I don't know, Tess. Women are complicated. I'm working on it."

"From where I was standing, it looked like you'd made short work of it." Gil leaned forward in the chair, rubbing a hand across his head. He shouldn't be here. Once Faith got them all on the same page, Luke would try to get him to the hotel. Ugh. They needed life to go back to whatever kind of normal they could piece together after this never-ending week.

Faith turned, her face drawn, eyes wary. "First, I feel I owe all of you an apology. I'm sure by now Luke has told you about Agent Estes and her total failure to do her job in a professional manner."

"You aren't responsible for Janice's stupidity," Jacob said. "Neither is Dale. I've already talked to him twice." He looked at the others. "You can't imagine how much guilt he's carrying. He feels like Michael's death is his fault."

Jacob looked each one of them in the eye before continuing. "Michael's death, Jared's death, the shootings, the arson—these things are someone's fault, but they aren't Janice's fault. Or the FBI's fault. Someone is behind this, and when we find them, then we will know where the blame lies."

Luke was listening to Jacob, but he was watching Faith. She had her head down, eyes on the floor, and she wouldn't make eye contact with anyone.

"Could the case have been handled better? Sure. Is it possible we could have solved Thad's murder by now? Yes. Is it possible doing so would have prevented Michael's and Jared's deaths and all that has come after? Maybe. Maybe not. Getting all worked up over it won't do anybody any good. We have murders to solve. We have an assailant on the loose. We don't know his motivation, and while we can guess, we can't know his next target."

Jacob rubbed his head. "If any of you have an issue with the FBI or with how this case has been handled, you are welcome to bring it to me privately. But we will not hash it out here, and we certainly will not hold Agent Malone responsible for things other people have done. Is that clear?"

All five agents, four Secret Service and one FBI, said, "Yes, sir."

Then Gil mock whispered, "Hear! Hear!" and a chuckle rippled around the table, and while Faith didn't join in, she did at least look like she wasn't carrying the weight of all of their trauma anymore.

Jacob cracked a smile, then nodded at Faith. "Please bring us up to speed."

Faith told them about her conversation with Sabrina, her suspicions about David Lee, and her concerns about Mi Cha's father, who still hadn't been located. As she was wrapping up, the iPad in front of her rang. "Perfect timing." Faith tapped a button on the screen, and Sabrina Campbell's face filled it. Faith set her iPad on a small tripod so they could all see Sabrina. While she worked, Luke couldn't shake the sensation that something was wrong. Sabrina was sitting at a desk and wore a Green Lantern T-shirt. Her glasses were sliding down her nose, and her hair was pulled away from her face in a haphazard fashion. She looked every bit the computer geek she was and pretty much the same way she'd looked the few times Luke had seen her in person, so it took Luke a few seconds to figure out what it was about her that was bothering him.

Sabrina was afraid.

"Faith. Hello. Who else am I speaking with?" Sabrina scanned the room. "Luke. How are you?"

"Fine. You?"

She didn't answer. Faith picked up the conversation. "Sabrina, I have the assistant resident agent in charge, Jacob Turner, as well as Special Agents Gil Dixon." Gil waved. "Zane Thacker." Zane gave her a small salute. "And Tessa Reed." Tessa smiled.

"Is everyone up to speed? Because we don't have time for backtracking."

Faith frowned. "Yes, they're up to speed. What have you found?"

"I wish I could present this to you in person. I have some slides I can email when we're finished. I won't get into the details of how I have this information, but it has all been legally obtained and can be used as evidence, should that be required."

Jacob seemed to appreciate Sabrina's thoroughness, but Luke didn't care anymore. He wanted this person caught, and he had a feeling that whenever they caught up to him, he wouldn't be interested in coming quietly.

Sabrina had barely paused for breath. "You were right about David Lee. He is most definitely not an accountant, and he's not American. I don't have anything conclusive to tell me where he was before July of last year, but I have confirmation that he was in Seoul in July. Then he showed up in the States in August."

"How did he get into the country?" Gil asked.

"No idea. What I do know is that David Lee was in the South Korean special forces."

"No offense intended, Dr. Campbell, but how high is your certainty on this?" Jacob asked.

"None taken, but it's one hundred percent. The tattoo was helpful, and I was able to pull one photo from Mi Cha's cloud storage. Combined with the information Mrs. Lin gave to Agent Malone, I'm confident this is the same guy."

"Is he active military?"

"No. And he's older than we suspected. He's thirty-nine. I've updated the local Raleigh officers with the information that this man is highly dangerous. I know you need him taken alive, but the officers going after him need to know that capturing him could be a deadly proposition."

Luke couldn't shake the knowledge that, in this moment, Sabrina wasn't talking as a professor or a consultant. She was talking as the wife of a sheriff's investigator. She wouldn't want anyone risking her husband's life, and she wasn't going to let anyone else's spouse face an unknown threat if she could help it.

"I cannot place David Lee at the initial bombing or at any of the attacks from this week. I'm still waiting on contact from my source in Seoul regarding Mi Cha's father. But we definitely need to find David Lee." She took off her glasses. "Are there any questions?"

So many, but none Sabrina could answer. When no one responded in the affirmative, she said, "Then I have nothing further at this time, and I need to get back to work. I'll be in touch. Please stay safe."

The video chat ended.

"Is she for real?" Tessa asked. It wasn't snarky. More admiring.

"Definitely for real. Okay, let's make a time line." Faith looked around the whiteboard. "Where do you guys hide the markers?"

Luke stood and reached into a drawer in the credenza behind him. "Marty makes us clean up after ourselves. We're well trained." There was a general murmur of agreement. "Want me to scribe?"

"Sure." Faith sat back in the chair and waited until Luke was ready at the whiteboard. "Okay. David Lee was in South Korea in July and in Raleigh in August. We need to find out from Ivy Collins when Mi Cha was awarded this internship. It may not matter, but I'd like to know when she started planning her stay in the States."

"I'll do that," Gil said.

"Great. We know Mi Cha had booked her room with Mrs. Lin at least a month before she arrived in Raleigh. And we know David Lee was in Raleigh in August, but he didn't stay with Mrs. Lin."

Luke drew a horizontal line across the board and then a hash mark labeled July. Under it he wrote down Faith's observations. Then he did the same for August.

Faith waited until he had everything recorded before she continued. "We know that Mi Cha began her internship in September. Ivy Collins told us she allows the interns to take time off to visit different parts of the country, but the only time Mi Cha took advantage of the opportunity was to visit a family friend in Seattle. According to Mrs. Lin, David Lee went with her in late October."

"Do we know who this friend of the family is? Maybe he could give us some insights into finding Mr. Park." Zane tapped the edge of the table. "I have a buddy in the Seattle office. I can have him look into it."

"That sounds great."

Zane scooted his chair back. "I'm going to get my laptop."

"Good idea." Gil pushed his chair back as well.

Tessa jumped to her feet. She held out one hand in Gil's direction and pressed the other down on Zane's shoulder. "Let me. I'll get all of them."

The fact that neither Zane nor Gil argued with Tessa told Luke how much both of them were sacrificing to be here. Not that any of them had a choice anymore. They had to find David Lee first—or wait for him to find them.

Tessa returned two minutes later with four laptops and a Cherry Coke. "You're an angel." Faith took the offered Cherry Coke and twisted the lid off. She took several sips as everyone powered up their computers.

"Where'd the Cherry Coke come from?" Gil asked.

Tessa grinned. "Leslie stocked the fridge last week. She said if Faith was going to be around so much, she needed to have her favorite on hand."

Faith put a hand on her chest. "She's so sweet. I'll thank her tomorrow." Faith's expression clouded, and Luke knew what she was thinking. Would there be a tomorrow? How much longer would this case take?

Zane and Gil typed away but gestured for Faith to continue.

"We aren't sure when Mi Cha reached out to Thad, but there's reason to believe they met more than once. I'm basing this on Mrs. Lin's comment that she'd covered for Mi Cha several times."

"What are we thinking about this David Lee?" Tessa asked. "Was Mi Cha clueless and had no idea that he wasn't an accountant? And what are we thinking about his role in her death? Are we saying he saw it all go down and he's been in hiding? And maybe now that we know who she is, he's . . . what? Trying to kill all of us? What would be the point? And do we have any proof that he's the one attacking us?"

Luke could not write fast enough to keep up with Tessa's questions.

"I hate this guy," Tessa said.

"Join the club," Gil said.

When Luke thought he'd captured the essence of Tessa's questions, he stepped back from the whiteboard. "I know it doesn't look like it, but we're much farther along than we were this morning."

Faith dropped her head to the table. "You're right. It doesn't look like it." Her words were muffled, but her frustration was clear. She straightened and looked at Tessa. "I hate him too."

They brainstormed for the next two hours. Somewhere along the way, Jacob must have messaged Marty, because around seven she walked in with two huge insulated baskets. "You people need to eat. Don't you understand that?"

She pulled out an assortment of takeout containers and set them on the table. "You can't heal when you're running on sugar and caffeine." Luke recognized his favorite Thai food, a few dishes from Gil and Tessa's favorite Indian restaurant, and what looked like a dozen tacos from Zane's favorite taqueria. "And that goes for you too, young lady." She cast a knowing look at Faith. "Have you eaten anything today?"

Faith flushed. "I've been busy."

Marty handed her a paper plate and a plastic fork. "Y'all can't get by without me. Don't forget it. Now, eat."

There was enough for everyone and then some. Once everyone had food on their plates, a mishmash sure to destroy their gastrointestinal systems, they resumed their conversation. There was only one new bit of information the entire time. Mrs. Lin answered Faith's call, and she did have a name for the family friend in Seattle, so Zane passed it on to the agent he'd emailed earlier.

After that, they kept circling. Every time, they landed back in the same spot. They still didn't know whether Thad or Mi Cha had been the target. And they still had no motive for anyone to come after them.

They needed a break in the case before someone else was killed.

— 30 —

FAITH HAD LOST track of time. Was it still Sunday? Had it been only one week since she'd gotten this case?

The faces around this table had become dear to her. One in particular.

Lord, is this why you brought him into my life? To help me see my own issues through his? Is it possible we can merge our messes and somehow come out better for it on the other side? Faith picked up another taco. She was two bites in when Zane's phone rang.

Everyone stopped talking, stopped eating, and openly stared as he answered it.

"Thacker." He listened for a moment. Then he started typing furiously. "No way. What?" More typing. "Who do you know at ATF out there?" More nodding. "Perfect." Zane sat back in his chair. "You're sure? This week? Okay. Yeah. Man, I owe you. Maybe my life. Literally. Holler at me tomorrow when the ME's done. Yeah. Will do. Thanks."

Zane set the phone on the table and shook his head. Whatever that call had been about, it had shocked him. Faith wanted to respect his need to process and then share, but if he didn't hurry up—

"Spit it out, man. We're dying over here." Luke was sitting to Faith's right, and she gave him a grateful smile.

"That was my buddy in Seattle. He got my message, grabbed an investigator friend from the sheriff's office, and went to pay Mi Cha's friend a visit. Found him dead. Their coroner estimates the time of death was sometime on Friday."

"A nice, natural death?" Gil clearly didn't expect the answer to be yes.

"Not even close. Evidence of torture." Everyone around the table winced. "When they cleared the house, they found a workshop—but not your regular woodworking workshop. This was a bomb-making workshop."

There was a collective intake of breath.

"And?" Faith prompted.

"My buddy has a friend at ATF. They're already on scene. He was able to tell the ATF team about the possible connection to our case. I wouldn't be surprised if we hear from them soon. They're already checking to see if they can find matching components to the bomb that killed Thad and Mi Cha, assuming it was her, the bomb that killed Jared, and the bombs on our cars. He said we could have preliminary results as early as this week."

Faith wanted to scream. As early as this week. If they were very, very lucky. Next week, or even next month, was more likely. She understood protocols and methods and how crucial it was for labs to follow their procedures, but they didn't have time for this.

"He did have one specific piece of information though."

"You're killing us slowly, man." Luke glared at Zane.

"I'm waiting for the email."

"You could give us a hint?" Tessa asked the question so sweetly that if you only heard her say it, you would think she was the gentlest creature in the world. But if you saw her face as Faith did, you would be afraid. There was some next-level crazy lurking under there, and based on the way Zane's hands lifted in a pacifying motion, Faith suspected he knew exactly how bad it could get.

"Hang on." Zane widened his eyes at Tessa. "It's coming."

Tessa leaned toward Faith and whispered loud enough for everyone to hear. "I'm going to kill him myself if this lasts much longer."

Zane crowed with delight—or was it relief?—when an image filled his screen. "I've seen that before."

Everyone stood and crowded around Zane's laptop. It was a bomb. Faith knew that much.

"So have I." Luke's confirmation came with a slight shudder that Faith doubted anyone but she had noticed.

"What's special about it?" Jacob removed his glasses and focused his attention on Luke and Zane.

"That's the bomb that was under Zane's car." Luke spoke with certainty.

"How do you know?" Jacob pushed back. "It looks like a block of C-4 with some wires."

"Yes, but it looks exactly like the one under the car. And this"—Luke pointed to a spot on the screen that showed a particularly nasty mass of wires—"is what convinced me that we had to move away from the car as fast as we could."

Gil reached around Zane and zoomed in on the wires. "What kind of wacky bomb is this? I thought most bomb makers were meticulous. How could you ever know which one—"

"Exactly." Zane agreed. "I think that's the point. There was no stopping it once it was set. Luke made the right call to drag us to the center of the space between the cars. It was the farthest we could get from either bomb."

"I can't pretend I was thinking that logistically," Luke said. "I was just reacting."

"But you reacted in the right direction, and you're both alive."

Tessa was standing behind Zane's chair, knuckles white from the grip she had on it.

One by one, people returned to their seats.

Gil was the first to speak. "If this is the guy Mi Cha went to see in Seattle—"

"Mi Cha *and* David Lee," Luke said.

"Yes, but that's my point. If the same bomb that blew up your cars is in this bomb maker's shop in Seattle, and we know David Lee was out there, then is it possible he killed Thad?"

"But why would he have risked killing Mi Cha?" Luke's frown made it clear that he wasn't convinced.

"He wouldn't have. He would have been targeting Thad. He wouldn't have known she would get in the car with him. Remember what Mrs. Lin told y'all? Mi Cha had shipped all her belongings and was flying home that night? All she had was a backpack and a purse, and she was going to Uber to the airport. I'd bet anything Thad offered to drive her. He might have even been planning to run by the house and introduce her to Rose. But if Mi Cha kept all the details about Thad from David Lee, then David Lee never could have anticipated that she would get in Thad's car."

"Okay, fine. Let's say, hypothetically, that David Lee blew up the car that Thad and Mi Cha were in. That he got the bomb when they flew out to Seattle. Although that doesn't explain how he got the thing home without her noticing, but we'll come back to that." Luke paced in front of the board as he talked. "If he killed her, why is he still here? Why didn't he get out of the country? We had nothing on him. In the first few hours after the explosion, we didn't even know there was another person in the car, much less who she was. This could have been the perfect crime."

Luke wrote, "Why is David Lee here?" on the board. If they could answer that, maybe they could get a handle on what was going on.

"Okay, but what does any of this have to do with who shot you?" Tessa held up a hand as Luke, Zane, and Gil all turned confused eyes in her direction. "I get the connection, but I don't get why. If this guy didn't like Thad, fine. But what did y'all ever do to him? You didn't know Mi Cha existed until he killed her." Tessa turned her attention to Faith. "And I don't understand why he would go after Janice."

"I do," Gil muttered.

Tessa ignored him. "What purpose does it serve to go after her other than to put him right back on our radar. We thought he was in DC. He shows up here and tries to kill the agent who . . ." She frowned at the table. "What if that's it?"

"Not following you, Tess." Zane said it more like a question than a dig.

"Okay, David Lee hooks up with Mi Cha and goes on this trip to Seattle with her. Comes home with a bomb. Blows her up. Goes dark. Maybe he kills the one buddy who could have talked to Janice about him. For all we know, Mrs. Lin might be in danger. She knew enough about him to tell us who he was and what was up with him and Mi Cha."

Faith kept listening, but she fired off a text to Hope.

LOCK EVERYTHING DOWN. STAY ALERT.

Warn Mrs. Lin. I may be overreacting, but
better safe than sorry.

Tessa was still talking. "Maybe we know something about the case we don't realize we know. And now David Lee is trying to kill off anyone who could connect him to Mi Cha and her death."

"That might have worked when it was just Mi Cha and Janice and his buddy." Zane looked around the room. "Now that we have the case, that ship has sailed. He can't kill every single Secret Service and FBI agent in the country. It doesn't make sense for him to try. We're missing something."

Frustration floated in the air like a contagion, infecting the mind and discouraging the heart. Faith could sense it pressing in on her, tempting her to give in. But she wouldn't. She couldn't. Not if she wanted to keep everyone alive.

"You're right." She stood. "It doesn't make sense, and there must be something we're missing, but we can't give up. Whatever is going on, you've survived an onslaught and you're going to continue to survive. This situation with the bomb maker is huge. It may finally give us the focus we need. We'll find David Lee, and when we find him, we will find out why he's done what he's done."

They wrapped up the meeting with plans to reconvene on Monday morning. Marty, bless her heart, had gone to her desk to work on some paperwork. Jacob checked her car before she drove away. When he returned to the building, he made it clear that no one was allowed to leave until he had their word they would check in when they were safe at their respective homes, or in the case of the Secret Service agents, a different hotel from the one they had been in the last several nights. All their belongings had been packed and moved to a new location while they were at the funeral.

"I think we should take separate cars," Gil said. "More targets. Better chance of survival."

"Wow. Getting shot in the head has turned you into a regular Pollyanna." Luke put the caps on all the dry-erase markers and tucked them in their drawer.

"I'm not wrong." Gil wasn't backing down. "While I respect that we have a limited number of agents and officers who can provide security, I'm not convinced we all need to be in the same location tonight."

"We didn't even know we were being moved until we got in the air," Zane said. "It will be fine for tonight, but I agree that if this drags on, we need to consider splitting up. And I agree that for now, let's call separate cars. Even if we're followed, he can't follow all of us."

Faith stood to the side as they all ordered a pickup. Two from Lyft, two from Uber. She should leave. This wasn't her office, and they were done for the night. But she couldn't imagine leaving anyone here alone.

The fact that Jacob wasn't leaving yet did make her reasoning a bit weak, but it was better than admitting to herself that she didn't want to leave until Luke did.

Zane and Gil had cars arriving in six minutes. Tessa in eight. Luke held his phone in the air to show her the app. "Twelve minutes. It's like my luck at the grocery store. I'm always in the longest line."

None of them had much to say. What could they say? "Hey, I hope you don't die tonight?" It was true, but it didn't instill hope into the situation.

When Luke was the last one waiting, he and Jacob checked Jacob's and Faith's cars for explosives. "I'm going to dream about that stupid bomb," Luke told her as he walked around her trunk.

Faith didn't think he was joking, and she wished she could do something to make it better. She had never been personally targeted. At least, not that she knew of. What would it be like to be staring at a bomb and knowing your only choice was to run into the open, dragging your friend, risking being killed by the concussive force of the bomb or the debris that rained down after it but knowing you were also risking being shot? It was a no-win situation.

But Luke had won.

Faith didn't know if she would be so lucky.

—31—

LUKE'S DRIVER pulled into the circular portion of the parking lot and waited. Faith's car was clear. Jacob's car was clear.

It was time to go, but he couldn't make himself leave Faith. He wanted to be sure she was okay. She didn't need him to, but he wanted to. He couldn't invite himself to her house for the night, but there was another option. "Come with us." The words were out of his mouth before he could stop them. "Stay at the hotel. Lots of security there. You'll sleep great."

"I'll sleep great in my own bed."

He knew he'd lost the battle. She was determined, and there was no point in making her as paranoid as he was. "Will you text me when you get home?" He tried to speak in a casual way, as if her answer didn't matter to him one way or the other. He failed. There was a hint of desperation in his voice, and he knew she'd picked up on it when she frowned and cocked her head to one side.

"Worried about me?" Her voice was light and friendly, but her eyes told a different story. If she kept looking at him that way, he was going to be in big trouble.

"Yes." There was no point in lying. "I know now isn't the time . . ."

Their eyes caught. Held. Had she moved closer to him?

"Luke . . ."

"Okay, see, that, right there. If you keep saying my name like that, then I'm going to—" He caught himself.

Her eyes widened in surprise but not anger. What was happening? Were they making up? Was she messing with him? He had no idea.

The driver honked the horn, and Faith waved Luke away. "Go. Text me when you get to where you're going."

He winked. "Yes, ma'am."

Three minutes later, he sent a text.

> I'm in the car. I will get where I'm going before you do. Why don't you call me in about ten minutes?

Her response was a bit too immediate for his taste. He wasn't doing anything reckless. She, however, shouldn't be texting and driving. It was dangerous.

> Sure.

At least it was just one word. She might have voice-to-text. Or she might have been at a red light.

Or he might be losing his mind stressing over whether Faith was texting while driving. What had happened to him? He wasn't a schoolboy hoping his crush would smile at him at lunch.

He was a federal agent.

So was she.

They were grown-ups doing grown-up work in a grown-up world. They knew how evil the world was, and they didn't hide from it. They ran straight for it. And notions of love and meeting

288

someone who could make you rethink your entire life plan were ridiculous.

He wasn't that guy. He should think about the case. David Lee. The dead bomb maker in Seattle. The dead guy in the Raleigh boardinghouse. They were connected. They had to be. And they were. To Mi Cha.

Had she been as innocent as they'd all assumed?

Could she have been up to something? Where Janice had been too quick to jump to conclusions, was it possible they hadn't been quick enough? She had claimed to be South Korean, but North Korea was known to have spies in the US. Her mother was dead, her father missing. What if they'd never existed to begin with?

He ran his good hand through his hair. His other arm wasn't as sore as it had been, and tomorrow he would see the doctor and be cleared to go back to his normal life.

Tomorrow was Monday, but there would be no morning run. *Sorry, Thad.*

The Uber driver hadn't been chatty, and Luke had been so busy trying not to think about Faith and to think about the case that he didn't notice that they'd arrived at the hotel until the Uber driver slammed the car into park and turned around.

"You okay, man?" The driver wasn't much younger than himself, but his face had a look of innocence that Luke envied.

"Yeah. Sorry. Wasn't paying attention." He was now though. Every nerve ending pinged. "Thanks." *I hope you don't see me get killed in the next thirty seconds.*

He did the best impersonation of a dash that his still-aching legs could manage and hit the revolving door with a gasp that was a combination of exhaustion and relief. He didn't acknowledge the uniformed Raleigh PD officer who fell into step with him and joined him on the elevator. Luke pressed the button for the fourteenth floor, then settled himself in the corner.

The police officer stood in front of him in a way that would be weird under normal circumstances. As it was, Luke appreciated the man's bulk as the doors opened on four different floors, with people entering and exiting each time. He was sweating by the time he got off on the fourteenth. The officer remained at the elevator.

"Am I the last one back?"

"Yes, sir."

"Thank you."

"Anytime."

Zane poked his head into the hall and blew out a breath in undisguised relief when he saw Luke. "Any trouble?"

"No." Luke entered the room, and Zane locked the door behind them. "You?"

"Nothing." Zane scooped ice from a bucket and filled a glass.

"Where's Gil?" Luke scanned the room.

"In his room. He's next door, but there's no connecting door. Our room connects to Tessa's like it did at the other place."

"Is Gil okay?"

"Sore and tired. Said he'd see us in the morning." Zane held the glass and stared at nothing. "It's weird. I know David Lee is out there. The waiting for him to attack is driving me bonkers."

"Seriously." Tessa spoke from the opposite corner of the room, and there was no humor in her remark.

"Drop it, Tess." Zane poured half a bottle of water into the small glass and took a long drink. Tessa stalked around them, through the adjoining door, and into her own space.

"You're going to have to explain that." Luke slipped off his shoes and scanned the room. It was much larger than where they'd been and had nicer amenities.

Zane poured the rest of the bottle into the glass and swirled it around. "Later."

"Keeping everything inside isn't healthy." Luke eyed his friend. "It's been a bad week all around, but you've taken the worst of it. It's okay to be—"

"To be what?" Zane slammed the glass on the counter. "Just because my life is a Dumpster fire doesn't mean I've lost my ability to do my job, and it doesn't mean I've turned into someone who can't distinguish the truth from a lie."

Luke didn't have to wonder who that last part had been for. Zane had practically yelled it at the door to Tessa's room. There was no response.

Zane rolled his head to the left, then the right. "I don't want to talk about it. Do you need the bathroom? I'm going to take a shower."

Luke waved him away.

Zane grabbed a small bag and stomped into the bathroom. Moments later the shower came on and seconds after that there was a soft knock on the adjoining door.

Luke opened it and Tessa jumped back, relaxing when she made eye contact with Luke. "I left my charger in your room."

Luke stepped back and she came through. "Tessa?"

"Hmm?" As if she didn't know what he wanted to know.

"Tessa." This time her name wasn't so much a question as a demand for information.

"Not case related. Nothing to worry about."

How little she knew about him. "I worry about my friends, and Zane is a friend. So are you. It may not be case related, but I don't believe there's nothing to worry about."

She unplugged the charger from the wall, turned, and walked back into her room as if she hadn't heard a word he'd said. "Good night." The door closed.

He stared at it in surprise. How could she? But before he could bang on the door and tell her off, the phone rang. He didn't bother with hello. "Faith."

"You know, if you keep saying my name like that . . ." Faith laughed in a low, throaty way that left Luke unprepared for what came next. "I might decide I like it."

And that left him without the ability to form coherent words.

"You still there?"

"Trying to breathe. You?"

She laughed again. If Luke didn't know better, he'd wonder if she'd been drinking. "I'm so tired, Luke. And I'm scared. I'm scared you're going to get killed, and I can't stay mad at you—and that scares me too."

"I'm scared too." And he was. Although there wasn't another soul in the universe he would admit it to. "I have a lot to live for, and I'd like to find out what that looks like."

Silence. Too much too soon? It had hardly been an ardent expression of love and devotion. But he did mean it.

"I don't know what that looks like either," Faith said.

"We'll figure it out as we go."

"But I like plans." Faith yawned as she spoke, but Luke thought he heard an undercurrent of teasing in her words.

"You could plan to see where it goes. Right?" *Please say right.*

"Yeah. I could plan to do that." There was a softness in the admission. A sweetness he doubted many people knew she was capable of.

"Are you at home?"

"I am." Another yawn.

"Did you clear your house?"

"Yes."

"Anything seem weird?"

"No."

Luke doubted she would have noticed if it was. She was about to fall asleep on the phone. "I'll call you in the morning and we'll . . ." He had no idea what they would do. But they would figure it out.

"Yeah." She got it. "Good night."

"'Night."

—32—

FAITH WASN'T SURE what had woken her. She slid her hand under the covers—slowly, silently—toward the gun under the pillow to her left.

It wasn't there.

She lay still, eyes closed, wide awake. Had she put it there? She'd been completely exhausted by the time she got home. But not too tired to remember to put a gun under the pillow when there was so much at stake.

"I'm not planning to hurt you, Agent Malone." The voice was soft. Spoken in a tone chosen carefully not to frighten her.

As if stealing into her bedroom, getting her gun, and then, based on the sound, hovering between her bed and the door wasn't terrifying. *Lord, I don't want to die. Help me. Please.*

There was still so much to do. So much life to live.

So many people to love. One in particular.

"I hear you're looking for me, and I need to set the record straight." The voice hadn't moved closer, but that brought no comfort.

Her eyes were wide now, and she was desperate for them to acclimate to the darkness and give her some hint of who her visitor was. It had to be either David Lee or the mysterious Tiger. Unless it was someone else entirely. "I would have been happy to chat in the office." Faith tried to keep her voice as calm and soft as his, as if they were both trying not to wake a sleeping baby.

"Well, your office isn't known for being an ideal location for people like me."

"And why is that?"

"You law-enforcement types get all antsy and jumpy. It's not like I'm walking around with a dirty bomb in my pocket."

A dirty bomb? A fresh horror chilled Faith, and she couldn't stop the shiver that rippled through her and rattled the bed frame against the wall. Had he killed the bomb maker? What other kinds of bombs had been in that workshop?

"It was a joke, Agent Malone. I'm not the one trying to kill the Secret Service agents."

She wasn't so sure about that, but she'd play along. "Then who is?"

"An injured party."

"What kind of injury?"

"The kind you need revenge to heal from."

"Mi Cha." In some way, everything came back to Mi Cha.

"And now we've come to it." The voice was closer and softer.

Faith took a breath and blew it out, slow and steady. *Think.* If he lunged at her now, he could trap her under the covers and suffocate her with her own pillow. Or he could shoot her in the head. Either way, she couldn't do much to protect herself.

She had to stay alert for any quick movement. "Do you mind if I sit up?" She didn't wait for him to answer. If he came for her, at least her arms would be free and she could fight back. She scooted herself into a seated position.

"Be my guest." He spoke in a courteous way. If there had been anyone to overhear their conversation, they never would have suspected he'd broken into her home and was holding her hostage in her own bedroom.

"Thanks." She crossed her legs and arranged the blankets off her knees in what she hoped appeared to be random movements. If he had night-vision goggles, then he could see every move she made.

Her phone was buried in the folds of the blankets. She'd fallen asleep with it on her chest between the sheet and the blanket, and now it was in front of her.

"I truly mean you no harm, Agent Malone. If he survives, that Agent Powell you got so friendly with in the parking lot would hunt me down. I'd rather not go to the trouble of killing him."

Her intruder had been watching them? How? No one could have seen them in the car. Not in that rain. How could he know? No one knew. Well, Hope knew.

Faith played with the blankets and the folds, hoping he assumed she was nervous and this was her way of dealing with the stress. If he knew she was repeatedly pressing the power button on her phone, then she was in big trouble.

"You keep saying you don't intend to harm me, but following me around, eavesdropping, and breaking into my house in the middle of the night? These things don't give me a feeling of comfort and security."

He laughed. "You're just embarrassed because you got caught making out in a parking lot like a teenager. Don't worry. I didn't see anything. Just put two and two together." He chuckled again. "You make a nice couple." He spoke in a conciliatory tone. "I'm sure you'll be very happy together and make very pretty babies. If he lives."

"You've mentioned that twice now. If you aren't here to kill me, and if you aren't trying to kill the Secret Service agents, then why are we having this lovely chat? If you wanted to leave a tip, we have a tip line. And my guess is you have my phone number. You could have sent a text."

He laughed again. "I do like you, Agent Malone. I do."

"Why don't you tell me your name?"

"You haven't guessed?"

"Guessing isn't a wise move in my line of work."

"Come on. Humor me."

"Fine. But I should tell you, David, you're getting on my nerves."

LUKE HAD NO IDEA how he'd come to be standing beside his bed, weapon in hand and pointing toward the door. But in the dim light sneaking through the heavy curtains, he could see Zane in the same position.

A knock, no, a pound on the door drew him to full attention. "Agents." Someone from the security detail outside yelled through the door. "Wake up. We have a situation."

"We're awake!" Zane yelled. "What's going on?"

"Check your phones, then come out."

"You check," Luke said to Zane. "I'll stay where I am."

Zane didn't turn on any lights, but Luke could hear him running his hands over his bed and pillows. "Got it." The light from the screen illuminated Zane's face, and Luke alternated between keeping his eyes on the door and stealing glances at Zane.

"No." Zane whispered the word.

"What is it?"

"Put the gun down and get dressed." Zane flipped on the lamp. "It's Faith."

DAVID LAUGHED again. A long chortle. If Faith survived, she'd be hearing that laugh in her nightmares. No doubt.

"Ah, Faith. I assume it's okay for me to call you Faith since we went straight to first names? I knew you knew it was me. But I'm curious. Who else might it have been?"

"I'm only actively hunting two people right now, David. You and the man they're calling the Tiger."

"Who says I'm not the Tiger?"

"I never said you weren't. Why did you kill the bomb maker?"

"Excuse me?"

"They told me a couple of the techs puked at the scene. It wasn't nice, what you did to him. Especially after he gave you all those lovely bombs for blowing up Luke and Zane and Jared." She was winging it. Poking the bear. Shooting, literally, in the dark.

"You've got it all wrong."

"So the Tiger did it?"

"No."

Was it possible that David Lee was the Tiger? Maybe he had some kind of personality disorder. Faith had dealt with some messed-up minds over the years, but she didn't know much about split personalities.

"He was found dead yesterday by a United States Secret Service agent and a Seattle sheriff's office investigator. There was evidence of torture. The body is going to be autopsied today. The bomb-making shop has been turned over to the ATF, and they're doing their own investigation into the types of explosives present. We'll know soon if there's a match. But there was one in the workshop, and it had a unique signature."

Why was she telling him this? She didn't know, but the compulsion was strong. Maybe the Lord *was* helping her and giving her the words? She pressed on. "Luke and Zane recognized it. Same kind of bomb was used to try to kill them on Monday. We're also checking to see if this is the same type of explosive that was used to kill Special Agent Baker. And Mi Cha, of course."

David Lee didn't respond.

"We know there's a connection, and we'll find it. And if you kill me now, you're right—someone will hunt you down. Even if you're innocent of killing Thad and Mi Cha, I doubt anyone would believe it. You'll need a good lawyer."

She was rambling now. Buying time. She had no idea if her phone had done what it was supposed to do. She continued to press the power button multiple times whenever she could do it in a way that seemed natural. And she continued to listen. When nothing but the silence and darkness filled her ears, she continued to ramble. "The thing I can't figure out is why you attacked Agent Estes."

"What?" The word ripped from his mouth.

She'd surprised him. Interesting. "I know you know who Agent Estes is. Going after her the way you did? I don't get it. I mean, she's not my favorite person either, but she's the connection I can't make sense of."

"I didn't attack Agent Estes."

That split-personality theory was starting to make sense now. "She saw you."

"She's lying."

"Why would she do that?"

"It wasn't me."

"So you've said, but she saw your tattoo. Not many people running around this corner of North Carolina with that kind of ink, David. You should have considered that."

"I'm not the only one with that type of tattoo. She didn't see me. I wasn't there."

"Then who did she see?"

"The one you need to look out for."

"The Tiger?"

"That's such a stupid name." Exasperation and disgust and frustration and fear were mingled in the words.

Faith still wasn't sure if they were talking about two different people or two manifestations of one very messed-up mind. "If it wasn't you who killed the bomb maker, and if it wasn't you who attacked Agent Estes, and it wasn't you who is trying to kill all the agents, then why are you here?"

"I'm not your guy. You need to look elsewhere. You'll never find me, and searching for me is wasting your time. Time, I might add, that you have precious little of."

She didn't believe this was his reasoning. "No one sneaks into an FBI agent's bedroom just to tell her he's innocent. You did this to prove a point."

He laughed again, this time with an edge of appreciation for her remark. "You're right, Faith. I knew you were smart, but I didn't expect you to be quite so perceptive. I've enjoyed our little chat, but it's time for me to head out, and I want to leave you with a final word of warning."

She waited. Ears straining for sirens. *Come on. Somebody.*

LUKE PLACED HIS WEAPON on the bed and grabbed his phone. Zane had already pulled on a pair of pants and pushed the door between their room and Tessa's open. He stayed back and called out, "Tess? Don't shoot anybody. Get up. We have a situation."

"I'm up," Tessa replied immediately, her voice strained. "Call Gil and see if he's awake."

"On it."

Luke was aware of everything happening, but at the same time he was scanning the message on his phone in disbelief. The text had come from Jacob.

> Got a call from Dale. There was an emergency call from Faith Malone's home. Details are slim. FBI on scene. I'm not going to tell you not to go to her house, but proceed with caution and make contact with the FBI before you get there. I'm headed there now.

Luke read the message twice, then threw the phone on the bed and grabbed his clothes. Two minutes in the bathroom and he emerged dressed and ready to . . . what? Whatever had to be done to get Faith back. He didn't care what happened after that.

Gil, Zane, and Tessa stood in a tight bunch in the corner of the room. All of them were dressed and armed. Like him, no one had bothered with the niceties. Gil's black hair had so many spikes, he looked like he could be trying out for a punk rock band. Zane's hair looked like a gerbil had nested in the back. And Tessa was . . . Tessa was a mess. Her long hair hung loose and wild down her back and kept falling into her eyes. She shoved a strand behind her ear, and when she looked at Luke, he saw his own terror mirrored back at him.

"I think we should pray." Tessa was terrified, but there was a strength in her words he hadn't expected.

Gil huffed. "Tessa, we don't have much time—"

"We don't have time to argue." She glared at Gil as she stretched out her hands.

Zane took one, and Gil grudgingly took the other. "Get in here, Powell. Prayer meeting time."

Luke joined them, grasping Gil's and Zane's hands.

"Jesus. Help us. Help Faith. Give her courage. Amen." Tessa

whispered the words, and when she said amen, they all echoed with their own amens.

"I liked that prayer meeting," Gil said as he checked his weapon. "Short. To the point."

"God doesn't need long, drawn-out prayers," Zane said. "Most of the time they're for the listeners, not God." He smiled at Tessa. It wasn't hostile. It was . . . sad.

The sight of it twisted something in Luke. His friend was hurting, but it would have to wait. "Let's go."

The same officer who'd come up with him last night stood at the elevator and joined them in the descent. "Does anyone have keys?" Gil asked.

Zane's and Luke's cars had been blown up a week ago. Gil's car was still parked at his house. Tessa reached into her pocket and removed a set of keys.

"You have keys. But do you have a car?" Gil asked. "You came straight here from the office like the rest of us."

"True." Tessa jingled the keys in Gil's direction. "But unlike the rest of you, I didn't like the idea of being here without my own wheels and asked one of the officers to bring my car over last night."

The officer in the elevator gave Tessa a fist bump. "Well played, Agent Reed. Your car is at the curb. There's an officer waiting for you."

"Thanks, Freddie. If we don't see you later, you've been great." She patted his arm and led the way off the elevator, with Zane, Gil, and Luke close on her heels.

DAVID LEE TOOK a step closer. "You're aware of your surroundings and trained to fight back." He took another step, and his voice lowered to a whisper. "And I got to you. I could have killed you as you slept. So, I know you'll believe me when I tell you that your sister—"

"Don't you dare touch my sister." Faith jumped to her knees as she spoke but froze when the tip of the barrel of a gun scraped none too gently down her temple.

His left hand twisted in her hair as he leaned close and whispered in her ear. "It's up to you, Faith. Hope is a beautiful woman. So full of vitality and joy, despite her condition. I'd hate to see that beautiful skin in shreds on those stunning cheekbones."

Bile churned in Faith's gut. She trembled—not out of fear but out of rage.

David's hand tightened in her hair and yanked her head back. "You are in charge of this investigation. Look for your Tiger"—he sneered the word—"and leave me out of it. Do you understand?"

When she didn't answer, he jammed the gun into the base of her skull. Tears leaked from her eyes and pain shot through her head as the gun pressed hard against her occipital bone.

"Do you understand?"

"Yes."

His hand traced across her back and arm before he stepped away, then he removed the gun. "You're quite a beautiful woman yourself. I'd love to stay and get to know you. But under the circumstances, let's never do this again, okay?" He laughed and turned for the door.

Faith blinked back the tears she'd had no control over, but otherwise remained still and silent.

Her eyes had adjusted, and she followed the darkness that was David Lee as he went through her door. She strained to hear his footfalls, but there was nothing. She pulled in a shaky breath, then bit back a scream as darkness filled the doorway.

"I forgot. In case you don't believe I'm capable of doing what I said, I've left a welcome gift for your friends. I hope they like it." This time, he left the room at a run, his laughter echoing back to her as he ran down the hall. Faith didn't wait to be sure he'd left the house. She scrambled to untangle her phone from the blankets.

She shifted the blankets and a low thud came from the floor on the other side of the bed. She scurried across the sheets, guided by the dim light from the screen, and snatched the phone.

She dialed 911. The dispatchers should be able to reach the—

An explosion shook the house, and outside her window a fireball rose into the sky.

—33—

TESSA FLOORED IT as Zane fed her directions. "Right at the next intersection. Left in two streets . . ."

From the back seat, Luke dialed Faith's number, but again and again it went straight to voice mail.

He slammed the phone on his leg. "She's not answering."

"We're almost there."

"But why isn't she answer—"

They came around a curve, and the back of the car shimmied as Tessa slammed the brakes and performed an impressive maneuver to keep them from careening into the row of police cars blocking them from going farther. A uniformed officer who looked like he should be getting ready for the prom, not manning a roadblock, approached. Tessa rolled down her window. "US Secret Service. We need to get in there. I'm reaching for my badge."

The officer took the badge and studied it. "How much do you want to bet he's never seen one of our badges?" Gil muttered.

"Just a minute," the officer said.

"We don't have a minute," Luke yelled from the back seat. "There's an FBI agent in trouble in that house, and we need to get through."

"I understand, sir."

"No, you don't!" Luke pulled on the door handle, but Gil grabbed his arm and Tessa hit the door locks before he could get the door open. "Let. Me. Out!"

Zane turned in the front seat. "We don't know what we're walking into."

"Exactly," Luke hissed back. "We don't know what's happening to Faith right now."

Gil elbowed him and showed Luke the phone. A text from Jacob.

Getting you cleared. Sit tight.

After an agonizing wait that felt like hours but was only minutes, the officer returned. "Sorry, agents." He pointed to a section of curb ten feet ahead. "Park there." Tessa did so, and they piled out of the car. The officer was still talking. "They told me not to let anyone through without authorization. Trying to keep from losing anybody else."

The words hit Luke like a kick to the sternum. He stumbled and put a hand on the car to catch his balance. Before he could pull in a breath, Gil and Zane were by his side. Tessa stood in front of him.

"Luke." Tessa's gentle voice frightened him more than the words from the officer because they meant Tessa thought Faith was gone, too.

He shoved away from the car. "I have to get over there."

"Okay." Tessa didn't move. "But we're going with you. I'll run interference." She cut her eyes toward Zane first, then Gil, then she turned and set a pace that had all three of them gasping.

"Should we remind her we all got shot this week?" Gil wheezed.

"Technically, it's Monday, and getting shot is so *last* week,"

Tessa said from ten feet ahead of them. But she did slow her steps. Slightly.

Luke scanned the area. Residential. Older homes. Large lots. He'd never been to Faith's house, but the police perimeter around it made it obvious to spot. Who was in charge? Where was Jacob? What was going on? And most importantly, where was Faith?

"There." Tessa pointed to the left. She had spotted the command center before any of the rest of them. Luke broke free from his escorts, and this time they let him go.

He found Jacob and Dale in conversation behind a series of vans. "Where's Faith?"

Both men looked at him, then each other.

No. This could not be happening.

FAITH NEVER WANTED to see anyone ever again.

She sat on the gurney in the ambulance. The paramedic had closed the doors to give them some privacy as she answered all his questions. No, she hadn't been physically assaulted. He'd pressed the barrel of the gun to her head. He'd pulled her hair. She had no other injuries. Nothing hurt except for a piercing headache.

She was not going to the hospital.

Forensics had taken samples from her skin, although she had no idea what good that would do. She knew what had happened. Knew who had done it. There was no mystery here.

She'd failed, and two people had died.

She'd been sure, cocky, and confident in her theory that she wasn't in danger. She should have stayed at the hotel. Shouldn't have believed she was beyond the reach of the terror stalking the Secret Service agents.

Now? Two officers would never go home.

End of watch.

Her fault.

"Are we done?" She tried to make the question sound like idle curiosity and not an agonized plea for release.

"I think so." The paramedic was older than she was, and he regarded her with a mixture of compassion and understanding. "But you're welcome to stay here as long as you'd—"

A pounding on the door startled both of them. "Faith? Faith? Are you in there?"

Luke!

"*Are* you in here?" the paramedic asked.

She appreciated the gesture. "He'll rip the door from the hinges to find out."

"Faith!"

"Partner or boyfriend?" The paramedic reached for the door. As soon as he unlatched it, the door flew open.

"Faith!"

Luke scrambled into the ambulance—eyes wild, frantic. "Are you—" He knelt before her, and his hands trembled as they reached for her face. His fingers were gentle and tentative as he tucked her hair behind her ear.

She should have cracked a joke about holes and how Gil wouldn't count a scratch as a real injury. But she couldn't.

His breathing was erratic and gasping as he scanned her face and body, obviously looking for bullet holes or knife wounds. When he spotted the scrape on her temple, his whispered "Oh, Faith" was the tipping point. She could pretend to be fine for everyone else, but it wasn't going to work with Luke. A few tears found their way between her clenched eyelids, and his thumbs wiped them away.

With a murmured "I'll give you two a minute," the paramedic slipped out of the ambulance.

When the door closed behind him, Faith lost her tenuous hold on her emotions. A sob tore from her throat, and she pressed her forehead against Luke's. "It's my fault."

"It isn't." His head moved back and forth across hers.

"Two officers died."

"You didn't kill them."

"I might as well have."

"No."

They sat there for a few moments, tears dripping from her face.

"Will you tell me what happened?" Luke whispered. It wasn't a demand. It was a plea for her to trust him with this.

And she did. At some point, her fingers and his got all twisted together, but other than that, he barely moved. It helped, not having to look at him. She stared at the top button of his polo shirt as she told him everything, even the part about how they would have beautiful babies, all the way to the point when her frantic call to 911 was interrupted by the explosion.

"They told me there was an IED in my driveway. The first car to respond—" She couldn't say it. She didn't have to. Luke knew what had happened. "I had to stay in the house while they brought the bomb dogs to clear the area. They wouldn't let me get off the phone. The entire time, all I could think about was who else would be blown up just so I could get out of my house."

LUKE SAT ON THE BENCH in the ambulance and couldn't free himself from the helplessness that held his heart and mind in a vise. *Lord, how do I help her?*

"I wish I'd been with you," he said. "I almost asked you if I could come here tonight."

"You did?"

"I should have trusted my gut."

"This isn't your fault," she said. "You tried to get me to come with you. This is all on me."

"It isn't. You didn't ask for this. David Lee is a twisted soul. He's convinced himself that some killings are justified while others aren't. He'll come into your bedroom—"

Luke had to stop for a second as the image Faith's words had painted settled into his mind. How much had she been through tonight? How much would she go through in the days ahead? Would she ever feel safe, anywhere, ever again?

He cleared his throat. "He'll come into your bedroom and make all sorts of threats, but he won't kill you because somehow in his twisted mind that would be wrong. But it isn't wrong to leave a bomb in your driveway designed to kill the occupants of the first car to pull in. That's sick—and not your fault."

"I shouldn't have called for help. He knew I would. He planned it."

"You did the right thing. It was brilliant. I didn't even know you could get a silent call out to 911 by pressing your power button over and over again."

"But—"

He pressed one finger to her lips, oh so gently. "I promise I will listen to you vent and worry and fret as much as you need in the days and weeks ahead, but I am never going to agree that you should have sat there and done nothing."

He twisted his hand to hold her face. "David Lee is evil. He's formidable. He's not opposed to going after innocents to get what he wants. And we didn't know anything much about him until when? Yesterday? Or the day before?" He couldn't remember. "The point is, he's been planning his attacks and schemes for weeks, maybe months. He's ahead of us, but now we know he's out there, and we know what he's capable of. We'll get him."

FAITH RESTED HER HEAD in Luke's hand. She wanted to believe him. Needed to believe him.

But she couldn't believe him. Not yet.

There was a soft tap at the door. Luke took his hand away from her face and put it on the weapon in the holster across his chest.

"Agent Malone?"

She knew the voice. "That's the paramedic," she whispered to Luke, ashamed that she didn't know his name.

"Enter." Luke spoke with authority, his left hand still holding hers, his right hand still on his weapon.

"My apologies, Agent Malone." The paramedic gave her a sly grin. "Are you okay?"

"Yes. Am I free to leave?"

He climbed in on the other side of the gurney, his eyes on Luke. "You seem to be in good hands, so I'll say yes. Don't hesitate to call your doctor if that headache won't ease up."

"Okay."

Luke climbed from the ambulance first, then offered his hand to her as she climbed down. When she was on the ground, he squeezed her hand. He gave her a little smirk when she held on a few seconds longer than necessary. He stayed by her side the rest of the night. Morning. Whatever it was. She didn't know anymore.

She answered questions and drank a Cherry Coke she suspected Luke had been responsible for procuring.

As the black sky began its slow fade into morning, she stood against a police car and watched Luke pace and talk and run his fingers through his hair as he followed up on the protective measures that were already being put into place for her family, and she tried to memorize his features while attempting not to imagine what her life would be like without him.

David Lee wouldn't disappear. Hope would be in danger. Her family would be in danger.

A cold realization filled her. David Lee had known that those officers' deaths would crush her—and that as she came to understand how devastating it was to be the cause of another's death, she would do anything to protect Hope, her mom, even her dad, Gail, and the boys.

Luke was right. David Lee was evil and brilliant. A formidable opponent she hadn't realized she had.

But she knew now.

—34—

IT WAS OFFICIAL. Faith hated Mondays.

She'd done what she had to do. She'd stood on the platform as Dale told the world about David Lee and asked people to turn him in.

Now she sat at her desk praying the same prayer over and over. *Protect them. Protect them.*

The *them* in question included Luke and all the agents working this case, her mom, Hope, her dad, Gail, and the boys. It was the first time she had ever prayed for Gail or the boys. And it was annoying that praying for them, even for something as basic as their protection, was making her feel less anger toward them. She'd made the phone calls, and all of them were away from their homes and in protective custody. For now.

Had she done the right thing? Made the right choices?

A Cherry Coke slid into her view, and the hand that held it moved to her right shoulder. "You're amazing." Luke's other hand came around her left side and opened in front of her. A small flash drive rested in his palm. "And we need to know what's on this. Now."

She turned, and Luke's face hovered so close that she had to force her head to keep from falling on his shoulder. He smelled clean and fresh. How was that even possible? They'd all been yanked from their beds in the middle of the night. There'd been no time for a shower. The only reason she had makeup on was because she'd had to be presentable for the 9:00 a.m. press conference, but her hair only looked good from the front.

Focus, Faith. Hair is not important. "Where did this come from?"

"Sabrina."

That drove all thoughts of hair and hands and lips from her mind. She inserted the drive into her computer and waited as the screen filled with the information Sabrina had compiled.

The first file listed said, "READ ME FIRST," so she clicked it. Luke continued to hover over her shoulder, and they read it together.

I am not supplying you with all the data I have because the file would be too large. I have documented everything— all admissible in court. I got a warrant over the weekend for some of this.

Bottom line: Mi Cha's father, Park Jae-ho, has not been seen in South Korea since a week after his wife's death. I have attached a few photographs. I found two that show that when he was younger, he may have had the same tattoo as David Lee. It isn't in current photos, but what looks like some type of birthmark could be where a tattoo was removed.

There is also a picture of a full tattoo—not from Mr. Park or David Lee—but if this is how their tattoo looks under their shirts, then it's proof of their involvement in a very secretive branch of Korean special forces. My source was positive Mr. Park was Korean special forces, and if he wanted to be in the United States, he would know how to get here without raising any suspicions.

Faith clicked on the photographs. There was Mi Cha with two people who must be her parents. Then she pulled up a photo of David Lee. And another photo that was split and showed the tattoos side by side with a note that the probability they were the same design was 90 percent. Then the picture of the full tattoo. On this unknown man, it began below his left ear and spread across his shoulder and down his chest. It was a tiger, and the tiny portion showing on the neck was the trailing end of the tail.

"Are you wondering if Mr. Park could be the Tiger?" Luke's whispered words sent a chill down her spine, and it wasn't just because his lips brushed her ear.

"Yes. And I'm thinking he could be the one David Lee told me about, and he's here to avenge Mi Cha's death."

"But we didn't kill her. We didn't even know she existed."

"I don't think he knows that."

WOULD THIS DAY EVER END?

Luke checked another number off the list he had in front of him. The tips had been coming in fast and furious since the press conference, and every tip was being chased down.

Everyone was working. This had turned into the biggest joint exercise he'd ever personally experienced. Losing two of their own had energized the local police force in a way that was both impressive and heartbreaking.

Zane, Tessa, Gil, Jacob, and even Marty were at the office

making phone calls to CIs and following up on leads, then sending local officers and FBI agents out to investigate any tips with merit.

But not him. He wasn't leaving Faith's side. He could work just as easily from the FBI office, and while it didn't follow any protocol, no one was complaining.

Especially Faith.

She sagged against her desk, and he longed to tell her to go take a nap, but he couldn't. Everyone was working and would continue to work until David Lee, and now Mr. Park, had been found.

Faith's private phone rang. She spun in her chair until her knees were touching Luke's. She frowned as she looked at the number and answered it with the speaker on so Luke could hear.

"Charles?" Faith's hand shook, and Luke rested it in his own.

"We're fine." The deep voice of the agent with Hope was calm and steady.

At the reassurance, Faith leaned forward, resting her forehead on Luke's good shoulder. "You scared me."

"Sorry about that. But I have a message for you."

Faith sat up quickly. "Okay."

"We left Hope's phone on in Raleigh, as a way to make her harder to track, and there's an agent keeping tabs on her email and messages. A little while ago, she received a text from Mrs. Lin.

"What does it say?"

"It says, 'The man you're looking for is here.'"

Faith set the phone on Luke's knee and reached for her iPad and pencil. "What time did the message come through?"

"Around two Eastern."

Luke glanced at his watch. Two hours ago.

"We'll be in touch." Faith's finger hovered over the End Call button.

Charles spoke quickly. "One more thing."

"Yes."

"She says to please be careful, because no matter how much she tries to convince you she can do life on her own, she doesn't want to do it without you."

Tears filled Faith's eyes. "I will. Take care of her."

"With my life."

The call disconnected.

Luke grabbed a tissue from the box on the edge of Faith's desk. "Here."

The tears hadn't fallen, and Faith dabbed the corner of each eye as she pulled in a shaky breath. When she looked at him again, all emotion had been chased back deep inside, where she kept it well controlled most of the time.

"Let's go find David Lee."

— 35 —

THREE HOURS LATER, Faith stood along the edge of a police barricade. Her FBI windbreaker hid the bulk of the bulletproof vest she wore. Her hair was pulled into a ponytail stuck through the back of her cap. It kept the wind from swirling her hair into her face, but it couldn't do much to stop the wind from blowing the misty rain against her cheeks.

This was the first time she'd been able to take a breath all afternoon. Everything ached. Her eyes, head, throat, hands, feet. Nothing was wrong with her that a solid forty-eight hours of sleep couldn't fix. Especially if she followed it up with a spa day. Or maybe a trip to the Caribbean.

She assumed those things would work. It wasn't like she ever took the time for anything like that. She wasn't a spa girl and hadn't used her vacation time for anything that wasn't family related in . . . well . . . ever.

She shifted her gaze to include Luke in it, but so it wouldn't look like she was ogling him. This thing she had with him would never work, and the realist in her knew it, but she was going to miss him so much when this was over. She had to solve the case to keep him alive, but that would take him away from her. He would go back to his life, and she would go back to her . . . work.

She'd never minded the work. But now? She would always wonder what it would be like to spend weekends not working. Maybe the Carrington guys would set her up with the best dive master around. She'd get her certification and then she and Luke could go to the Outer Banks and dive shipwrecks. Or maybe they could remodel her house. She could picture it. Luke, with paint on his face, laughing as they ripped out a countertop or—

Luke looked up and caught her staring. A smile spread slowly across his face, and his step had a bit of swagger in it as he made his way toward her. He stopped a professional distance away and leaned against her car. "See something you like?"

"Yes. Can you introduce me to that officer you were talking to? He's cute."

Luke glared, but there was a twinkle in his eyes. "He's a baby. You need a real man in your life."

"Know any?"

"Now you're just being mean." He took a step closer, and his arm brushed against hers. "I don't like the waiting." The happy-go-lucky façade was gone. "That baby over there"—he inclined his head toward the officer he'd been speaking to—"told me they've confirmed that all the houses between us and Mrs. Lin's house are clear."

"Thank goodness." She'd insisted on a wide perimeter. David Lee, and possibly Mr. Park, were known to be explosives-happy. For all she knew, they could have Mrs. Lin's house wired to blow the entire block.

"Faith." Luke turned to face her. "I need to tell you something."

"Malone!" The shout came from behind Luke. His face twisted in frustration, and his shoulders slumped.

319

She squeezed his forearm as she stepped around him and responded to Dale's yell. "Yes, sir!"

It was time.

IDIOT. What kind of moron decides to profess his undying devotion right before they attempt to capture a vicious murderer? He was relieved that Dale had stopped him. Now, if this worked out the way he hoped it would, Faith wouldn't be spending the rest of their lives reminding him of that time he told her he loved her under the romantic blue glow of a police cruiser's flashing light.

Mrs. Lin was safely in FBI custody. When David Lee arrived earlier that afternoon and asked her for a room, she hadn't panicked or bolted. She settled him into a corner room, and then she'd told her entire kitchen staff to take the night off and leave immediately. As soon as the house was clear, she left as well. When she felt like she could safely pause for breath, she darted into a coffee shop and texted Hope. Then she called her two boarders and told them not to return until she gave them the all clear.

An agent had picked up Mrs. Lin and she'd been taken to the local FBI office and given a polygraph, which she passed with flying colors. She might even wind up with a commendation for her efforts. They weren't sure why David Lee had returned to her establishment, but the theory was that he might have been planning to kill her, given that he seemed to be on a mission to eliminate everyone who had known that he and Mi Cha were friends. Regardless of his purpose, David Lee had seriously underestimated how much Mrs. Lin despised him, and now they had him surrounded.

After all the boarders and kitchen staff had been accounted

for, the SWAT team had done a flyover with a heat-sensing drone. Pretty cool contraption. If it was working properly, only one individual was left in the house.

The trick was going to be getting him out.

Night was coming fast, hastened by the cloud cover.

Luke was excited that they could have the murders solved and all this madness could end tonight—and terrified he would lose friends in the process.

They'd discussed the possibility that this was all a trap, but they couldn't wait forever. They couldn't endanger more people, innocents, while they stalled.

Faith waved him over. "We're tightening the perimeter. SWAT's prepared to breach."

The FBI had gotten all grouchy over the presence of the Secret Service agents. And to be fair, their argument was valid. They were the targets, and they shouldn't be within five miles of this place.

However, the FBI needed all the help they could get, so the agents had been allowed to stay—provided they agreed to stay away from the closest perimeter and from one another. "Let's not give them an easy way to take all of you out," Dale had said.

Encouraging guy.

Fifteen minutes later, the house was in view. SWAT was ready. Faith was standing thirty feet away, leaning against a cruiser, megaphone in hand.

Lord, protect us. Protect us all.

"David Lee!" Faith's voice echoed through the damp air. "David Lee, come out with your hands up."

Nothing happened. Not that they'd expected it to.

Faith checked her watch, and Luke glanced at his. One minute passed, then Faith spoke again. "David Lee! Don't make this worse than it is. Come out with your hands up."

Another minute.

One corner of the house exploded.

Shrieks and yells filled the night air. If he had been looking anywhere else, like, say, for example, at the burning house like a normal person, he would have missed it.

But he was looking at Faith.

And he couldn't breathe.

"DON'T EVEN ATTEMPT to get to that weapon, young lady." The cold voice was clipped and sure. And it was not the voice of David Lee.

The knife at her throat was sharp and had already pricked her skin. It would hurt later, but right now there was no pain.

He reached under her windbreaker and removed her weapon. She had a small gun at her ankle, but it wasn't much use to her at the moment.

"I don't want to hurt you."

"Yeah right." She whispered the words.

"Move." He had one arm around her neck, holding the knife flat against her skin, and he was pressing a gun, probably her own, into her side with his other hand. His knee landed in the back of her thigh, and she stumbled forward. One step. Two.

"Keep going."

What was he doing? Another two steps, and they were twenty feet from the house. The cacophony that had followed the explosion died away as if an invisible conductor had cut them off midperformance.

Her captor called out in Korean. At least she assumed it was

Korean. It was something she didn't understand. She hoped this was being recorded, and they'd get a translation eventually.

He switched to English and spoke loudly enough for the assembled agents and law enforcement officers to hear him. "I don't want anyone else to die. David and I will leave here. Agent Malone will accompany us. When we're gone, we will release her."

His words were met with silence. No one moved.

"Mr. Park! Why are you protecting him? He killed your daughter!" Luke's voice rang out in the tense stillness.

The flat of the blade pressed harder against Faith's throat. So, this was Mi Cha's dad. She was as good as dead. All she could hope for now was to keep anyone else from dying.

And then Luke stepped into the space between them and the house.

LUKE STOOD WITH FAITH and Mr. Park on his left and the house on his right. "Take me. I'm what you want. Faith has nothing to do with this. Let her go."

The arm around Faith tightened, and Mr. Park hissed. Luke could see the frustration in his eyes, the temptation to take him up on the offer.

"I'll come willingly. I don't know why you want us dead, but I know you don't want Faith dead."

"You killed my daughter."

"We didn't kill your daughter. We didn't know anything about her. We didn't know she was related to our agent, and we didn't know she was in the car until a few days ago."

"What is he talking about?" Mr. Park growled the question at Faith, but Luke answered.

"Your wife. Her father was half-Korean, half-American. Mi Cha found Thad Baker, a distant cousin, here in the States. She was hoping some of her American relatives might be a match for a transplant for her mother."

Faith gave a tiny nod of her head to some question that Mr. Park asked her.

And then the ground rumbled as another corner of the house exploded.

—36—

THE KNIFE NEVER WAVERED from her neck, but the blade was flat on her skin.

Luke continued to stand between her and the house.

"Why did you kill the bomb maker?"

"I don't know what you're talking about."

"In Seattle." Luke took one step closer. "I thought he was a family friend. Mi Cha and David went to see him back in October. From what I heard, you tortured him. No mercy at all. Why would you do that?"

"I didn't." He switched from English to Korean and yelled something again. Faith forced herself not to flinch away.

"We can't prove it yet"—Luke's tone was persuasive, friendly— "but we're pretty sure David killed your daughter."

"David had nothing to do with it. He was here to protect her."

Luke grimaced. "Yeah. Well. I think he got the bomb that killed your daughter from your bomb maker buddy. And then he killed her with it. I don't know why. Maybe she refused to sleep with him, and he was mad? Or maybe he was trying to get back at you for something. And then he hightailed it to Seattle this week to kill off your buddy before he could tell you that he'd given David the bomb. Are you sure you're safe with David? He's definitely a bit of a loose cannon, blowing up things left and right."

"Is this true?"

The cold voice at her ear wasn't so sure anymore. Faith didn't nod but whispered, "Yes. All of it."

A yell of triumph came from the house. They must have David Lee in custody. Unless that yell had come from David.

Fifteen interminable seconds later, she had her answer.

DAVID LEE OPENED the front door, hands in the air, shotgun grasped tightly in one raised fist. He surveyed the scene, and his expression shifted from one of triumph to one of confusion.

He said something in Korean to Mr. Park.

Mr. Park answered, and his voice was cold and filled with fury. The men argued, but there was no way to know what was being said. What was clear was that both men were beyond reason.

On TV, when a scene turned to chaos, everything slowed down. But that's not how it worked in real life.

Everything blurred. Mr. Park shoved Faith toward Luke and in the same moment took aim at David Lee. David Lee lowered the shotgun. They both fired.

They both went down.

— 37 —

FAITH LAY FACE DOWN on the ground. Luke was draped across her with his arms wrapped securely around her head. She pulled her head up and peered through the spaces of the cocoon Luke had formed around her.

David Lee and Mr. Park were both splayed on the ground. There was a lot of blood. Neither of them moved.

For the space of a heartbeat, no one else moved either. Then Dale and Jacob approached the bodies and secured the weapons that had fallen beside David Lee and Mr. Park.

Then they checked for signs of life, the whole scene playing out like a silent movie until Dale yelled, "I've got a pulse!"

And Jacob's Jersey accent called out, "I've got one too!"

Somehow both men were still alive.

Pandemonium broke out. Paramedics rushed forward while everyone else was kept back as far as possible from the house.

In the chaos, Luke's cheek rested against hers. "Faith?" His voice was shaking. "Can you move?"

In answer, she rolled onto her back and punched Luke's good shoulder. "What were you thinking? You could have been killed!"

Luke smiled—that slow, soft smile that made her forget she

was lying on the wet ground with the smell of smoke and blood thick in the air. His thumb brushed her cheek. "I love you, Faith."

Before she could respond, they were surrounded. Dale, Jacob, Tessa, Gil, and Zane encircled them, all talking at once.

"Are you all right?"

"Were you hit?"

"We need to get the paramedics over here to check Faith's neck."

"We need to move."

Faith couldn't tell who was talking, but it didn't matter. No matter how they worded it, they were all saying the same thing. "You scared us. We're glad you're okay."

Luke moved to his knees, then offered her a hand and helped her into a sitting position. Then they both got to their feet, aided—or more accurately, hindered—by five other sets of hands.

Once they had succeeded in convincing everyone from Dale and Jacob to the paramedics to their friends that they were not in need of emergency medical services, the rest of the evening was a blur.

David Lee and Mr. Park were taken to the hospital. If either of them survived, it would be hours if not days before they could be questioned.

Faith waited with Luke and the others as the bomb techs cleared the house. While they worked, she called Hope, then her mom, then her dad to let them know that no matter what they might see on television, she was fine and their respective security details would ensure they were all returned home tomorrow.

An agent approached them. "Agent Malone. I was told to give this to you."

Faith opened the folder. Inside was the translation of the conversation between David Lee and Mr. Park. From what they could piece together, David Lee had believed that Mi Cha had fallen in love with Thad. He'd killed Thad because he thought that was the only way to ensure that she would never return to the States and to clear the way for her to fall in love with him, but he swore that Mi Cha's death had been an accident. After that, he'd killed the bomb maker in Seattle and his friend, Jesse Thomas, presumably because they knew too.

It was clear that Mr. Park had believed the Secret Service agents had endangered Mi Cha's life by dragging her into a dangerous situation. One that ultimately resulted in her death. He had come to the US to exact revenge on the agents he believed most culpable. He was responsible for the deaths of Jared Smith and Michael Weaver, as well as the attempted murders of Gil, Zane, and Luke.

The saddest part in the transcript was when Mr. Park had said, "I killed them. For nothing! How could you let me kill innocent men?"

Those were the last words he'd spoken.

They could all go home now—all except Zane, who had nowhere to go. Instead, they picked up takeout and drove to Luke's house, convening in his spacious den. Gil and Zane claimed the recliners. Tessa curled up on one end of the sofa, her concerned gaze flickering around the room but resting most often on Zane. Luke settled Faith into an oversized chair and then squeezed in beside her. She wasn't complaining.

They ate their burgers and shakes and talked about the case and what the days and weeks ahead would look like if either of the men survived their injuries.

"Can we do this again? Not the getting shot at and blown up parts." Gil closed his eyes. "I mean the dinner at Luke's part."

"I think that could be arranged." Luke spoke the words against Faith's hair. "Assuming you do the cooking."

"Excellent." Gil smiled. "It's a date. Friday night. Does that work for everyone?"

Zane and Tessa grunted agreement.

"Faith?" Gil grinned but didn't look at her. "I'm assuming you'll be here too?"

Luke turned to look at her, Gil's question mirrored in his eyes. "Definitely."

"Excellent. Then I'm going to get Tessa to give me a ride home, and I'll see y'all tomorrow." He popped the recliner back into a sitting position.

"I'm already tired of being everyone's chauffeur." Tessa grumbled the words, but she jumped up and stretched out a hand to help Gil to his feet. "I guess since no one has a car, you'll need me to pick all of you up in the morning. I expect payment in coffee."

Zane clambered from his recliner and said good night to everyone before shuffling up the stairs to what Faith assumed was one of Luke's guest rooms. Gil and Tessa left a few minutes later after Tessa gave Faith directions to her house. Faith was going to crash at Tessa's place since Faith's house was still a crime scene.

Luke kept an arm around Faith as he walked her to her car. "I'm going to miss having you around tomorrow, being all bossy and argumentative. It's going to be boring."

"You can't get rid of me that easily, Special Agent Powell." Faith leaned against him. "We'll have hours of debriefing, you'll have to give official statements, who knows how long this will drag out."

Luke wrapped both arms around her and pressed his lips to the tip of her nose. "I never imagined I would say this, but it would be all right with me if you dragged this out forever."

She knew she should respond, but she couldn't form a coherent thought.

"I'll leave the details up to you. I'm sure you'll figure something out." He traced her cheek with his index finger, then moved his finger to her lips. "I don't care, as long as we're together."

She forgot that she wanted to tell him she loved him too. That she trusted him. That she'd never imagined anyone would literally try to give his life for hers and she couldn't believe she was lucky enough to have someone like him in her life. She wanted to tell him she was scared and excited, and she was sure she'd get it wrong some of the time, but she would never, ever stop fighting for them and she would be the safest place for him to leave his heart and she would cherish every moment.

She grabbed the sides of his shirt and pulled him against her. "Shut up and kiss me."

Luke Powell was very good at following orders he liked.

She would have to remember that.

— 38 —

FOUR MONTHS LATER

It hadn't been the longest Monday ever, but she wasn't sorry to see it come to an end. Faith opened her garage door and spotted Luke's car parked on one side. He was back! He'd been called in on Wednesday to support a protective detail in Charlotte, and she hadn't seen him since.

Her heart rate sped up as she parked, grabbed her bag, and jogged inside. She found him in the kitchen, paintbrush in hand, humming as he cut in the new paint they'd picked out last week. He had his back to her, and she paused a moment to admire this man who had captured her heart so completely.

The last few months hadn't been easy. There'd been many nights when she'd awakened in a cold sweat, David Lee's laughter ringing in her ears. There'd been long days filled with paperwork and interviews and filling in the missing pieces of the puzzle.

They'd been able to conclusively tie the bomb that killed Thad and Mi Cha to the bomb maker in Seattle, and they'd found evidence that David Lee had killed both the bomb maker and Jesse Thomas.

Sabrina found proof that while Mi Cha had flown home from

their trip to Washington State, David had decided to drive home, which explained how he got the bomb back to North Carolina. They would never know exactly what he took, but he must have taken enough explosive material for several bombs, because the chemical signature of the bomb used on Thad's car matched what Mr. Park had used on Luke's and Zane's cars, as well as what David had used on Mrs. Lin's house. They could only guess at his reasoning, but assumed that he'd taken advantage of the opportunity to procure the bomb ingredients in case he ever needed them, and then he'd offered them to Mr. Park to use against the Secret Service.

Sabrina had also found a gold mine with David Lee's computer. Between what they knew for sure and what an FBI profiler had surmised, the going theory was that David Lee had been infatuated, not with Mi Cha, but with her father. Mr. Park had been his mentor and father figure, and when he'd asked David to watch over Mi Cha, David had decided this was his chance to insert himself into the family.

But Mi Cha hadn't cooperated. She hadn't fallen in love with him, so he'd gotten more possessive and intrusive in her life. Sabrina located a screenshot that he'd taken of Mi Cha's phone where she was gushing about how excited she was that Thad was in her life and how she couldn't wait to introduce him to her family.

Taken out of context, it could easily have been misconstrued to be a text between a romantic couple. Thad was killed two days later. The profiler believed that in David Lee's twisted mind, killing Thad would have been the logical step to ensuring his own happiness and place in the Park family.

Even after killing Mi Cha, he had been determined to fill the role of son in the family and had stayed behind in the Raleigh area to help Mr. Park on his mission of vengeance.

Janice Estes had admitted that David Lee threatened to torture and kill her mother if she didn't drag her feet on the investigation. Janice had been moved to an FBI office across the country, and Faith could honestly say she wished her well. She wouldn't have made the same choices Janice had made, but she could understand them.

Zane had moved into Luke's house and was still waiting on his transfer to Phase 2. Jacob had been made the resident agent in charge, and a new assistant RAIC had been assigned to their office. Gil had made a full recovery and taken over most of the electronic crimes investigations.

Faith and Tessa had become good friends, but Tessa continued to struggle with some personal issues that she remained unwilling to share. Faith couldn't help but wonder if Tessa's tense relationship with Zane was part of the problem, but she didn't think that was the whole story.

When Luke introduced Faith to his mom and his sister, he made it clear that if they had a problem with Faith being an FBI agent, then they would have to get over it. Luke's sister had been easy. And his mom was coming around. Luke's stepdad was a sweetheart, and he and Faith had hit it off immediately. Faith suspected he was the real reason Luke's mom was softening.

Luke had gone with her to Georgia to see her dad, Gail, and the boys. He'd sat on the sofa beside her until he was sure she wasn't going to lose it, and then he'd cajoled Gail and the boys into showing him around the large backyard, giving Faith some time alone with her dad. Faith had accepted that it was never going to be an easy relationship. Some hurts were too deep to heal properly. But she didn't ignore her dad's calls anymore. And her younger brothers weren't all bad. Gail was . . . tolerable.

Of course, Hope adored Luke. He'd even won over her mom, who now thought he could do no wrong.

"When you get done staring at my butt, could you bring some more paint?" Luke hadn't turned around, but she could hear the laughter threatening to break free.

She couldn't resist teasing him. "Happy to, but it may be a while."

He balanced the paintbrush on top of the ladder and climbed down, then stalked toward her.

"No way." She backed away. "You have paint all over your hands."

Luke didn't stop. He backed her into a corner, and without laying a hand on her, he kissed her senseless. "I missed you."

She might have thought that he'd been too busy to miss her, but he'd sent her a bouquet of flowers on Friday and they'd made her smile every time she saw them—and made her blush every time she reread the note.

"I missed you too. When did you get back?"

"Around two. I started some laundry and changed clothes at my place. Thought I'd surprise you."

"You did." She reached for another kiss, and he complied. When he pulled away, she grabbed his shirt. "I love you."

"I love you too." He pulled a rag from his pocket and wiped his hands. "Go change clothes. I have something I want to show you."

"Okay. Five minutes." Faith hurried to her room, curiosity spurring her to pull on some old yoga pants and a T-shirt and rush back to the kitchen.

She froze in the doorway.

Luke was on one knee, holding a ring. "Faith."

She didn't give him a chance to say more. "If you promise to say my name like that forever, then I say yes."

He smiled his slow smile, the one that was just for her, and stood. He rested the ring at the tip of her finger and squeezed her hand. "Faith." He winked and stage whispered, "Did I say it right?"

At her nod, he continued. "Will you marry me?"

"Yes!"

He slid the ring on her finger and kissed his way from the sparkling diamond, up her arm, to her earlobe, and down her chin, until he finally found her lips.

She only kissed him for a moment before she pulled away. "How do you feel about short engagements?"

His eyes lit. "I'm in favor of them."

"Are you sure you don't want to stay engaged for a couple of years to see if things—"

"Don't." He was not amused now. His mouth flattened into a thin line, and he shook his head. "I know what I need to know. I know I need you. I know I love you. I know I'm not going to ever feel this way about anyone else." He traced the ring on her hand. "And I know I don't want to wait one second longer than necessary to commit to you forever."

Maybe someday Faith would be able to express herself as well as Luke did. For now, she'd have to keep it simple and hope he understood everything she couldn't say. "Short it is."

If Luke's answering kiss was any indication, he'd understood just fine.

Acknowledgments

No one ever writes a book on their own. My eternal gratitude to:

The experts who wish to remain anonymous but without whom I would never have attempted to write this story.

Brian, Emma, James, and Drew, for loving me through another story.

Ken and Susie Huggins and Sandra Blackburn, for frequently taking your grandchildren off my hands so I could concentrate and for continuing to believe in me.

Jennifer Huggins, for not freaking out when I ask where the best place is to shoot someone without killing them and for being my resident medical advisor/best sister ever.

Lynette Eason, for every text, email, phone call, and evening escape to brainstorm—or not!

Carrie Stuart Parks, Colleen Coble, Robin Caroll, Pam Hillman, Edie Melson, Emme Gannon, Linda Gilden, Alycia Morales, Tammy Karasek, Erynn Newman, Michelle Cox, Molly Jo Realy, Lisa Carter, Alison Hendley, Mindy Song Houng, Holly Dowling,

Angie Poole, Ginny Hodel, and Dr. Judy Melinek, for your willingness to share your creativity and knowledge.

My sisters of The Light Brigade, for your unfailing encouragement and ceaseless prayers on my behalf.

Deborah Clack and Debb Hackett, for crying with me until I laugh and for laughing with me until I cry. #HackersClackers Blackers4ever

The extraordinary publicity and marketing teams at Revell who work so tirelessly to help get my stories into the world.

Kelsey Bowen, for seeing what was needed to make this story all it could be and for being a true pleasure to work with.

Amy Ballor, for making sure every word is where it's supposed to be.

Tamela Hancock Murray, for being the best agent I could ask for.

My fabulous readers, who have waited not so patiently for this book. Your enthusiasm and delight keep me motivated and encouraged!

My Savior, the Ultimate Storyteller, for allowing me to write stories for you.

> Let the words of my mouth and the meditation of my heart
> be acceptable in your sight,
> O Lord, my rock and my redeemer. (Psalm 19:14)

READ ON
FOR CHAPTER 1

OF THE NEXT BOOK
IN THIS SERIES!

— 1 —

THE STACK OF CASH on his desk was as close to genuine currency as squeeze cheese was to Brie.

US Secret Service Special Agent Gil Dixon turned one of the fraudulent twenties over and studied the back. There were a few similarities to the real thing, but not enough to confuse anyone paying attention.

"Free money?" Special Agent Zane Thacker asked as he passed Gil's cubicle for his own.

"Hardly enough to fool with." Gil glanced back at the file. Two hundred dollars in twenties. Even if the person who had deposited it had been trying to do something illegal, no prosecutor would touch the case. It simply wasn't worth it.

"Where did it come from?" Zane asked the question, but his tone indicated that he was making conversation to pass the time, not because he really cared about the answer.

"Hedera, Inc."

Zane's head appeared over the top of the cubicle wall they shared. "You're kidding."

"Nope."

"No way she's running counterfeit bills."

"I agree."

"When are you going to see her?"

"This afternoon. I thought I'd swing by her office first since the cash came from a business deposit."

"What's a company like Hedera doing depositing cash anyway?" Zane's question was the same one Gil had been pondering since the case hit his desk.

"No idea." Hedera's accounts should have been almost entirely digital. The deposit had been for a little over two thousand dollars in cash, only two hundred of which were fake. "That's the reason I want to talk to Dr. Collins."

One reason, but not the only reason.

Hedera, Inc. was owned by Dr. Ivy Collins. Gil only knew her by reputation, but he'd chatted with her assistant briefly a few months earlier when she was helping them with a case.

Was that before or after he'd been shot? Before. No. After.

He'd volunteered to follow up with her, in part because he wanted to hear her voice. As if that would tell him what he wanted to know. But she hadn't been in the office, and her assistant had answered the question. There'd been no reason to insist on meeting in person just to satisfy his curiosity. Staying alive had been the priority that week, but in the months since, he hadn't been able to stop the wondering.

He'd known an Ivy once upon a time. Was it possible that the eight-year-old Ivy from his memory had grown into the delicately boned woman with intense eyes that sparkled from the home page of Hedera, Inc., the company she'd founded four years earlier?

If it was her, she'd been his best friend. They'd had their whole life planned. School, college, marriage. It had all been so simple. Next to Emily, his twin sister, Ivy was his favorite person in the world, so it only made sense that he would spend the rest of his life with her.

It never occurred to either of them that anything could tear them apart . . . until the day she'd said goodbye and climbed into her mom's sedan.

He'd scampered up a tree and watched until the car disappeared from view and his nine-year-old heart had broken.

He never saw her again.

Ivy Collins. The last name was wrong, but that was easily explained. She might be married. Or divorced.

Or more likely, not the same Ivy at all.

He'd thought about tracking her down before, but he'd never followed through. What would he say if he found her? "I missed you?" or "Can we be friends?" or "Marry me?" He had no idea what might fly out of his mouth. Hopefully it wouldn't be anything too stupid.

Regardless, he needed to put the wondering to rest. What was the worst thing that could happen?

Six hours later, he and Zane pulled into an empty Hedera parking lot. Zane waved a hand to indicate the empty spaces. "It's only four thirty. Why isn't anyone here?"

Gil parked in a visitor space and dialed the Hedera number. A recorded feminine voice with the barest hint of Southern drawl told him that Hedera's business hours were 7:00 a.m. to 4:00 p.m. and encouraged him to leave a message, assuring him that he would be contacted during normal business hours.

"These people work seven to four? I wonder if they're hiring?" Zane glanced at his watch. "What now?"

Gil wasn't ready to let this go. Not yet. "Do you have time to swing by her house?"

"What else do I have to do?" Zane laughed, but there was a bite in the words. Zane was usually a fun guy, but he'd grown somber and withdrawn over the last few months. Most people assumed it was because of the trauma they'd all been through in the spring. Zane had been shot, then he'd lost his car, his home, and almost everything he owned. And if that hadn't been bad enough, his transition to the protective detail had been delayed indefinitely. All solid reasons for a guy to be in a funk.

But their other fellow agent Luke Powell was convinced it had more to do with Zane's tense relationship with the only female agent in the office, Tessa Reed, and Gil was increasingly sure he was right.

This wasn't the time to pry, but the time was coming. For now, he let it go. "She lives about five minutes from here. Let's see if she's home."

Gil slowed as he approached the house but didn't stop. The house was in an older part of Raleigh where the lots were large and the subdivision delineations weren't clear. Two stories. Probably with a basement. Sitting on a wooded acre of land.

He drove past five more houses, turned around in a driveway, and came back. He pulled into her driveway and parked near the walkway to the front porch.

Gil and Zane exited the car and walked to the front door. There was no reason to think this would be anything other than a friendly chat. But when Gil knocked, the door swung open.

He pulled his weapon from his hip.

Zane was already dialing for backup. He put his phone back in his pocket and gave Gil a quick nod.

Gil pushed the door all the way open. It swung silently. He concentrated all his senses on this new environment. The foyer was small, with a hexagon-shaped library/office to his left. To his right sat a formal living room. Both were empty.

There were two distinct and wildly contrasting odors in the hall. Cinnamon and . . . charred flesh.

Zane lifted his chin in a quick up and to the left. Gil followed, and Zane cleared the two bedrooms and small bathroom. Then Gil took the lead and went to the right. A door opened at the back of the house and feet pounded down steps. But someone was moving in the room just beyond the kitchen.

Was that a drawer being opened?

He swung into the next room. The kitchen.

Across the large island stood Ivy Collins.

His Ivy.

It was as if no time had passed. No years of silence. The decades of longing were erased. Something strong and true pulled him to her. His body tried to close the gap between them, but his mind resisted. Years of training refused to be ignored, and Gil forced himself to scan the room around them. Zane shifted to the left to clear the remaining room—her bedroom?

Blood ran down her right temple and trickled from puffy lips. The sweater she was wearing was ripped and hung off one shoulder, revealing a nasty burn. Something was very wrong with her right hand, but Gil couldn't focus on that, because in her left hand, she held a gun.

Before he could tell her he was a friend, she pulled the trigger.

Lynn H. Blackburn is the author of *Beneath the Surface*, *In Too Deep*, and *One Final Breath*. Winner of the 2016 Selah Award for Mystery and Suspense and the 2016 Carol Award for Short Novel, Blackburn believes in the power of stories, especially those that remind us that true love exists, a gift from the Truest Love. She's passionate about CrossFit, coffee, and chocolate (don't make her choose) and experimenting with recipes that feed both body and soul. She lives in Simpsonville, South Carolina, with her true love, Brian, and their three children.

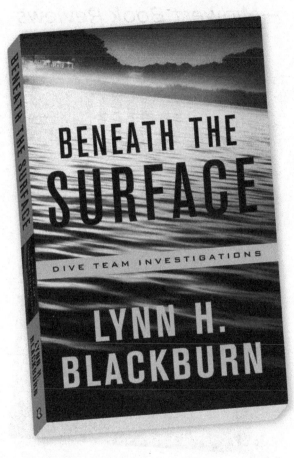

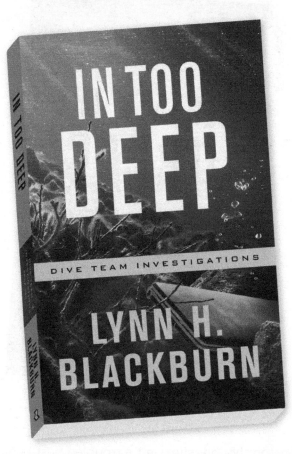

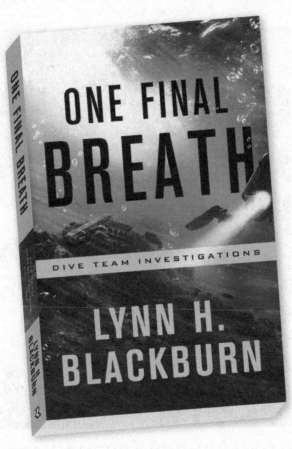

CONNECT WITH LYNN

WWW.LYNNHBLACKBURN.COM